SPELL OF THE DRUIDS' SWORDS

Marcus braced for Viridovix's attack, but the Celt was staring at his sword. "How is it that a Roman comes by the blade of a Druid?"

"The Druid who bore it found he could not stand against me," Marcus replied.

"Of its own free will—like mine," Viridovix murmured. He drifted forward in a fencer's crouch as Marcus brought his weapon to guard position.

Suddenly the Druid's marks stamped down the length of the blades glowed with a hot golden light that grew stronger with every step Viridovix took.

The two blades met with a roar louder than thunder. A dome of red-gold light sprang from the crossed blades to surround the duelists and the legionaries.

When the dome of light faded away, the space where the men had stood was empty.

Book One of *The Videssos Cycle*

The Misplaced Legion

Harry Turtledove

A Del Rey Book

BALLANTINE BOOKS • NEW YORK

A Del Rey Book
Published by Ballantine Books

Copyright © 1987 by Harry Turtledove

All rights reserved under International and Pan-American Copyright Conventions. Published in the United States of America by Ballantine Books, a division of Random House, Inc., New York, and simultaneously in Canada by Random House of Canada Limited, Toronto.

Library of Congress Catalog Card Number: 86-91385

ISBN 0-345-33067-6

Manufactured in the United States of America

First Edition: February 1987

Cover Art by Romas

In various ways, this book is dedicated
to L. Sprague de Camp,
J. R. R. Tolkien, Speros Vryonis, Jr.,
and, above all, Laura.

SHAUMKHIIL

N

SHAUM RIVER

PARDRAYA

DEGIRD RIVER

MYLASA

THE GODS'
DUNG HEAP

KOUPHIS RIVER

GELOS RIVER

SEA

MAIOTIC
BAY

YEZD

GUNIB

MOUSH R.

ERZERUM
MTS.

PRISTA

VIDESSIAN
SEA

DILBAT
MTS.

TUTUB

TIB

SEA

MASHIZ

VASPURAKAN
MTS.

KHLIAT

MARAGHA

RHAMNOS R.

PITYOS

SOLI

NAKOLEIA

APTOS

VAX

RHYAX

CAVAS

RESAINA

GARSAVRA

TZOUX

EBER

EMPIRE

ITHOME

AMORION

ARANDOS R.

KYZIKOS

SEA
OF
SALT

KYBISTRA

DOXON

SAILORS'

I

THE SUN OF NORTHERN GAUL WAS PALE, NOTHING LIKE THE hot, lusty torch that flamed over Italy. In the dim stillness beneath the trees, its light came wan, green, and shifting, almost as if undersea. The Romans pushing their way down the narrow forest track took their mood from their surroundings. They moved quietly; no trumpets or bawdy marching songs announced their coming. The daunting woods ignored them.

Peering into the forest, Marcus Aemilius Scaurus wished he had more men. Caesar and the main Roman army were a hundred miles to the southwest, moving against the Veneti on the Atlantic coast. Scaurus' three cohorts—"a reconaissance in force," his superior had called them—were more than enough to attract the attention of the Gauls, but might be unable to deal with it, once attracted.

"Only too right," Gaius Philippus answered when the tribune said that aloud. The senior centurion, hair going gray and face tanned and lined by a lifetime on campaign, had long ago lost optimism with the other illusions of his youth. Though Scaurus' birth gave him higher rank, he had the sense to rely on his vastly experienced aide.

Gaius Philippus cast a critical eye on the Roman column. "Close it up, there!" he rasped, startlingly loud in the quiet. His gnarled vine-staff badge of office thwacked against his greave to punctuate the order. He quirked an eyebrow at Scaurus. "You've nothing to worry about anyway, sir. One

1

look and the Gauls will think you're one of theirs on a masquerade."

The military tribune gave a wry nod. His family sprang from Mediolanum in northern Italy. He was tall and blond as any Celt and used to the twitting his countrymen dished out. Seeing he'd failed to hit a nerve, Gaius Philippus took another tack. "It's not just your looks, you know—that damned sword gives you away, too."

That hit home. Marcus was proud of his blade, a three-foot Gallic longsword he had taken from a slain Druid a year ago. It was fine steel and better suited to his height and reach than the stubby Roman *gladii*. "You know full well I had an armorer give it a decent point," he said. "When I use a sword, I'm not such a fool as to slash with it."

"A good thing, too. It's the point, not the edge, that brings a man down. Hello, what's this about?" Gaius Philippus added as four of the small army's scouts dashed into the woods, weapons in hand. They came out a few moments later, three of them forcibly escorting a short, scrawny Gaul while the fourth carried the spear he had borne.

As they dragged their captive up to Scaurus, their leader, an underofficer named Junius Blaesus, said, "I'd thought someone was keeping an eye on us this past half hour and more, sir. This fellow finally showed himself."

Scaurus looked the Celt over. Apart from the bloody nose and puffed eye the Romans had given him, he could have been any of a thousand Gallic farmers: baggy woolen trousers, checked tunic—torn now—long, fair hair, indifferently shaven face. "Do you speak Latin?" the military tribune asked him.

The only answer he got was a one-eyed glare and a headshake. He shrugged. "Liscus!" he called, and the unit's interpreter trotted up. He was from the Aedui, a clan of south central Gaul long friendly to Rome, and wore a legionary's crested helm over bright curls cut short in the Roman fashion. The prisoner gave him an even blacker stare than the one he had bestowed on Scaurus. "Ask him what he was doing shadowing us."

"I will that, sir," Liscus said, and put the question into the musical Celtic speech. The captive hesitated, then answered in single short sentence. "Hunting boar, he says he was," Liscus reported.

"By himself? No one would be such a fool," Marcus said.

"And this is no boarspear, either," Gaius Philippus said, grabbing it from a scout. "Where's the crosspiece below the head? Without one, a boar will run right up your shaft and rip your guts out."

Marcus turned to Liscus. "The truth this time, tell him. We'll have it from him, one way or another. The choice is his: he can give it or we can wring it from him." Marcus doubted he could torture a man in cold blood, but there was no reason to let the Celt know that.

But Liscus was only starting to speak when the prisoner, with a lithe twist and a kick, jerked free of the men holding him. His hand flashed to a leaf-shaped dagger cunningly slung below his left shoulder. Before the startled Romans could stop him, he thrust the point between his ribs and into his heart. As he toppled, he said, "To the crows with you," in perfect Latin.

Knowing it would do no good, Scaurus shouted for a physician; the Celt was dead before the man arrived. The doctor, a sharp-tongued Greek named Gorgidas, glanced at the protruding knife hilt and snapped, "You ask too much of me, you know. I'll close his eyes for him if you like."

"Never mind. Even while I called, I knew there was nothing you could do." The tribune turned to Junius Blaesus. "You and your men did well to find the spy and bring him in—not so well in not searching him carefully and keeping a lax hold on him. The Gauls must have something in the wind, though we've lost the chance to find out what. Double your patrols and keep them well out in front—the more warning of trouble we have, the better." Blaesus saluted and hurried off, thankful to get away with no harsher reprimand.

"Full battle readiness, sir?" Gaius Philippus asked.

"Yes." Marcus cocked an eye at the westering sun. "I hope we can find a clearing before dusk for an encampment. I'd feel safer behind earthworks."

"And I. I'd feel safer still with a couple of legions at my back." The centurion went off to make the needful changes in the Romans' marching order, bringing his spear-throwers forward and tightening up the distance between each maniple and its neighbor. An excited hum ran through the ranks. Here a

man hastily sharpened his sword, there another cut short a
leather sandal strap that might trip him in action, still another
took a last swig of sour wine.

Shouts came from up ahead, out of sight beyond a bend in
the path. A minute or so later a scout jogged back to the main
body of troops. "We spied another skulker in the bushes, sir.
I'm afraid this one got away."

Marcus whistled tunelessly between his teeth. He dismissed the scout with a word of thanks, then looked to Gaius
Philippus, sure the centurion felt the same certainty of trouble
he did himself. Gaius Philippus nodded at his unspoken
thought. "Aye, we're for it, right enough."

But when another of the advance guards came back to report the path opening out into a sizable clearing, the military
tribune began to breathe more easily. Even the small force he
led—not quite a third of a legion—could quickly build field
fortifications strong enough to hold off many times its number
of barbarians.

The clearing was large, several hundred yards of meadow
set in the midst of the deep wood. The evening mist was
already beginning to gather above the grass. A stream trickled
through the center of the clearing; half a dozen startled teal
leaped into the air as the Romans began emerging. "Very good
indeed," Scaurus said. "Perfect, in fact."

"Not quite, I'm afraid," Gaius Philippus said. He pointed
to the far edge of the clearing, where the Celtic army was
coming out.

Marcus wasted a moment cursing; another hour and his
men would have been safe. No help for it now. "Trumpets and
cornets together!" he ordered the buccinators.

As the call to action rang out, Gaius Philippus' voice rang
with it. The senior centurion was in his element, readying his
troops. "Deploy as you debouch!" he shouted. "Three lines—
you know the drill! Skirmishers up ahead, then you front-
rankers with your *pila*, then the heavy infantry, then reserves!
Come on, *move*—yes, *you* there, you worthless whoreson!"
His vine-stave thudded down on the slow legionary's corseleted back. Junior centurions and underofficers echoed and
amplified his commands, yelling and prodding their men into
place.

The deployment took only minutes. Beyond posting an

extra squad of slingers and some protecting spearmen on the slightly higher ground to his right, Scaurus kept a symmetrical front as he waited to see how many enemies he faced.

"Is there no end to them?" Gaius Philippus muttered by his side. File after file of Gauls moved into the clearing, slowly going into line of battle. Well-armored and powerfully armed nobles shouted and waved as they tried to position their bands of retainers but, as always among the Celts, discipline was tenuous. Most of the men the nobles led had gear far poorer than theirs: a spear or slashing sword, perhaps a large oblong shield of wood painted in bright spirals. Except for the nobles, few wore more armor than a leather jerkin, or at most a helmet. Of the cuirasses to be seen, most were Roman work, the spoil of earlier battles.

"What do you make of them? About three thousand?" Marcus asked when the Celtic flood at last stopped flowing.

"Aye, about two for our one. It could be worse. Of course," Gaius Philippus went on, "it could be a damned sight better, too."

On the far side of the clearing the Gauls' commander, splendid in armor of black and gold and a cape of crimson-dyed skins, harangued his men, whipping them up into a fighting frenzy. He was too far away for the Romans to make out his words, but the fierce yells of his listeners and the deep thudding of spearshafts on shields told of the fury he was rousing.

Heads turned Scaurus' way as he strode out in front of his own troops. He paused for a moment, gathering his thoughts and waiting for the full attention of his men. Though he had never given a pre-combat oration, he was used to public speaking, having twice run for a magistracy in his home town —the second time successfully. The technique, if not the occasion, seemed similar.

"We've all of us heard Caesar," he began, and at the mention of their beloved marshal of legionaries they shouted approval as he had hoped. He went on, "We all know I can't talk that well, and I don't intend to try." He quieted the small laugh from the men with an upraised hand. "No need, anyhow—things are very simple. Caesar is five days' march from here at most. We've beaten the Gauls time and again. One more win here, now, and there's not the chance of a frog at a snake symposium that they'll be able to put anything in our way before we can link up with him again."

The Romans cheered. The Gauls shouted back, shaking their fists, waving their spears, and yelling bloodthirsty threats in their own language.

"I've heard worse," Gaius Philippus said of the speech. From him it was high praise, but Scaurus only half heard him. Most of his attention was on the Celts, who, behind their tall leader, were trotting at the Romans. He would have liked to meet them at the streamlet in mid-clearing, but to do so he would have had to pull his line away from the woods which anchored its flanks.

Only skirmishers contested the crossing. Slingers sent leaden bullets whizzing into the ranks of the Gauls, to bang off shields or slap into flesh. Archers added their fire, drawing back to the breast and emptying quivers as fast as they could. Here and there along the barbarians' line a man stumbled and fell, but the damage was only a pinprick to the onrushing mass.

The Celts raised a cheer as one of their archers transfixed a Roman slinger as he was letting fly. The bullet he had been about to loose flew harmlessly into the air.

The Celts drew nearer, splashing through the ankle-deep water of the rivulet. The Roman skirmishers fired a last few shots, then scampered for the protection of their line.

The long Gallic sword felt feather light in Marcus' hands. The druids' marks stamped down the length of the blade seemed to glow with a life of their own in the red sunlight of late afternoon. An arrow buried itself in the ground beside the tribune's feet. Almost without thinking, he shuffled a couple of steps to one side.

The barbarians were so near he could see the scowls darkening their mustachioed faces, could tell their leader bore a sword twin to his own, could all but count the spokes of the bronze wheel cresting that leader's high-crowned helm. The beat of the Gauls' feet against the grass was a growing thunder.

"At my command!" Marcus shouted to his first line, raising his blade high over his head. They hefted their *pila* and waited, quiet and grimly capable. Already, with wild whoops, the Celts were starting to fling their spears, most falling short of the Roman line.

The tribune studied the oncoming mass. A moment more . . . "Loose!" he cried, sword-arm flailing down. Half a thousand arms flung their deadly burdens against the Gauls as one.

The enemy line staggered. Men screamed as they were pierced. Others, luckier, blocked the Romans' casts with their shields. Yet their luck was mixed, for the soft iron shanks of the *pila* bent as their points bit, making the weapons useless for a return throw and fouling the shields so they, too, had to be discarded.

"Loose!" Scaurus shouted again. Another volley leaped forth. But the Gauls, brave as they were unruly, kept coming. Their spears were flying too, many of them, even if not in tight volleys. Next to Marcus a man pitched backwards, his throat spurting blood around the javelin that had found its way over his shield. The legionaries pulled stabbing-swords from their scabbards and surged forward as the fighting turned hand-to-hand.

A cry of triumph rose from the Gauls as, spearheaded by two huge blond-maned warriors, they hewed their way through the first Roman rank. Even as the buccinators' horns trumpeted a warning, a maniple of the second line was moving into the gap. Their short swords flickered now forward, now back, fast and sure as striking snakes; their tall, semi-cylindrical *scuta* turned the strokes of the foe. The Celtic champions died in moments, each beset by half a dozen men. Surrounded on three sides, most of their followers fell with them. The Romans, in their turn, raised the victory shout.

Marcus sent another maniple to the left flank to deal with a breakthrough. They contained it, but that part of the line still sagged. The Celtic chieftain was there, fighting like a demon. Red light flashed from his sword as he lopped off a legion-ary's hand, then killed the man as he stood stupidly staring at the spouting stump.

A Gaul charged Scaurus, swinging his sword over his head in great circles as if it were a sling. As the tribune ducked under his wild slash, he caught the reek of ale from the man. He whirled for an answering blow, only to see Gaius Philippus tugging his blade from the Gaul's body.

The centurion spat contemptuously. "They're fools. Fight-

ing is far too serious a business to take on drunk." He looked
about. "But there's so damned many of them."

Scaurus could only nod. The Roman center was holding,
but both flanks bent now. In close fighting the slingers on the
right were more liability than asset, for their covering spearmen had to do double duty to keep the Celts off them. Worse
yet, bands of Celts were slipping into the woods. Marcus did
not think they were running. He was afraid they were working
their way round to attack the Roman rear.

Gorgidas the doctor slipped by him to drag a wounded
legionary from the line and bandage his gashed thigh. Catching the tribune's eye, he said, "I'd have been as happy without
this chance to ply my trade, you know." In the heat of the
moment he spoke his native Greek.

"I know," Marcus answered in the same tongue. Then another Celt was on him—a noble, by his bronze breastplate.
He feinted low with his spear, thrust high. Scaurus turned the
stab with his shield. The spearpoint slid past him off the *scutum*'s rounded surface; he stepped in close. The Gaul backpe-
daled for his life, eyes wide and fearfully intent on the motion
of the tribune's sword.

Marcus lunged at the opening under the arm of his corselet.
His aim was not quite true, but the thrust punched through his
foe's armor and into his vitals. The barbarian swayed. Bright
blood frothed from his nose and mouth as he fell.

"Well struck!" Gaius Philippus shouted.

His sword-arm was red almost to the elbow. Marcus
shrugged, not thinking his blow had carried that much force.
More likely some smith had jobbed the Gaul, though most
Celtic metalworkers took pride in their products.

It was growing dark fast now. Marcus set some men not yet
fighting to make torches and passing them forward. His soldiers used them for more than light—a Celt fled shrieking, his
long, greasy locks ablaze.

Liscus went down, fighting against the countrymen he had
abandoned for Rome. Scaurus felt a stab of remorse. The interpreter had been bright, jolly, and recklessly brave—but
then, of how many on both sides might that have been said?
Now he was merely dead.

The Gauls pushed forward on either wing, slashing, stabbing, and chopping. Outnumbered, the Romans had to give

ground, their line bending away from the covering forest. As he watched them driven back upon themselves, the growing knowledge of defeat pressed its icy weight on Scaurus' shoulders. He fought on, rushing now here, now there, wherever the fighting was fiercest, shouting orders and encouragement to his men all the while.

In his learning days he had studied under scholars of the Stoic school. Their teachings served him well now. He did not give way to fright or despair, but kept on doing his best, though he knew it might not be enough. Failure, in itself, was not blameworthy. Lack of effort surely was.

Gaius Philippus, who had seen more bumbling young officers than he could remember, watched this one with growing admiration. The fight was not going well, but with numbers so badly against the Romans it was hard to see how it could have gone much better.

The buccinators' horns blew in high alarm. The woods were screen no more; leaping, yelling Celts burst forward, storming at the Roman rear. Tasting the cup of doom in earnest, Marcus wheeled his last reserves to face them, shouting, "Form circle! Form circle!"

His makeshift rear defense held somehow, beating back the ragged Celtic charge until the Roman circle could take shape. But the trap was sprung. Surrounded deep within the land of their foes, the legionaries could expect but one fate. The night was alive with the Celts' exultant cries as they flowed round the Roman ring like the sea round a pillar of hard black stone it would soon engulf.

Druids' marks on his blade flashing in the torchlight, the Gallic chieftain leaped like a wolf against the Roman line. He hewed his way through three ranks of men, then spun and fought his way back to his own men and safety.

"There's a warrior I'd sooner not come against," Gaius Philippus said, somberly eyeing the twisted bodies and shattered weapons the Gaul had left behind him.

Marcus gave tribute where it was due. "He is a mighty one."

The battle slowed, men from both sides leaning on spear or shield as they tried to catch their breath. The moans of the wounded floated up into the night. Somewhere close by, a cricket chirped.

Marcus realized how exhausted he was. His breath came in panting sobs, his legs were leaden, and his cuirass a burden heavier than Atlas had borne. He itched everywhere; dried, crusted sweat cracked whenever he moved. He had long since stopped noticing its salt taste in his mouth or its sting in his eyes.

His hand had been clenched round his sword hilt for so long he had to will it open to reach for the canteen at his side. The warm, sour wine stung his throat as he swallowed.

The moon rose, a couple of days past full and red as if reflecting the light of this grim field.

As if that had been a signal, the Celtic chieftain came up once more. The Romans tensed to receive his onslaught, but he stopped out of weapon range. He put down his sword, raised his bare right hand above his head. "It's well you've fought," he called to the Romans in fair Latin. "Will you not yield yourselves to me now and ha' done with this foolish slaughter? Your lives you'll save, you know."

The military tribune gave surrender a few seconds' honest thought. For some reason he was inclined to trust the Gaul's good intentions, but doubted the barbarian would be able to control his followers after they had the Romans in their power. He remembered all too well the Gallic custom of burning thieves and robbers alive in wickerwork images and knew it would be easy for the Romans, once captive, to be judged such.

One legionary's comment to his linemate rang loud in the silence: "Bugger the bastard! If he wants us, let him come winkle us out and pay the bill for it!"

After that, Marcus did not feel the need for any direct reply. The Celt understood. "On your heads it will be, then," he warned.

He turned to his own troops, shouting orders. Men who had chosen to sit for a moment heaved themselves up off their haunches, tightened their grips on spears, swords, clubs. They tramped forward, and the insane smithy's din of combat began again.

The Roman ring shrank, but would not break. The still bodies of the slain and thrashing forms of the wounded impeded the Gauls' advance; more than one stumbled to his death trying to climb over them. They came on.

"Give yourselves up, fools, while there's the most of you alive!" their chieftain yelled to his foes.

"When we said 'no' the first time, did you not believe us?" Marcus shouted back.

The Gaul swung up his sword in challenge. "Maybe after the killing of you, the Roman next in line to your honor will have more sense!"

"Not bloody likely!" Gaius Philippus snarled, but the big Celt was already moving. He cut down one Roman and kicked two more aside. He ducked under a broken spear swung club-fashion, lashing out with his blade to hamstring the swinger. Then he was inside the Roman line and loping at Marcus, longsword at the ready.

A score of legionaries, first among them Gaius Philippus, moved to intercept him, but the tribune waved them back. Fighting died away as, by unspoken common consent, both armies grounded their weapons to watch their leaders duel.

A smile lit the Celt's face when he saw Marcus agree to single combat. He raised his sword in salute and said, "A brave man you are, Roman dear. I'd know your name or ever I slay you."

"I am called Marcus Aemilius Scaurus," the tribune replied. He felt more desperate than brave. The Celt lived for war, where he himself had only played at it, more to further his political ambitions than from love of fighting.

He thought of his family in Mediolanum, of the family name that would fail if he fell here. His parents still lived, but were past the age of childbearing, and after him had three daughters but no son.

More briefly, he thought of Valerius Corvus and how, almost three hundred years before, he had driven a Celtic army from central Italy by killing its leader in a duel. He did not really believe these Gauls would flee even if he won. But he might delay and confuse them, maybe enough to let his army live.

All this sped through his mind as he raised his blade to match the Gaul's courtesy. "Will you give me your name as well?" he asked, feeling the ceremony of the moment.

"That I will. It's Viridovix son of Drappes I am, a chief of the Lexovii." The formalities done, Marcus braced for Virido-vix's attack, but the Celt was staring in surprise at his sword.

"How is it," he asked, "that a Roman comes by the blade of a druid?"

"The druid who bore it tried to stand against me and found he could not," Marcus replied, annoyed that his enemies, too, found it odd for him to carry a Celtic sword.

"It came of its own free will, did it?" Viridovix murmured, more surprised now. "Well, indeed and it's a brave blade you have, but you'll find mine no weaker." He drifted forward in a fencer's crouch.

Celtic nonsense, the tribune thought; a sword was a tool, with no more will of its own than a broom. But as he brought his weapon to the guard position, he suddenly felt unsure. No trick of the setting sun now made the druids' marks stamped down the length of the blade flicker and shine. They glowed with a hot golden light of their own, a light that grew stronger and more vital with every approaching step Viridovix took.

The Gaul's sword was flaring, too. It quivered in his hand like a live thing, straining to reach the blade the Roman held. Marcus' was also twisting in his hand, struggling to break free.

Awe and dread chased each other down Viridovix's long face, harshly plain in the hellish light of the swords. Marcus knew his own features bore a similar cast.

Men in both armies groaned and covered their eyes, caught in something past their comprehension.

The two blades met with a roar louder than thunder. The charms the druids had set on them, spells crafted to keep the land of the Gauls ever free of foreign rule, were released at their meeting. That one sword was in an invader's hands only powered the unleashing further.

The Celts outside the embattled circle of Romans saw a dome of red-gold light spring from the crossed blades to surround the legionaries. One Gaul, braver or more foolish than his fellows, rushed forward to touch the dome. He snatched his seared hand back with a howl. When the dome of light faded away, the space within was empty.

Talking in low voices over the prodigy they had witnessed, the Celts buried their dead, then stripped the Roman corpses and buried them in a separate grave. They drifted back to their villages and farms by ones and twos. Few spoke of what they had seen, and fewer were believed.

Later that year Caesar came to the land of the Lexovii, and from him not even miracles could save the Gauls. The only magic he acknowledged was that of empire; for him it was enough. When he wrote his commentaries, the presumed massacre of a scouting column did not seem worth mentioning.

Inside the golden dome, the ground faded away beneath the Romans' feet, leaving them suspended in nothingness. There was a queasy feeling of motion and imbalance, though no wind of passage buffeted their faces. Men cursed, screamed, and called on their gods, to no avail.

Then, suddenly, they stood on dirt again; Marcus had the odd impression it had rushed up to meet his sandals. The dome of light winked out. The Romans found themselves once more in a forest clearing, one smaller and darker than that which they had so unexpectedly left. It was dark night. Though Scaurus knew the moon had risen not long before, there was no moon here. There were no massed Celts, either. For that he gave heartfelt thanks.

He realized he was still sword-to-sword with Viridovix. He stepped back and lowered his blade. At his motion, Viridovix cautiously did the same.

"A truce?" Marcus said. The Gaul was part and parcel of the magic that had fetched them to this place. Killing him out of hand would be foolish.

"Aye, the now," Viridovix said absently. He seemed more interested in looking around at wherever this was than in fighting. He also seemed utterly indifferent to the danger he was in, surrounded by his foes. Marcus wondered whether the bravado was real or assumed. In the midst of Gauls, he would have been too terrified to posture.

He glanced from his sword to Viridovix'. Neither, now, seemed more than a length of edged steel.

The Romans milled about, wandering through the open space. To the tribune's surprise, none came rushing up to demand putting Viridovix to death. Maybe, like Scaurus, they were too stunned at what happened to dare harm him, or maybe that confident attitude was paying dividends.

Junius Blaesus came up to Marcus. Ignoring Viridovix altogether, the scout gave his commander a smart salute, as if by clinging to legionary routine he could better cope with the terrifying unknown into which he had fallen. "I don't believe this is Gaul at all, sir," he said. "I walked to the edge of the clearing, and the trees seem more like the ones in Greece, or some place like Cilicia.

"It's not a bad spot, though," he went on. "There's a pond over there, with a creek running into it. For a while I thought we'd end up in Tartarus, and nowhere else but."

"You weren't the only one," Marcus said feelingly. Then he blinked. It had not occurred to him that whatever had happened might have left him and his troops still within land under Roman control.

The scout's salute and his speculation gave the tribune an idea. He ordered his men to form a camp by the pond Blaesus had found, knowing that the routine labor—a task they had done hundreds of times before—would help take the strangeness from this place.

He wondered how he would explain his arrival to whatever Roman authorities might be here. He could almost hear the skeptical proconsul: "A dome of light, you say? Ye-ss, of course. Tell me, what fare did it charge for your passage . . . ?"

Earthworks rose in a square; inside them, eight-man tents sprang up in neat rows. Without being told, the legionaries left a sizeable space in which Gorgidas could work. Not far from where Marcus stood, the Greek was probing an arrow wound with an extracting-spoon. The injured legionary bit his lips to keep from crying out, then sighed in relief as Gorgidas drew out the barbed point.

Gaius Philippus, who had been supervising the erection of the camp, strolled over to Scaurus' side. "You had a good idea there," he said. "It keeps their minds off things."

So it did, but only in part. Marcus and Gorgidas were educated men, Gaius Philippus toughened by a hard life so he could take almost anything in stride. Most legionaries, though, were young, from farms or tiny villages, and had neither education nor experience to fall back on. The prodigy that had swept them away was too great for the daily grind to hold off for long.

The Romans murmured as they dug, muttered as they carried, whispered to one another as they pounded tentpegs. They made the two-fingered sign against the evil eye, clutching the phallic amulets they wore round their necks to guard themselves from it.

And more and more, they looked toward Viridovix. Like the anodyne of routine, his immunity slowly wore away. The mutters turned hostile. Hands started going to swords and spears. Viridovix' face turned grim. He freed his own long blade in its scabbard, though even with his might he could not have lasted long against a Roman rush.

But the legionaries, it seemed, wanted something more formal and awesome than a lynching. A delegation approached Scaurus, at its head a trooper named Lucilius. He said, "Sir, what say we cut the Gaul's throat, to take away the anger of whatever god did this to us?" The men behind him nodded.

The tribune glanced at Viridovix, who looked back, still unafraid. Had he cringed, Marcus might have let his men have their way, but he was a man who deserved better than being sacrificed for superstition's sake.

Scaurus said so, adding, "He could have stood by while his men slew us all, but instead he chose to meet me face to face. And the gods have done the same thing to him they did to all of us. Maybe they had their reasons."

Some legionaries nodded, but most were still unsatisfied. Lucilius said, "Sir, maybe they left him with us just so we could offer him up, and they'll be angry if we don't."

But the more he thought about it, the more Marcus hated the idea of deliberate human sacrifice. As a Stoic, he did not believe it would do any good, and as a Roman he thought it archaic. Not since the desperate days a hundred fifty years ago, after Hannibal crushed the Romans at Carthage, had they resorted to it. In even more ancient days, they sacrificed old men to relieve famine, but for centuries they had been throwing puppets made of rushes into the Tiber instead.

"That's it!" he said out loud. Both Viridovix and his own men eyed him, the one warily, the others expectantly. Remembering his fear of what the Gauls would do to his men if they surrendered, he went on, "I won't make us into the savage image of the barbarians we were fighting."

He left everyone unhappy. Viridovix let out an angry snort; Lucilius protested, "The gods should have an offering."

"They will," the tribune promised. "In place of Viridovix here, we'll sacrifice an image of him, as the priests do to mark festivals where the victim used to be a man. If the gods take those offerings, they'll accept this one as well—and in this wilderness, wherever it is, we may need the Gaul's might to fight with us now, not against us."

Lucilius was still inclined to argue, but the practicality of Scaurus' argument won over most of the men. Without backing, Lucilius gave up. To keep from having a disaffected soldier in the ranks, Marcus detailed him to gather cloth and, from the edges of the pond, rushes to make the effigy. Self-importance touched, Lucilius bustled away.

"I thank your honor," Viridovix said.

"He didn't do it for *your* sake," said Gaius Philippus. The senior centurion had stayed in the background, quiet but ready to back Marcus at need. "He did it to hold his leadership over the troops."

That was not altogether true, but Marcus knew better than to dilute Gaius Philippus' authority by contradicting him. He kept quiet. Why the Gaul thought he had saved him did not matter; the result did.

Viridovix looked down his nose at the short, stocky centurion. "And what would you have had him do with me, now? Chop me into dogmeat? The dogs'll feed on more than me if you try that—a deal more, if himself sends runts like you against me."

Scaurus expected Gaius Philippus to fly into a killing rage, but instead he threw back his head and laughed. "Well said, you great hulk!"

"Hulk, is it?" Viridovix swore in Gaulish, but he was grinning too.

"What then?" Marcus said. "Do you aim to join us, at least till we find out where we are? The gods know, you're a warrior born."

"Och, the shame of it, a Roman asking for my comradeship and me saying aye. But these woods are a solitary place for a puir lone Celt, and you Romans are men yourselves, for all that you're dull."

Gaius Philippus snorted.

"There's another score," Viridovix said. "Will your men

have me, after my sending more than one of them to the next world?"

"They'd better," the senior centurion said, smacking his vine-stave into a callused palm.

"Dull," Viridovix repeated. "Never the chance to tell your officer be damned to him—and the day you try ordering me about you'll remember forever. Nay, it's always march in line, camp in line, fight in line. Tell me, do you futter in line as well?"

Having done so more than once, the centurion maintained a discreet silence.

The more they snipe, Marcus thought, the sooner they'll grow used to each other. He slapped at a mosquito. He must have missed, because he heard it buzz away.

Lucilius hurried up, carrying in his arms a bundle of rushes tied here and there with linen strips. It did not look much like a man, but again Scaurus had no intention of criticizing. If it satisfied Lucilius, that was good enough.

"What will you do with it, sir?" the trooper asked. "Throw it into the water the way the priests in Rome fling the puppets off the Sublician Bridge into the Tiber?"

Marcus rubbed his chin, thinking briefly. He shook his head. "In view of the color of the dome of light we were in, I think I ought to cast it into the flames instead."

Lucilius nodded, impressed by the tribune's reasoning. "Here, sir." He handed Scaurus the effigy, falling in behind him to make the beginning of a procession. More men joined it as Scaurus walked slowly and ceremoniously toward one of the campfires.

He paused in front of it so more of the legionaries could gather. Others looked up from their tasks to watch. Then he raised the crude rush-puppet high over his head, proclaiming loudly, "Whatsoever god or goddess is responsible for the wonder that has overtaken us, by whatever name or names you wish to be called, accept this offering in propitiation!" He hurled the image into the fire.

The flames leaped as they burned the effigy. "See how the god receives the sacrifice!" Lucilius cried. Marcus hid a smile; it was as if the legionary himself had thought of substituting the puppet for the man.

Yet the tribune wondered for a moment if Lucilius saw

something he was missing. An effigy of damp rushes should have burned slowly instead of being consumed like so much tinder.

Marcus scowled, suppressing his superstitious maunderings. One miracle in an evening, he told himself firmly, is enough. He turned his back on the fire and went over to see how Gorgidas was doing with the wounded.

"How does it look like I'm doing?" Gorgidas snarled at him.

"Not well," Scaurus admitted. Gorgidas was rushing from one injured man to the next, bandaging here, suturing there, tossing his head in despair at a head wound he had no hope of treating. The tribune asked, "What help can I give you?"

The Greek looked up, as if just realizing Marcus was there. "Hmm? Let me think. . . . If you order a couple of troopers to work with me, that might help a little. They'd be clumsy, but better than nothing—and sometimes, whether he wants to or not, a man writhes so much he needs to be held."

"I'll take care of it," the tribune said. "What happened to Attilius and Publius Curtianus?"

"My assistants? What do you suppose happened to them?"

His face hot, Marcus beat a hasty retreat. He almost forgot to send the legionaries over to Gorgidas.

Gaius Philippus and Viridovix were still arguing, away from most of the men. The senior centurion drew his sword. Scaurus dashed over to break up the fight. He found none to break up; Gaius Philippus was showing the Gaul the thrusting-stroke.

"All well and good, Roman dear," Viridovix said, "but why then are you spoiling it by using so short a blade?"

The veteran shrugged. "Most of us aren't big enough to handle the kind of pigsticker you swing. Besides, a thrust, even with a *gladius*, leaves a man farther from his foe than a cut from a longsword."

The two lifelong warriors might have been a couple of bakers talking about how to make bread rise highest. Marcus smiled at the way a common passion could make even deadly foes forget their enmity.

One of the junior centurions, a slim youngster named Quintus Glabrio, came up to him and said, "Begging your pardon, sir, could you tell me where this is so I can pass the word along to the men and quiet them down? The talk is getting wild."

"I'm not sure, precisely. From the terrain and the trees, one of the scouts thinks this may be Cilicia or Greece. Come morning we'll send out a detail, track down some peasants, and find out what we need to know."

Glabrio gaped at him. Even in the starlight Marcus could see the fear on his face, fear intense enough to make him forget the pain of a slashed forearm. "Cilicia, sir? Greece? Have you—?" Words failed him. He pointed to the sky.

Puzzled, Marcus looked up. It was a fine, clear night. Let's see, he thought, scanning the heavens, north should be . . . where? Cold fingers walked his spine as he stared at the meaningless patterns the stars scrawled across the sky. Where was the Great Bear that pointed to the pole? Where were the stars of summer, the Scorpion, the Eagle, the Lyre? Where were the autumn groupings that followed them through the night, Andromeda, Pegasus? Where even were the stars of winter, or the strange constellations that peeped above the southern horizon in tropic lands like Africa or Cyrenaica?

Gaius Philippus and Viridovix stared with him, shared his will to disbelieve. The Gaul cursed in his native speech, not as he had at Gaius Philippus, but softly, as if in prayer. "Gods on Olympus," the senior centurion murmured, and Marcus had to fight hysterical laughter. This place was beyond the Olympians' realm. And his own as well; his vision of an angry proconsul blew away in the wind of the unknown.

Few Romans slept much that night. They sat outside their tents, watching the illegible heavens wheel and trying, as men will, to tame the unknown by drawing patterns on it and naming them: the Target, the Ballista, the Locust, the Pederasts.

The naming went on through the night as new stars rose to replace their setting fellows. The east grew pale, then pink. The forest ceased to be a single dark shape, becoming trees, bushes, and shrubs no more remarkable than the ones of Gaul, if not quite the same. The sun rose, and was simply the sun.

And an arrow flashed out of the woods, followed an instant later by a challenge in an unknown tongue.

II

FROM THE WAY THEIR CHALLENGER BRUSHED THE BUSHES aside and strode toward the Romans, Marcus was sure he was no skulking woods-bandit, but a man who felt the full power of his country behind him. It showed in the set of his shoulders, in the watchful suspicion on his face, in the very fact that he dared come out, alone, to defy twelve hundred men.

"You're right enough," Gaius Philippus agreed when the tribune put his thought into words. "He's not quite alone, though—or if I were in his boots, I'd not be so lackwitted as to leave my bow behind. He'll have friends covering him from the woods, I'd wager."

So it seemed, for the warrior stopped well within arrow range of the trees from which he'd come and waited, arms folded across his chest. "Let's see what he has to say," Marcus said. "Gaius, you'll come with me, and you, Viridovix— maybe he understands Celtic. Gorgidas!"

The doctor finished a last neat knot on the bandage he was tying before he looked up. "What do you need *me* for?"

"If you'd rather I relied on my own Greek—"

"I'm coming, I'm coming."

The tribune also picked Adiatun, an officer of the slingers. Like his men, he was from the Balearic Islands off the coast of Spain and had their strange tongue as his birthspeech. One of the legionaries who had served in the east had picked up a bit of Syrian and Armenian. That would have to do, Marcus decided. Any more and the waiting soldier would think them an attack, not a parley.

As it was, he drew back a pace when he saw half a dozen men approaching from the Roman camp. But Marcus and his companions moved slowly, right hands extended before them at eye level, palms out to show their emptiness. After a moment's hesitation, he returned the gesture and advanced. He stopped about ten feet from them, saying something that had to mean, "This is close enough." He studied the newcomers with frank curiosity.

Marcus returned it. The native was a lean man of middle height, perhaps in his mid-thirties. Save for a proud nose, his features were small and fine under a wide forehead, giving his face a triangular look. His olive skin was sun-darkened and weathered; he carried a long scar on his left cheek and another above his left eye. His jaw was outlined by a thin fringe of beard, mostly dark, but streaked with silver on either side of his mouth.

But for that unstylish beard, Marcus thought, by his looks he could have been a Roman, or more likely a Greek. He wore a shirt of mail reaching halfway down his thighs. Unlike the Romans', it had sleeves. Over it was a forest-green surcoat of light material. His helm was a businesslike iron pot; an apron of mail was riveted to it to cover his neck, and a bar nasal protected his face. The spurs on the heels of his calf-length leather boots said he was a horseman, as did the saber at his belt and the small round shield slung on his back.

The soldier asked something, probably, Marcus thought, "Who are you people, and what are you doing here?" The tribune looked to his group of would-be interpreters. They all shook their heads. He answered in Latin, "We have no more idea where we are than you do who we are."

The native spread his hands and shrugged, then tried what sounded like a different language. He had no better luck. The Romans used every tongue at their command, and the soldier seemed to speak five or six himself, but they held none in common.

The warrior finally grimaced in annoyance. He patted the ground, waved his hand to encompass everything the eye could see. "Videssos," he said. He pointed at Marcus, then at the camp from which he had come, and raised his eyebrows questioningly.

"Romans," the tribune answered.

"Are you after including me in that?" Viridovix asked. "The shame of it!"

"Yes, we all feel it," Gaius Philippus told him.

"Enough, you two," Gorgidas said. "I'm no more Roman than you, my mustachioed friend, but we need to keep things as simple as we can."

"Thank you," Marcus said. "Romans," he repeated.

The Videssian had watched the byplay with interest. Now he pointed at himself. "Neilos Tzimiskes."

After echoing him, Scaurus and his companions gave their names. Viridovix grumbled, "A man could choke to death or ever he said 'Tzimiskes,'" but Neilos had no easier time with "Viridovix son of Drappes."

Tzimiskes unbuckled his swordbelt and laid it at his feet. There was a cry of alarm from the woods, but he silenced it with a couple of shouted sentences. He pointed to the sword, to himself, and to Marcus, and made a gesture of repugnance.

"We have no quarrel with you," Scaurus agreed, knowing his words would not be understood but hoping his tone would. He reached into his pack for a ration biscuit, offering it and his canteen, still half-full of wine, to Tzimiskes.

The Videssian nodded and grinned, shedding years as he did so. "Not so happy will he be when he eats what you give him," Adiatun said. "The *bucellum* tastes all too much like sawdust."

But Tzimiskes bit into the hard-baked biscuit without complaint, drank a long swallow of wine with the air of a man who has had worse. He patted himself apologetically, then shouted into the forest again. A few moments later another, younger, Videssian emerged. His equipment was much like that of Tzimiskes, though his surcoat was brown rather than green. He carried a short bow in his left hand and bore a leather sack over his right shoulder.

The young Videssian's name was Proklos Mouzalon. From his sack he brought out dried apples and figs, olives, smoked and salted pork, a hard yellow cheese, onions, and journey-bread differing from the Romans' only in that it was square, not round—all normal fare for soldiers on the move. He also produced a small flask of thick, sweet wine. Marcus found it cloying, as he was used to the drier vintage the Roman army drank.

Before they raised the flask to their lips, the Videssians each spat angrily on the ground, then lifted their arms and eyes to the sky, at the same time murmuring a prayer. Marcus had been about to pour a small libation, but decided instead to follow the custom of the country in which he found himself. Tzimiskes and Mouzalon nodded their approval as he did so, though of course his words were gibberish to them.

By signs, Neilos made it clear there was a town a couple of days' travel to the south, a convenient place to establish a market to feed the Roman soldiers and lodge them for the time being. He sent Mouzalon ahead to prepare the town for their arrival; the clop of hoofbeats down a forest path confirmed the Videssians as horsemen.

While Tzimiskes was walking back to his own tethered mount, Marcus briefed his men on what had been arranged. "I think we'll be able to stay together," he said. "As far as I could understand all the finger-waving, these people hire mercenaries, and they're used to dealing with bodies of foreign troops. The problem was that Tzimiskes had never seen our sort before, and wasn't sure if we were invaders, a free company for hire, or men from the far side of the moon."

He stopped abruptly, mentally cursing his clumsy tongue; he was afraid the Romans were farther from home than that.

Gaius Philippus came to his rescue, growling, "Another thing, you wolves. On march, we treat this as friendly country—no stealing a farmer's mule or his daughter just because they take your fancy. By Vulcan's left nut, you'll see a cross if you bugger that one up. Till we know we have a place here, we walk soft."

"Dull, dull, dull," Viridovix said. The centurion ignored him.

"Are you going to sell our swords to these barbarians?" someone called.

Gaius Philippus glared as he tried to spot the man who had spoken, but Scaurus said, "It's a fair question. Let me answer this way: our swords are all we have to sell. Unless you know the way back to Rome, we're a bit outnumbered." It was a

feeble jest, but so plainly true the legionaries nodded to themselves as they began breaking camp.

Marcus was not eager to take up the mercenary's trade, but
an armed force at his back lent him bargaining power with the
Videssians he would not have had otherwise. It also gave him
the perfect excuse for keeping the Romans together. In this
strange new land, they had only themselves to rely on.

The tribune also wondered about Videssos' reasons for hir-
ing foreign troops. To his way of thinking, that was for deca-
dent kingdoms like Ptolemaic Egypt, not for healthy states.
But Tzimiskes and Mouzalon were soldiers and were also
plainly natives.

He sighed. So much to learn—

At Gorgidas' request, Scaurus detailed a squad to cut poles
for litters; more than a score of Romans were too badly
wounded to walk. "Fever will take some," the Greek said,
"but if they get decent food and treatment in this town, most
should pull through."

Tzimiskes rode up to the edge of the makeshift earthwork
the Romans had made. Atop his horse, he was high enough
off the ground to see inside. He seemed impressed by the
bustle and the order of the camp.

Though canny enough not to say so, Scaurus was struck by
the equipment of the Videssian's saddle and horse. Even at a
quick glance, there were ideas there the Romans had never
had. For one thing, Neilos rode with his feet in irons shaped to
hold them, which hung from his saddle by leather straps. For
another, when his mount lifted a forefoot, the tribune saw that
its hoof was shod in iron to help protect it from stones and
thorns.

"Isn't that the sneakiest thing?" Gaius Philippus said as he
strolled up. "The whoreson can handle a sword or a bow—or
even a spear—with both hands, and stay on with his feet.
Why didn't we ever think of that?"

"It might be a good idea not to let on that we didn't know
of such things."

"I wasn't born yesterday."

"Yes, I know," Marcus said. Not a glance had his centurion
given to Tzimiskes' gear while he spoke of it. The Videssian,
looking from one of them to the other, could have had no clue
to what they were talking about.

* * *

About an hour's march west along a narrow, twisting woods-path got the Romans free of the forest and into the beginnings of settled country. His horizon widening as he moved into open land, Marcus looked about curiously. The terrain he was passing through was made up of rolling hills and valleys; to the north and northeast real mountains loomed purple against the horizon.

Farmhouses dotted the hillsides, as did flocks of sheep and goats. More than one farmer started driving his beasts away from the road as soon as he caught sight of an armed column of unfamiliar aspect. Tzimiskes shouted reassurance at them, but most preferred to take no chances. "Looks like they've been through it before," Gaius Philippus said. Marcus gave a thoughtful nod.

The weather was warmer and drier than it had been in Gaul, despite a brisk breeze from the west. The wind had a salt tang to it; a gull screeched high overhead before gliding away.

"We'll not be having to take ship to come to this town, will we?" Viridovix asked Marcus.

"I don't think so. Why?"

"For all I've lived by the ocean the whole of my life, it's terrible seasick I get." The Celt paled at the thought of it.

The narrow path they had been following met a broad thoroughfare running north and south. Used to the stone-paved highways the Romans built, Marcus found its dirt surface disappointing until Gaius Philippus pointed out, "This is a nation of horsemen, you know. Horses don't care much for hard roads; I suppose that still holds true with iron soles on their feet. Our roads aren't for animal traffic—they're for moving infantry from one place to another in a hurry."

The tribune was only half-convinced. Come winter, this road would be a sea of mud. Even in summer, it had disadvantages—he coughed as Tzimiskes' horse kicked up dust.

He stepped forward to try to talk with the Videssian, pointing at things and learning their names in Tzimiskes' tongue while teaching him the Latin equivalents. To his chagrin, Tzimiskes was much quicker at picking up his speech than he was in remembering Videssian words.

In the late afternoon they marched past a low, solidly built stone building. At the eastern edge of its otherwise flat roof, a blue-painted wooden spire leaped into the air; it was topped by a gilded ball. Blue-robed men who had shaved their pates but kept full, bushy beards worked in the gardens surrounding the structure. Both building and occupants were so unlike anything Marcus had yet seen that he looked a question to Tzimiskes.

His guide performed the same ritual he had used before he drank wine, spitting and raising his arms and head. The tribune concluded the blue-robes were priests of some sort, though tending a garden seemed an odd way to follow one's gods. He wondered if they did such work full time. If so, he thought, they took their religion seriously.

There was little traffic on the road. A merchant, catching sight of the marching column as he topped a rise half a mile south, promptly turned his packhorses round and fled. Gaius Philippus snorted in derision. "What does he think we can do? Run down his horses, and us afoot?"

"Dinna even think of it," Viridovix said earnestly. "A mess o' blisters bigger than goldpieces, my feet must be. I think you Romans were born so you couldna feel pain in your legs. My calves are on fire, too."

To Scaurus, on the other hand, the day's march had been an easy one. His men were slowed by the litters they bore in teams. Many were walking wounded, and all bone-weary. Four of the soldiers in the litters died that day, as Gorgidas had known they would.

Tzimiskes appeared pleased at the pace the legionaries had been able to keep. He watched fascinated, as they used the last sunshine and the purple twilight to create their square field fortifications. Marcus was proud of the skill and discipline his exhausted troops displayed.

When the sun dipped below the western horizon, Neilos went through his now-familiar series of actions, though his prayer was longer than the one he had made at wine. "That explains the golden ball back down the road," Gorgidas said.

"It does?" Marcus' mind had been elsewhere.

"Of course it does. These people must be sun-worshipers."

The tribune considered it. "There are worse cults," he said. "Reverencing the sun is a simple enough religion." Gorgidas

dipped his head in agreement, but Marcus would long remember the naïveté and ignorance behind his remark.

A thin sliver of crescent moon slid down the sky, soon
leaving it to the incomprehensible stars. Marcus was glad to
see there was a moon, at least, even if it was out of phase with
the one he had known. A wolf bayed in the distant hills.

The day had been warm, but after sunset it grew surprisingly chilly. When added to the ripe state of the grainfields he
had seen, that made Marcus guess the season to be fall,
though in Gaul it had been early summer. Well, he thought, if
this land's moon doesn't match my own, no good reason its
seasons should, either. He gave it up and slept.

The town's name was Imbros. Though three or four ball-
topped blue spires thrust their way into sight, its wall was high
enough to conceal nearly everything within. The fortifications
seemed sturdy enough, and in good condition. But while most
of the gray stonework was old and weathered, much of the
northern wall looked to have been recently rebuilt. The tribune
wondered how long ago the sack had taken place and who the
foe had been.

He knew the local leaders would not let any large numbers
of his men into the town until they were convinced the legionaries could be trusted, but he had expected Imbros would
ready a market outside the walls for the Romans' use. Where
were the scurrying peasants, the bustling merchants, the approaching wagonloads of grain and other supplies? The city
was not shut up against a siege, but it was not looking to the
arrival of a friendly army either.

That could mean trouble. His troops were nearly through
the iron rations they carried in their packs, and the fields and
farms round Imbros looked fat. Not even Roman discipline
would hold long in the face of hunger.

With his few words and many gestures, he tried to get that
across to Tzimiskes. The Videssian, a soldier himself, understood at once; he seemed puzzled and dismayed that the messenger he had sent ahead was being ignored.

"This is good brigand country," Gaius Philippus said. "I
wonder if young Mouzalon was bushwhacked on his way
here."

Viridovix said, "Wait—is that not the youngling himself, galloping out toward us?"

Mouzalon was already talking as he rode up to Tzimiskes. The latter's answers, short at first, grew longer, louder, and angrier. The word or name "Vourtzes" came up frequently; when at last it was mentioned once too often, Tzimiskes spat in disgust.

"He must be truly furious, to vent his rage by perverting a prayer," Gorgidas said softly to Marcus. The tribune nodded, grateful for the Greek's insights.

Something was happening to Imbros now. There was a stir at the north gate, heralding the emergence of a procession. First came a fat man wearing a silver circlet on his balding head and a robe of maroon brocade. Parasol bearers flanked him on either side. They had to be for ceremony, as it was nearing dusk. Tzimiskes gave the fat man a venomous glance —was this, then, Vourtzes?

Vourtzes, if it was he, was followed by four younger, leaner men in less splendid robes. From their inkstained fingers and the nervous, nearsighted stares they sent at the Romans, Marcus guessed they were the fat man's secretaries.

With them came a pair of shaven-headed priests. One wore a simple robe of blue; the other, a thin-faced man with a graying beard and bright, burning eyes, had a palm-wide circle of cloth-of-gold embroidered on the left breast of his garment. The plain-robed priest swung a brass thurible that gave forth clouds of sweet, spicy smoke.

On either side of the scribes and priests tramped a squad of foot soldiers: big, fair, stolid-looking men in surcoats of scarlet and silver over chain mail. They carried pikes and wicked-looking throwing axes; their rectangular shields had various devices painted on them. Mercenaries, the tribune decided— they looked like no Videssians he had yet seen.

Behind the soldiers came three trumpeters, a like number of flute-players, and a man even fatter than Vourtzes pushing a kettledrum on a little wheeled cart.

Vourtzes stopped half a dozen places in front of the Romans. His honor-guard came to a halt with a last stomped step and a loud, wordless shout; Marcus felt his men bristling at the arrogant display. Trumpeters and flautists blew an elabo-

rate flourish. The tubby drummer smote his instrument with
such vim that Scaurus waited for it or its cart to collapse.

When the fanfare stopped, the two Videssians with the
Roman army put their right hands over their hearts and bent
their heads to the plump official who led the parade. Marcus
gave him the Roman salute, clenched right fist held straight
out before him at eye level. At Gaius Philippus' barked command, the legionaries followed his example in smart unison.

Startled, the Videssian gave back a pace. He glared at
Scaurus, who had to hide a grin. To cover his discomfiture,
the official gestured his priests forward. The older one pointed
a bony finger at Marcus, rattling off what sounded like a
series of questions. "I'm sorry, my friend, but I do not speak
your language," the tribune replied in Latin. The priest
snapped a couple of queries at Tzimiskes.

His reply must have been barely satisfactory, for the priest
let out an audible sniff. But he shrugged and gave what
Marcus hoped were his blessings to the Romans, his censer-
swinging comrade occasionally joining in his chanted prayer.

The benediction seemed to complete a prologue the Videssians felt necessary. When the priests had gone back to their
place by the scribes, the leader of the parade stepped up to
clasp Marcus' hands. His own were plump, beringed, and
sweaty; the smile he wore had little to do with his feelings, but
was the genial mask any competent politician could assume at
will. The tribune understood that face quite well, for he wore
it himself.

With patience and Tzimiskes' help, Scaurus learned this
was indeed Rhadenos Vourtzes, *hypasteos* of the city of
Imbros—governor by appointment of the Emperor of Videssos. The Emperor's name, Marcus gathered, was Mavrikios, of the house of Gavras. The Roman got the impression
Tzimiskes was loyal to Mavrikios, and that he did not think
Vourtzes shared his loyalty.

Why, Marcus struggled to ask, had the *hypasteos* not begun
to prepare his town for the arrival of the Romans? Vourtzes,
when he understood, spread his hands regretfully. The news of
their appearance had only come the day before. It was hard to
believe in any case, as Vourtzes had no prior reports of any
body of men crossing Videssos' border. And finally, the *hypasteos* did not place much faith in the word of an *akrites*, a

name which seemed to apply to both Mouzalon and Tzi-miskes.

Young Proklos reddened with anger at that and set his hand on the hilt of his sword. But Vourtzes turned his smile to the soldier and calmed him with a couple of sentences. In this case, it seemed, he had been wrong; matters would be straightened out shortly.

Without liking the man who gave it, Marcus had to admire the performance. As for delivery on the promises, he would see.

Gorgidas plucked at the tribune's arm. His thin face was haggard with exhaustion. "Have they physicians?" he demanded. "I need help with our wounded, or at least poppy juice to ease the pain for the ones who are going to die no matter what we do."

"We can find out," Scaurus said. He had no idea of the words to tell Vourtzes what he needed, but sometimes words were unnecessary. He caught the *hypasteos'* eye, led him to the litters. The official's retinue followed.

At the sight of the injured legionaries, Vourtzes made a choked sound of dismay. In spite of the soldiers with him, Marcus thought, he did not know much of war.

To the tribune's surprise, the lean priest who had prayed at the Romans stooped beside a litter. "What's he mucking about for?" Gorgidas said indignantly. "I want another doctor, not spells and flummeries."

"You may as well let him do what he wants," Gaius Philippus said. "Sextus Minucius won't care."

Looking at the moaning legionary, Marcus thought the senior centurion was right. A bandage soaked with blood and pus was wrapped over a spear wound in Minucius' belly. From the scent of ordure, Scaurus knew his gut had been pierced. That sort of wound was always fatal.

Gorgidas must have reached the same conclusion. He touched Minucius' forehead and clicked his tongue between his teeth. "A fever you could cook meat over. Aye, let's see what the charlatan does for him. Poor bastard can't even keep water down, so poppy juice won't do him any good either. With the dark bile he's been puking up, at most he only has a couple of bad days left."

The wounded soldier turned his head toward the sound of

the Greek's voice. He was a big, strapping man, but his features bore the fearful, dazed look Marcus had come to recognize, the look of a man who knew he was going to die.

As far as the Videssian priest was concerned, all the Romans but Minucius might have disappeared. The priest dug under the stinking bandages, set his hands on the legionary's torn belly, one on either side of the wound. Scaurus expected Minucius to shriek at the sudden pressure, but the legionary stayed quiet. Indeed, he stopped his anguished thrashing and lay still in the litter. His eyes slid shut.

"That's something, anyhow," Marcus said. "He—"

"Hush," Gorgidas broke in. He had been watching the priest's face, saw the intense concentration build on it.

"Watch your mouth with the tribune," Gaius Philippus warned, but halfheartedly—not being in the chain of command, Gorgidas had more liberty than a simple solider.

"It's all right—" Scaurus began. Then he stopped of his own accord, the skin on his arms prickling into gooseflesh. He had the same sense of stumbling into the unknown that he'd felt when his blade met Viridovix'. That thought made him half draw his sword. Sure enough, the druids' marks were glowing, not brilliantly as they had then, but with a soft, yellow light.

Thinking about it later, he put that down to the magic's being smaller than the one that had swept him to Videssos, and to his being on the edge of it rather than at the heart. All the same, he could feel the energy passing from the priest to Minucius. Gaius Philippus' soft whistle said he perceived it too.

"A flow of healing," Gorgidas whispered. He was talking to himself, but his words gave a better name to what the priest was doing than anything Marcus could have come up with. As with the strange stars here, though, it was only a label to put on the incomprehensible.

The Videssian lifted his hands. His face was pale; sweat ran down into his beard. Minucius' eyes opened. "I'm hungry," he said in a matter-of-fact voice.

Gorgidas leaped at him like a wolf on a calf. He tore open the bandages the priest had disturbed. What they saw left him speechless, and made Scaurus and Gaius Philippus gasp. The

great scar to the left of **Minucius'** navel was white and puckered, as if it had been there five years.

"I'm hungry," the legionary repeated.

"Oh, shut up," Gorgidas said. He sounded angry, not at
Minucius but at the world. What he had just witnessed
smashed the rational, cynical approach he tried to take to
everything. To have magic succeed where his best efforts had
been sure failures left him baffled, furious, and full of an awe
he would not admit even to himself.

But he had been around Romans long enough to have
learned not to quarrel with results. He grabbed the priest by
the arm and frogmarched him to the next most desperately
hurt man—this one had a sucking wound that had collapsed a
lung.

The Videssian pressed his hands to the legionary's chest.
Again Marcus, along with his comrades, sensed the healing
current pass from priest to Roman, though this time the contact lasted much longer before the priest pulled away. As he
did, the soldier stirred and tried to stand. When Gorgidas ex-
amined his wound, it was like Minucius': a terrible scar, but
one apparently long healed.

Gorgidas hopped from foot to foot in anguished frustration.
"By Asklepios, I have to learn the language to find out how he
does that!" He looked as though he wanted to wring the answer from the priest, with hot irons if he had to.

Instead, he seized the Videssian and hauled him off to another injured legionary. This time the priest tried to pull away.
"He's dying, curse you!" Gorgidas shouted. The cry was in
his native Greek, but when Gorgidas pointed at the soldier, the
priest had to take his meaning.

He sighed, shrugged, and stooped. But when he thrust his
hands under the Roman's bandages, he began to shake, as
with an ague. Marcus thought he felt the healing magic begin,
but before he could be sure, the priest toppled in a faint.

"Oh, plague!" Gorgidas howled. He ran after another blue-
robe and, ignoring the fellow's protests, dragged him over to
the line of wounded soldiers. But this priest only shrugged and
regretfully spread his hands. At last Gorgidas understood he
was no healer. He swore and drew back his foot as if to boot
the unconscious priest awake.

Gaius Philippus grabbed him. "Have you lost your wits?

He's given you back two you never thought to save. Be grateful for what you have—look at the poor wretch, too. There's no more help left in him than wine in an empty jar."

"Two?" Gorgidas struggled without success against the veteran's powerful grip. "I want to heal them all!"

"So do I," Gaius Philippus said. "So do I. They're good lads, and they deserve better than the nasty ways of dying they've found for themselves. But you'll kill that priest if you push him any more, and then he won't be able to fix 'em at all. As is, maybe he can come back tomorrow."

"Some will have died by then," Gorgidas said, but less heatedly—as usual, the senior centurion made hard, practical sense.

Gaius Philippus went off to start the legionaries setting up camp for the night. Marcus and Gorgidas stood by the priest until, some minutes later, he came to himself and shakily got to his feet.

The tribune bowed lower to him than he had to Vourtzes. That was only fitting. So far, the priest had done more for the Romans.

That evening, Scaurus called together some of his officers to hash out what the legionaries should do next. As an afterthought, he added Gorgidas to Gaius Philippus, Quintus Glabrio, Junius Blaesus, and Adiatun the Iberian. When Viridovix ambled into the tent, he did not chase the Gaul away either—he was after as many different viewpoints as he could find.

Back in Gaul, with the full authority of Rome behind him, he would have made the decision himself and passed it on to his men. He wondered if he was diluting his authority by discussing things with them now. No, he thought—this situation was too far removed from ordinary military routine to be handled conventionally. The Romans were a republican people; more voices counted than the leader's.

Blaesus raised that point at once. "It grates on me, sir, it does, to have to hire on to a barbarian king. What are we, so many Parthians?"

Gaius Philippus muttered agreement. So did Viridovix; to him, even the Romans followed their leaders too blindly. He and the senior centurion looked at each other in surprise. Neither seemed pleased at thinking along with the other. Marcus smiled.

"Did you see the way the local bigwig was eyeing us?" Quintus Glabrio put in. "To him, *we* were the barbarians."

"I saw that too," Scaurus said. "I didn't like it."

"They may be right." That was Gorgidas. "Sextus Minucius would tell you so. I saw him in front of his tent, sitting there mending his tunic. Whatever these Videssians are, they know things we don't."

"Gaius Philippus and I already noticed that," Marcus said, and mentioned the iron riding-aids and horseshoes on Tzimiskes' mount. Glabrio nodded; he had spotted them too. So had Viridovix, who paid close attention to anything related to war. Blaesus and Adiatun looked surprised.

"The other problem, of course, is what happens to us if we don't join the Videssians," Glabrio said. The junior centurion had a gift for going to the heart of things, Scaurus thought.

"We couldn't stay under arms, not in the middle of their country," Gaius Philippus said with a reluctant nod. "I'm too old to enjoy life as a brigand, and that's the best we could hope for, setting up on our own. There aren't enough of us to go conquering here."

"And if we disarm, they can deal with us piecemeal, turn us into slaves or whatever they do to foreigners," Marcus said. "Together we have power, but none as individuals."

Ever since they'd met Tzimiskes, he had been looking for a more palatable answer than mercenary service and failing to find one. He'd hoped the others would see something he had missed, but the choice looked inescapable.

"Lucky we are they buy soldiers," Adiatun said. "Otherwise they would be hunting us down now." As a foreign auxiliary, he was already practically a mercenary; he would not earn Roman citizenship till his discharge. He did not seem much upset at the prospect of becoming a Videssian instead.

"All bets are off if we find out where Rome is, though," Gaius Philippus said. Everyone nodded, but with less hope and eagerness than Scaurus would have thought possible a few days before. Seeing alien stars in the sky night after night painfully reminded him how far from home the legionaries were. The Videssian priest's healing magic was an even stronger jolt; like Gorgidas, the tribune knew no Greek or Roman could have matched it.

Gaius Philippus was the last one to leave Scaurus' tent. He threw the tribune a salute straight from the drillfield. "You'd best start planning to live up to it," he said, chuckling at Marcus' bemused expression. "After all, *you're* Caesar now."

Startled, Marcus burst out laughing, but as he crawled into his bedroll he realized the senior centurion was right. Indeed, Gaius Philippus had understated things. Not even Caesar had ever commanded all the Romans there were. The thought was daunting enough to keep him awake half the night.

The market outside Imbros was established over the next couple of days. The quality of goods and food the locals offered was high, the prices reasonable. That relieved Marcus, for his men had left much of their wealth behind with the legionary bankers before setting out on their last, fateful mission.

Nor were the Romans yet in the official service of Videssos. Vourtzes said he would fix that as soon as he could. He sent a messenger south to the capital with word of their arrival. Scaurus noticed that Proklos Mouzalon disappeared about the same time. He carefully did not remark on it to Tzimiskes, who stayed with the Romans as an informal liaison despite Vourtzes' disapproval. Faction against faction . . .

Mouzalon's mission must have succeeded, for the imperial commissioner who came to Imbros ten days later to inspect the strange troops was not a man to gladden Vourtzes' heart. No bureaucrat he, but a veteran warrior whose matter-of-fact competence and impatience with any kind of formality reminded Marcus of Gaius Philippus.

The commissioner, whose name was Nephon Khoumnos, walked through the semipermanent camp the Romans had set up outside Imbros' walls. He had nothing but admiration for its good order, neatness, and sensible sanitation. When his inspection was done, he said to Marcus, "Hell's ice, man, where did you people spring from? You may know the tricks of the soldier's trade better than we do, you're no folk we've set eyes on before, and you appear inside the Empire without seeming to have crossed the border. How does this happen?"

Scaurus and his officers had been spending every free moment studying Videssian—with Tzimiskes, with Vourtzes' scribes, and with the priests, who seemed surprised the tribune wanted to learn to read and at how quickly he picked up the written language. After working with both the Roman and Greek alphabets, another script held no terrors for him. He found following a conversation much harder. Still, he was beginning to understand.

But he had little hope of putting across how he had been swept here, and less of being believed. Yet he liked Khoumnos and did not want to lie to him. With Tzimiskes' help, he explained as best he could and waited for the officer's disbelief.

It did not come. Khoumnos drew the sun-sign on his breast. "Phos!" he muttered, naming his people's god. "That is a strong magic, friend Roman; you must be a nation of mighty sorcerers."

Surprised he was not being laughed at, Marcus had to disagree. Khoumnos gave him a conspiratorial wink. "Then let it be your secret. That fat slug of a Vourtzes will treat you better if he thinks you may turn him into a newt if he crosses you."

He went on, "I think, outlander, the Imperial Guards could have use for such as you. Maybe you can teach the Halogai—" he named the blond northerners who made up Vourtzes' honor guard, and evidently much of the Emperor's as well, "—that there's more to soldiering than a wild charge at anything you don't happen to like. And I tell you straight out, with the accursed Yezda—may Skotos take them to hell!—sucking the blood from our westlands, we need men."

Khoumnos cocked an eye to the north. Dirty gray clouds were gathering there, harbingers of winter storms to come. He rubbed his chin. "Would it suit you to wait until spring before you come to the city?" he asked Marcus. By the slight emphasis he laid on "the," Scaurus knew he meant the town of Videssos itself. "That will give us time to be fully ready for you . . ."

Time to lay the political groundwork, Marcus understood him to mean. But Khoumnos' proposal suited him, and he said so. A peaceful winter at Imbros would allow his men a full refit and recovery, and let them learn their new land's ways and tongue without the pressure they would face in the capital. When Khoumnos departed, they were on the best of terms.

Rhadenos Vourtzes, Marcus noted, was very polite and helpful the next few days. He was also rather anxious and spent much of the time he was near the Roman looking back over his shoulder. Scaurus liked Nephon Khoumnos even more.

The autumn rains began only a few days after the last of the harvest was gathered in. One storm after another came blustering down from the north, lashing the last leaves from the trees, turning every road and path into an impassable trough of mud, and pointing out all the failures of the Romans' hasty carpentry. The legionaries cursed, dripped, and patched. They scoured the ever-encroaching rust from armor, tools, and weapons.

When the real cold came, the muddy ground froze rock-hard, only to be covered by a blanket of snow that lay in drifts taller than a man. Marcus began to see why, in a climate like this, robes were garments of ceremony but trousers the every-day garb. He started wearing them himself.

In such freezing weather, exercises were not a duty to be avoided, but something avidly sought to put warmth in a man's bones. The Romans trained whenever they could. Gaius Philippus worked them hard. Except when the blizzards were at their worst, they went on a twenty-mile march every week. The senior centurion was one of the oldest men among them, but he fought his way through the snow like a youngster.

He also kept the Romans busy in camp. Once he'd learned enough Videssian to get what he needed, he had the locals make double-weight wicker shields and wooden swords for the legionaries to practice with. He set up pells, against which they continually drilled in the thrusting stroke. Trying to keep the men fresh and interested, he even detailed Adiatun to teach them the fine points of slinging.

The only traditional legionary exercise from which he ex-cused the men was swimming. Even his hardiness quailed at subjecting his men to the freezing water under the ice that covered streams and ponds.

The legionaries did stage mock fights, with the points on their swords and spears covered. At first, they only worked

against one another. Later, they matched themselves against
the two hundred or so Halogai who made up Imbros' usual
garrison.

The tall northerners were skilled soldiers, as befitted their
mercenary calling. But, like the Gauls, they fought as individuals and by clans, not in ordered ranks. If their first charge
broke the Roman line they were irresistible but, more often
than not, the legionaries' large shields and jabbing spears held
them at bay until they tired and the Romans could take the
offensive.

In the drills Marcus was careful never to cross blades with
Viridovix, fearful lest they and all around them be swept away
again by the sorcery locked in their swords. His own weapon
seemed utterly ordinary when he practiced with his fellow
Romans. But when he was working against the garrison troops
he left behind such a trail of shattered shields and riven chain
mail that he gained a reputation for superhuman strength. The
same, he noticed, was true of Viridovix.

The garrison commander was a one-eyed giant of a man
named Skapti Modolf's son. The Haloga was not young, but
his hair was so fair it was hard to tell silver crept through the
gold. He was friendly enough and, like any good fighting
man, interested in the newcomers' ways of doing things, but
he never failed to make Scaurus nervous. With his long, dour
features, rumbling voice, and singleminded concentration on
the art of war, he reminded the Roman all too much of a wolf.

Viridovix, though, took to the Halogai. "It's a somber lot
they are," he admitted, "and more doomful than I'm fond of,
but they fight as men do, and they perk up considerable wi' a
drop of wine in 'em, indeed and they do."

That, Marcus found a few days later, was an understatement. After a day and most of a night of drinking, the Gaul
and half a dozen northern mercenaries staged a glorious brawl
that wrecked the tavern where it happened and most of the
participants.

One aftermath of the fight was a visit from Vourtzes to the
Roman camp. Marcus had not seen much of him lately and
would have forgone this occasion, too, when he learned the
hypasteos wanted him to pay for all the damage the grogshop
had taken. Annoyed, he pointed out that it was scarcely just

for him to be saddled with all the charges when only one of his men was involved, as opposed to six or seven under the *hypasteos'* jurisdiction. Vourtzes let the matter drop, but Marcus knew he was unhappy.

"Maybe you should have compromised and saved trouble," Gorgidas said. "If I know our Celtic friend, he raised more than his share of the ruction."

"I shouldn't be a bit surprised. But Vourtzes is the sort to bleed you to death a drop at a time if you let him. I wonder," Marcus mused, "how he'd look as a newt."

Like the rest of the Empire of Videssos, Imbros celebrated the passing of the winter solstice and the turning of the sun to the north once more. Special prayers winged their way heavenward from the temples. Bonfires blazed on street corners; the townsfolk jumped over them for luck. There was a huge, disorderly hockey match on the surface of a frozen pond. Falling and sliding on the ice seemed as much a part of the game as trying to drive the ball through the goal.

A troupe of mimes performed at Imbros' central theater. Marcus saw he was far from the only Roman there. Such entertainments were much like those his men had known in Italy, and the fact that they had no dialogue made them easier for the newcomers to understand.

Venders climbed up and down the aisles, crying their wares: good-luck charms, small roasted birds, cups of hot spiced wine, balls of snow sweetened with syrups, and many other things.

The skits were fast-paced and topical; a couple in particular stuck in Scaurus' mind. One showed an impressive-looking man in a cloth-of-gold robe—the Emperor Mavrikios, the tribune soon realized—as a farmer trying to keep a slouching nomad from running off with his sheep. The farmer-Emperor's task would have been much easier had he not had a cowardly son clinging to his arm and hindering his every move, a fat son in a robe of red brocade . . .

The other sketch was even less subtle. It involved the devastation of Imbros itself, as carried out in a totally inadvertent and unmalicious fashion by a tall, skinny fellow who wore a red wig and had a huge fiery mustache glued over his upper lip.

Viridovix was in the audience. "'Twas not like that at all,

at all!" he shouted to the mummer on stage, but he was laughing as hard as anyone around him.

Venders of food and drink were not the only purveyors to circulate through the crowd. Though exposed flesh would have invited frostbite, women of easy virtue were not hard to spot. Paint, demeanor, and carriage made their calling clear. Marcus caught the eye of a dark-haired beauty in a sheepskin jacket and clinging green gown. She smiled back and pushed her way toward him through the crowd, squeezing between a couple of plump bakers.

She was only a few feet from Scaurus when she abruptly turned about and walked in another direction. Confused, he was about to follow when he felt a hand on his arm. It was the angular prelate who had blessed and healed the Romans when they first came to Imbros.

"A fine amusement," he said. Scaurus was thinking of a better one, but did not mention it. This priest was a powerful figure in the city. The man continued, "I do not believe I have seen you or many of your men at our shrines. You have come from afar and must be unfamiliar with our faith. Now that you have learned something of our language and our ways, would it please you to discuss this matter with me?"

"Of course," Marcus lied. He had a pair of problems as he walked with the hierarch through the frosty, winding streets of Imbros toward its chief temple. First, he was anything but anxious for a theological debate. Like many Romans, he gave lip service to the veneration of the gods, but wasted little serious belief on them. The Videssians were much more earnest about their cult and harsh with those who did not share it.

Even more immediate was his other dilemma; for the life of him, he could not recall his companion's name. He kept evading the use of it all the way to the doorway of Phos' sanctuary, meanwhile flogging his memory without success.

The sweet savor of incense and a choir's clear tones greeted them at the entrance. Scaurus was so bemused he hardly noticed the cleric who bowed as his ecclesiastical superior came in. Then the young priest murmured, "Phos with you, elder Apsimar, and you as well, outland friend." The warmth and gratitude Marcus put into his handclasp left the little shaven-headed man blinking in puzzlement.

A colonnade surrounded the circular worship area, at

whose brightly lit center priests served the altar of Phos and led the faithful in their prayers. Apsimar stayed in the semi-darkness outside the colonnade. He led Marcus around a third of the circle, stopping at an elaborately carved door of dark, close-grained wood. Extracting a finger-long iron key from the pouch at his belt, he clicked the door open and stood aside to let the Roman precede him.

The small chamber was almost pitch-dark until Apsimar lit a candle. Then Marcus saw the clutter of volumes everywhere, most of them not the long scrolls he was used to, but books after the Videssian fashion, with small, square pages bound together in covers of wood, metal, or leather to form a whole. He wondered how Apsimar could read by candlelight and have any sight left at his age, though the priest had given no sign of failing vision.

The room's walls were as crowded with religious images as its shelves were with books. The dominant theme was one of struggle: here a warrior in armor that gleamed with gold leaf felled his foe, whose mail was black as midnight; there, the same gold-clad figure drove its spear through the heart of a snarling black panther; elsewhere, the disc of the sun blazed through a roiling, sooty bank of fog.

Apsimar sat in a hard, straight chair behind his overloaded desk, waving Scaurus to a more comfortable one in front of it. The priest leaned forward. He said, "Tell me, then, somewhat of your beliefs."

Unsure where to begin, the Roman named some of the gods his people followed and their attributes: Jupiter the king of heaven, his consort Juno, his brother Neptune who ruled the seas, Vulcan the smith, the war god Mars, Ceres the goddess of fertility and agriculture . . .

At each name and description Apsimar's thin face grew longer. Finally he slammed both hands down on the desk. Startled, Marcus stopped talking.

Apsimar shook his head in dismay. "Another puerile pantheon," he exclaimed, "no better than the incredible set of miscegenating godlets the Halogai reverence! I had thought better of you, Roman; you and yours seemed like civilized men, not barbarians whose sole joy in life is slaughter."

Marcus did not understand all of that, but plainly Apsimar thought little of his religious persuasions. He thought for a moment. To his way of looking at things, Stoicism was a philosophy, not a religion, but maybe its tenets would please Apsimar more than those of the Olympian cult. He explained its moral elements: an insistence on virtue, fortitude, and self-control, and a rejection of the storms of passion to which all men were liable.

He went on to describe how the Stoics believed that Mind, which among the known elements could best be equated with Fire, both created and comprised the universe in its varying aspects.

Apsimar nodded. "Both in its values and in its ideas, this is a better creed, and a closer approach to the truth. I will tell you the truth now."

The tribune braced himself for a quick course on the glory of the divine sun, kicking himself for not mentioning Apollo. But the "truth," as Apsimar saw it, was not tied up in heliolatry.

The Videssians, Marcus learned, viewed the universe and everything in it as a conflict between two deities: Phos, whose nature was inherently good, and the evil Skotos. Light and darkness were their respective manifestations. "Thus the globe of the sun which tops our temples," Apsimar said, "for the sun is the most powerful source of light. Yet it is but a symbol, for Phos transcends its radiance as much as it outshines the candle between us."

Phos and Skotos warred not only in the sensible world, but within the soul of every man. Each individual had to choose which he would serve, and on this choice rested his fate in the next world. Those who followed the good would gain an afterlife of bliss, while the wicked would fall into Skotos' clutches, to be tormented forever in his unending ice.

Yet even the eternal happiness of the souls of the deserving might be threatened, should Skotos vanquish Phos in this world. Opinions over the possibility of this differed. Within the Empire of Videssos, it was orthodox to believe Phos would emerge victorious in the ultimate confrontation. Other sects, however, were less certain.

"I know you will be traveling to the city," Apsimar said. "You will be meeting many men of the east there; fall not into their misbelief." He went on to explain that, some eight hundred years before, nomadic barbarians known as the Kha-

morth flooded into what had been the eastern provinces of the
Empire. After decades of warfare, devastation, and murder,
two fairly stable Khamorth states, Khatrish and Thatagush,
had emerged from the chaos, while to their north the Kingdom
of Agder was still ruled by a house of Videssian stock.

The shock of the invasions, though, had caused all these
lands to slip into what Videssos called heresy. Their theologians, remembering the long night of destruction their lands
had undergone, no longer saw Phos' victory as inevitable, but
concluded that the struggle between good and evil was in perfect balance. "They claim this doctrine gives more scope to
the freedom of the will." Apsimar sniffed. "In reality, it but
makes Skotos as acceptable a lord as Phos. Is this a worthwhile goal?"

He gave Marcus no chance to reply, going on to describe
the more subtle religious aberration which had arisen on the
island Duchy of Namdalen in the past couple of centuries.
Namdalen had escaped domination by the Khamorth, but fell
instead, much later, to pirates from the Haloga country, who
envied and aped the Videssian style of life even as they
wrested away Videssian land.

"The fools were seeking a compromise between our views
and the noxious notions which prevail in the east. They refuse
to accept Phos' triumph as a certainty, yet maintain all men
should act as if they felt it assured. This, a theology? Call it,
rather, hypocrisy in religious garb!"

It followed with a certain grim logic that, as any error in
belief gave strength to Skotos, those who deviated from the
true faith—whatever that happened to be in any given area—
could and should be brought into line, by force if necessary.
Accustomed to the general tolerance and indeed disregard for
various creeds he had known in Rome, Marcus found the notion of a militant religion disturbing.

Having covered the main variants of his own faith, Apsimar spoke briefly and slightingly of others the Videssians
knew. Of the beliefs of the Khamorth nomads still on the
plains of Pardraya, the less said the better—they followed
shamans and were little more than demon-worshipers. And
their cousins who lived in Yezd were worse yet; Skotos was
reverenced openly there, with horrid rites.

All in all, the Halogai were probably the best of the heathen. Even if incorrect, their beliefs inclined them to the side of Phos by fostering courage and justice. "Those they have in abundance," Apsimar allowed, "but at the cost of the light of the spirit, which comes only to those who follow Phos."

The barrage of strange names, places, and ideas left Marcus' head spinning. To get time to regain his balance, he asked Apsimar, "Do you have a map, so I may see where all these people you mention live?"

"Of course," the priest said. As with his theological discussion, he gave Scaurus more than the tribune had bargained for. Apsimar gestured toward one of the crowded bookshelves. Like a called puppy, a volume wriggled out from between its neighbors and floated through the air until it landed gently on his desk. He bent over it to find the page he wanted.

The tribune needed those few seconds to try to pull his face straight. Never in Mediolanum, never in Rome, never in Gaul, he knew, would he have seen anything to match that casual flick of the hand and what came after it. Its very effortlessness impressed him in a way even the healing magic had not.

To Apsimar it was nothing. He turned the book toward Marcus. "We are here," he said, pointing. Putting his face close to the map, the tribune made out the word "Imbros" beside a dot.

"My apologies," Apsimar said courteously. "Reading by candlelight can be difficult." He murmured a prayer, held his left hand over the map, and pearly light sprang from it, illuminating the parchment as well as a cloudy day.

This time, Scaurus had all he could do not to flee. No wonder, his mind gibbered, eyestrain did not trouble Apsimar. The priest was his own reading lamp.

As the first shock of amazement and fear faded, a deeper one sank into the tribune's bones. The map was very detailed: better, by the looks of it, then the few Marcus had seen in Rome. And the lands it showed were utterly unfamiliar. Where was Italy? No matter how crude the map, the shape of the boot was unmistakable. He could not find it, or any of the other countries he knew.

Seeing the curious outlines of the Empire of Videssos and its neighbors, reading the strange names of the seas—the

Sailors' Sea, the Northern Sea, the almost landlocked Videssian Sea, and the rest—drove home to the tribune what he had
feared since the two swords swept him and his legionaries
here, had suspected since Apsimar's first sorcery. This was a
different world from Rome's, one from which he could never
go back.

His good-byes to the priest were subdued. Once out in the
street, he made for a tavern. He needed a cup of wine, or
several, to steady his nerves. The grape worked a soothing
magic of its own. And even with magic, he told himself, men
were still men. An able one might go far.

He took another pull at the mug. Presently he remembered
the business Apsimar had interrupted. He wondered whether
he could still find the bright-eyed girl in the green gown. He
laughed a little. Men were still men, he thought.

On his way out of the tavern, he wondered for a moment
how venery counted in the strife between Phos and Skotos. He
decided he did not care and closed the tavern door behind
him.

III

AFTER A LAST SERIES OF BLIZZARDS THAT TRIED TO BATTER Imbros flat, winter sullenly left the stage to spring. Just as they had at the outset of fall, the Empire's roads became morasses. Marcus, anxious for word from the capital, grumbled about the sense of a nation which, to protect its horses' hooves, made those hooves all but worthless over much of the year.

The trees' bare branches were beginning to clothe themselves in green when a mud-splattered messenger splashed his way up from the south. As Nephon Khoumnos had predicted and Marcus hoped, he bore in his leather message-pouch an order bidding the Romans come to *the* city, Videssos.

Vourtzes did not pretend to be sorry to see the last of them. Though the Romans had behaved well in Imbros—for mercenary troops, very well—it had not really been the fat governor's town since they arrived. For the most part they followed his wishes, but he was too used to giving orders to enjoy framing requests.

To Marcus' surprise, Skapti Modolf's son came to bid him farewell. The tall Haloga clasped Scaurus' hand in both his own, after his native custom. Fixing his wintry gaze on the Roman, he said, "We'll meet again, and in a less pleasant place, I think. It would be better for me if we did not, but we will."

Wondering what to make of that, the tribune asked him if he'd had news of the coming summer's campaign.

Skapti snorted at such worry over details. "It will be as it is," he said, and stalked away toward Imbros. Staring at his back, Marcus wondered if the Halogai were as spiritually blind as Apsimar thought.

The march to Videssos was a pleasant week's travel through gently rolling country planted in wheat, barley, olives, and grapevines. To Gorgidas the land, the crops, and the enameled blue dome of the sky were aching reminders of his native Greece. He was by turns sullen with homesickness and rhapsodic over the beauty of the scenery.

"Will you not cease your endless havering?" Viridovix asked. "In another month it'll be too hot for a man to travel by day unless he wants the wits fried out of him. Your grapevine is a fine plant, I'll not deny, but better in the jug than to look at, if you take my meaning. And as for the olive, if you try to eat him his pit'll break your teeth. His oil stinks, too, and tastes no better."

Gorgidas grew so furious working up a reply to this slander that he was his old self for the next several hours. Marcus caught Viridovix grinning behind the irascible doctor's back. His respect for the Celt's wits went up a couple of notches.

The road to Videssos came down by the seaside about a day's journey north of the capital. Villages and towns, some of respectable size, sat athwart the highway at increasingly frequent intervals. After passing through one large town, Gaius Philippus commented, "If these are the suburbs, what must Videssos be like?"

The mental picture Marcus carried of the Empire's capital was of a city like, but inferior to, Rome. In the afternoon of the eighth day out from Imbros, he was able to compare his vision with the reality, and it was the former which paled in the comparison.

Videssos owned a magnificent site. It occupied a triangle of land jutting out into a strait Tzimiskes called the Cattle-Crossing. The name was scarcely a misnomer, either—the opposite shore was barely a mile away, its suburbs plain to the eye despite sea-haze. The closest of those suburbs, the tribune had learned, was simply called "Across."

But with Videssos at which to marvel, the strait's far shore was lucky to get a glance. Surrounded on two sides by water, the capital's third, landward, boundary was warded by fortifications more nearly invulnerable than any Marcus had imagined, let alone seen.

First came a deep ditch, easily fifty feet wide; behind it stood a crenelated breastwork. Overlooking that was the first wall proper, five times the height of a tall man, with square towers strategically sited every fifty to a hundred yards. A second wall, almost twice as high and built of even larger stones, paralleled this outwork at a distance of about fifty yards. The main wall's towers—not all of these were square; some were round, or even octagonal—were placed so that fire from them could cover what little ground those of the outwall missed.

Gaius Philippus stopped dead when he saw those incredible works. "Tell me," he demanded of Tzimiskes, "has this city ever fallen to a siege?"

"Never to a foreign foe," the Videssian replied, "though in our own civil wars it's been taken twice by treachery."

The great walls did not hide as much of the city as had Imbros' fortifications, for Videssos, coincidentally like Rome, had seven hills. Marcus could see buildings of wood, brick, and stucco like those in the latter town, but also some splendid structures of granite and multicolored marble. Many of those were surrounded by parks and orchards, making their pale stone shine the brighter. Scores of shining gilded domes topped Phos' temples throughout the city.

At the harbors, the beamy grainships that fed the capital shared dockspace with rakish galleys and trading vessels from every nation Videssos knew. There and elsewhere in the city, surging tides of people went about their business. Tiny in the distance, to Scaurus they seemed like so many ants, preoccupied with their own affairs and oblivious to the coming of the Romans. It was an intimidating thought. In the midst of such a multitude, how could his handful of men hope to make a difference?

He must have said that out loud. Quintus Glabrio observed, "The Videssians wouldn't have taken us on if they didn't think we mattered." Grateful for Glabrio's calm good sense, the tribune nodded.

Tzimiskes led the Romans past the first two gates that opened into the city. He explained, "An honor guard will escort us into Videssos from the Silver Gate."

Marcus had no idea why the Silver Gate was so called. Its immense portals and spiked portcullis were of iron-faced wood; from their scars, they had seen much combat. Over each wall's entryway hung a triumphant icon of Phos.

"Straighten up there, you shambling muttonheads!" Gaius Philippus growled to the already orderly legionaries. "This is the big city now, and I won't have them take us for gawking yokels!"

As Tzimiskes had promised, the guard of honor was waiting, mounted, just inside the main wall. At its head was Nephon Khoumnos, who stepped up smiling to clasp Scaurus' hand. "Good to see you again," he said. "The march to your barracks is a couple of miles. I hope you don't mind us making a parade of it. It'll give the people something to talk about and get them used to the look of you as well."

"Fine," Marcus agreed. He had expected something like this; the Videssians were inordinately fond of pomp and ceremony. His attention was only half on Khoumnos anyhow. The rest was directed to the troops the imperial officer led.

The three contingents of the honor guard seemed more concerned over watching each other than about the Romans. Khoumnos' personal contingent was a squadron of *akritai*—businesslike Videssians cut in the mold of Tzimiskes or Mouzalon. They wanted to give the Romans their full attention, but kept stealing quick looks to the right and left.

On their left was a band—Marcus rejected any word with a more orderly flavor than that—of nomads from the Pardrayan plains. Dark, stocky men with curly beards, they rode shaggy steppe ponies, wore breastplates of boiled leather and foxskin caps, and carried double-curved bows reinforced with horn. "Foot soldiers!" one said in accented Videssian. He spat to show his contempt. Marcus stared at him until the nomad flushed and jerked his eyes away.

The tribune had a harder time deciding the origin of the escorting party's last group. They were big, solid men in heavy armor, mounted on horses as large as any Marcus had seen, and armed with stout lances and straight slashing swords. They had something of the look of the Halogai to them, but seemed rather less—what was the word Viridovix had used?—doomful than the northern mercenaries. Besides, about half their number had dark hair. They were the first clean-shaven men Scaurus had seen. The only nation that might have spawned them, he decided at last, was Namdalen. There Haloga overlords mixed blood with their once-Vedessian subjects, from whom they had learned much.

Their leader was a rugged warrior of about thirty, whose dark eyes and tanned skin went oddly with his mane of wheat-colored hair. He swung himself down from his high-cantled saddle to greet the Romans. "You look to have good men here," he said to Marcus, taking the tribune's hand between his own in a Haloga-style grip. "I'm Hemond of Metepont, out of the Duchy." That confirmed Marcus' guess. Hemond went on, "Once you're settled in, look me up for a cup of wine. We can tell each other stories of our homes—yours, I hear, is a strange, distant land."

"I'd like that," Marcus said. The Namdalener seemed a decent sort; his curiosity was friendly enough and only natural. All sorts of rumors about the Romans must have made the rounds in Videssos during the winter.

"Come on, come on, let's be off," Khoumnos said. "Hemond, your men for advance guard; the Khamorth will take the rear while we ride flank."

"Right you are." Hemond ambled back to his horse, flipping the Videssian a lazy salute as he went. Khoumnos' sudden urgency bothered Marcus; he had been in no hurry a moment before. Could it be he did not want the Romans friendly toward the Namdaleni? Politics already, the tribune thought, resolving caution until he learned the local rules of the game.

A single Videssian with a huge voice led the procession from the walls of the city to the barracks. Every minute or so he bellowed, "Make way for the valiant Romans, brave defenders of the Empire!" The thoroughfare down which they strode emptied in the twinkling of an eye; just as magically, crowds appeared on the sidewalks and in every intersection. Some people cheered the valiant Romans, but more seemed to wonder who these strange-looking mercenaries were, while the largest number would have turned out for any parade, just to break up the monotony of the day.

Eyes front and hands raised in salute, the legionaries marched west. They passed through two large, open squares, by a marketplace whose customers scarcely looked up to notice them, and past monuments, columns, and statues commemorating long-past triumphs and Emperors.

The only bad moment in the procession came near its end. An emaciated monk in a tattered, filthy robe leaped into the roadway in front of the Romans' herald, who perforce stopped. Eyes blazing, the monk screeched, "Beware Phos' wrath, all traffickers with infidels such as these! Woe unto us, that we shelter them in the heart of Phos' city!"

There was a mutter from the crowd, at first confused, then with the beginning of anger in it. Out of the corner of his eye Marcus saw a man bend to pick up a stone. The mutter grew louder and more hostile.

Intent on heading off a riot before it could start, the tribune elbowed his way through the halted Namdalener horsemen to confront the monk. As if he were some demon, the scrawny cleric drew back in horror, sketching his god's sign on his breast. Someone in the crowd yelled, "Heathen!"

Hands empty before him, Scaurus bowed low to the monk, who stared at him suspiciously. Then he drew the sun-circle over his own heart, at the same time shouting, "May Phos be with you!"

The amazement on the monk's face was comical. He ran forward to fold the Roman in a smelly embrace he would have been as glad not to have. For a horrible instant Marcus thought he was about to be kissed, but the monk, after a few quick, babbled prayers, vanished into the crowd, which was now cheering lustily.

Marcus gave himself the luxury of a sigh of relief before he went back to his men. "Quick thinking, outlander," Hemond said as he walked by. "We could all have been in a lot of trouble there."

"Tell me about it," the tribune said feelingly.

"Make way for the valiant Romans!" the herald cried, and the parade advanced once more.

"I did not know you had decided to follow Phos," Tzimiskes said.

"I said nothing at all about me," Marcus replied.

Tzimiskes looked scandalized.

They traversed a last forum, larger than either of the previous two, and passed by a tremendous oval amphitheater before entering a district of elegant buildings set among wide

expanses of close-cropped emerald lawn and tastefully
trimmed shrubs and vines.

"Another few moments and I'll show you to your barracks," Khoumnos said.

"Here?" Marcus asked, startled. "Surely this is much too
fine."

It was the Videssian's turn for surprise. "Why, where else
would a unit of the Imperial Guards lodge, but in the Imperial
Palaces?"

The buildings devoted to the Emperors of Videssos made
up a vast, sprawling complex which itself comprised one of
the imperial capital's many quarters. The Romans were bil-
leted some distance from the Emperor's residence proper, in
four stuccoed barracks halls set among citrus trees fragrant
with flowers.

"I've had worse," Gaius Philippus said with a laugh as he
unslung his marching kit and laid it by his fresh straw pallet.

Marcus understood the centurion's way of speaking—he
could not remember arrangements to compare with these. The
barracks were airy, well lit, and roomy. There were baths
nearby, and kitchens better equipped than some eateries. Only
the lack of privacy made the long halls less comfortable than
an inn or a hostel. If anything, they were too luxurious. "In
quarters this fine, the men may lose their edge."

Gaius Philippus gave a wolfish grin. "I'll see to that, never
fear." Scaurus nodded, but wondered how well-drilled the rest
of the Imperial Guards were.

He had some of his answer within minutes, for cornets
blared while the Romans were still stowing their possessions.
A plump functionary appeared in the doorway and bawled,
"His Highness the Sevastos Vardanes Sphrantzes! His Majesty
the Sevastokrator Thorisin Gavras! All abase themselves for
his Imperial Majesty, the Avtokrator of the Videssians, Mavrikios Gavras!"

The cornets rang out again. Over them Gaius Philippus
yelled, "Whatever you've got, drop it!" The Romans, used to
snap inspections, sprang to attention.

Preceded by a dozen Halogai, the rulers of the Empire
came into the barracks hall to examine their new warriors.
Before they set foot in it, Marcus stole a glance at their

guardsmen and was favorably impressed. For all the gilding on their cuirasses, for all the delicate inlaywork ornamenting their axes, these were fighting men. Their eyes, cold as the ice of their northern home, raked the barracks for anything untoward. Only when he was satisfied did their leader signal his charges it was safe to enter.

As they did so, Tzimiskes went to his knees and then to his belly in the proskynesis all Videssians granted their sovereign. Marcus, and his men after his example, held to their stiff brace. It did not occur to him to do otherwise. If the Videssians chose to prostrate themselves before their lord, it was their privilege, but not one the Romans, a republican people for four and a half centuries, could easily follow.

The Haloga captain stared at Scaurus, his face full of winter. But now the tribune had no time to try to face him down, for his attention was focused on the triumvirate in the doorway.

First through it, if they were coming in the order announced, was Vardanes Sphrantzes, whose title of Sevastos was about that of prime minister. Heavyset rather than fat, he wore his gem-encrusted robes of office with a dandy's elegance. A thin line of beard framed his round, ruddy face. His eyes did not widen, but narrowed in surprise when he saw the Romans still on their feet.

He turned to say something to the Emperor, but was brushed aside by Mavrikios' younger brother, the Sevastokrator Thorisin Gavras. In his late thirties, the Sevastokrator looked as if he would be more at home in mail than the silks and cloth-of-gold he had on. His hair and beard were carelessly trimmed; the sword at his side was no ceremonial weapon, but a much-used saber in a sheath of plain leather.

His reaction to the sight of the standing Romans was outrage, not surprise. His bellowed, "Who in Phos' holy name do these baseborn outland whoresons think they are?" cut across Sphrantzes' more measured protest: "Your Majesty, these foreigners fail to observe proper solemnity..."

Both men stopped in confusion; Scaurus had the impression they had not agreed on anything in years. From behind them he heard the Emperor's voice for the first time: "If the two of you will get out of my way, I'll see these monsters for myself." And with that mild comment the Avtokrator of the Videssians came in to survey his newest troop of mercenaries.

He was plainly Thorisin's brother; they shared the same long face, the same strong-arched nose, even the same brown hair that thinned at the temples. But at first glance Marcus would have guessed Mavrikios Gavras fifteen years older than his brother. Lines bracketed his forceful mouth and creased his forehead; his eyes were those of a man who slept very little.

A second look told the Roman much of the apparent difference in age between the two Gavrai was illusion. Like the massy golden diadem he wore on his head, Mavrikios bore responsibility's heavy weight, and it had left its mark on him. He might once have shared Thorisin's quick temper and headlong dash, but in him they were tempered by a knowledge of the cost of error.

As the Emperor approached, Tzimiskes rose to stand beside Marcus, ready to help interpret. But Mavrikios' question was direct enough for Scaurus to understand: "Why did you not make your obeisance before me?"

Had Sphrantzes asked that, Marcus might have talked round the answer, but this, he felt instinctively, was a man to whom one gave truth. He said, "It is not the custom in my land to bend the knee before any man."

The Avtokrator's eye roved over the Romans as he considered Scaurus' reply. His gaze stopped on a battered shield; on the stiff peasant face of a young legionary; on Viridovix, who stood out because of his inches and his Celtic panoply.

At last he turned to the waiting Sevastos and Sevastokrator, saying quietly, "These are soldiers." To Thorisin Gavras that seemed to explain everything. He relaxed at once, as did the Haloga guardsmen. If their overlord was willing to let these outlanders keep their rude habits, that was enough for them.

Sphrantzes, on the other hand, opened his mouth for further protest before he realized it would do no good. His eyes locked resentfully with the tribune's, and Marcus knew he had made an enemy. Sphrantzes was a man who could not stand to be wrong or, more to the point, to be seen to be wrong. If he made a mistake, he would bury it . . . and maybe its witnesses, too.

He covered his slip adroitly, though, nodding to Marcus in a friendly way and saying, "At sunset tomorrow evening we have tentatively scheduled a banquet in the Hall of the Nine-teen Couches, in honor of your arrival. Would it be convenient for you and a small party of your officers to join us then?"

"Certainly," Marcus nodded back. The Sevastos' smile made him wish he could bring, not his officers, but a food-taster instead.

The Hall of the Nineteen Couches was a square building of green-veined marble not far from the actual living quarters of the imperial family. There had been no couches in it for gener-ations, Marcus learned, but it kept its name regardless. It was the largest and most often used of the palace compound's sev-eral reception halls.

When Scaurus and his companions—Gaius Philippus, Quintus Glabrio, Gorgidas, Viridovix, and Adiatun, the cap-tain of slingers, along with Tzimiskes—came to the Hall's double doors of polished bronze and announced themselves, a servitor bowed and flung the doors wide, crying, "Ladies and gentlemen, the Ronams!"

There was a polite spatter of applause from the guests al-ready present. Scaurus suppressed an urge to kick the bun-gling fool and resigned himself to being called a Ronam for the next year.

The Videssian custom was to talk, nibble, and drink for a time before settling down to serious eating. Marcus took a chilled cup of wine from the bed of snow on which it rested, accepted a small salted fish from a silver tray proffered by the most bored-looking servant he had ever seen, and began to circulate through the crowd.

He soon became aware that four distinct groups were present, each largely—and sometimes pointedly—ignoring the other three.

In the corner by the kitchens, civil servants, gorgeous in their bright robes and colorful tunics, munched hors d'oeuvres as they discussed the fine art of government by guile.

They sent supercilious glances toward the crowd of army officers who held the center of the hall like a city they had stormed. Though these sprang from several nations, they, too, had a common craft. Their shoptalk was louder and more pungent than that of the bureaucrats, whose sneers they re-turned. "Plague-taken pen-pushers," Marcus heard a young

Videssian mutter to a Haloga clutching a mug of mead almost as big as his head. Already half-drunk, the northerner nodded solemnly.

Over half the Roman party vanished into this group. Gaius Philippus and Nephon Khoumnos were talking about drill fields and training techniques. Glabrio, gesturing as he spoke, explained Roman infantry tactics to a mixed audience of Videssians, Namdaleni, and Halogai. And Adiatun was trying to persuade a buckskin-clad Khamorth that the sling was a better weapon than the bow. The nomad, a better archer than any Adiatun had imagined, was obviously convinced he'd lost his mind.

If the councilors were peacocks and the soldiers hawks, then the ambassadors and envoys of foreign lands who made up the third contingent were birds of various feathers. Squat, bushy-bearded Khamorth wore the wolfskin jackets and leather trousers of the plains and mingled with a couple of other, more distant, plainsmen whose like Marcus had not seen before: slim, swarthy, flat-faced men with draggling mustaches and thin, wispy beards. The tribune learned they were known as Arshaum.

Marcus recognized desert nomads from the southwest, and more from the distant lands across the Sailors' Sea. There were several envoys in strange costumes from the valleys of Erzerum, north and west from Videssos' western borders. There were Haloga princelings, and one man the tribune would have guessed a Videssian but for his northern clothing and the perpetually grim expression Scaurus had come to associate with the Halogai.

A giant in the swirling robes of the desert was so swathed even his face was obscured. He sipped wine through a straw and moved in a circle of silence, for even his fellow ambassadors gave him a wide berth. Marcus understood when he found out the man was an emissary out of Mashiz, the capital of Videssos' deadly western foe, Yezd.

With his insatiable curiosity, Gorgidas had naturally gravitated toward the ambassadors. He was in earnest conversation with a rabbity little man who would have made a perfect Videssian ribbon clerk had he not affected the unkempt facial foliage of the Khamorth.

That takes care of just about all my men, Marcus thought,

and when he turned his head at a burst of laughter to his left he found Viridovix was rapidly making himself popular with the last group at the banquet: its women. Looking quite dashing with his cape of scarlet skins flung back over his wide shoulders, the big Gaul had just finished an uproariously improper tale his brogue only made funnier. A pretty girl was clinging to each arm; three or four more clustered round him. He caught Scaurus' eye over the tops of their heads and threw him a happy tomcat's smile.

The tribune returned it, but did not feel like emulating the Celt. Nor did the other groups attract him any more. The bureaucrats snubbed soldiers on principle, but Scaurus himself was not enough of a professional warrior to delight in discussing the fine points of honing a broadsword. And unlike Gorgidas, he could not turn his inquisitiveness to distant lands when he was still so ignorant of Videssos. Thus, while he spent a minute here and two more there in polite small talk, he was bored before the evening was very old.

Feeling like the spare wheel on a wagon, he drifted over to get more wine. He had just taken it when a voice behind him asked, "The music tonight is very fine, don't you think?"

"Hmm?" He wheeled so fast the wine slopped in its cup. "Yes, my lady, it's very fine indeed." In fact he had no ear for music and had ignored the small tinkling orchestra, but a "no" would have ended the conversation, and that he suddenly did not want at all.

She was as tall as many of the men there. She wore her straight black hair bobbed just above the shoulder, a far simpler style than the elaborate piles of curls most of the women preferred, but one that suited her. Her eyes were very blue. Her gown was a darker shade of the same color, with a bodice of white lace and wide, fur-trimmed sleeves. A fine-looking woman, Marcus thought.

"You Romans—" He noticed she said the name correctly, despite the botched announcement at the door. "—are from quite far away, it's said. Tell me, is your homeland's music much like what's played here?"

Wishing she would find another topic, Scaurus considered the question. "Not a great deal, my lady—?"

"Oh, I crave your pardon," she said, smiling. "My name is Helvis. You are called Marcus, is that right?"

Marcus admitted it. "From Namdalen, are you not?" he asked. It was a reasonable guess. Her features were less aquiline than the Videssian norm, and she certainly did not bear a Videssian name.

She nodded and smiled again; her mouth was wide and generous. "You've learned a good deal about this part of the world," she said, but then, as the tribune had feared, she returned to her original thought. "In what ways do your music and ours differ?"

Scaurus grimaced. He knew little of Roman music and less of the local variety. Worse, his vocabulary, while adequate for the barracks, had huge holes when it came to matters musical.

At last he said, "We play—" He pantomimed a flute.

Helvis named it for him. "We have instruments of that kind, too. What else?"

"We pluck our stringed instruments instead of playing them with the thing your musicians use."

"A bow," Helvis supplied.

"And I've never seen anything like the tall box that fellow is pounding."

Her eyebrows lifted. "You don't know the clavichord? How strange!"

"He's two days in the city, darling, and you're tormenting him about the clavichord?" The guards' officer Hemond came up to put his arm round Helvis' waist with a casual familiarity that said they had been together for years.

"I wasn't being tormented," Scaurus said, but Hemond dismissed his protest with a snort.

"Don't tell me that, my friend. If you let this one carry on about music, you'll never get your ears back. Come on, love," he said to Helvis, "you have to try the fried prawns. Incredible!" He was licking his lips as they walked off together.

Marcus finished his wine in one long gulp. He was bitter and resentful, the more so because he knew his feelings had no justifiable basis. If Helvis and Hemond were a pair, then they were, and no point worrying about it. It was only that she had seemed so friendly and open and not at all attached . . . and she really was beautiful.

Many Namdalener men, Hemond among them, shaved their scalps from the ears back so their heads would fit their helmets better. It was a remarkably ugly custom, the tribune decided, and felt a little better.

Sphrantzes the Sevastos came in a few minutes later. As if his arrival was a signal—and it probably was—servants leaped forward to remove the tables of hors d'oeuvres and wine, substituting long dining tables and gilded straight-backed chairs.

They worked with practiced efficiency and had just finished putting out the last place setting when the doorman cried, "His Majesty the Sevastokrator Thorisin Gavras and his lady, Komitta Rhangavve! Her Majesty the Princess Alypia Gavra!" Then, in the place his rank deserved, "His Imperial Majesty, Avtokrator of the Videssians, Mavrikios Gavras!"

Marcus expected the entire room to drop to the floor and braced himself to shock everyone in it. But as the occasion was social rather than formal, the men in the hall merely bowed from the waist—the Romans among them—while the women dropped curtsies to the Emperor.

Thorisin Gavras' companion was an olive-skinned beauty with flashing black eyes, well matched to the hot-blooded Sevastokrator. She quite outshone the Princess Alypia, Mavrikios' only surviving child by a long-dead wife. Her lineage was likely the reason Alypia was still unwed—she was a political card too valuable to play at once. She was not unattractive, with an oval face and eyes of clear green, rare among the Videssians. But her attention appeared directed inward, and she walked through the dining hall scarcely seeming to notice the feasters in it.

Not so her father. "The lot of you have been standing around munching while I've had to work," he boomed, "and I'm hungry!"

Scaurus had thought he and his men would be seated with the other mercenary captains, well down the ladder of precedence. A eunuch steward disabused him of the notion. "This festivity was convened in your honor, and it would be less than appropriate were you to take your place elsewhere than at the imperial table."

As his knowledge of elegant Videssian manners was small, the tribune would willingly have forgone the distinction, but, of course, the gently irresistible steward had his way. Instead of soldiers, the tribune found himself keeping company with the leading nobles and foreign envoys in Videssos' court.

The straight-backed chairs were as hard as they looked.

Marcus found himself between the skinny little fellow with whom Gorgidas had been talking and the tall dour man who looked like a Videssian in Haloga clothing. The latter introduced himself as Katakolon Kekaumenos. Going by the name, the tribune asked, "You are of Videssos, then?"

"Nay, 'tis not so," Kekaumenos replied in his archaic accent. "I am his Majesty King Sirelios of Agder's embassy to Videssos; in good sooth, his blood is higher than most in this mongrel city." The man of Agder looked round to see if anyone would challenge his statement. The smaller fragment of the Empire of old had learned more from its Haloga neighbors than wearing snow-leopard jackets: its ambassador spoke with a bluntness rare in the city. He was also taciturn as any northerner, subsiding into moody silence after speaking his piece.

Marcus' other seatmate nudged him in the ribs. "You'd think old Katakolon had a poker up his arse, wouldn't you?" he stage-whispered, grinning slyly. "Ah, you don't know who I am, do you, to get away with such talk? Taso Vones is my name, envoy of Khagan Vologes of Khatrish, and so I have a diplomat's privilege. Besides, Kekaumenos has reckoned me daft for years—isn't that right, you old scoundrel?"

"As well for you I do," Kekaumenos rumbled, but his stern features could not hide a smile. Evidently he was used to making allowances for Vones.

The fast-talking ambassador gave his attention back to Scaurus. "I saw you admiring my beard a few minutes ago."

That was not the emotion Marcus had felt for the untidy growth. "Yes, I—"

"Horrible, isn't it? My master Vologes thinks it makes me look a proper Khamorth, instead of some effete Videssian. As if I could look like that!" He pointed across the table at the emissary of the Khaganate of Thatagush. "Ha, Gawtruz, you butterball, are you drunk yet?"

"Not yet I am," Gawtruz replied, looking rather like a bearded boulder. His Videssian was heavily accented. "But will I be? Haw, yes, to be sure!"

"He's a pig," Taso remarked, "but a pleasant sort of pig,

and a sharp man in the bargain. He can also speak perfectly good Videssian when he wants to, which isn't often."

A trifle overwhelmed by the voluble little Khatrisher, Marcus was glad to see the food brought in. The accent was on fish, not surprising in a coastal town like Videssos. There were baked cod, fried shark, lobsters and drawn butter, a tangy stew of clams, crab, and shrimp, as well as divers other delicacies, among them oysters on the half-shell.

Viridovix, a few chairs down from the tribune, took one of these from the crushed ice on which it reposed. After a long, dubious look he gulped it down, but seemed less than pleased he'd done so. With a glance at the girl by his side, he said to Marcus, "If you're fain to be eating something with that feel to it, it's better warm."

Scaurus, *sans* oyster, gulped himself. He was wondering why the Celt had not stopped conversation in its tracks all along the table when the Princess Alypia, who was sitting almost directly across from him, asked, "What does your comrade think of the shellfish?" and he realized Viridovix had spoken Latin.

Well, fool, he said to himself, you thought music a poor topic. How do you propose to cope with *this*? His answer unhesitatingly sacrificed the spirit to the letter: "He said he would prefer it heated, your Highness."

"Odd, such an innocent comment making you start so," she said, but to his relief she did not press him further.

A gray-haired servant tapped the Roman on the shoulder. Setting a small enamelware dish before Marcus, he murmured, "Herrings in wine sauce, my lord, courtesy of his Highness the Sevastos. They are excellent, he says."

Recalling only too vividly his idle thought of the day before, Marcus looked down the table to Vardanes Sphrantzes. The Sevastos raised his glass in genial salute. Scaurus knew he had to take the dainty and yet could not forget the veiled look of menace he had seen in Sphrantzes' eyes.

He sighed and ate. The herrings were delicious.

Alypia noticed his hesitation. "Anyone watching you would say you thought that your final meal," she said.

Damn the observant woman! he thought, flushing. Would he never be able to tell her any truth? It certainly would not do here. "Your Majesty, I could not refuse the Sevastos' gift, but

I fear herring and my innards do not blend well. That was why I paused." The tribune discovered he had only told half a lie. The spicy fish *were* making his stomach churn.

The princess blinked at his seeming frankness, then burst into laughter. If the Roman had seen the slit-eyed look Sphrantzes sent his way, he would have regretted the herrings all over again. That it might be dangerous for a mercenary captain to make a princess of the blood laugh had not yet occurred to him.

Although the Sevastokrator Thorisin stayed to roister on, the Emperor and his daughter, having arrived late, left the banquet early. After their departure things grew livelier.

Two of the desert nomads, relegated to a far table by the insignificance of their tribes, found nothing better to do than quarrel with each other. One of them, a ferret-faced man with waxed mustaches, screamed a magnificent guttural oath and broke his winecup over his rival's head. Others at the table pulled them apart before they could go for their knives.

"Disgraceful," Taso Vones said. "Why can't they leave their blood-feuds at home?"

Snatches of drunken song floated up throughout the Hall of the Nineteen Couches. Viridovix began wailing away in Gaulish, loud enough to make the crockery shiver. "If you can't hit the damned notes, at least scare them as they go by," Gaius Philippus growled. The Celt pretended not to hear him.

Several Khamorth were singing in the plains speech. Lifting his face from his cup, Gawtruz of Thatagush looked up owlishly and joined them.

"Disgraceful," Taso said again; he, too, understood the plainsmen's tongue. "You can't have Khamorth at a feast without them getting sozzled and calling on all sorts of demons. Most of them follow Skotos in their hearts, you know; cleaving to the good is too dull to be tolerable."

The wine was starting to go to the Roman's head; he was losing track of how many times he had filled his goblet from the silver decanter in front of him. On his left, Katakolon Kekaumenos had left some time ago. Marcus did not miss him. The strait-laced northerner's disapproving gaze could chill any gathering.

Viridovix was also gone, but not by himself. Scaurus could not remember if he'd left with the talkative brunette who'd sat beside him or the statuesque serving maid who had hovered over him all evening long. A bit jealous, the Roman took a long pull at his wine. His own contacts with women tonight had been less than successful, from any point of view.

He climbed slowly to his feet, filling his glass one last time to keep him warm on the ten-minute walk back to the barracks. Vones stood too. "Let me accompany you," he said. "I'd like to hear more about your leader—Kizar, was it? A fascinating man, from what you've told me."

Marcus hardly remembered what he'd been saying, but Vones was good company. They made their way down toward the end of the imperial table. There someone had spilled something greasy on the mosaic floor; the tribune slipped, his arms waving wildly for balance. He kept his feet, but the wine he was carrying splattered the white robes of Yezd's ambassador.

"I beg your pardon, my lord—" he began, then stopped, confused. "Your pardon twice—I do not know your name."

"Do you not?" A fury the more terrible for being cold rode the Yezda's words. He rose in one smooth motion, to tower over even the Roman's inches. So thick was his veiling that his eyes were invisible, but Scaurus knew he was seen; the weight of that hidden gaze was like a blow. "Do you not, indeed? Then you may call me Avshahin."

Taso Vones broke in with a nervous chuckle. "My lord Avshar is pleased to make a pun, calling himself 'king' in Videssos' language and his own. Surely he will understand my friend meant no offense, but has seen the bottom of his winecup perhaps more often than he should—"

Avshar turned his unseen stare on the Khatrisher. "Little man, this does not concern you. Unless you would have it so . . . ?" His voice was still smooth, but there was menace there, like freezing water under thin ice. Vones, pale, flinched and shook his head.

"Good." The Yezda dealt Marcus a tremendous roundhouse buffet, sending him lurching back with blood starting from the corner of his mouth. "Dog! Swine! Vile, crawling insect! Is it not enough I must dwell in this city of my foes? Must I also be subject to the insults of Videssos' slaves? Jackal of a mercenary, it shall be your privilege to choose the weapon that will be your death."

The feasting hall grew still. All eyes were on the Roman, who abruptly understood Avshar's challenge. In an odd way he was thankful the Yezda had struck him; the blow and the rage that followed were burning the wine from his blood. He was surprised at the steadiness of his voice as he answered, "You know as well as I, I spilled my wine on you by accident. But if you must take it further, sword and shield will do well enough."

Avshar threw back his head and laughed, a sound colder and more cruel than any of the winter blizzards that had howled down on Imbros. "So be it—your doom from your own mouth you have spoken. Mebod!" he shouted, and a frightened-looking Yezda servant appeared at his side. "Fetch my gear from my chambers." He gave the Roman a mocking bow. "The Videssians, you see, would not take it kindly if one who bears them no love were to come armed to a function where their precious Emperor was present."

Taso Vones was plucking at Scaurus' arm. "Have you lost your wits? That is the deadliest swordsman I have ever seen, the winner in a score of duels, and a sorcerer besides. Crave his forgiveness now, before he cuts a second mouth in your throat!"

"I asked his pardon once, but he hardly seems in a forgiving mood. Besides," Marcus said, thinking of the potent blade at his side, "I may know something he doesn't."

Gaius Philippus was so drunk he could hardly stand, but he still saw with a fighting man's knowledge. "The big son of a pimp will likely try to use his reach to chop you to bits from farther out than you can fight back. Get inside and let the air out of him."

Marcus nodded; he had been thinking along those lines himself. "Send someone after my shield, will you?"

"Adiatun is already on his way."

"Fine."

While everyone waited for the fighters' gear to be fetched, a double handful of high-ranking officers, like so many servants, shoved tables around, clearing a space for combat.

Wagers flew thick and fast. From the shouts, Marcus knew he was the underdog. He was pleased, though, when he heard Helvis' clear contralto announce, "Three pieces of gold on the Roman!" Gawtruz of Thatagush covered her bet.

The Sevastokrator Thorisin Gavras called to Vardanes Sphrantzes, "Whom do you like, seal-stamper?"

The dislike on the Sevastos' face covered Gavras, Avshar, and Scaurus impartially. He rubbed his neatly bearded chin. "Though it grieves me to say so, I think it all too likely the Yezda will win."

"Are you a hundred goldpieces sure?"

Sphrantzes hesitated again, then nodded. "Done!" Thorisin exclaimed. Marcus was glad to have the Sevastokrator's backing, but knew the Emperor's brother would have been as quick to favor Avshar if Sphrantzes had chosen him.

A cry rang out when the Yezda ambassador's servant returned with his master's arms. Marcus was surprised that Avshar favored a long, straight sword, not the usual scimitar of the westerners. His shield was round, with a spiked boss. The emblem of Yezd, a leaping panther, was painted on a background the color of dried blood.

Moments later, Adiatun was back with the tribune's *scutum*. "Cut him into crowbait," he said, slapping Scaurus on the shouder.

The Roman was drawing his blade when something else occurred to him. He asked Taso Vones, "Will Avshar not want me to shed my cuirass?"

Vones shook his head. "It's common knowledge he wears mail himself, under those robes. He's not the envoy of a friendly country, you know."

Marcus spent a last second wishing he had not drunk so much. He wondered how much wine was in Avshar. Then it was too late for such worries. There was only a circle of eager, watching faces, with him and the Yezda in the middle of it—and then he forgot the watchers, too, as Avshar leaped forward to cut him down.

For a man so tall, he was devilishly quick, and strong in the bargain. Marcus caught the first slash on his shield and staggered under it, wondering if his arm was broken. He thrust up at Avshar's unseen face. The Yezda danced back, then came on again with another overhand cut.

He seemed to have as many arms as a spider and a sword in every hand. Within moments Marcus had a cut high up on his sword arm and another, luckily not deep, just above the top of his right greave. His shield was notched and hacked. Avshar wielded his heavy blade like a switch.

Fighting down desperation, Marcus struck back. Avshar turned the blow with his shield. It did not burst as the Roman had hoped, but at the contact Avshar gave back two startled paces. He swung his blade up in derisive salute. "You have a strong blade, runagate, but there are spells of proof against such."

Yet he fought more cautiously after that and, as the hard work of combat helped banish the wine from Scaurus' system, the Roman grew surer and more confident of himself. He began to press forward, blade flicking out now high, now low, with Avshar yielding ground step by stubborn step.

The Yezda, who had kept silent while all around him voices rose in song, began to chant. He sang in some dark language, strong, harsh, and freezing, worse even than his laugh. The torchlight dimmed and almost died in a web of darkness spinning up before Marcus' eyes.

But along the length of the Roman's blade, the druids' marks flared hot and gold, turning aside the spell the wizard had hurled. Scaurus parried a stroke at his face.

The episode could only have taken an instant, for even as he was evading the blow, a woman in the crowd—he thought it was Helvis—called out, "No ensorcelments!"

"Bah! None are needed against such a worm as this!" Avshar snarled, but he chanted no further. And now the tribune had his measure. One of his cuts sheared away the tip of Avshar's shield-boss. The Yezda envoy's robes grew tattered, and red with more than wine.

Screaming in frustrated rage, Avshar threw himself at the Roman in a last bid to overpower his enemy by brute force. It was like standing up under a whirlwind of steel, but in his wrath the Yezda grew careless, and Marcus saw his moment come at last.

He feinted against Avshar's face, then thrust quickly at his belly. The Yezda brought his blade down to cover, only to see, too late, that this too was a feint. The Roman's sword hurtled at his temple. The parry he began was far too slow, but in avoiding it, Scaurus had to turn his wrist slightly. Thus the flat of his blade, not the edge, slammed into the side of Avshar's head.

The Yezda tottered like a lightning-struck tree, then toppled, his sword falling beside him. Scaurus took a step forward to finish him, then shook his head. "Killing a stunned man is butcher's work," he said. "The quarrel was his with me, not mine with him." He slid his blade back into its scabbard.

In his exhaustion afterwards, he only remembered a few pieces of flotsam from the flood of congratulations that washed over him. Gaius Philippus' comment was, as usual, short and to the point. "That is a bad one," he said as Avshar, leaning on his servant, staggered from the hall, "and you should have nailed him when you had the chance."

Her winnings ringing in her hand, Helvis squeezed and kissed the tribune while Hemond pounded his back and shouted drunkenly in his ear.

And Taso Vones, though glad to see Avshar humbled, also had a word of warning. "I suppose," the mousy little man from Khatrish grumbled, "now you think you could storm Mashiz singlehanded and have all the maidens from here to there fall into your arms."

Marcus' mind turned briefly to Helvis, but Vones was still talking. "Don't you believe it!" he said. "A few years ago Avshar was leading a raiding-party along the western marches of Videssos, and a noble named Mourtzouphlos handled him very roughly indeed. The next spring, the biggest snake anyone in those parts had ever seen swallowed Mourtzouphlos down."

"Happenstance," Marcus said uneasily.

"Well, maybe so, but the Yezda's arm is long. A word to the wise, let us say." And he was off, brushing a bit of lint from the sleeve of his brown robe as if amazed anyone could think there was a connection between himself and this outlander rash enough to best Avshar.

IV

When he returned for Marcus' shield, Adiatun must have wakened the Romans in their barracks. Torches were blazing through the windows, everyone was up and stirring, and by the time Marcus got back to his quarters a good score of legionaries were fully armed and ready to avenge him.

"You don't show much confidence in your commander," he told them, trying to hide how pleased he was. They gave him a rousing cheer, then crowded close, asking for details of the duel. He told the story as best he could, peeling off his belt, corselet, and greaves while he talked. Finally he could not keep his sagging eyelids open any longer.

Gaius Philippus stepped into the breach. "That's the nub of it. The rest you can all hear in the morning—early in the morning," he half threatened. "There's been nothing but shirking the past couple of days while we've got settled, but don't get the notion you can make a habit of it."

As the centurion had known it would, his announcement roused a chorus of boos and groans, but it also freed Scaurus from further questions. Torches hissed as they were quenched. The tribune, crawling under a thick woolen blanket, was as glad of sleep as ever he had been in his life.

It seemed only seconds later when he was shaken awake, but the apricot light of dawn streamed through the windows. Eyes still blurred with sleep, he saw Viridovix, looking angry, crouched above him. "Bad cess to you, southron without a heart!" the Gaul exclaimed.

Marcus raised himself onto one elbow. "What have I done

to you?" he croaked. Someone, he noted with clinical detachment, had raced a herd of goats through his mouth.

"What have you done, man? Are you daft? The prettiest bit of fighting since we came here, and me not there to see it! Why did you no send a body after me so I could watch the shindy my own self and not hear about it second hand?"

Scaurus sat up gingerly. While he had made no real plans for the morning, he had not intended to spend the time pacifying an irate Celt. "In the first place," he pointed out, "I had no notion where you were. You had left some little while before I fell foul of Avshar. Besides, unless I misremember, you didn't leave alone."

"Och, she was a cold and clumsy wench, for all her fine chest." It had been the servingmaid, then. "But that's not the point at all, at all. There's always lassies to be found, but a good fight, now, is something else again."

Marcus stared at him, realizing Viridovix was serious. He shook his head in bewilderment. He could not understand the Celt's attitude. True, some Romans had a taste for blood, but to most of them—himself included—fighting was something to be done when necessary and finished as quickly as possible. "You're a strange man, Viridovix," he said at last.

"If you were looking through my eyes, sure and you'd find yourself a mite funny-looking. There was a Greek once passed through my lands, a few years before you Romans—to whom it doesn't belong at all—decided to take it away. He was mad to see the way things worked, was this Greek. He had a clockwork with him, a marvelous thing with gears and pullies and I don't know what all, and he was always tinkering with it to make it work just so. You're a bit like that yourself sometimes, only you do it with people. If you don't understand them, why then you think it's them that's wrong, not you, and won't have a bit to do with them."

"Hmm." Marcus considered that and decided there was probably some justice to it. "What happened to your Greek?"

"I was hoping you'd ask that," Viridovix said with a grin. "He was sitting under an old dead tree, playing with his clockwork peaceful as you please, when a branch he'd been ignoring came down on his puir foolish head and squashed him so flat we had to bury the corp of him between two doors, poor lad. Have a care the same doesn't befall you."

"A plague take you! If you're going to tell stories with morals in them, you can start wearing a blue robe. A blood-thirsty Celt I'll tolerate, but the gods deliver me from a preaching one!"

After his work of the previous night, the tribune told himself he was entitled to leave the morning drills to Gaius Philippus. The brief glimpse of Videssos the city he'd had a few days before had whetted his appetite for more. This was a bigger, livelier, more brawling town even than Rome. He wanted to taste its life, instead of seeing it frozen as he tramped by on parade.

Seabirds whirled and mewed overhead as he left the elegant quiet of the imperial quarter for the hurly-burly of the forum of Palamas, the great square named for an Emperor nine centuries dead. At its center stood the Milestone, a column of red granite from which distances throughout the Empire were reckoned. At the column's base two heads, nearly fleshless from the passage of time and the attentions of scavengers, were displayed on pikes. Plaques beneath them set forth the crimes they had plotted while alive. Marcus' knowledge of Videssos' written language was still imperfect, but after some puzzling he gathered the miscreants had been rebellious generals with the further effrontery to seek aid for their revolt from Yezd. Their present perches, he decided, were nothing less than they deserved.

The people of Videssos ignored the gruesome display. They had seen heads go up on pikes before and expected these would not be the last.

Scaurus, on the other hand, was anything but ignored. He had thought he would be only one among a thousand foreigners, but the mysterious network that passes news in any great city had singled him out as the man who beat the dreaded Avshar. People crowded forward to pump his hand, to slap his back, or simply to touch him and then draw back in awe. From their reaction to him, he began to realize how great an object of fear the Yezda was.

It was next to impossible to get away. At every stall he passed, merchants and hucksters pressed samples of their wares on him: fried sparrows stuffed with sesame seeds; candied almonds; a bronze scalpel; amulets against heartburn, dysentery, or possession by a ghost; wines and ales from every corner of the Empire and beyond; a book of erotic verse, unfortunately addressed to a boy. No one would hear him say no and no one would take a copper in payment.

"It is my honor, my privilege, to serve the Ronam," declared a ruddy-faced baker with sweeping black mustachioes as he handed the tribune a spiced bun still steaming from his ovens.

Trying to escape his own notoriety, Marcus fled the forum of Palamas for the back streets and alleyways of the city. In such a maze it was easy to lose oneself, and the tribune soon did. His wandering feet led him into a quarter full of small, grimy taverns, homes once fine but now shabby from neglect or crowding, and shops crammed with oddments either suspiciously cheap or preposterously expensive. Young men in the brightly dyed tights and baggy tunics of street toughs slouched along in groups of three and four. It was the sort of neighborhood where even the dogs traveled in pairs.

This was a more rancid taste of Videssos than the tribune had intended. He was looking for a way back toward some part where he could feel safe without a maniple at his back when he felt furtive fingers fasten themselves to his belt. As he was half expecting such attention, it was easy to spin round and seize the awkward thief's wrist in an unbreakable grip.

He thought he would be holding one of the sneering youths who prowled here, but his captive was a man of about his own age, dressed in threadbare homespun. The would-be fingersmith did not struggle in his grasp. Instead he went limp, body and face alike expressing utter despair. "All right, you damned hired sword, you've got me, but there's precious little you can do to me," he said. "I'd have starved in a few days anyways."

He *was* thin. His shirt and breeches flapped on his frame and his skin stretched tight across his cheekbones. But his shoulders were wide, and his hands strong-looking—both his carriage and his twanging speech said he was more used to walking behind a plow than skulking down this alley. He had borne arms, too; Marcus had seen the look in his eyes before, on soldiers acknowledging defeat at the hands of overwhelming force.

"If you'd asked me for money, I would gladly have given it to you," he said, releasing his prisoner's arm.

"Don't want nobody's charity, least of all a poxy mercenary's," the other snapped. "Weren't for you mercenaries, I wouldn't be here today, and I wish to Phos I wasn't." He hesitated. "Aren't you going to give me to the eparch?"

The city governor's justice was apt to be swift, sure, and drastic. Had Scaurus caught one of the street-rats, he would have turned him over without a second thought. But what was this misplaced farmer doing in a Videssian slum, reduced to petty thievery for survival? And why did he blame mercenaries for his plight? He was no more a thief than Marcus was a woodcutter.

The tribune came to a decision. "What I'm going to do is buy you a meal and a jug of wine. Wait, now—you'll earn it." He saw the other's hand already starting to rise in rejection. "In exchange, you'll answer my questions and tell me why you mislike mercenaries. Do we have a bargain?"

The rustic's larynx bobbed in his scrawny neck. "My pride says no, but my belly says yes, and I haven't had much chance to listen to it lately. You're an odd one, you know— I've never seen gear like yours, you talk funny, and you're the first hired trooper I've ever seen who'd feed a hungry man instead of booting him in his empty gut. Phostis Apokavkos is my name, and much obliged to you."

Scaurus named himself in return. The eatery Phostis led them to was a hovel whose owner fried nameless bits of meat in stale oil and served them on husk-filled barley bread. It was better not to think of what went into the wine. That Apokavkos could not afford even this dive was a measure of his want.

For a goodly time he was too busy chewing and swallowing to have much to say, but at last he slowed, belched enormously, and patted his stomach. "I'm so used to empty, I near forgot how good full could feel. So you want to hear my story, do you?"

"More now than I did before. I've never seen a man eat so much."

"If the hole is big, it takes a deal to fill it." He took a pull at his wine. "This is foul, isn't it? I was too peckish to notice

before. I grew better grapes than this my own self, back on
my farm—

"That's a good place to start, I guess. I had a steading in
the province of Raban, not far from the border with Yezd—do
you know the country I mean?"

"Not really," Marcus admitted. "I'm new to Videssos."

"Thought you were. Well, then, it's on the far side of the
Cattle-Crossing, about a month's foot-travel from here. I
should know—I did the hike, fool that I was. Anyway, that
farm had been in my family for longer than we could remember any more. We weren't just peasants, either—we'd
always been part of the provincial militia. We had to send a
man to war if the militia got called and to keep up a horse and
gear ready to fight any time, but in exchange we got out of
paying taxes. We even got paid sometimes, when the government could afford it.

"That's how my grandfather told it, anyhow. It sounds too
good to be real, if you ask me. It was in granddad's day the
Mankaphas family bought out about every farm in the village,
us included. So we served the Mankaphai instead of the government, but things still weren't bad—they kept the tax col-
lectors off our backs well enough."

Marcus thought of how it was in Rome, with retiring soldiers depending not on the Senate but on their generals for
land allotments on mustering out. All too familiar with the
turmoil his own land had endured, he could guess Apokavkos'
next sentence before it was spoken.

"Of course, the pen-pushers weren't happy over losing our
taxes, and the Mankaphai were even less happy about paying
in our place now that they owned the land. Five years ago
Phostis Mankaphas—I'm named for him—rebelled along
with a fair pile of other nobles. That was the year before
Mavrikios Gavras raised a ruction big enough to work, and we
were swamped," Apokavkos said bleakly; the tribune noted
how he took his patron's side without hesitation. He also
learned for the first time that the reigning Emperor held his
throne thanks to a successful rebellion.

"The pen-pushers broke up the Mankaphas estates and said
things would be like they were in granddad's time. Hah! They
couldn't trust us for militia no more—we'd fought for the
nobles. So in came the taxmen, wanting everything due since

the days when Phostis' great-grandfather bought our plot in
the first place. I stuck it out as long as I could, but once the
bloodsuckers were through, I couldn't keep the dirt under my
feet, let alone anything growing on it.

"I knew it was hopeless there and I thought it might not be
here, so a year ago I left. Fat lot of good it did me. I'm not
much for lying or cheating; all I know is fighting and farming.
I commenced to starve just as soon as I got here and I've been
at it ever since. I was getting right good at it, too, till you
came along."

Scaurus had let Apokavkos spin his tale without interrup-
tion. Now that he was through, the Roman found he'd raised
as many questions as he'd answered. "Your lord's lands were
on the border with Yezd?"

"Near enough, anyway."

"And he rebelled against the Emperor. Did he have backing
from the west?"

"From those dung-eaters? No, we fought them at the same
time we took on the seal-stampers. That's one of the reasons
we lost."

Marcus blinked; the strategy implied was not of the finest.
Something else troubled him. "You—and I suppose a good
many like you—made up a militia, you said?"

"That's what I told you, all right."

"But when you revolted, the militia was broken up?"

"Say, you did listen, didn't you?"

"But—you're at war with Yezd, or as close as makes no
difference," the tribune protested. "How could you disband
troops at a time like that? Who took their place?"

Apokavkos gave him an odd look. "You ought to know."

A great many things suddenly became clear to Scaurus. No
wonder the Empire was in trouble! Its rulers had seen its own
warriors used by power-hungry nobles against the central government and decided native troops were too disloyal to trust.
But the Empire still had foreign foes and had to quell revolts
as well. So the bureaucrats of Videssos hired mercenaries to
do their fighting for them, a cure the tribune was certain
would prove worse than the disease.

Mercenary troops were fine—as long as they got paid reg-
ularly and as long as their captains did not grow greedy for
power rather than money. If either of those things happened

. . . the mercenaries had been hired to check the local soldiery, but who would put them down in turn?

He shook his head in dismay. "What a mess! Oh, what a lovely mess!" And we Romans in the middle of it, he thought, disquieted.

"You are *the* most peculiar excuse for a mercenary I ever did see," Apokavkos observed. "Any of them other buggers would be scheming like all get out to see what he could squeeze out of this for him and his, but from the noises you're making, you're trying to figure out what's best for the Empire. I do confess to not understanding."

Marcus thought that over for a minute or two and decided Apokavkos was right. How to explain it, though? "I'm a soldier, yes, but not a mercenary by trade. I never really planned to make a career of war. My men and I are from farther away than you—or I, for that matter—can imagine. Videssos took us in, when we could have been slain out of hand. As much as we have one, the Empire has to be our home. If it goes under, we go under with it."

"Most of that I could follow and I like the sound of it. What do you mean, though, when you're talking of how far you're from? I already said you were a new one on me."

So now for perhaps the twentieth time the tribune told of how the Romans—and a cantankerous Gaul—had come to Videssos. By the time he was through, Apokavkos was staring at him. "You must be telling the truth; no one would make up a yarn like that and figure to be believed. Phos above, there's thousands could tell my story or one about like it, but in all my born days I never heard any to come close to yours." His hand sketched the sun-disc over his breast.

"That's as may be," Scaurus shrugged. "There still remains the problem of what to do with you." He had taken to this strangely met acquaintance, appreciating his matter-of-factness in the face of trouble. Even if he knew it would not be good enough, Apokavkos would give his best. In that, Marcus mused, he's like most of my own men.

The thought gave him his answer; he snapped his fingers in satisfaction. The few seconds of his deliberation had been bad ones for Apokavkos, with new-found hope struggling against the visions of misfortune he had learned to expect.

"I'm sorry," Scaurus said, for all this was painfully clear

on the Videssian's face. "I didn't mean for you to worry. Tell me, how would you like to become a Roman?"

"Now I know I don't follow you."

"That's what you will do—follow me. I'll take you back to our barracks, get you some gear, and quarter you with my men. You've soldiered before; the life won't come hard for you. Besides, you haven't done any too well as a Videssian, so what do you have to lose?"

"I'd be a liar if I said I'd be much worse off," Apokavkos admitted. His unhappy stay in the capital had given him a share of big-city cynicism, for his next question was, "What do you get out of the deal?"

Scaurus grinned. "For one thing, a good fighting man—I am a mercenary, remember? There's more to it than that, though. Your scales have got weighted on the wrong side, and it hasn't been your fault. Somehow it seems only fair to even them a little if I can."

The displaced farmer clasped Marcus' hands in a grip that still held the promise of considerable strength. "I'm your man," he said, eyes shining. "All I ever wanted was an even chance and I never came close to one till now. Who would have thought it'd be a foreigner to give it to me?"

After the Roman paid the taverner's score—an outrageous one, for food and drink so vile—he let Apokavkos lead him from the unsavory maze into which he'd wandered. They were not long out of it before the Videssian said, "It's your turn now. That rat's nest is the only part of the city I really know. I never had the money to see the rest."

With some fumbling and the help of passers-by, they made their way back to Palamas' forum. There, to his annoyance, Marcus was promptly recognized again. Apokavkos' mouth fell open when he found his companion had bested the fearsome Avshar with swords. "I saw the son of a snake in action once or twice, leading part of King Wulghash's army against us. He's worth half an army all by his lonesome, 'cause he's as strong as he is sly, which is saying a lump. He beat the boots off us."

The gardens, grounds, and buildings of the palace quarter awed the rustic even more. His comment was, "Now I know what to look forward to, if I'm kindly judged when I die."

Another thought struck him. "Phos' light! I'll be bedded down right in the middle of it all! Can you imagine that? Can you?" Marcus was sure he was talking to himself.

When they reached the Roman barracks, they found Tzimiskes and Viridovix outside, a game board between them. Many of the Romans—and the Gaul as well—had become fond of the battle game the Videssians played. Unlike the ones they had known before, it involved no luck, only the skill of the player.

"Glad I am to see you," Viridovix said, sweeping the pieces from the board. "Now I can tell our friend here 'I would have got you in the end' and there's no way for him to make a liar of me."

The tribune had seen how few of his own pieces the Celt had removed, and how many of Tzimiskes'. The Videssian had the game firmly controlled, and all three of them knew it—no, all four, if Apokavkos' raised eyebrows meant anything.

Tzimiskes started to say something, but Viridovix interrupted him. "Where did you come by this scarecrow?" he asked, pointing at Apokavkos.

"There's a bit of a story to that." The Roman turned to Tzimiskes. "Neilos, I'm glad I found you. I want you to take charge of this fellow," he named Apokavkos and introduced him to the other two, "feed him as much as he'll hold, get him weapons—and clothes, too, for that matter. He's our first honorary Roman. He—what is it? You look like you're about to explode."

"Scaurus, I'll do everything you say, and you can tell me the wherefores later. The Emperor has been sending messengers here every hour on the hour since early this morning. Something to do with last night's activities, I gather."

"Oh." That put a different light on matters. Whether or not he was a hero in the city, he realized the Emperor might have to take a dim view of one of his soldiers brawling with a neighboring land's ambassador. "I wonder how much trouble I'm in. Phostis, go with Tzimiskes here. If I have to see the Emperor, I'd best get shaved—" He was still refusing to grow his beard. "—cleaned, and changed."

* * *

The next imperial messenger arrived while Marcus was scraping the last whiskers from under his chin. He waited with ill-concealed impatience while the Roman bathed and donned a fresh mantle. "It's about time," he said when Marcus emerged, though he and the tribune both knew how quick the ablutions had been.

He led Scaurus past the Hall of the Nineteen Couches, past the looming Grand Courtroom with its incredible bronzework doors, past a two-story barracks complex—Namdaleni were wandering about here, and Marcus looked for but did not see Hemond—and through a grove of cherry trees thick with sweet, pink blossoms to a secluded building deep within it— the private chambers of the imperial family, Marcus realized.

His worries lessened slightly. If Mavrikios was ging to take strong action against him, he would do it publicly, so Yezd's honor could be seen to be satisfied.

A pair of lazy-looking sentries, both Videssians, lounged by the entranceway of the private chambers. They had doffed their helmets so they could soak up the sun; the Videssians deemed a tanned, weathered look a mark of masculine, though not of feminine, beauty.

Scaurus' guide must have been well-known to the guards, who did not offer even a token challenge as he led the tribune inside. It was not his job, though, to conduct Scaurus all the way to the Emperor. Just inside the threshold he was met by a fat chamberlain in a maroon linen robe with a pattern of golden cranes. The chamberlain looked inquiringly at the Roman.

"He's the one, all right," the messenger said. "Took long enough to find, didn't he?" Without waiting for an answer, he was off on his next mission.

"Come with me, if you please," the chamberlain said to Scaurus. His voice was more contralto than tenor, and his cheeks were beardless. Like many of the Videssian court functionaries, he was a eunuch. Marcus presumed this was for the same reason eunuchs were common in the oriental monarchies of his own world; being ineligible for the throne because of their castration, they were thought to be more trustworthy in close contact with the person of the ruler.

Like all such rules, the tribune knew, that one had its dreadful exceptions.

The long corridor down which the chamberlain led him was lit by translucent panes of alabaster set into the ceiling. The milky light dimmed and grew bright as clouds chased across the sun. It was, Marcus thought, a bit like seeing underwater.

And there was much to see. As was only natural, many of the finest gauds of a thousand years and more of empire were displayed for the pleasure of the Emperors themselves. The passageway was crowded with marble and bronze statuary, pottery breathtakingly graceful and painted with elegant precision, busts and portraits of men Scaurus guessed to be bygone Emperors. religious images lavish with gold leaf and polished gems, a rearing stallion as big as Marcus' hand that had to have been carved from a single emerald, and other marvels he did not really see because he had too much pride to swivel his head this way and that like a goatherd on holiday in the city. Even the floor was a bright mosaic of hunting and farming scenes.

In that company, the rusted, dented helmet on a pedestal of its own seemed jarringly out of place. "Why is this here?" he asked.

"That is the helmet of King Rishtaspa of Makuran—we would say 'Yezd' now—taken from his corpse by the Emperor Laskaris when he sacked Mashiz seven hundred and— let me think a moment—thirty-nine years ago. A most valiant warrior, Laskaris. The portrait above the helmet is his."

The painting showed a stern-faced, iron-bearded man in late middle life. He wore gilded scale-mail, the imperial diadem, and the scarlet boots that marked the Emperors of Videssos, but for all that he looked more like a senior centurion than a ruler. His left hand was on the hilt of his sword; in his right was a lance. The spear carried a pennant of sky-blue, with Phos' sun-symbol large on its field.

The chamberlain continued, "Laskaris forcibly converted all the heathen of Makuran to the true faith but, as Videssos proved unable to establish lasting rule over their land, they have relapsed into error."

Marcus thought that over and liked none of his thoughts. War for the sake of religion was a notion that had not crossed his mind before. If the people of Makuran were as resolute about their faith as Videssians were for the worship of Phos, such a struggle would be uncommonly grim.

The eunuch was ushering him into a small, surprisingly spare chamber. It held a couch, a desk, a couple of chairs but, save for an image of Phos, was bare of the artwork crowding the hallway. The papers on the desk had been shoved to one side to make room for a plain earthen jug of wine and a plate of cakes.

Seated on the couch were the Emperor, his daughter Alypia, and a big-bellied man of about sixty whom Marcus had seen but not met the night before.

"If you will give me your sword, sir—" the chamberlain began, but Mavrikios interrupted him.

"Oh, run along, Mizizios. He's not out for my head, not yet, anyway—he doesn't know me well enough. And you needn't stand there waiting for him to prostrate himself. It's against his religion, or some such silly thing. Go on, out with you."

Looking faintly scandalized, Mizizios disappeared.

Once he was gone, the Emperor waved a bemused Scaurus in. "I'm in private now, so I can ignore ceremony if I please —and I do please," Gavras said. This was Thorisin's brother after all; though Thorisin's fiery impetuosity was banked in him, it did not fail to burn.

"You might tell him who I am," the aging stranger suggested. He had an engagingly homely face; his beard was snow streaked with coal and reached nearly to his paunch. He looked like a scholar or a healer, but from his robes only one office could be his; he wore gem-strewn cloth-of-gold, with a large circle of blue silk on his left breast.

"So I might," the Emperor agreed, taking no offense at his aggrieved tone. Here, plainly, were two men who had known and liked each other for years. "Outlander, this tub of lard is called Balsamon. When I took the throne I found him Patriarch of Videssos and I was fool enough to leave him on his seat."

"Father!" Alypia said, but there was no heat in her complaint.

As he bowed, Marcus studied the patriarch's features, looking for the fanaticism he had seen in Apsimar. He did not find it. Wisdom and mirth dominated Balsamon's face; despite his years, the prelate's brown eyes were still keen and among the shrewdest the tribune could recall.

"Bless you, my heathen friend," he said. In his clear tenor the words were a friendly greeting with no trace of condescension. "And do sit down. I'm harmless, I assure you."

Quite out of his depth, Marcus sank into a chair. "To business, then," Gavras said, visibly reassuming part of his imperial dignity. He pointed an accusing finger at the Roman. "You are to know you are reprimanded for assaulting the ambassador of the Khagan of Yezd and offering him gross insult. You are fined a week's pay. My daughter and the patriarch Balsamon are witnesses to this sentence."

The tribune nodded, expressionless; this was what he had expected. The Emperor's finger dropped and a grin spread across his face. "Having said that, I'll say something else—good for you! My brother came storming in here to wake me out of a sound sleep and show me every thrust and parry. Wulghash sent Avshar here as a calculated insult, and I'm not sorry to see his joke turn and bite him."

He grew sober once more. "Yezd is a disease, not a nation, and I intend to wipe it from the face of the earth. Videssos and what was once Makuran have always fought—they to gain access to the Videssian Sea or the Sailors' Sea, we to take their rich river valleys, and both sides to control the passes, the mines, and the fine fighting men of Vaspurakan between us. Over the centuries, I'd say, honors were evenly divided."

Scaurus chewed on a cake as he listened. It was excellent, full of nuts and raisins and dusted over with cinnamon, and went very well with the spiced wine in the jug. The tribune tried to forget the stale slop he'd drunk before, in the Videssian slums.

"Forty years ago, though," the Emperor went on, "The Yezda from the steppe of Shaumkhiil sacked Mashiz, seized all of Makuran, and rammed their way through Vaspurakan into the Empire. They kill for the sport of it, steal what they can carry, and wreck what they can't. And because they are nomads, they gleefully lay waste all the farmland they come across. Our peasants, from whom the Empire gets most of its taxes, are murdered or driven into destitution, and our western cities starve because no peasants are left to feed them."

"Worse yet, the Yezda follow Skotos," Balsamon said. When Marcus made no reply, the patriarch cocked a bushy gray eyebrow at him in sardonic amusement. "You think, perhaps, this is something I would be likely to say of anyone who does not share my creed? You must have seen enough of our priests to know most of them do not take kindly to unbelievers."

Marcus shrugged, unwilling to commit himself. He had an uneasy feeling the patriarch was playing a game with him and an even more uncomfortable certainty that Balsamon was much the smarter.

The patriarch laughed at his noncommital response. He had a good laugh, inviting everyone within earshot to share the joke. "Mavrikios, it is a courtier, not a solider!"

His eyes still twinkling, he gave his attention back to the Roman. "I am not a typical priest, I fear. Time was when the Makurani gave reverence to their Four Prophets, whose names I forget. I think their faith was wrong, I think it was foolish, but I do not think it damned them or made them impossible to treat with. The Yezda, though, worship their gods with disemboweled victims writhing on their altars and summon demons to glut themselves on the remains. They are a wicked folk and must be suppressed." If anything convinced Marcus of the truth in Balsamon's words, it was the real regret his voice bore . . . that, and the memory of Avshar's chill voice, incanting as they fought.

"And suppress them I shall," Mavrikios Gavras took up the discussion. In his vehemence he pounded right fist into left palm. "The first two years I held the throne, I fought them to a standstill on our borders. Last year, for one reason and another—" He did not elaborate and looked so grim that Marcus dared not ask for details. "—I could not campaign against them. We suffered for it, in raids and stings and torments. This year, Phos willing, I will be able to hire enough mercenaries to crush Yezd once and for all. I read your arrival here as a good omen for that, my proud friend from another world."

He paused, awaiting the Roman's reply. Scaurus recalled his first impression of this man, that giving him the truth served best. "I think," he said carefully, "you would do better to restore the peasant militias you once had than to spend your coin on foreign troops."

The Emperor stared, jaw dropping. Sneaking a glance at Balsamon, Marcus had the satisfaction of knowing he'd managed to startle the patriarch as well. The princess Alypia, on the other hand, who so far had held herself aloof from the conversation, looked at the tribune in appraisal and, he thought, growing approval.

The patriarch recovered before his sovereign. "Be glad this one is on your side, Gavras. He sees things clearly."

Mavrikios was still shaking his head in wonder. He spoke not to Scaurus, but to Balsamon. "What is he? Two days in the city? Three? There are men who have been in the palaces longer than he's been alive who cannot see that far. Tell me, Marcus Aemilius Scaurus—" It pleased but did not surprise the tribune that Gavras knew his full name. "—how did you learn so much about our woes so quickly?"

Marcus explained how he had met Phostis Apokavkos. He did not mention the peasant-soldier's name or what he had done about him.

By the time the Roman was done, the Emperor was angry. "May Phos fry all pen-pushers! Until I took the throne, the damned bureaucrats ruled the Empire for all but two years of the last fifty, in spite of everything the nobles in the provinces could do against them. They had the money to hire mercenaries and they held the capital, and that proved enough for the puppet-Emperors they raised to keep their seats. And to ruin their rivals in the power struggle, they turned our militiamen into serfs and taxed them to death so they couldn't fight for their patrons. A plague on every one of them, from Vardanes Sphrantzes on down!"

"It's not as simple as that, Father, and you know it very well," Alypia said. "A hundred years ago the peasantry was really free, not bound to our nobles. When magnates began buying up peasant land and making the farmers their dependents, it cost the central government dear. Would any Emperor, no matter how simple, want private armies raised against him, or want to see the taxes rightfully his siphoned into the hands of men who dream of the throne themselves?"

Mavrikios looked at her with a mixture of exasperation and fondness. "My daughter reads history," he said to Marcus, as if in apology.

The Roman did not think any was necessary. Alypia had

spoken well and to the point. There was plainly a keen wit behind her eyes, though she kept it on a short rein of words. The tribune was also grateful for any facts he could get. The Videssos he and his men entered was a maze of interlocking factions more twisted than any Rome had known.

The princess had turned to face her father; Scaurus admired her clean profile. It was softer than Mavrikios' both because of her sex and the influence of her mother's looks, but she was still a distinguished young woman. A cat can look at a king, Marcus thought, but what of a king's daughter? Well, he told himself, no one's yet been killed for thinking, and a good thing too, or the world would be a lonely place.

"Say what you want," the Emperor told Alypia, "about how things were a hundred years ago. Ten years ago, when Strobilos Sphrantzes had his fat fundament on the throne—"

"You'd say 'arse' to anyone but me," Alypia said. "I've heard the word before."

"Probably from my own mouth, I fear." Gavras sighed. "I do try to watch my tongue, but I've spent too many years in the field."

Marcus ignored the byplay. A Sphrantzes ruling Videssos just before Mavrikios forcibly took power? Then what in the name of Jove—or even Phos—was Vardanes Sphrantzes doing as the present Emperor's chief minister?

"Where was I?" Gavras was saying. "Oh yes, that cretin Strobilos. He was a bigger booby than his precious nephew. Fifty thousand peasants on the border of Vaspurakan he converted from soldiers to serfs in one swoop, and overtaxed serfs at that. Is it any wonder half of them went over to the Yezda, foul as they are, on their next raid? There's such a thing, Alypia, as taking too long a view."

Damn it, thought Scaurus, there was no graceful way to ask the question that was consuming him with curiosity. He squirmed in his seat, so busy with unsuccessful tries at framing it that he did not notice Balsamon watching him.

The patriarch came to his rescue. "Your Majesty, before he bursts, will you tell the poor lad why there's still a Sphrantzes in your service?"

"Ah, Scaurus, then there *is* something you don't know? I'd started to wonder. Balsamon, you tell it—you were in things up to your fuzzy eyebrows."

Balsamon assumed a comic look of injured innocence "I? All I did was point out to a few people that Strobilos had, perhaps, not been the ideal ruler for a land in a time of trouble."

"What that means, Roman, is that our priestly crony here broke a hole in the ranks of the bureaucrats you could throw *him* through, which is saying something. Half the pen-pushers backed me instead of the old Sphrantzes; their price was making the younger one Sevastos. Worth it, I suppose, but he wants the red boots for himself."

"He also wants me," Alypia said. "It is not mutual."

"I know, dear, I know. I could solve so many problems if it were, but I'm not sure I'd give you to him even so. His wife died too conveniently last year. Poor Evphrosyne! And as soon as was decent—or before, thinking back on it—there was Vardanes, full of praises for the notion of 'cementing our two great houses.' I do not trust that man."

Marcus decided he too would like to cement Vardanes Sphrantzes—by choice, into the wall of a fortress.

Something else occurred to him. Mavrikios, it seemed, was a man who liked to speak the truth as well as hear it, so the tribune felt he could inquire, "May I ask, my lord, what became of Strobilos Sphrantzes?"

"You mean, did I chop him into chitterlings as he deserved? No, that was part of the bargain Balsamon forged. He lived out his worthless life in a monastery north of Imbros and died a couple of years ago. Also, to his credit, Vardanes swore he would not serve me if I killed his uncle, and I needed him, worse luck for me.

"Here, enough of this—I neglect my hostly duties. Have another cake." And the Emperor of Videssos, like any good host, extended the platter to the Roman.

"With pleasure," Scaurus said, taking one. "They're delicious."

"Thank you," said Alypia. When Marcus blinked, she went on, a bit defensively: "I was not raised in the palaces, you know, with a servant to squirm at every crook of my finger. I learned womens' skills well enough, and after all—" She smiled at her father. "—no one can read history all the time."

"Your Highness, I said they were very good cakes before I knew who who made them," Marcus pointed out. "You've only given me another reason to like them." As soon as the words were out of his mouth he wished he had not said them. Where his daughter was concerned, Mavrikios could not help but be suspicious of everyone.

Though Alypia dropped her eyes, if the remark annoyed the Emperor he showed no sign of it. "A courtier indeed, Balsamon," he chuckled. As he bowed his way from the imperial audience, Marcus concluded that any soldier of Videssos who had no turn for diplomacy would hardly last long enough to face her foes.

V

Mizizios the eunuch led the Roman back to the entranceway of the imperial quarters, then vanished back into the building on some business of his own. The messenger who had led the tribune hither was nowhere to be seen. The Videssians, apparently, took less care over exits than entrances.

Their sentries were also less careful than Marcus found tolerable. When he emerged into the golden sunshine of late afternoon, he found both guards sprawled out asleep in front of the doorway. Their sword belts were undone, their spears lay beside the helmets they had already shed when Scaurus first saw them.

Their sloth infuriated the tribune. With an Emperor worth protecting—and that for the first time in years—these backcountry louts could do no better than doze the day away. It was more than the Roman could stand. "On your feet!" he roared. At the same time he kicked their discarded helms, making a fine clatter.

The sentries jerked and scrambled upright, fumbling for the weapons they had set aside. Marcus laughed scornfully. He cursed the startled warders with every bit of Videssian foulness he had learned. He wished Gaius Philippus were at his side; the centurion had a gift for invective. "If you were under my command, you'd be lashed with more than my tongue, I promise you that," he finished.

Under his tirade, the Videssians went from amazement to sullenness. The older one, a stocky, much-scarred veteran, muttered to his companion, "Who does this churlish barbarian think he is?"

A moment later he was on the ground, flat as he'd been while napping. Marcus stood over him, rubbing a sore knuckle and watching the other sentry for any move he might make. Save for backing away, he made none.

Seeing the still-standing guard was safe to ignore, Marcus hauled the man he had felled to his feet. He was none too gentle about it. The sentry shook his head, trying to clear it. A bruise was already forming under his left eye.

"When do your reliefs arrive?" Scaurus snapped at the two of them.

"In about another hour, sir," the younger, milder guard answered. He spoke very carefully, as one might to a tiger which had asked the time of day.

"Very well, then. Tell them what happened to you and let them know someone will be by to check on them sometime during their watch. And may your Phos help them and you if they get caught sleeping!"

He turned his back on the sentries and stalked off, giving them no chance to question or protest. In fact, he did not intend to send anyone to spy on the next watch. The threat alone should be enough to keep them alert.

As he walked back past the barracks hall belonging to the mercenaries from the Duchy of Namdalen, he heard his name called. Helvis was leaning out of a top-story window, holding something in her hand. The Roman was too far away to see what it was until the sun gave back the bright glint of gold— probably some trinket she'd bought with what she'd won betting on him. She smiled and waved.

Grinning himself, he waved back, his anger at the sentries forgotten for the moment. She was a friendly lass, and he had only himself to blame for thinking her unattached the night before. Hemond was a good sort, too; Marcus had liked him from their first meeting at the Silver Gate. His grin turned wry as he reflected that the two women who had interested him most in Videssos both seemed thoroughly unapproachable. It's hardly the end of the world, you know, he told himself, seeing that you've been in the city less than a week.

His mood of gentle self-mockery was suddenly erased by the sight of the tall, white-robed figure of Avshar. His hand reached the hilt of his sword before he knew he had moved it. The envoy of Yezd, though, did not appear to see him in return. Avshar was some distance away in deep conversation with a squat, bowlegged man in the furs and leather of the Pardrayan nomads. The tribune had the feeling he'd seen the plainsman before, but could not recall when or where— maybe at last night's banquet, he thought uncertainly.

He was so intent on Avshar that he forgot to pay attention to where his feet were taking him. The first knowledge he had that he was not alone on his pathway came when he bounced off a man coming in the opposite direction. "Your pardon, I pray!" he exclaimed, taking his eye off the Yezda to see whom he'd staggered.

His victim, a short chubby man, wore the blue robes of the priesthood of Phos. His shaven head gave him a curious age- less look, but he was not old—gray had not touched his beard, and his face was hardly lined. "Quite all right, quite all right," he said. "It's my own fault for not noticing you were full of your own thoughts."

"That's good of you, but it doesn't excuse my clumsiness."

"Don't trouble yourself about it. Am I not right in recog- nizing you as the leader of the new company of outland mer- cenaries?"

Marcus admitted it.

"Then I've been wanting to meet you for some time." The priest's eyes crinkled at the corners as he smiled. "Though not so abruptly as this, perhaps."

"You have the advantage of me," the tribune observed.

"Hmm? Oh, so I do—no reason you should know me, is there? I'm called Nepos. I wish I could claim my interest in you was entirely unselfish, but I fear I can't. You see, I hold one of the chairs in sorcery at the Videssian Academy."

Scaurus nodded his understanding. In a land where wiz- ardry held so strong a place, what could be more logical than its taking its place alongside other intellectual disciplines such as philosophy and mathematics? And since the Romans were widely known to have come to Videssos by no natural means, the Empire's sorcerers must be burning with curiosity about their arrival. For that matter, so was he—Nepos might be able to make him better understand the terrifying moment that had whisked him to this world.

He gauged the setting sun. "It should be about time for my men to sit down to supper. Would you care to join us? After we've eaten, you can ask questions to your heart's content."

"Nothing would please me more," Nepos answered, beaming at him. "Lead on, and I'll follow as best I can—your legs are longer than mine, I'm afraid."

Despite his round build, the little priest had no trouble keeping up with the Roman. His sandaled feet twinkled over the ground, and as he walked, he talked. An endless stream of questions bubbled from him, queries not only about the religious and magical practices of Rome and Gaul, but about matters social and political as well.

"I think," the Roman said, wondering at the relevance of some of the things Nepos was asking, "your faith plays a larger part in everything you do than is true in my world."

"I'd begun to reach that conclusion myself," the priest agreed. "In Videssos you cannot buy a cup of wine without being told Phos will triumph in the end, or deal with a jeweler from Khatrish without hearing that the battle between good and evil is evenly matched. Everyone in the city fancies himself a theologian." He shook his head in mock annoyance.

At the Roman barracks Marcus found the sentries alert and vertical. He would have been astounded had it been otherwise. Far less dangerous for a legionary to face an oncoming foe than Gaius Philippus' wrath, which fell unerringly on shirkers.

Inside the hall, most of the legionaries were already spooning down their evening meal, a thick stew of barley, boiled beef and marrowbones, peas, carrots, onions, and various herbs. It was better food than they would have had in Caesar's barracks, but of similar kind. Nepos accepted his bowl and spoon with a word of thanks.

Marcus introduced the priest to Gaius Philippus, Viridovix, Gorgidas, Quintus Glabrio, Adiatun, the scout Junius Blaesus, and several other Romans. They found a quiet corner and talked while they ate. How many times now, the tribune wondered, had he told some Videssian his tale? Unlike almost all the others, Nepos was no passive audience. His questions were good-natured but probing, his constant effort aimed toward piecing together a consistent account from the recollections of his table companions.

Why was it, he asked, that Gaius Philippus and Adiatun both remembered seeing Scaurus and Viridovix still trading swordstrokes inside the dome of light, yet neither the tribune nor the Gaul had any such memory? Why had it been hard for Gorgidas to breathe, but for no one else? Why had Junius Blaesus felt piercing cold, but Adiatun broken into a sweat?

Gaius Philippus answered Nepos patiently for a time, but before long his streak of hard Roman practicality emerged. "What good does it do you, anyway, to learn that Publius Flaccus farted while we were in flight?"

"None whatever, very possibly," Nepos smiled, taking no offense. "Did he?"

Amid general laughter, the centurion said, "You'd have to ask him, not me."

"The only way to understand anything in the past," Nepos went on in a more serious vein, "is to find out as much as one can about it. Often people have no idea how much they can remember or, indeed, how much of what they think they know is false. Only patient inquiry and comparing many accounts can bring us near the truth."

"You talk like a historian, not a priest or a wizard," Gorgidas said.

Nepos shrugged, as puzzled by the Greek doctor's comment as Gorgidas was by him. He answered, "I talk like myself and nothing else. There are priests so struck by the glory of Phos' divinity that they contemplate the divine essence to the exclusion of all worldly concerns, and reject the world as a snare Skotos laid for their temptation. Is that what you mean?"

"Not exactly." Priest and physician viewed things from such different perspectives as to make communication all but impossible, but each had a thirst for knowledge that drove him to persist.

"To my mind," Nepos continued, "the world and everything in it reflects Phos' splendor, and deserves the study of men who would approach more nearly an understanding of Phos' plan for the Empire and all mankind."

To that Gorgidas could make no reply at all. To his way of thinking, the world and everything in it was worth studying for its own sake, and ultimate meanings, if any, were likely unknowable. Yet he had to recognize Nepos' sincerity and his goodness. "'Countless are the world's wonders, but none more wonderful than man,'" he murmured, and sat back with his wine, soothed as always by Sophokles' verse.

"Being a wizard, what have you learned from us?" Quintus Glabrio asked Nepos; until then he'd sat largely silent.

"Less than I'd have liked, I must admit. All I can tell you is the obvious truth that the two blades, Scaurus' and yours, Viridovix, brought you hither. If there is a greater purpose behind your coming, I do not think it has unfolded yet."

"Now I know you're no ordinary priest," Gorgidas exclaimed. "In my world, I never saw one admit to ignorance."

"How arrogant your priests must be! What greater wickedness than claiming to know everything, arrogating to yourself the privileges of godhood?" Nepos shook his head. "Thanks be to Phos, I am not so vain. I have so very much to learn! Among other things, my friends, I would like to see, even to hold, the fabled swords to which we owe your presence here."

Marcus and Viridovix exchanged glances filled with the same reluctance. Neither had put his weapon in another's hands since coming to Videssos. There seemed no way, though, to decline such a reasonable request. Both men slowly drew their blades from their scabbards; each began to hand his to Nepos. "Wait!" Marcus said, holding out a warning hand to Viridovix. "I don't think it would be wise for our swords to touch, no matter what the circumstance."

"Right you are," the Gaul agreed, sheathing his blade for the moment. "One such mischance cools the appetite for another, indeed and it does."

Nepos took the Roman's sword, holding it up to a clay lamp to examine it closely. "It seems altogether plain," he said to Marcus, some perplexity in his voice. "I feel no surge of strength, nor am I impelled to travel elsewhere—for which I have no complaint, you understand. Save for the strange characters cut into the blade, it is but another longsword, a bit cruder than most. Is the spell in those letters? What do they say?"

"I have no idea," Scaurus replied. "It's a Celtic sword, made by Viridovix's people. I took it as battle spoil and kept it because it fits my size better than the shortswords most Romans use."

"Ah, I see. Viridovix, would you read the inscription for me and tell me what it means?"

The Gaul tugged at his fiery mustache in some embarrassment. "Nay, I canna, I fear. With my folk letters are no common thing, as they are with the Romans—and with you too, I
should guess. Only the druids—priests, you would say—
have the skill of them, and never a druid I was, nor am I sorry
for it. I will tell you, my own blade is marked as well. Look,
if you will."

But when his sword came free of its scabbard the runes set
in it were gleaming gold, and those on the other blade sprang
to glowing life with them. "Sheathe it!" Marcus shouted in
alarm. He snatched his own sword from Nepos' hand and
crammed it back into its sheath. There was a bad moment
when he thought it was fighting against his grip, but then it
was securely back in place. Tension leaked from the air.

Sudden sweat beaded Nepos' forehead. He said to Gorgidas, "Of such a thing as that I was indeed ignorant, nor, to
quote your red-haired friend, am I sorry for it." His laugh was
shaky and rang loud in the awed and fearful hush that had
fallen over the barracks. He soon found an excuse to make an
early departure, disappearing after a few quick good-byes.

"There goes a fellow who set his nets for rabbit and found
a bear sitting in them," Gaius Philippus said, but even his
chuckle sounded forced.

Almost all the Romans, and Marcus with them, sought
their pallets early that night. He snuggled beneath his blanket
and slowly drifted toward sleep. The coarse wool made him
itch, but his last waking thought was one of relief that he still
had a blanket—and a barracks, for that matter—over him.

The tribune woke early the next morning to the sound of an
argument outside the barracks hall. He flung on a mantle,
belted his sword round his middle, and, still rubbing sleep
from his eyes, went out to see what the trouble was.

"No, sir, I'm sorry," a Roman guard was saying, "but you
cannot see my commander until he wakes." He and his mate
held their spears horizontally across their bodies to keep their
unwanted guest from entering.

"Phos fry you, I tell you this is urgent!" Nephon
Khoumnos shouted. "Must I—oh, there you are, Scaurus. I
have to talk to you at once, and your thickskulled sentries
would not give me leave."

"You cannot blame them for following their standard orders. Don't worry about it, Gnaeus, Manlius—you did right." He returned his attention to Khoumnos. "If you wanted to see me, here I am. Shall we stroll along the path and give my men a chance to go back to sleep?"

Still fuming, Khoumnos agreed. The Roman sentries stepped back to let their commander by. The path's paving stones were cool on his bare feet. He gratefully sucked in the early morning air. It was sweet after the close, smoky atmosphere inside the hall.

A gold-throated thrush in a nearby tree greeted the sun with a burst of sparkling notes. Even as unmusical a soul as Scaurus found it lovely.

The Roman did not try to begin the conversation. He ambled along, admiring now the delicate flush the early light gave to marble, now the geometric precision of a dewspangled spiderweb. If Khoumnos had so pressing a problem, let him bring it up.

He did, rising to the bait of Marcus' silence. "Scaurus, where in Phos' holy name do you get the authority to lay your hands on my men?"

The Roman stopped, hardly believing he'd heard correctly. "Do you mean the guards outside the Emperor's dwelling yesterday?"

"Who else could I possibly mean?" Khoumnos snapped. "We take it very ill in Videssos when a mercenary assaults native-born soldiers. It was not for that I arranged to have you come to the city; when I saw you and your men in Imbros, you struck me as being out of the common run of barbarians."

"You take it ill, you say, when a mercenary strikes a native Videssian soldier?"

Nephon Khoumnos gave an impatient nod.

Marcus knew Khoumnos was an important man in Videssos, but he was too furious to care. "Well, how do you take it when your fine Videssian soldiers are snoozing the afternoon away in front of the very chambers they're supposed to guard?"

"What?"

"Whoever was telling you tales out of school," the tribune said, "should have gone through the whole story, not just his half of it." He explained how he had found both sentries napping in the sun as he left his audience with the Emperor. "What reason would I have for setting upon them? Did they give you one?"

"No," Khoumnos admitted. "They said they were attacked from behind without warning."

"From above would be more like it." Marcus snorted. "They can count themselves lucky they were your troops, not mine; stripes are the least they could have hoped for in Roman service."

Khoumnos was not yet convinced. "Their stories hang together very well."

"What would you expect, that two shirkers would give each other the lie? Khoumnos, I don't much care whether you believe me or not. You ruined my sleep, and, from the way my guts are churning right now, I'd wager you've ruined my breakfast as well. But I'll tell you this—if those guards were the best men Videssos can offer, no wonder you need mercenaries."

Thinking of Tzimiskes, Mouzalon, Apokavkos—yes, and Khoumnos himself—Scaurus knew how unfair he was being, but he was too nettled to watch his tongue. The incredible gall the sentries had shown—not merely to hide their guilt, but to try to put it on him! He shook his head in wonder.

Anger cloaked by expressionless features, Khoumnos bowed stiffly from the waist. "I will look into what you've told me, I promise you that," he said. He bowed again and strode away.

Watching his rigid back, Marcus wondered if he had made another enemy. Sphrantzes, Avshar, now Khoumnos—for a man who'd aspired to politics, he told himself, you have a gift for the right word at the wrong time. And if Sphrantzes and Khoumnos are both your foes, where in Videssos will you find a friend?

The tribune sighed. As always, it was too late to unsay anything. All he could do now was live with the consequences of what he'd already done. And in that context, he thought, breakfast did not seem such a bad idea after all. He walked back toward the barracks.

Despite his Stoic training, despite his efforts to take things as they came, the rest of that morning and early afternoon were hard for him to wait through. To try to drown his worries in work, he threw himself into the Romans' daily drill with such nervous energy that he flattened everyone who stood against him. At any other time he would have been proud. Now he barked at his men for lying down against their commander. "Sir," one of the legionaries said, "if I was going to lie down against you, I would have done it sooner." The man was rubbing a bruised shoulder as he limped away.

Scaurus tried to unburden himself to Viridovix, but the big Celt was scant help. "I know it's a bad thing," he said, "but what can you do? Give 'em half a chance and the men'd sooner sleep nor work. I would myself, if there's no fighting or women to be had."

Gaius Philippus had come up during the last part of this speech and listened to it with obvious disagreement. "If your troops won't obey orders you have a mob, not an army. That's why we Romans were conquering Gaul, you know. Man for man, the Celts are as brave as any I've seen, but you can't work together worth a turtle turd."

"Aye, it's not to be denied we're a fractious lot. But you're a bigger fool or ever I thought, Gaius Philippus, if you think your puny Romans could be holding the whole of Gaul in despite of its people."

"Fool, is it?" As with a terrier, there was no room for retreat in the senior centurion. "Watch what you say."

Viridovix bristled back. "Have a care with your own mouth, or I'll cut you a new one, the which you'd not like at all."

Before his touchy comrades heated further, Marcus quickly stepped between them. "The two of you are like the dog in the fable, snapping after the reflection of a bone. None of us here will ever know whether Caesar or the Gauls prevailed. There's not much room for enmity among us, you know—we have enough foes outside our ranks. Besides, I tell you now that before you can go for each other, you'll go through me first."

The tribune carefully did not see the measuring stares both his friends gave him. But he had eased the friction; centurion and Celt, after a last, half-friendly snarl, went about their own affairs.

It occurred to Scaurus that Viridovix had to feel far more lost and alone in ther new land than the Romans felt. There were more than a thousand of them to but a solitary Gaul; not a soul in this land even spoke his tongue. No wonder his temper slipped from time to time—the wonder was the Celt keeping up his spirits as well as he did.

At about the time when the Emperor had summoned him to audience the day before, Tzimiskes sought out the tribune to tell him that Khoumnos begged leave to speak with him. There was wonder on the dour Videssian's face as he conveyed the message. "'Begged leave,'" he said. I don't think I've heard of Nephon Khoumnos begging leave of anyone. 'Begged leave,'" Tzimiskes repeated, still not believing it.

Khoumnos stood outside the barracks, one square hand scratching his iron-bearded chin. When Marcus walked up to him, he jerked the hand away as if caught doing something shameful. His mouth worked a couple of times before words came out. "Damn you," he said at last. "I owe you an apology. For what it's worth, you have it."

"I accept it gladly," Marcus replied—just how glad he was, he did not want to show the Videssian. "I would have hoped, though, that you'd know I had better things to do than breaking your guardsmen's heads."

"I'd be a liar if I said I wasn't surprised when Blemmydes and Kourkouas came to me with their tale. But you don't go disbelieving your men without some good reason—you know how it is."

Scaurus could only nod; he did know how it was. An officer who refused to back up his troops was useless. Once his men lost confidence in him, he could not rely on their reports, which only made them less confident . . . That road was a downward spiral which had to be stopped before it could start. "What made you change your mind?" he asked.

"After the pleasant little talk I had with you this morning, I went back and gave those two scoundrels separate grillings. Kourkouasa cracked, finally."

"The younger one?"

"That's right. Interesting you should guess—you notice things, don't you? Yes, Lexos Blemmydes kept playing the innocent wronged up until the last minute, Skotos chill his lying heart."

"What do you plan to do with the two of them?"

"I've already done it. I may have made a mistake before, but I fixed it. As soon as I knew what the truth was, I had their corselets off their backs and shipped them over the Cattle-Crossing on the first ferry. Between brigands and Yezda, the west country should be lively enough to keep them away. Good riddance, say I, and I'm only sorry such wastrels made me speak hastily to you."

"Don't let it trouble you," Marcus answered, convinced Khoumnos' apology came from mind and heart both. He also realized he had let his anger put him in the wrong with that vicious gibe about Videssian troops. "You weren't the only one who said things he regrets now, you know."

"Fair enough." Khoumnos extended his hand, and the tribune took it. The Videssian's palm was even harder than his own, callused not only from weaponwork but also by years of holding the reins. Khoumnos slapped him on the back and went about his business. Marcus suspected it would be a good long while before the next set of sentries dropped off to sleep before the Emperor's quarters.

His own sleep that night, after tension well relieved, was deep and untroubled for several hours. Ordinary barracks chatter and the noise of men rising to make water or find a snack never bothered his rest. That was as well; if they had, sleep would have been impossible to come by.

The noise that woke him now was no louder than the usual run of nightly sounds. But it was one which did not belong— the soft slide of a booted foot across the flooring. Romans were either barefoot and silent or wore clattering nail-soled sandals. The sound of a footfall neither one nor the other pierced Marcus' slumber and pried his eyelids apart.

Only a couple of torches burned in the hall, giving just enough light to keep the Romans from stumbling over each other in the night. But the crouched figure sneaking between the sleeping soliders was no legionary. The squat silhouette and bushy beard could only belong to a Khamorth; Marcus felt cold fear as he recognized the nomad who had been talking to Avshar the night before. He was coming toward the tribune, a dagger in his hand.

The nomad shook his head, muttering something under his breath. He saw Scaurus as the Roman flung back his blanket and grabbed for his sword. The Khamorth roared and charged. Naked as a worm, Marcus scrambled to his feet. There was no time to pull his blade from its sheath. He used it as a club to knock aside the Khamorth's first stab, then closed with the shorter man, seizing his assailant's knife-wrist with his left hand.

He caught a glimpse of his foe's face. The nomad's dark eyes were wide with a consuming madness and something more, something the tribune would not identify until some time later as stark terror.

They rolled to the floor, still holding tightly to each other.

There were shouts all through the barracks now—the Khamorth's bellow and the sound of struggle routed the men from their mattresses. It took a few seconds, though, for the sleep-fuzzed soldiers to grasp where the hubbub came from.

Marcus held his grip with all his strength, meanwhile using the pommel of his sword to try to batter the nomad into submission. But his enemy seemed to have a skull hard as rock. For all the blows he took, he still writhed and twisted, trying to plant his knife in the tribune's flesh.

Then a second strong hand joined Marcus' on the nomad's wrist. Viridovix, as naked as Scaurus, squeezed down on the Khamorth's tendons, forcing his fingers to open. The knife dropped to the floor.

Viridovix shook the Khamorth like a great rat. "Why would he be after having a grudge against you, Roman dear?" he asked. Then, to his prisoner, "Don't wriggle, now!" He shook him again. The Khamorth, eyes riveted on the fallen dagger, ignored him.

"I don't know," Marcus answered. "I think he must be in Avshar's pay, though. I saw them walking together yesterday."

"Avshar, is it? The why of that omadhaun's misliking for you everyone knows, but what of this kern? Is he a hired knife, or did you do something to raise his dander, too?"

Some of the Romans gathered round grumbled at the Gaul's tone of voice, but Marcus waved them to silence. He was about to say he had only seen the Khamorth that once with Avshar, but there was still a nagging familiarity about him, about the way he kept his gaze fixed on the knife he no longer held.

Scaurus snapped his fingers. "Remember the plainsman at the Silver Gate who tried to stare me down when we came into Videssos?"

"I do that," Viridovix said. "You mean—? Hold still, blast your hide!" he snapped at the prisoner, who was still struggling to break free.

"There's no need to hold him all night," Gaius Philippus said. The senior centurion had found a length of stout rope. "Titus, Sextus, Paulus, give me a hand. Let's go get our bird trussed."

It took all four Romans and the big Gaul to bind the Khamorth. He fought the rope with more fury than he had shown against Scaurus himself, shrieking and cursing in his harsh native tongue. So frenziedly did he kick, scratch, and bite that none of his captors was left unmarked, but in the end to no avail. Even after the ropes were tight around him, he still thrashed against their unyielding grip.

No wonder, the tribune thought, Avshar had chosen to use this man against him. The nomad's already-existing contempt for infantry of any sort must have become a personal hatred when Scaurus won their battle of wills at the city gate. As Viridovix had said, the Khamorth had a reason for furthering the schemes of the envoy of Yezd.

But still—at the Silver Gate the plainsman had been in full control of his faculties, while now he acted for all the world like a madman. Had Avshar given him a drug to heighten his fury? There might be a way to find out. "Gorgidas!" he called.

"What is it?" the Greek answered from the fringes of the crowd around the tied-up Khamorth.

Marcus explained his idea to the doctor, adding, "Can you examine him and find out why his nature has changed so greatly since the last time we saw him?"

"What do you think I've been trying to do? But all these gawkers here are too tightly packed to let me through." The physician was too slight to have much luck elbowing his way into a crowd.

"Let him by. Make way, there," the tribune ordered, moving his men out of the way so Gorgidas could reach the nomad, who lay across Scaurus' own pallet. The physician knelt beside him, touching his forehead, peering into his eyes, and listening to his breathing.

When he stood, his face was troubled. "You were right, sir," he said. Marcus knew how concerned he was when he used the title of respect; Gorgidas was a man with no time for formality. "The poor devil is at the point of death, from some toxic potion, I would say."

"At the point of death?" Scaurus said, startled. "He was lively enough a few minutes ago."

Gorgidas made an impatient gesture. "I don't mean he's liable to die in the next hour, maybe even not in the next day. But die he will—his eyes are sunk in his head, and one pupil is twice the other's size. He breathes like a delirious man, deep and slow. And between his bellows you can hear him grinding his teeth fit to break them. As anyone who has read the writings of Hippokrates will tell you, those are fatal signs.

"Yet he has no fever," the doctor continued, "and I see no sores or pustules to indicate some disease has him in its clutches. Therefore, I must conclude he has been drugged— poisoned would be a better word."

"Can you cure him, do you think?" Marcus asked.

Gorgidas tossed his head in an imperious Greek negative. "I've told you before, I am a doctor, not a worker of miracles. Without knowing what hell-brew is in him, I wouldn't know where to start, and, if I did, it would probably still be useless."

"'Worker of miracles,' your honor said?" Viridovix put in. "Could it be the priests of Phos might save him, where you canna?"

"Don't be ridi—" Gorgidas began, and then stopped in confusion. Marcus had to admire the way he faced up to an idea he did not like. He reluctantly admitted, "That might not be foolish after all. Some of them can do what I'd not have believed—isn't that right, Minucius?"

The legionary a priest had saved outside of Imbros was a stalwart young man whose stubbly whiskers were black almost to blueness. "So you keep telling me," he answered. "I don't recall a bit of it—the fever must have made my wits wander."

"That Nepos fellow you brought over last night seemed a man of sense," Gorgidas suggested to Marcus.

"I think you're right. Nephon Khoumnos will have to know of this, too, though I wouldn't blame him for thinking I'm trying to tear down Videssos' army from the inside out."

"If this sort of garbage goes on, I'd say the Videssian army could use some tearing down," Gaius Philippus said. Privately, his superior officer was beginning to agree with him, but Scaurus had already found that was not something he could tell the Videssians.

The tribune bent to pick up the dagger forced from the Khamorth. He misliked the blade even before he touched it. The pommel was carved into a leering, evil cat's-face, while the hilt was covered by a green, velvety leather that must have come from the skin of a serpent. The blade itself was badly discolored, as if it had been tempered too long or too often.

No sooner had Marcus' fingers folded round the hilt than he dropped the weapon with a cry of alarm. The discolored blade had begun to gleam, not an honest red-gold like the Druids' marks on his sword and Viridovix', but a wavering yellowish green. The tribune was reminded of some foul fungus shining with the sickly light of decay. He sniffed . . . no, it was not his imagination. A faint corrupt reek rose from the dagger.

He thanked every god he knew that the baneful weapon had not pierced his flesh; the death it would have dealt would not have been clean.

"Nepos must see this at once," Gorgidas said. "Magic is his province."

Marcus agreed, but could not nerve himself to pick up the wicked blade again. Magic was no province of his.

"It came to life when you touched it," Gorgidas said. "Was it glowing when the nomad assailed you?"

"Truth to tell, I have no idea. I had other things on my mind at the moment."

Gorgidas sniffed. "Well, I suppose you can't be blamed," he said, but his tone belied his words. The Greek was a man who, if it befell him to lose his head, would notice the color of the headsman's eyes behind his mask.

Now he stooped down to take the vicious dagger gingerly by the handle. The blade flickered uncertainly, like a half-asleep beast of prey. The doctor tore a strip of cloth from a solider's mantle and wrapped it several times round the dagger's hilt, tying it with an elegant knot he usually used to finish a bandage on an arm or leg.

Only when the knot was done did he touch the hilt with his bare hand. He grunted in satisfaction as the blade remained dark. "That should keep it safe enough," he said, carefully handing the weapon to Scaurus, who took it with equal caution.

Holding the knife well away from his body, Scaurus started for the door, only to be stopped by a guffaw from Viridovix. "Would your honor not think it a good idea to put on a cloak, ere he scandalize some early-rising lass?"

The tribune blinked; he had had too much else to worry about in the commotion to think of clothes. Not sorry to be rid of it, he put the dagger down for a moment to wrap himself in a mantle and strap on his sandals. Then he picked it up again with a sigh and stepped out into the crisp sunrise coolness.

As soon as he reached the door, he discovered how the nomad hád been able to get into the barracks without the Roman sentries stopping him or raising the alarm. Both of them were lying in front of the entrance, fast asleep. Amazed and furious, Marcus prodded one none too gently with his foot. The man murmured faintly but would not wake, even after another, harsher, prod. Nor could his fellow guard be roused. Neither seemed harmed in any way, but they could not be brought to consciousness.

When Marcus summoned Gorgidas, the Greek physician was also unable to make the guards stir. "What's happened to them, do you think?" the tribune asked.

"How in blazes do I know?" Gorgidas sounded thoroughly harried. "In this bloody country you have to be a he-witch as well as a doctor, and it puts me at a disadvantage. Go on, go on, fetch Napos—they're breathing well and their pulses are strong. They won't die while you're gone."

The sun's first rays were just greeting the tops of the city's taller buildings when the tribune began his walk to the Vides-sian Academy, which was on the northern edge of the palace complex. He did not know whether he would find Nepos there so early, but could think of no better place to start looking for the priest.

As he walked, he watched the sun creep down the walls of the structures he passed by, watched it caress the flowering trees in the palace gardens and orchards, watched their blossoms begin to unfold under its light. And as he walked out from behind the long blue shadow of a granite colonnade, the sun reached him as well.

The dagger he carried was suddenly hot in his hand. At the

sun's first touch the blade began to burn, giving off clouds of acrid yellow smoke. The Roman threw it to the ground and backed away, coughing and gasping for breath—the smoke felt like live coals in his lungs.

He thought he heard the metal wail as if in agony and resolved to clamp down on a runaway imagination.

The fire was so furious it soon burned itself out. After the breeze had dispersed the noxious fumes, Marcus warily approached the sorcerous weapon. He expected to see only a lump of twisted, fused metal, but found to his dismay that hilt, pommel, and even Gorgidas' wrappings were still intact, as was a thin rod of steel extending the length of what had been the blade.

A cautious touch revealed the dagger to be cool enough to handle. Fighting back a shudder, the tribune picked it up and hurried on to the Academy.

A four-story building of gray sandstone housed the Videssian center of learning. Though both secular and religious knowledge were taught there, a spire and golden sphere surmounted the structure; here as elsewhere in the Empire, its faith had the last word.

The doorman, half-asleep over his breakfast of bread and hot wine, was surprised his first guest should be a mercenary captain, but polite enough to try to hide it. "Brother Nepos?" he said. "Yes, he's here—he's always an early riser. You'll probably find him in the refectory, straight down this hall, the third door on your right."

This early in the day, the Academy hallway was almost deserted. A young blue-robe looked intrigued as the Roman strode past him but, like the doorman, offered no comment.

Sunlight streamed through the tall, many-paned windows of the refectory and onto its battered tables and comfortably dilapidated chairs. But somehow, instead of accenting their shabbiness, the warm light gave the old furniture the effect of being freshly varnished and newly reupholstered.

Except for the fat, unshaven cook sweating behind his pots, Nepos was alone in the room as Marcus stepped in. The priest stopped with a steaming spoonful of porridge halfway to his mouth. "You look like grim death," he told the tribune. "What has brought you here so early?"

By way of answer, Scaurus dropped what was left of the

Khamorth's dagger with a clank onto the priest's table. Nepos'
reaction could not have been more emphatic had it been a fat
viper in front of him. Forgetting the spoon in his hand, he
shoved his chair back as fast as he could. Porridge splattered
in all directions. The priest went first red, then pale, to the
crown of his shaven head. "Where did you come by this?" he
demanded; the sternness his light voice could assume was
amazing.

His round face grew more and more grave as the Roman
told his tale. When at last Marcus was done, Nepos sat silent
for a full minute, his chin cupped in the palms of his hands.
Then he bounced to his feet, crying, "Skotos is among us!"
with such fervor that the startled cook dropped his spoon into
a pot and had to fish for it with a long-handled fork.

"Now that you've been informed," Marcus began, "I
should also pass my news on to Nephon Khoumnos so he can
question—"

"Khoumnos question?" Nepos interrupted. "No! We need
subtlety here, not force. I will put the question to your nomad
myself. Come!" he snapped, scooping up the dagger and
moving for the door so quickly Marcus had to half trot to
catch him up.

"Where are you going, your excellency?" the Academy
doorman asked the priest as he hurried by. "Your lecture is to
begin in less than an hour, and—"

Nepos did not turn his head. "Cancel it!" Then, to Marcus,
"Hurry, man! All the freezing furies of hell are at your back,
though you know it not!"

When they got back to the barracks, the bound Khamorth
screamed in despair as he saw the consumed weapon Nepos
carried. The prisoner shrank in upon himself, drawing his
knees up against his belly and tucking his head down into the
hollow of his shoulder.

Gaius Philippus, a firm believer in the saving value of routine, had already sent most of the Romans out to the drill
field. Now Nepos cleared the barracks of everyone save himself, the nomad, the two unconscious Roman sentries, and
Gorgidas, allowing the doctor to act as his assistant.

"Go on, go on," he said, shooing them out before him.
"You can do nothing to help me, and a word at the wrong
moment could do great harm."

"Sure and he's just like a druid," Viridovix grumbled, "always thinking he knows twice as much as anyone else."

"I notice you're out here with the rest of us," Gaius Philippus said.

"That I am," the Celt admitted. "All too often, your druid is right. It's a rare chancy thing, going against one."

Only a few minutes passed before the sentries came out of the barracks hall. They seemed none the worse for what they had undergone, but had no memory of how their unwilled sleep had begun. As far as they knew, one moment they were on guard, while in the next Nepos was bending over them in prayer. Both of them were angry and embarrassed at failing in their duty.

"Don't trouble yourselves about it," Marcus told them. "You can't be blamed for falling victim to wizardry." He sent them on to exercise with their comrades, then settled back to wait for Nepos to emerge.

And wait he did; the fat little priest did not come forth for another two hours and more. When he appeared at last, Scaurus bit back a shocked exclamation. Nepos' gait was that of a man in the last throes of exhaustion; he clutched Gorgidas' elbow as a shipwreck victim clings to a plank. His robe was soaked with sweat, his eyes black-circled. Blinking at the bright sunlight, he sank gratefully onto a bench. There he sat for several minutes, gathering his strength before he began to speak.

"You, my friend," he told Marcus wearily, "have no notion of how lucky you were to wake, and how much luckier still not to be touched by that accursed knife. Had it pierced you, had it even pricked you, it would have drawn the soul from your body into the deepest pits of hell, there to lie tormented for all eternity. A demon was bound in that blade, a demon to be set free by the taste of blood—or destroyed by Phos' sun, as in fact befell."

In his own world, the tribune would have taken all that as a metaphor for poison. Here he was not so sure . . . and suddenly more than half believed, as he remembered how the dagger had shrieked when struck by sunlight.

The priest continued, "You were right in blaming Avshar for setting upon you the poor, damned nomad inside your hall. Poor lost soul—the wizard linked his life to that of the demon he bore, and when it failed, he began to gutter out, like a candle in air unable to sustain a flame. But the destruction of the demon severed the hold Avshar had on him, and I learned much before his flame fell into nothingness."

"Is your honor saying he's dead?" Viridovix said. "Hardly hurt, he was, in the taking of him."

"He's dead," Gorgidas said. "His soul, his will to live— call it what you like—there was none in him, and he died."

Marcus recalled the doom-filled cry on the Khamorth's lips when he saw the ruin of the weapon he had carried, recalled how he had crumpled in on himself. "Can you trust the knowledge you get from a dying man who was your foe's tool?" he asked Nepos.

"A good question," the priest nodded. Little by little, as he sat, his voice and manner were losing their haggard edge. "The chains the Yezda put on him were strong—I would curse him, but he has cursed himself beyond my power to damn. Nonetheless, Phos has granted those who follow him a means of cutting through such chains—"

"A decoction of henbane is what we used," Gorgidas put in, impatient at Nepos' elliptical phrasing. "I've used it before, Phos notwithstanding. It dulls pain and frees the guard on a man's tongue. You have to be careful, though—too high a dose, and you've put your patient out of pain forever."

The priest plainly did not care for Gorgidas' casual revelation of a secret of his magical craft. But, impelled by larger concerns, he kept his temper, saying, "It is enough that we know two things: Avshar loosed this treacherous assault on you; and he is a sorcerer more powerful in his wickedness than any we have met for years uncounted. Yet by the first action I named, he forfeited the protections all envoys, no matter how evil, enjoy."

A smile of anticipation flitted across Nepos' face as he went on, "So, my outland friends, the fiend has delivered himself into our hands! *Now* we send for Nephon Khoumnos!"

VI

THE THOUGHT OF AVSHAR'S HEAD GOING UP ON THE MILE-stone had so ferocious an appeal to Marcus that he charged away from the barracks hall before he realized he was not sure where to find Khoumnos. Neither was Nepos, who puffed along gamely beside him. "I know of the man, you understand," he said to the Roman, "but I do not know him personally."

Scaurus was not overly worried at his ignorance. He felt sure any soldier in Videssos for longer than a week could give him the directions he needed. The first group he saw was a squad of Namdaleni returning from the practice field. At their head was Hemond of Metepont, his conical helm tucked under his arm. He had seen the tribune, too—he waved his men to a halt and sauntered over to Scaurus.

"For a newly come mercenary, you make the oddest set of acquaintances," he observed with a smile. "It's a long road to travel from the wizard-envoy of Yezd to a priest of the Academy."

Nepos' robes were no different from those of any other priest of similar rank; Hemond, Marcus thought, was uncommonly well informed.

The Namdalener acknowledged his introduction of Nepos with a friendly nod. "Actually," Scaurus continued, "you can do us a favor, if you will."

"Name it," Hemond said expansively.

"We need to see Nephon Khoumnos as quickly as we can, and neither of us is sure where he might be."

"Ho-ho!" Hemond laid a finger alongside his nose and winked. "Going to twist his beard some more over his sleepy sentries, are you?"

Uncommonly well informed indeed, Marcus thought, but this time not quite well enough. He considered for a moment. Remembering that Hemond and Helvis had backed him against Avshar, he decided he could tell the Namdalener his story. "It's not that—" he began.

When he was done, Hemond rubbed the shaven back of his head and swore in the broad dialect of his homeland. "The snake has really overreached himself this time," he said, more to himself than to Marcus or Nepos. His face suddenly was that of a hunter about to bag his prey. "Bors! Fayard!" he snapped, and two of his men stiffened to attention. "Get back to quarters and let the men know the rest of us will be delayed." As the soldiers hurried away, their captain turned back to the Roman. "I'd have given a year's pay to drag that losel down, and here you offer me a free chance!"

He grabbed Scaurus' hand in his double clasp, barked to his troopers, "First for Khoumnos and some help, then we peg out Avshar the wizard over a slow fire!" Their full-throated shout of approval made Marcus see again how widely the Yezda was detested.

Hemond may have preferred to fight on horseback, but there was nothing wrong with his legs. He set a pace Marcus was hard pressed to match, one that had Nepos in an awkward half-trot to keep up.

Ten minutes and three expostulating sentries later, they were in Khoumnos' office, a well-lit room attached to the Grand Courtroom of the palace complex. The Videssian looked up from the paperwork he had been fighting. His heavy brows lowered to see Scaurus and Nepos with Hemond and his squad. "You keep odd company," he said to the tribune, unconsciously paraphrasing the easterner he mistrusted.

"That's as may be," the Roman shrugged. "They helped me find you, though, when I needed to." And he told Khoumnos the same tale he had spun out to Hemond shortly before.

Long before he was through, the same predatory eagerness that gripped him and Hemond had communicated itself to the Videssian. A triumphant grin spread over his face; he slammed his fist down onto his desk. Ink slopped out of its pot to mar the sheets over which he had been working. He did not care.

"Zigabenos!" he shouted, and his aide appeared from another room. "If there's not a squad here double-quick, you'll find out if you remember which end of a plow you stand behind."

Zigabenos blinked, saluted, and vanished.

"My men and I want a piece of the wizard," Hemond warned.

"You'll have it," the Videssian officer agreed. Marcus had expected Khoumnos to argue, but if the Videssian was unsure of the Namdaleni's loyalty to the Empire, he had no doubt they hated Avshar more.

Khoumnos was still buckling on his swordbelt when a sweating Zigabenos led a squad of *akritai* into his superior's office. Their arrival filled it almost to overflowing. The native Videssian troops sent suspicious looks at Hemond's mercenaries.

But Khoumnos was master of the situation. He knew he had a cause bigger than any rivalry within the imperial army. A single sentence was enough to electrify his men: "What we and the islanders are going to do, boys, is march over to the Hall of the Ambassadors, winkle our *dear* friend Avshar the Yezda out of his hole, and clap him in irons."

After a second's disbelieving silence, the Videssians burst into cheers. Hemond and his Namdaleni, although they had already cheered once, were more than willing to do so again. In the confined space, the noise was deafening. All dissension forgotten, the double squad—and Nepos and Marcus with it —rushed for the Hall of the Ambassadors like hounds upon a leopard's den.

The Hall, as was only natural, lay close by the Grand Courtroom, so foreign envoys could attend the Emperor at their mutual convenience. Above it flapped, fluttered, or simply hung the emblems of twoscore nations, tribes, factions, and other political entities less easily defined; among them was the leaping panther of Yezd.

The diplomatic calm ambassadors cultivate was not altogether proof against two dozen armed men swarming toward Avshar's dwelling-place. Taso Vones of Khatrish was on the

Hall's steps discussing trade in spices and furs with a nomad from the far western plains of Shaumkhiil when he heard the troopers clattering toward him. He looked up, saw the source of the pother, murmured to the Arshaum, "You will excuse me, I hope," and ran for his life.

The nomad ran, too—for the bow he kept in his chamber, to sell himself as dearly as he could.

But the warriors ignored him, just as they ignored the shouts of alarm that rang out in the Hall's lobby as they rushed through it behind Nephon Khoumnos. The Videssian led them up the wide stairway of polished marble at the lobby's back. As they climbed, he panted, "The whoreson's suite is on the second story. More than once I've been here to ransom prisoners—this is a job I'd rather do!" The men with him yelled their agreement.

Gawtruz of Thatagush was carrying a silver tray loaded with fried meats and candied fruits back to his own suite of rooms when the stairs erupted soldiers behind him. Though fat and past fifty, he still had a warrior's reflexes. He hurled his tray, food and all, at what he thought were his attackers.

Hemond knocked the spinning tray aside with his shield. A man or two cried out as they were hit by hot meat. Another tripped over the trail of grease a skidding fowl had left behind and went sprawling.

"Phos!" Khoumnos muttered. He cried to Gawtruz, "Mercy, valiant lord! We have no quarrel with you—it's Avshar we seek."

At his words, Gawtruz lowered the knife he had drawn from his belt. His eyes widened. "The man of Yezd? He and you are enemies, yes, but he is an embassy and cannot be assailed." Marcus noted Taso Vones had been correct at the ill-fated banquet a few days before—at need, Gawtruz' Videssian was perfect, polished, and unaccented.

"Ambassadors who live within the law of nations enjoy its protections," Khoumnos returned. "Sorcerers who hire knives in the night do not." His men and Hemond's were already gathered before a stout door on which stood Yezd's panther. Khoumnos ordered, "Rap gently once. I would not have it said we invaded the suite without giving warning."

The warning rap was scarcely gentle; a dozen heavy fists slammed into the door. There was no response. "Break it down!" Khoumnos snapped. But the portal so staunchly resisted shoulders and booted feet that Scaurus wondered whether it was merely a strong bar or magic which held it closed.

"Enough of this foolery! Out of my way!" One of the Namdaleni, a dark-haired giant with tremendous forearms, preferred the axe of his Haloga cousins. Men scurried back to give him room to swing. Chips flew and boards split as his axe buried itself helve-deep.

Within a dozen strokes, the door sagged back in defeat. The troopers stepped into their enemy's chambers, weapons at the ready. Khoumnos stood outside the door, repeatedly explaining to the startled, frightened, or angry diplomats who threw questions at him why the Videssians had come.

Marcus' first thought was that, while Avshar's lusts for power and destruction were boundless, he had no corresponding desire for personal luxury. Except for a Videssian desk, the embassy of Yezd was furnished nomad-style. Pillows took the place of chairs, and tables were low enough for men sitting on the ground to use. Cushions and tables alike were black, the walls of the room a smoky gray.

The door between Yezd's public offices and Avshar's private quarters was locked, but a few strokes of the axe dealt with that. But Avshar was no more to be found in his chambers than in the embassy portion of Yezd's suite. Marcus was not surprised; the rooms had a dead feel, a feel of something discarded and forgotten. The Videssians had come too late.

The Yezda's room was as sparely equipped as the office: more black-lacquered low tables, pillows, and a sleeping mat of felt stuffed with horsehair. Above the mat hung the image of a fierce-faced warrior dressed all in black and hurling a livid blue thunderbolt. He strode against the fleeing sun over a pile of naked, bloody victims. "Skotos!" the Videssian soldiers murmured to themselves; their fingers moved in signs against evil.

On one of the tables stood a small brazier and another icon of the dark god Yezd followed. Beside the icon lay the pitiful figure of a white dove with its neck wrung. The brazier was full of ashes; Avshar had left not intending to return and burned those papers he did not wish his foes to see.

Neither Videssians nor Namdaleni would go near that table, but when Marcus walked around it he saw on the floor a scrap of parchment scorched at one edge; it must have fallen from the brazier before the fire could sieze it. He bent to pick it up and shouted in sudden excitement: it was a sketch-map of the city and its walls, with a spidery red line leading from the Hall of the Ambassadors to a tower by the sea.

His companions crowded round him at his yell, peering over his shoulder and asking what he'd found. Their letdown at not trapping Avshar in his lair disappeared when they understood what the Roman was holding. They shook his hand and slapped his back in congratulations. "A second chance!" Hemond whooped. "Phos is truly with us today!"

"There's still no time to lose," Nepos said. "We should celebrate after we catch the Yezda, not before."

"Well said, priest," Hemond agreed. Leaving a couple of his men and a like number of Videssians to search the embassy quarters further, he led the rest out past Nephon Khoumnos, who was still justifying the soldiers' presence to the diplomats crowding around him.

Marcus stuck the fragment of parchment under his nose. Khoumnos' eyes crossed as he snatched it from the Roman's hands and tried to focus on it. "The game is still in play, then!" he exclaimed. He bowed to the envoys and their aides, saying, "Gentles, further explanations must wait on events." He pushed his way through the crowd, shouting to his men, "Wait, fools, I have the map!"

The tower Avshar's sketch had shown was at Videssos' northwest corner, where the city jutted furthest into the strait called the Cattle-Crossing. It was about half a mile north and slightly west of the Hall of the Ambassadors, through the palace complex and the streets of the town, and it seemed mostly uphill.

The tribune felt his heart race and the sweat spring from his brow as he trotted through the city. The troopers with him suffered far more than he, for he was in mantle and sandals while they loped along fully armored. One Namdalener could not stand the pace and fell back, his face flushed lobster-red.

As he ran, Scaurus was spurred on by the knowledge that so cold-blooded a calculator as Avshar could blunder—and blunder badly. Not only had his attempt at assassination gone for nought, but when he set about destroying his papers the most crucial one of all, the route of his escape, failed to burn and gave his pursuers another chance at him. If only he knew, Marcus thought—he'd gnash his teeth behind those veils of his.

The path turned down, bringing the sea wall of Videssos into sight. "That one!" Khoumnos panted, pointed at the square tower straight ahead. But when he sucked in wind, the middle-aged officer had enough breath to shout, "Ho the tower guards! Any sign of Avshar the Yezda?"

No answering shout came. When the soldiers wove their way through the last of the buildings between themselves and the wall, they saw the four-man watch contingent lying motionless in front of the guard tower's open gate. Khoumnos swore horribly. To Marcus he said, "The past five years I can recall no dozing sentries. Now I find them twice in two days, and you as witness both times. In Phos' holy name, I stand ashamed before you."

But the sprawled-out guards suggested only one thing to the tribune—the magic Avshar's nomad tool had used to get into the Roman barracks. He explained quickly, adding, "I don't think they are asleep through any fault of their own; it's some spell the westerner knows. His map did not lie—there may still be time to catch him before he can get down the seaward side of the wall."

Nephon Khoumnos reached out to press his arm. "Outlander, you are a man of honor."

"Thank you," Marcus said, surprised and touched.

"Come on, the two of you!" Hemond exclaimed, tugging his straight sword free of its scabbard. "Time enough for pretty speeches later!" He charged toward and through the gate, the rest of the warriors close behind. Nepos fell behind for a moment to revive the guardsmen Avshar had entranced.

Marcus was almost blind for a few seconds in the sudden gloom of the tower's interior. He stumbled up the tight spiral staircase; the only light in the stairwell came from small arrow slits let into the wall.

"Hold up!" Hemond called from above him. Men cursed as they bumped and tripped trying to stop quickly.

"What is it?" asked Khoumnos, who was several men below the Namdalener.

"I'm at the mouth of a corridor," Hemond replied. "It must lead to a weapons store, or something like that—and, square in the strip of sun from a firing slit, there's a scrap of white wool, just what might get torn from a nomad's robes if he ran past something stickery. We have the bastard hooked!" He laughed aloud in sheer exultation.

An excited hum ran up and down the spiral line of hunters. More swords slid from their scabbards. One by one, the men stepped into the passage Hemond had found.

The narrow corridor within the wall ran about fifty feet before ending in a single doorway. Clutching his sword hilt, Marcus moved forward with the rest of the warriors. He no longer saw Avshar as the dreaded evil mage Nepos had depicted, but as a wicked, frightened fool who had slipped at every turn in his escape attempt and, at the end, managed to close himself in a chamber with but one entrance. He could nearly pity the trapped Yezda on the other side of the door.

Hemond gave that door a tentative push. It swung open easily. The mercenary had been right in his guess at the chamber's function; it was indeed an armory. Through the doorway Marcus could see neat sheaves of arrows, piled spears, rows of maces and swords, and, as he came nearer and gained a wider view, the tip of an outstretched foot upon the floor.

Along with the rest of the soldiers, Scaurus pushed into the storeroom to see better. Unlike most of them, he recognized the dead man lying by the back wall—it was Mebod, Avshar's ever-frightened body servant. His head was twisted at an impossible angle, his neck broken like that of the dove on Skotos' altar in the Yezda's private chamber.

The senselessness and wanton cruelty of slaying this inoffensive little man bewildered the tribune. So did something else—Avshar had surely been here, but was no longer. There was no place to hide among the glittering weapons. Where, then, was the fugitive emissary of Yezd?

At nearly the same moment that thought crossed his mind, the door slammed shut behind them. Though it had opened invitingly to Hemond's lightest touch, now it would not yield to the frantic tugging of all the warriors caught behind it. Suddenly trapped instead of trapper, Marcus felt dread course through his veins.

"Ah, how pleasant. My guests have arrived." At the sound of that deep voice, full of chilly hate, the soldiers' hands fell from the bronze doorlatch. They turned as one, in disbelief and terror. Head still lolling on its right shoulder, eyes blind and staring, the corpse of Mebod was on its feet, but through its dead lips came Avshar's voice.

"You were so kind—and so clever—to answer the invitations I left for you," the wizard went on, bending his servant to his will in death as in life, "that I thought I should prepare fitting hospitality for you." With the jerky grace of a stringed puppet, what had been Mebod threw its hands wide. At their motion the weapons of the armory came alive, flying against the stunned men who, minutes before, had thought themselves about to seize Yezd's wizard-envoy.

One of the Videssians fell at once, a spear driven through chain mail and flesh alike. An instant later a Namdalener was on the ground beside him, his neck pierced from behind by a dagger. Another screamed in fear and pain as a mace laid open his arm.

Never had Marcus imagined—never had he wanted to imagine—a fight like that one, men against spears and swords that hovered in the air and struck like giant angry wasps. It did no good to strike back against them; there was no wielder to lay low. Worse, there was no shuffle of foot, no telltale shift of eye, to give a clue where the next blow would fall. The warriors were reduced to a purely defensive fight and, thus constrained in their very thoughts, suffered wounds from strokes they would have turned with ease had a body been behind them.

With his usual quickness of thought, Hemond slashed at Mebod's animate lich, but his blow did no good—the weapons still came on.

At first clash of enchanted steel, the druids' marks on Scaurus' blade flamed into fiery life. The sword his brand had met clattered to the floor and did not rise again. The same things happened again and yet again. So many blades were hovering for a chance to bite, though, that the unarmored Roman had all he could do to stay alive. He gave the best protection he could to his mates, but when he tried to follow Hemond's lead and strike down Mebod with his potent sword, the disembodied weapons kept him at bay and drove him back, bleeding from several cuts.

Someone was pounding on the door from the outside. Marcus shouted a warning to whoever it was, but his shout was drowned by a bellow of anguish from Hemond. A sword stood hilt-deep in the Namdalener's chest. His hands grabbed at the hilt, then fell limply to his side as he went down.

From the other side of the door came a cry louder even than Hemond's. "Open, in Phos' holy name!" Nepos roared, and the portal sprang back as if kicked. The priest-mage bounded into the weapons store, his arms upraised. He was a short man, but the power crackling from his rotund frame seemed to give him inches he did not possess.

Recognizing the danger in Nepos, Avshar's swooping armory abandoned the mere men-at-arms to dart at this new foe. But the priest was equal to them. He moved his hands in three swift passes, shouting a fraction of prayer or spell with each. Before the blades could touch him, they fell, inert, to the floor. As they did so, Mebod's body sank with them, to become again nothing more than a corpse.

It was like waking from a nightmare. The soldiers still on their feet held their guard for several seconds, hardly daring to believe the air empty and quiet. But quiet as it was, the weapons strewn like jackstraws and the bodies on the ground showed it had been no dream.

As the dazed survivors of the sorcerous assault bent to the fallen, they learned four were dead: the Videssian killed in the first instant of attack and three Namdaleni, Hemond among them. The mercenary officer had died as rescue stood outside the door. Marcus shook his head as he closed Hemond's set eyes. Had he not happened on the Namdalener in his search for Nephon Khoumnos, a good soldier who was becoming a good friend would still be alive.

Still looking down at Hemond's body, the tribune flinched when someone touched his arm. It was Nepos, his chubby features haggard and drawn. "Let me tie those up for you," he said.

"Hmm? Oh, yes, go ahead." Lost in his thoughts, Scaurus had almost forgotten his own wounds. Nepos bandaged them with the same dexterity Gorgidas might have shown.

As the priest worked, he talked, and Marcus learned he

was not the only one carrying a burden of self-blame. Nepos could have been talking to anyone or no one; as it happened, the Roman heard his struggle to understand the why of what had taken place.

"Had I not paused to end a small enchantment," the priest said bitterly, "I could have checked this far more wicked one. Phos knows his own ways, but it is an untasty thing to rouse four men from sleep only to see four others die."

"You did what was in your nature, to help wherever you first saw it needed," Marcus told him. "You could not be what you are and have done otherwise. What happened afterwards could not be helped."

Nepos did not agree. "You feel as do the Halogai, that there is a fate no man can hope to escape. But we who follow Phos know it is our god who shapes our lives and we seek to make out his purposes. There are times, though, when those are hard, hard to understand."

Moving slowly, as if still caught up in the bad dream from which they had just escaped, the warriors bound one another's wounds. Almost in silence, they lifted their fallen comrades' bodies—and that of Mebod as well—and awkwardly brought them down the watchtower's spiral stair and out into the sunlight once more.

The sentries Nepos had awakened met them there. One of the watchmen, alarm on his face, said to Marcus, "Please do not blame us for failing, sir. One moment we were all standing to arms, and the next this priest was bending over us, undoing the magic that laid us low. We didn't doze by choice."

At any other time the Roman would have been gladdened by the way his reputation had shot through the Videssian army. As it was, he could only say tiredly, "I know. The wizard who tricked you gulled us all. He got clean away, and I don't doubt many throughout the Empire will have cause to regret it."

"The son of nobody's not safe yet," Nephon Khoumnos declared. "Though he's crossed the strait, he has five hundred miles of travel through our western provinces before he reaches his accused borders. Our fire-beacons can flash word to seal the frontiers long before even a wizard could reach them. I'll go have the beacons fired now; we'll see what kind of welcome our *akritai* ready for that fornicating sorcerer!" And Khoumnos was off, shoulders hunched forward like a determined man walking into a gale.

Scaurus could only admire his tenacity, but did not think much would come of it. If Avshar could get free of the most strongly fortified city this world knew, the Roman did not believe Videssos' border troops, no matter how skilled, would keep him from slipping across the frontier into his own dark land.

He turned to the Namdaleni. Though he shrank from it, there was something he felt he had to do, something for which he needed the good will of these men. He said, "It was an unlucky chance that led me to you this morning. Now three of you have died, thanks to that unlucky chance. I had not known him long, but I was happy to call Hemond my friend. If it is not against your customs, it seems only right for me to be one of those who carries news of his loss to his lady. I bear the blame for it."

"A man lives as long as he lives and not a day more," said one of the men of the Duchy. Whether or not he followed the cult of Phos, some of the ways of his Haloga ancestors still lived in him. The Namdalener went on, "You were doing the best you could for the state that bought your sword. So were we. Service honorably done may cause hurt, but it is no matter for blame."

He paused for a moment to read his countrymen's eyes. Satisfied by what he saw, he said, "There is nothing in our usages to keep you from being the man who brings Hemond's sword to Helvis." Seeing Scaurus' lack of understanding, he explained, "That is our way of saying without word what words are too painful to carry. No blame rests with you," the mercenary repeated, "but were it there, what you are doing now would erase it. I am called Embriac Rengari's son and I am honored to know you."

The other six Namdaleni nodded soberly; one by one, they spoke their names and gave the tribune the two-handed clasp all men of northern descent seemed to share. That brief formality over, they lifted their burdens once more and began the somber journey back to their quarters.

News of what had happened spread like windblown fire, as always in Videssos. Before the soldiers had finished half their short course, the first cries of "Death to Yezd!" began ringing through the city. Scaurus saw a band of men armed with clubs and daggers dash down an alley after some foreigner or other —whether a Yezda or not, he never knew.

As he trudged toward the palace complex, the dead weight of Hemond's body made the tribune's shoulders ache, though he shared it with a Namdalener. He and his companions were all wounded. They slowly made their way to the mercenaries' barracks, pausing more than once to lay down the bodies of the dead and rest for a moment. Their load seemed heavier after each halt.

Marcus kept turning over in his mind why he had taken on himself the task of telling Hemond's woman of his death. What he had said to the Namdalener was true, but he was uneasily aware it was not the entire truth. He remembered how attractive he had found Helvis before he knew she was attached and had a guilty suspicion he was letting that attraction influence his behavior.

Stop it, lackwit, he told himself, you're only doing what has to be done. But . . . she was very beautiful.

The barracks of the Namdaleni were an island of ironic peace in the ferment rising in Videssos. Because they were outlanders and heretics, the men of the Duchy had few connections with the city's ever-grinding rumor mill and had no notion of the snare Avshar had sprung on their countrymen. A couple of men were wrestling outside the barracks. A large crowd cheered them on, shouting encouragements and bets. Two other soldiers practiced at swords, their blades clanging off one another. From a nearby smithy, Marcus heard the deeper ring of a hammer on hot steel. Several islanders were on their knees or haunches shooting dice. It occurred to Marcus that he had seen dicing soldiers whenever he passed their barracks, and they were quick to bet on almost anything. Gambling appealed to them, it appeared.

Someone in the back of the crowd looked up from the half-naked wrestlers and saw the approaching warriors and their grim burden. His startled oath lifted more eyes; one of the fencers whipped his head around and dropped his sword in surprise and shock. His opponent's blade was beginning its victory stroke when its owner, too, caught sight of the bodies the returning troopers bore. The stroke went undelivered.

The Namdaleni rushed up, crying out questions in the broad island patois they spoke among themselves. Marcus could hardly make out their dialect at the best of times; now he was too full of his own misery to make the effort. He and the mercenary who had helped him carry Hemond put down their burden for the last time. The Roman freed Hemond's sword and scabbard from his belt and made his way through the Namdaleni toward their barracks.

Most of the mercenaries stood back to let him pass when they saw what he bore, but one came up and grasped his arm, shouting something in his own speech. Scaurus could not catch more than a word or two, but Embriac replied, "He took it on himself, and his claim to it is good." He spoke in clear Videssian so his countryman and the tribune could both understand him. The islander nodded and let Marcus go.

The barracks of the Namdaleni were, if anything, even more comfortable than the Romans' quarters. Part of the difference, of course, was that there had been a Namdalener contingent in the Videssian army for many years, and over those years the men of the Duchy had lavished much labor on making their dwelling as homelike as they could. By contrast, the Romans had not yet made their hall their own.

Because many of the mercenaries spent a large portion of their lives in Videssian service, it was not surprising that they formed families in the capital, either with women of the Empire or with wives or sweethearts who had accompanied them from Namdalen. Their barracks reflected this. Only the bottom floor was a common hall like that of the Romans, a hall in which dwelt warriors who had formed no household. The upper story was divided into apartments of varying size.

Remembering Helvis waving to him from a window above —was it only a couple of days before?—Marcus climbed the stairway, a wide, straight flight of steps nothing like the spiral stair that had led to Avshar's trap. He felt more misgivings now than he had on the wizard's trail; Hemond's sword in his hand was heavy as lead.

Thanks to his memory of Helvis displaying for him the jewelry she'd brought with her winnings, the tribune knew about which turns to take through the upper story's corridors. From an open doorway ahead, he heard a clear contralto he knew. "Now stay there for a few minutes," Helvis was saying firmly. "I want to find out what the commotion down below is all about."

He and she came into the doorway at the same moment. Helvis drew back a pace, laughing in surprise. "Hello, Marcus!" she said. "Are you looking for Hemond? I don't know where he is—he should have been back from the drill-field some time ago. And what's going on outside? My window won't let me see."

She came to a halt, really seeing him for the first time. "Why so grim? Is anything the . . ." Her voice faltered as she finally recognized the sheathed blade he carried. "No," she said. "No." The color faded from her face; her knuckles whitened as her hand clutched at the doorlatch, seeking a support it could not give her.

"Who is this man, Mama?" A naked boy of about three came up to peer at Scaurus from behind Helvis' skirts. He had her blue eyes and Hemond's shock of blond hair. Marcus had not imagined he could be more wretched, but then he had not known Hemond had a son. "Aren't you going downstairs?" the tot asked his mother.

"Yes. No. In a minute." Helvis searched the tribune's features, her eyes pleading with him to give her some other, any other explanation than the one she feared for Hemond's sword in his hands. He bit his lip until the pain made him blink, but nothing he could say or do would erase his mute message of loss.

"Aren't you going downstairs, mama?" the child asked again.

"Hush, Malric," Helvis said absently. "Go back inside." She stepped into the hall, closing the door behind her. "It's true, then?" she said, more wonder in her voice than anything else. Though she said the words, it was plain she did not believe them.

Marcus could only nod. "It's true," he answered as gently as he could.

Not looking at the tribune, moving in a slow, dreamlike fashion, she took Hemond's sword from his hands into her own. She caressed the blade's worn, rawhide-wrapped hilt. Her hand, Marcus noticed in one of those irrelevant flashes he knew he would remember forever, though large for a woman's, was much too small for the grip.

Her head still bent, she leaned the sword against the wall by the closed door of her rooms. When at last she looked at the tribune, tears were running down her cheeks, though he had not heard her start to weep. "Take me to him," she said. As they walked down the hall, she clasped his arm like a drowning man seizing a spar to keep himself afloat a few minutes longer.

She was still looking for small things she did not under-stand to keep from facing the great incomprehensibility that lay, cold and stiffening, outside the barracks. "Why did you bring me his sword?" she asked the tribune. "I mean no harm, no insult, but you are not of our people or our ways. Why you?"

Scaurus heard the question with a sinking feeling. He would have given a great deal for a plausible lie but had none ready; in any case, such false kindness was worse than none. "It seemed only right I should," he said, "becasue it is all too much my fault he fell."

She stopped as short as if he had struck her; her nails were suddenly claws digging into his flesh. Only by degrees did the misery on the Roman's face and in his voice reach her. Her face lost the savage look it had assumed. Her hand relaxed; Marcus felt blood trickle down his arm from where her nails had bitten him.

"Tell me," she said, and as they walked down the stairs he did so, hesitantly at first but with growing fluency as the tale went on.

"The end was very quick, my lady," he finished lamely, trying to find such consolation as he could. "He could hardly have had time to feel much pain. I—" The upwelling futility of any apology or condolence he might make silenced him effectively as a gag.

Helvis' touch on his arm was as gentle as it had been fierce a minute before. "You must not torment yourself for doing what was only your duty," she said. "Had your roles been reversed, Hemond would have asked the same of you. It was his way," she added softly, and began to cry again as the truth of his death started forcing its way past the defenses she had flung up.

That she could try to comfort him in her own anguish amazed Marcus and made him feel worse at the same time.

Such a woman did not deserve to have her life turned upside down by a chance meeting and a wizard's scheme. Another score against Avshar, he decided, as if more were needed.

After the dimness of the interior of the barracks, the bright sun outside dazzled the Roman. Seeing the crowd still ringing the bodies of Hemond and his squadmates, Helvis dropped Scaurus' arm and ran toward them. Suddenly alone among strangers, the tribune felt another burst of empathy for Viridovix' plight. As quickly as he could, he found an excuse to get away and, wishing he had this day back to live over in some other way, went back to the Roman barracks.

As he stood sweating in his full regalia on the elevated central spine of Videssos' amphitheater, Scaurus decided he had never seen such a sea of people gathered together in one place. Fifty thousand, seventy thousand, a hundred twenty thousand—he had no way to guess their numbers. For three days criers ran through the city to proclaim the Emperor would speak this noon; the great arena had begun to fill at dawn and now, a few minutes before midday, almost every inch of it was packed with humanity.

The only clear spaces in all that crush were a lane leading from the Emperor's Gate at the western end of the amphitheater's long oval to its spine and that spine itself. And the clearing of that latter was only relative. Along with statues of marble, bronze, and gold, along with a needle of gilded granite reaching for the sky, the spine held scores of Videssian functionaries in their gaudy robes of state, priests of various ranks in blue regalia, and contingents of troops from every people who soldiered for the Empire. Among them, Scaurus and the maniple he led had pride of place this day, for they stood just below the elevated rostrum from which Mavrikios Gavras would soon address the throng.

To either side of the Romans were squadrons of tall Halogai, unmoving as the statuary they fronted. All the discipline in the world, though, could not keep resentment from their faces. The place of honor the Romans were usurping was at most times theirs, and they were not happy to be displaced by these newcomers, men who would not even show proper respect for the Emperor they served.

But today that central place was rightfully the Romans';

they, indeed, were the reason this assemblage had been called. News of Avshar's sorcerous assault on Scaurus and the deadly snare he had set to make good this escape had raced through the city like fire through parched woodlands. The mob Marcus saw chasing a fleeing foreigner was but the start of troubles. Many Videssians concluded that, if Yezd could reach into their capital to assail them, it was their Phos-given right to take vengeance on anyone they imagined a Yezda—or, at a pinch, on any other foreigners they could find.

Nearly all the folk from what was now Yezd who lived in Videssos were of trading houses that had been in the capital since the days when the Empire's western neighbor was still called Makuran. They hated their ancestral homeland's nomadic conquerors more bitterly than did the people of the Empire. Their hatred, however, was of no avail when the Videssian rabble came roaring up to loot and burn their stores. "Death to the Yezda!" was the mob's cry, and it did not ask questions of its victims.

It had taken troops to quell the riots and douse the flames —native Videssian troops. Knowing his people, the Emperor had known the sight of outlanders trying to quell them would only inflame them further. And so the Romans, the Halogai, the Khamorth, and the Namdaleni kept to their barracks while Khoumnos used his *akritai* to restore order to the city. Marcus gave him credit for a good, professional job. "Well, why not?" Gaius Philippus had said. "He's probably had enough practice at it."

Those three days had not been altogether idle. An imperial scribe came to record depositions from all the Romans who had been a part of subduing Avshar's luckless pawn of a plainsman. Another, higher-ranking scribe questioned Marcus minutely over every tiny detail he could recall about the nomad, about Avshar himself, and about the spell the Yezda had unleashed in the sea-wall armory. When the tribune asked what point the questions had, the scribe shrugged, blandly said, "Knowledge is never wasted," and returned to the interrogation.

The gabble in the amphitheater rose suddenly as a pair of parasol-carriers stepped from the shadows behind the Emperor's Gate into the sight of the crowd. Another pair emerged, and another, and another, until twelve silk flowers

of varied hues bloomed in the narrow passage which twin
lines of *akritai* kept open. Rhadenos Vourtzes had been proud
of the two sunshades to which his provincial governor's rank
entitled him; the imperial retinue was more splendid by six-
fold.

The cheering which had begun at first glimpse of the parasol bearers rose to a crescendo of shouting, clapping, and
stamping as the Emperor's party proper came into view.
Marcus felt the arena's spine quiver beneath his feet; the noise
the crowd put forth transcended hearing. It could only be felt,
stunning the ears and the mind.

First behind the escort was Vardanes Sphrantzes. It might
have been Marcus' imagination, but he did not think many of
the cheers went to the Sevastos. Far more beloved by the
people was their patriarch Balsamon. In matters of ceremony
he outranked even the prime minister, and thus had his place
between Sphrantzes and the imperial family itself.

The fat old priest flowered in adulation like a lilac in the
sun. His shrewd eyes crinkled into a mischievous grin; he
beamed out at the crowd, his hands raised in blessing. When
people reached between the tight ranks of guardsmen to touch
his robes, more than once he stopped to take hold of their
hands for a moment before moving on.

Thorisin Gavras, too, was popular in the city. He was
everyone's younger brother, with all the amused toleration that
went with that status. Had the Emperor brawled in a tavern or
tumbled a serving wench, he would have forfeited all respect
due his office. The Sevastokrator, without his brother's burdens, could—and did—enjoy himself to the fullest. Now he
strode along briskly, with the air of a man fulfilling an important task he nonetheless found boring and wanted to finish
quickly.

His niece, Mavrikios' daughter Alypia, came just before
her father. From her demeanor, the amphitheater might as well
have been still and empty, not packed to its rearmost benches
with screaming citizens. The same air of preoccupation she
had shown entering the banquet held her now. Marcus wondered if shyness was at its root rather than indifference; she
had been far less reserved in the closer setting of the banquet
table and in the imperial chambers.

Several times now the tribune had thought the tumult in the

arena could not grow greater, and several times was wrong. And with the entrance of the Emperor, he found himself mistaken once more. The noise was a real and urgent pain, as if someone were driving dull rods through his ears and into his brain.

Mavrikios Gavras was not, perhaps, the ideal Emperor for a land in turmoil. No long generations strengthened his family's right to the throne; he was but a usurping general more successful than his predecessors. Even as he ruled, his government was divided against him, with his highest civil ministers standing to profit most from his fall and doing their best to stifle any reforms which might weaken their own positions.

But ideal or not, Mavrikios was what Videssos had, and in the hour of crisis its people rallied to him. With every step he took, the crescendo of noise rose. Everyone in the amphitheater was standing and screaming. A group of trumpeters followed the Emperor, but in the bedlam they must have been inaudible even to themselves.

Behind the Sevastos, the patriarch, and his family, the Emperor mounted the twelve steps up onto the arena's spine. Each compay of soldiers presented arms to him as he passed, the Khamorth and native Videssians drawing empty bows, the Halogai lifting their axes in salute, and the Namdaleni and at last the Romans holding their spears out at arm's length before them.

Thorisin Gavras gave Marcus an eager, predatory grin as he walked by. His thoughts were easy to read—he wanted to fight Yezd, Scaurus had furnished a valid reason for fighting, and so the Roman stood high in his favor. Mavrikios was more complex. He said something to Scaurus, but the crowd's din swept it away. Seeing he could not hope to make himself understood, the Emperor shrugged almost sheepishly and moved on.

Gavras halted for a few seconds at the base of his speaking platform while his retinue, parasols bobbing, arranged themselves around it. And when the Emperor's foot touched its wooden step, Marcus wondered whether Nepos and his wizardly colleagues had worked a potent magic or whether his ill-used ears had given out at last. Sudden, aching silence fell, broken only by the ringing in his head and the thin shout of a fishmonger outside the arena: "Fre-esh squi-id!"

The Emperor surveyed the crowd, watching it settle back into its seats. The Roman thought it hopeless for one man to be heard by so many, but he knew nothing of the subtlety Videssian craftsmen had invested in their amphitheater. Just as the center of the spine was the focus where every sound in the arena reverberated, so words emanating from that one place were plain throughout.

"I'm not the man for fancy talk," the Emperor began, and Marcus had to smile, remembering how, in a Gallic clearing not so long ago, he had used a disclaimer like that to start a speech.

Mavrikios went on, "I grew up a soldier, I've spent all my life among soldiers, and I've come to prize a soldier's frankness. If it's rhetoric you're after, you don't have far to look today." He waved his hand to take in the rows of seated bureaucrats. The crowd chuckled. Turning his head, Scaurus saw Vardanes Sphrantzes' mouth tighten in distaste.

Though unable to resist flinging his barb, the Emperor did not sink it deeply. He knew he needed such unity as he could find in his divided land and spoke next in terms all his subjects could understand.

"In the capital," he said, "we are lucky. We are safe, we are well fed, we are warded by walls and fleets no land can match. Most of you are of families long-settled in the city and most of you have lacked for little in your lives." Marcus thought of Phostis Apokavkos, slowly starving in Videssos' slums. No king, he reflected, not even one so recent and atypical as Mavrikios, could hope to learn of all his country's troubles.

The Emperor was only too aware of some of them, however. He continued, "In our western lands, across the strait, they envy you. For a man's lifetime now, Yezd's poisons have spilled into our lands, burning our fields, killing our farmers, sacking and starving cities and towns, and desecrating the houses of our god.

"We've fought the followers of Skotos whenever we could catch them laden with their plunder. But they are like so many locusts; for every one that dies, two more spring up to take his place. And now, in the person of their ambassador, they spread their canker even into Videssos itself. Avshar the Phosforsaken, unable to withstand one soldier of the Empire in honest combat, cast his web of deception over another and sent him like a viper in the night to murder the man he dared not face in open battle."

The multitude he addressed growled ominously, a low, angry sound, like the rumble just before an earthquake. Mavrikios let the rumble build a moment before raising his arms for silence.

The anger in the Emperor's voice was real, not some trick of speechmaking. "When his crime was found out, the beast of Yezd fled like the coward he is, with more of his unclean magic to cover his trail—and to once more kill for him so he need not face danger himself!" This time the crowd's ire did not subside at once.

"Enough, I say, enough! Yezd has struck too often and taken too few blows in return. Its brigands need a lesson to learn by heart: that while we are patient with our neighbors, our memory for wrongs is also long. And the wrongs Yezd has given us are far beyond forgiveness!" His last sentence was almost drowned by the rancor of the crowd, now nearly at the boil.

Scaurus' critical side admired the way the Emperor had built up his audience's rage step by step, as a mason erects a building with course after course of bricks. Where the Roman had drawn on the speeches he made before becoming a soldier to hearten his troops, Gavras was using his memory of field orations to stir a civilian crowd. If the bureaucrats were the models the people of the city were used to, Mavrikios' gruff candor made for an effective change.

"War!" the assemblage shouted. "War! War!" Like the savage tolling of an iron bell, the word echoed and re-echoed in the amphitheater. The Emperor let the outcry last as long as it would. Perhaps he was enjoying to the fullest the rare concord he had brought into being; perhaps, thought Marcus, he was trying to use this outpouring of hatred for Yezd to overawe the bureaucrats who opposed his every action.

At last the Emperor raised his hands for quiet, and slowly it came. "I thank you," he told the throng, "for bidding me do what is right in any case. The time for half-measures is past. This year we will strike with all the strength at our command; when next you see me here, Yezd will be a trouble no more!"

The arena emptied after a last rousing cheer, people still

buzzing with excitement. Only after the last of them had gone could the guard units, too, stand down and return to their more usual duties.

"What did you think?" Scaurus asked Gaius Philippus as they marched back toward the barracks.

The senior centurion rubbed the scar on his cheek. "He's good, there's no doubt of that, but he's not Caesar, either." Marcus had to agree. Mavrikios had fired the crowd, yes, but Scaurus was sure the Emperor's foes within the government had neither been convinced by his words nor intimidated by the passions he had roused. Such theatrics meant nothing to cold calculators like Sphrantzes.

"Besides," Gaius Philippus unexpectedly added, "it's fool-hardy to speak of your triumphs before you have them in hand." And to that thought, too, the tribune could take no exception.

VII

"THERE'S A NAMDALENER OUT FRONT WANTS TO SEE YOU," Phostis Apokavkos told Scaurus on the morning of the second day after the Emperor's declaration of war. "Says he's Soteric somebody's son."

The name meant nothing to Marcus. "Did he say what he wanted of me?"

"No; didn't ask him, either. Don't much like Namdaleni. Far as I can see, the most of them aren't any more than so many—" and Apokavkos swore a ripe Latin oath.

The ex-farmer was fitting in among the Romans even better than Marcus could have hoped when he plucked him from his miserable life in Videssos' thieves' quarter. His face and frame were losing their gauntness, but that was only to be expected with regular meals.

It was, however, the least of his adaptation. Having been rejected by the nation that gave him birth, he was doing everything he could to become a full part of the one that had taken him in. Even as the Romans had learned Videssian to make life within the Empire easier, Phostis was picking up Latin to blend with his new surroundings. He was working hard with the thrusting-sword and throwing-spear, neither of them weapons he was used to.

And ... Marcus' brain finally noticed what his eyes had been telling him. "You shaved!" he exclaimed.

Apokavkos sheepishly rubbed his scraped jaw. "What of it? Felt right odd, being the only hairy-cheeks in the barracks. I'll never be pretty, with whiskers or without. Can't see why you

131

people bother, though—hurts more than it's worth, if you ask me. But my naked chin isn't what I came to show you. Are you going to talk to that damned Namdalener, or shall I tell him to take himself off?"

"I'll see him, I suppose. What was it that priest said a few days ago? 'Knowledge is never wasted.'" Just listen to you, he thought; anyone would think it was Gorgidas talking.

Leaning comfortably against the side of the barracks hall, the mercenary from the eastern islands did not seem much put out at having had to wait for Scaurus. He was a solidly built man of middle height, with dark brown hair, blue eyes, and the very fair skin that bespoke the northern origins of the Namdaleni. Unlike many of his countrymen, he did not shear the back of his head, but let his hair fall in long waves down to the nape of his neck. Marcus doubted he could be more than a year or two past thirty.

When he recognized the tribune, he straightened and came up to him, both hands extended for the usual Namdalener clasp. Scaurus offered his own, but had to say, "You have the better of me, I'm afraid."

"Do I? I'm sorry; I gave your man my name. I'm Soteric Dosti's son, from Metepont. In the Duchy, of course."

Apokavkos had forgotten Soteric's patronymic, but the mercenary's name meant no more to Scaurus with it. But the Roman had heard of his native town somewhere before. "Metepont?" he groped. Then he found the memory. "Hemond's home?"

"The same. More to the point, Helvis' as well. She's my sister, you see."

And Marcus did see, once he knew of the relationship. Helvis had not mentioned her brother in his hearing, or her father's name to let him guess the kinship, but now it was easy to pick out Soteric's resemblance to her. That their coloring was alike was not enough; many Namdaleni had similar complexions. But Soteric had a harder version of Helvis' ample mouth, and his face, like hers, was wide with strong cheekbones. His nose, on the other hand, was prominent enough to make any Videssian proud, where hers was short and straight.

He realized he was staring rudely. "Your pardon. Will you

come in and tell me your business over an early mug of wine?"

"Gladly." Soteric followed the tribune into the barracks; Scaurus introduced him to the legionaries they passed. The Namdalener's greetings were friendly, but Marcus noticed he was unobtrusively taking the measure both of the Romans and of the hall in which they lived. It did not upset the tribune— he would have done the same.

When they sat, Soteric picked a chair whose back faced no doors. With a smile, Marcus said, "Now that you're quite sure you won't be suddenly killed, will you risk a glass of red with me? I think it's too sweet, but everyone hereabouts swears by it."

Soteric's clear skin made his flush easy to see. "Am I as easy to read as that?" the Namdalener asked, shaking his head ruefully. "I've been long enough among the Videssians to mistrust my own shadow, but not long enough, it seems, to keep the fact to myself. Yes, the red will do excellently, thank you."

They sipped a while in silence. The barracks hall was almost empty, as most of the Romans were at their exercises. As soon as he saw the Namdalener come in the front way, Phostis Apokavkos had vanished out the back, wanting nothng more to do with the mercenary.

Finally Soteric put down his wine and looked at Marcus over his steepled fingertips. "You aren't what I thought you'd be," he said accusingly.

"Ah?" To a statement of that sort, no real answer seemed possible. The Roman lifted his glass to his lips once more. The wine, he thought, really was sticky.

"Hemond—Phos rest him—and my sister both claimed you had no patience for the poisonous subtlety the Empire so loves, but I own I didn't believe them. You were too friendly by half with the Videssians and too quick to win the Emperor's trust. But having met you, I see they were right after all."

"I'm glad you think so, but in fact my subtlety is so great you take it for frankness."

Soteric flushed again. "I had that coming."

"You would know better than I. Don't think too little of your own delicacy, either; it's half an hour now, and I have no more idea of why you're here than when I first set eyes on you."

"Surely you must know that—" the Namdalener began, but then he saw he was judging Marcus by the standards of his own people. "No, there's no reason why you should," he decided, and explained, "Our custom is to offer formal thanks to the man who brings a slain warrior's sword back to his family. Through Helvis, I am Hemond's closest male kin here, so the duty falls on me. Our house is in your debt."

"You would be deeper in my debt if I hadn't seen Hemond that morning," Marcus said bitterly. "You owe me no debt, but rather I one to you. Thanks to that unlucky meeting, a man who was becoming my friend is dead, a fine woman widowed, and a lad I didn't even know existed is an orphan. And you speak of debts?"

"Our house is in your debt," Soteric repeated, and Marcus realized the obligation was real to him, whatever the circumstances. He shrugged and spread his hands, unwillingly accepting it.

Soteric nodded, his part in the Namdalener usage satisfactorily completed. Marcus thought he would now rise and take his leave, but he had other things on his mind besides his custom-assumed debt.

He poured himself a second glass of wine, settled back in his seat, and said, "I have some small rank among my countrymen, and I speak for all of us when I tell you we've watched your men on the practice field. You and our cousins the Halogai are the only folk we know who prefer to fight on foot. From what we've seen, your style of war is different from theirs, and a good deal more precise. Would you be interested in exercising your men against ours and showing us some of what you know? We're horsemen by choice, true, but there are times and terrains where fighting has to be on foot. What say you?"

Here was a proposal to which the tribune could agree with pleasure. "We might learn something from you as well," he said. "Your warriors, from the little I know of them, are brave, well armed, and better ordered than most of the troops I've seen here."

Soteric dipped his head, acknowledging the compliment.

After a few minutes of discussion to find a time and day suit-able to Romans and Namdaleni alike, they arranged to meet three days hence, three hundred men to a side. "Would you care to lay a stake on the outcome?" Soteric asked. Not for the first time, Marcus thought that the Namdaleni seemed fond of betting.

"Best keep it a small one, lest tempers in the skirmish flare higher than they should," he said. He thought briefly. "What do you say to this: let the losing side treat the winners to a feast at their barracks—food and drink both. Does that sound fair?"

"Outstandingly so," Soteric grinned. "It's better than a money bet, because it should cure any ill feelings left from the fight instead of letting them fester. By Phos' Wager, Roman, I like you."

The oath puzzled Marcus for a moment. Then he remem-bered Apsimar's slighting reference to the Namdalener belief that, though the battle between good and evil was of unsure result, men should act as though they felt good would win. With a theology of that sort, the tribune thought, no wonder the men of the Duchy enjoyed gambling.

Soteric emptied his glass and started to rise, then seemed to think better of it. "There is one other message I bear," he said slowly.

He was quiet so long Marcus asked, "Do you intend to give it to me?"

The islander surprised him by saying, "When I was coming here, I did not. But, as I said before, you Romans—and you yourself—are not what I'd pictured you to be, and so I can pass it on. It comes from Helvis, you see."

That was enough to gain Scaurus' complete attention. With no idea what to expect, he did his best to keep everything but polite interest from his face. Soteric went on, "She asked me, if I thought it suitable, to tell you that she bears no grudge against you for what befell, and that she feels the sword-bringer's debt extends to her as well as to me."

"She is gracious, and I'm grateful," Marcus replied sin-cerely. It would have been all too easy, after a few days of bitter reflection, for Helvis to grow to hate him for his part in Hemond's death.

* * *

At drill, the Romans proved as eager to scrimmage with the Namdaleni as Scaurus had thought they would. They did their best to catch an officer's eye for inclusion in the select three hundred, working harder than they had in weeks. Marcus' wager touched their pride; in their skirmishes at Imbros they had become convinced they were better soldiers than any other infantry the Empire had. They were keen to prove it again at the capital.

"You'd not be leaving me out of the shindy for misliking fighting in line, now would you?" Viridovix asked anxiously as they trudged back through the city from the field.

"I wouldn't think of it," Scaurus assured him. "If I tried to, you'd come after me with that sword of yours. Better you should use it on the Namdaleni."

"All right, then."

"Why this passion for carving up your fellow man?" Gorgidas asked the Celt. "What satisfaction do you take from it?"

"For all your bark, my Greek friend, you're a cold-blooded man, I ween. Fighting is wine and women and gold all rolled up into one. Never do you feel more alive than after beating your foe and seeing him drop before you."

"And never more dead than when he beats you," Gorgidas retorted. "It would open your eyes to see war from a doctor's view—the filth, the wounds, the pus, the arms and legs that will never be sound again, the face of a man dying over days with a stab in his belly."

"The glory!" Viridovix cried.

"Tell it to a bloodsoaked boy who's just lost a hand. Don't speak to me of glory; I patch the bodies you build it on." The physician stamped off in disgust.

"If you'd lift your face from the muck you'd see more!" Viridovix called after him.

"Were you not strewing corpses through it, the muck and I would never meet."

"He hasn't the proper spirit at all, at all," Viridovix sadly told Scaurus.

The tribune's thoughts kept slipping back to Hemond. "Hasn't he? I wonder." The Gaul stared at him, then moved away as if afraid he might have something catching.

Nepos was waiting for them back at the barracks. The fat

priest's face was too jowly to grow truly long, but he was not a happy man. After polite greetings, his voice became beseeching as he asked Marcus, "Tell me, have you recalled anything of any relevance whatever to Avshar in the time since the Emperor's investigators questioned you? Anything at all?"

"I don't think I'll ever recall any more of Avshar than they pulled out of me," Marcus said, remembering the interrogation he had undergone. "They couldn't have wrung more from me with pincers and red-hot irons."

Nepos' shoulders slumped. "I feared you would say as much. Then we are stymied, and the accursed Yezda—may Phos turn his countenance from him—has won another round. Like a weasel, he slips through the tiniest holes."

The Roman had thought that, once Avshar reached the western shore of the Cattle-Crossing, any chance of laying hold of him was gone. He put no faith in Khoumnos' firebeacons to the frontier; the border was too long, too weakly held, and too often punctured by raiders—and even armies— out of Yezd. But from Nepos' disappointment, it seemed the priest had held real hopes of locating the wizard, hopes now dashed. When Scaurus asked him about this, he got a dispirited nod as answer.

"Oh, indeed. There should have been nothing easier than to trace him. When he fled the Hall of the Ambassadors, he had to leave nearly all his gear behind, not least the smoking altar to his dark god. What was once his, of course, retains its affinity for him, and through the possessions, our mages have the skill to find their owner. Or so they should, at any rate. But there was only a great emptiness awaiting their search, a void as wide as the land where Avshar could be hiding. He has baffled seven of our most potent wizards, your servant among them. His sorcery keeps to none of the scruples that those who follow good needs must observe, and the fiend is strong, strong."

Nepos looked so gloomy Marcus wanted to cheer him in some way, but he could find nothing cheerful to say. Like a giant pursued by pygmies, Avshar had shaken loose of those who would check him and was free to unleash whatever blows against the Empire his foully fertile mind could devise.

"In the days before the Yezda swallowed them down," Nepos said, "the folk of Makuran had a favorite curse: 'May you live in interesting times.' Until you and yours came to Videssos, my friend from far away, it never struck me what a potent curse that could be."

The field where Videssos' soldiers trained for war was just outside the southern end of the great city wall. Looking southeast, it was easy to see the island the Videssians called the Key, a purple mass on the gray horizon. Lying between the Empire's eastern and western dominions, it also commanded the approach to the capital from the Sailors' Sea. It was, Marcus knew, second only to the city itself as center for the imperial fleets.

But the tribune's thoughts were not really on the distant Key, not when more urgent matters were so much closer. His handpicked band of three hundred legionaries was eyeing the Namdaleni limbering themselves up at the far end of the drillfield. Gorgidas had wanted to call the troop "the Spartans," for their numbers were the same as those of the gallant company which had faced Xerxes' Persians at Thermopylae.

Scaurus demurred, saying, "I know they are part and parcel of your Greek pride, but we need a name of better omen—as I recall, none of those men survived."

"No, two did live, it's said. One made up for it with a brave fight at Plataia the next year; the other hanged himself for shame. Still, I take your point."

As he watched the Namdaleni stretch and twist, the tribune thought, not for the first time, how physically impressive they were. At least as much taller than the Romans as were the Celts, their height was made still more intimidating by the conical helms they preferred. They were wider in the shoulder and thicker in the chest than the Gauls, too, and wore heavier armor. That, though, was partly because they liked to fight from horseback; afoot, so much mail might tire them quickly.

Between the Namdaleni and Romans paced a score of umpires, Videssians and Halogai of known integrity. They bore whistles made of tin and white wands. It was easy for the combatants to carry spears without points, but swordplay, even in sport, could grow bloody unless controlled.

Marcus was getting used to the way rumors of all sorts flashed through Videssos, but he was still surprised by the crowd round the drill field's edge. There were Romans and

Namdaleni in plenty, of course, and officers and men from Videssos' native soldiery as well. But how had the colorfully dressed civil servants and the large numbers of ordinary city folk learned of the impending match? And the last time Scaurus had seen the skinny envoy of the Arshaum, he was running for his bow at the Hall of the Ambassadors. How had he heard of this meeting?

The tribune had his answer to that, at least, within moments. The nomad shouted something in the Romans' direction and Viridovix replied with a wave. The tall, fair Gaul and swarthy little plainsman were odd to think of as a pair, but they had plainly come to know and like each other.

The chief umpire, a Haloga commander called Zeprin the Red, beckoned the two leaders to the center of the field. The burly Haloga took his name not from his hair, which was blond, but from his complexion. Atop a thick neck, his face was almost the color of poached salmon. Gorgidas would have called him a good candidate for apoplexy, but he was not a man to argue with.

Marcus was pleased to see Soteric as his opposite number. There were higher-ranking Namdaleni, true, but Dosti's son had the privilege of heading the men of the Duchy because he had arranged their meeting with the Romans.

Zeprin looked sternly from one leader to the other. His slow, drawling Haloga accent lent his words gravity. "This frolic is for pride and for sport. You know that, and your men know it—now. See they remember it after they take a spear-shaft in the ribs. We want no riots here." He flicked his eyes about to see if any of his Videssian colleagues were close enough to hear. Satisfied, he lowered his voice to resume, "I've no real fears—there's not a city man among you. Have fun—I only wish I had a sword in my hand to join you, not this puny wand."

Scaurus and Soteric trotted back to their troops. The Romans were aligned in three maniples, two side by side at the fore and the third in reserve behind them. Their opponents formed in a single deep column with a forward fence of spears. Soteric was in the center of the first rank.

When he was sure both sides were ready, Zeprin swung his wand in a circle over his head. His fellow umpires scrambled out of the way as the Romans and Namdaleni bore down on each other.

Just as the chief umpire had said, it was hard to remember this was not real combat. The faces of the Namdaleni were set and grim under their bar nasals. The forward thrust of their bodies, their white-knuckled hands tight on their long spears —*poles*, the tribune reminded himself—their yells to terrify their foes—only the cold glint of steel from their spearheads was missing.

Closer and closer they came. "Loose!" the tribune shouted, and his front rank flung their dummy *pila*. Most bounced harmlessly from the shields of the Namdaleni. That was not as it should be; with their points and soft-iron shanks, real *pila* would have fouled the islanders' bucklers and forced the mercenaries to discard them.

Here and there a spear thudded home against mail or flesh. Umpires tooted frantically and waved their wands, ordering "killed" warriors to the sidelines. One islander, who felt his armor would safely have turned the spear, screamed abuse at the referee who had declared him dead. The umpire was a Haloga half a head taller than the incensed man of the Duchy. He listened for a few moments, then planted a huge hand on the Namdalener's chest and shoved. His attention was back to the skirmish before the mercenary hit the ground.

The Namdaleni did not use their pikes as throwing weapons. Standing up under the Roman volleys, they accepted their mock casualties until they could close with the legionaries. The weight of their phalanx and the length of their thrusting-spears began to tell then. Unable to get close enough to their foes to use their swords with any effect, the Romans saw their line begin to sag in the middle. More and more now, the whistles and the waving, tapping wands of the umpires ushered Scaurus' men from the field.

The men of the Duchy shouted in anticipated victory. Gaius Philippus was beset by two Namdaleni at once. His sword darted like an adder's tongue as he desperately held them off. Then Viridovix came rampaging up behind the easterners. One he flattened with a brawny fist; he traded sword strokes with the other for a few hot seconds, then, delicate as a surgeon, barely touched the islander's neck with the edge of his blade. Ashen-faced, the Namdalener staggered away. He heard the umpire's whistle with nothing but relief. The Romans—and some of the Namdaleni as well—yelled applause for the Celt's swordplay.

More than one man had really fallen; even without their points, the spearshafts both sides used were effective weapons. Here a man staggered away clutching a broken arm, there another was stretched full length on the ground, stunned or worse by a blow to the side of the head. A couple on each side had real sword wounds, too. The men were doing their best to use the flats of their blades instead of edges or points, but accidents had to happen.

Marcus paid scant heed to the casualties. He was too busy trying to keep the Namdaleni from splitting his wider battle line and beating the Romans in detail. Also, thanks to his high-crested helm and red cape of rank, he was a primary target for the islanders. Some fought shy of his already fabled sword, but to the bravest of the brave it was challenge, not deterrent.

Soteric had leaped for him at the outset, high glee on his face. The Roman ducked the lunge of his spear. Before he could reply with his own shorter weapon, the swirl of fighting swept them apart. Another Namdalener clouted him with a broken spearshaft. The tribune saw stars and waited for wand or whistle to take him out of action, but none of the referees spotted the stroke.

Scaurus fought his way through the press to his senior centurion, who had just sent an islander from the fray by slipping past his thrust and thumping him on the chest with his sword. The tribune bellowed his plan at the top of his lungs. Some of the Namdaleni must have heard him, but he did not care— where in this world would they have learned Latin?

When he was through, Gaius Philippus raised a startled eyebrow. "You're sure?"

"I'm sure. They're certain to beat us if we keep fighting on their terms."

"All right." The centurion brushed the sweat from his forehead with his sword arm. "This puts it all on one throw, doesn't it? But I think you're right—we've got nothing to lose. The bastards are just too big to deal with, straight up. You want me to lead it, I hope?"

"No one else. Take the Gaul along, too, if you find him."

Gaius Philippus grinned wolfishly. "Aye, if it works he'd be just the man I want. Wish me luck." He slipped back through the Roman ranks, shouting orders as he went.

The third, rearmost, maniple had not yet been entirely committed to the fighting, despite the pressure at the front. Gaius Philippus pulled about thirty men from the last couple of ranks and led them at a fast trot round the left side of the Romans' line. As he ran, he caught Viridovix's eye and waved for him to join them.

"Good-bye to you, now," the Celt told the man he was fighting; he checked his slash inches from the flinching Namdalener's face. Before a nearby umpire could tap his victim, Viridovix was free of the crush and loping after the centurion and his flanking party.

The next minute or two would tell the story, Marcus knew. If the Namdaleni could break through his suddenly thinned line before Gaius Philippus took them in flank, it would be all over. If not, though, he would have built himself a miniature Kynoskephalai. Just as Flaminius had against King Philip of Macedon's phalanx one-hundred-forty years before, he was using his troops' ability to maneuver and fight in small units to overcome a more heavily-armed, less wieldy foe.

Learning Greek was good for something after all, he thought irrelevantly. If it hadn't been for Polybios, I might never have thought of this.

It was going to be very close, though. The Roman center was stretched almost to the breaking point. There in the very heart of the fire stood the legionary Minucius like a stone wall. His helmet was jammed down over one ear by some blow he had taken and his shield was almost beaten to bits, but he was holding the Namdaleni at bay. Other Romans, driven back by the men of the Duchy, rallied to him and kept the line intact.

Then the pressure on them suddenly eased as Gaius Philippus and his little band crashed against the easterners' flank. The pikes which had given the Romans so much trouble now proved the bane of the islanders. Hampered by their long shafts, the Namdaleni could not spin to meet the new threat without fouling each other and throwing their lines into chaos. Yelling their own victory paean, the Romans slid into the gaps thus exposed and worked what would have been a ghastly slaughter. Behind them came sweating, panting referees to reckon up their victims.

In this sort of fight, with all order fallen by the wayside, Viridovix was at his best. Like some runaway engine of destruction, he howled through the disintegrating Namdalener ranks, smashing pikeshafts to kindling and caving in shields with blows of his mighty sword. His long red locks streamed from under his helmet, a private battle banner.

As the Namdaleni faltered, the Romans' main line surged forward too, completing the work the flanking column had begun. The demoralized islanders could not stand against them. Soon those whose dooms the umpires had not decreed were a small, struggling knot almost surrounded by their conquerors.

Soteric was still there, fighting with the best of them. When he saw Marcus prowling round the Namdaleni looking for an opening, he cried with a laugh, "Vile foe, you'll not take me alive!" He rushed at the tribune, sword held high over his head. Grinning in return, Scaurus stepped up to meet him.

Helvis' brother was quick and strong and as skillful a user of the slashing style as any Marcus had faced. The Roman had all he could do to keep himself untouched, parrying with his own blade and blocking Soteric's cuts with his shield. He was panting at once, as was the islander—mock-fighting, it seemed, was about as tiring as the real thing.

A legionary ran up to help his commander. Distracted by the new threat, Soteric left himself unguarded for an instant, and Marcus' blade snaked past his shield to ring off his breastplate. Zeprin the Red tooted his whistle and pointed at the Namdalener with his wand.

Soteric threw both hands in the air. "Beset by two at once, your valiant leader falls," he shouted to his men. "The time has come to ask the enemy for mercy." Quite realistically, he tumbled to the ground. The few easterners still in the fray doffed their helmets in token of surrender.

"A cheer for our enemies in this fight, our friends in the next!" Marcus called, and the Romans responded with a will. The Namdaleni gave back the compliment. The two groups left the field as one. Marcus saw a man of the Duchy help a hobbling Roman along, watched one of his legionaries demonstrating the thrusting stroke to a pair of easterners, and decided the morning's work had been a great success.

Miraculously risen from the slain, Soteric caught up with the tribune. "Congratulations," he said, taking the Roman's hand. "I have to ask your indulgence in putting off payment of our stake for a day or two. I felt so sure we would win, I fear I laid in no supplies for a feast I didn't think we'd have to give."

"No hurry," Marcus said. "Your men fought very well." He meant it; the Namdaleni, not natural foot soldiers, had given the Romans all they wanted.

"Thank you. I thought we were going to push straight through you until you sprang that flanking maneuver on us. That was quick thinking."

"The idea wasn't altogether mine, I'm afraid." He explained how he had borrowed Flaminius' solution to a similar tactical problem.

Soteric nodded thoughtfully. "Interesting," he commented. "You're drawing on knowledge of war no one here can match. That could be precious one day."

It was the Roman's turn to nod; the same thought had crossed his mind. And because his nature was one to grapple with all sides of a question, he also wondered what the Videssians and their neighbors knew of war that Rome had never learned . . . and what price he would have to pay for instruction.

Torches, lamps, and fat beeswax candles kept the courtyard in front of the Namdalener barracks bright as day, though by now the sun was a couple of hours gone. The courtyard, most of the time a pleasant open place, was full of splintery benches and tables hastily made by throwing boards over trestles. The benches were full of feasters and the tables piled high with food.

Except for an unlucky handful who had drawn sentry duty, all the Romans were there to collect the prize they'd won from the Namdaleni. They and the easterners seemed to have nothing but respect for each other. Seating arrangements intermingled the two groups, and those on both sides who had been in the bout three days before swapped stories and proudly displayed their bandages to their admiring comrades.

Roast pork, beef, mutton, and goat were the main courses, eked out with fowl and the fish and other seafood so easily available in the city. To the dismay of the Namdaleni, most of the Romans gave everything a liberal dousing with the spicy sauce of fermented fish the Videssians loved. The men of the Duchy kept the puritan palates of their northern ancestors, but to the Romans liquamen was a condiment known and loved for many years.

"I suppose you like garlic, too," Soteric said with a shudder.

"Don't you?" Marcus replied, amazed anyone could not.

Wine, ale, and mead flowed like water. Thanks to the sweetness of the local wines, the tribune found he was developing a real taste for the thick, dark ale the Videssians brewed. But when he said that to Soteric, it was the islander's turn for surprise. "This bilgewater?" he exclaimed. "You should come to the Duchy, my friend, where you drink your ale with a fork."

Viridovix, an earthenware mug in his hand, said, "Why anyone would drink ale—with a fork or no, mind you—when there's the blood of the grape to be had is past my understanding. In the land where I was born, ale was a peasant's drink. For the chiefs, now, it was wine, when we could get it and when we could afford it. A dear thing it was, too, that I'll tell you."

Some fine wines came from Narbonese Gaul, with its warm Mediterranean climate, but Marcus realized he had seen no vines in Viridovix's northern homeland. Like most Romans, the tribune had drunk wine from childhood and took it very much for granted. For the first time, it occurred to him how precious it could be when hard to come by.

At the Celt's right hand sat his nomad friend from the far northwest; the Arshaum had given his name as Arigh, son of Arghun. The night was mild, but he wore a wolfskin jacket and a hat of red fox. His hard, lean frame and the lithe, controlled intensity of his movements reminded Scaurus of a hunting hawk. Until now he had been too busy with heroic eating to say much, but the talk of drink gained his interest.

"Ale, mead, wine—what difference does it make?" he said. He spoke Videssian fairly well, with a clipped, quick accent in perfect accord with the way he carried himself. "Kavass, now, is a man's drink, made from his horses' milk and with a kick as strong."

The stuff sounded ghastly, Marcus thought. He also noticed that Arigh's derisive comment about the drinks before him was not keeping him from downing quite a lot of them.

At the rate food was vanishing, it was no easy task to keep the tables loaded. Almost as if they were a bucket brigade battling a fire, the Namdalener women made never-ending trips from the kitchens with full platters and pitchers and back to them with empties. Marcus was surprised to see that Helvis was one of them. When he remarked on it, Soteric said with a shrug, "She told me she would sooner distract herself than sit alone and ache. What could I say to that?"

The servers were, most of them, much like the soldiers' women Scaurus had known in Rome's dominions. They thought nothing of trading bawdry with the men they were attending; pats and pinches brought as many laughs as squeaks of outrage. Through all that Helvis passed unaffronted; she wore her mourning like invisible armor. Her look of quiet sorrow and her air of remoteness, even when bending over a man's shoulder to fill his winecup, were enough to deter the most callous wencher.

More and more drink was fetched as time went by, and less and less food. Never sedate to begin with, the feast grew increasingly boisterous. Romans and Namdaleni learned each other's curses, tried to sing each other's songs, and clumsily essayed each other's dances. A couple of fights broke out, but they were instantly quelled by the squabblers' neighbors— good feelings ran too high tonight to give way to quarrels.

More than a few people wandered into the courtyard to see what the racket was about, and most of them liked what they found. Scaurus saw Taso Vones several tables away, a mug of wine in one hand and a partridge leg in the other. He waved to the ambassador of Khatrish, who made his way through the crowd and squeezed in beside him.

"You're kind to want anything to do with me," he said to the tribune, "especially if you recall that the last time I set eyes on you, I did nothing but flee."

Marcus had drunk enough wine and ale to make him brush aside such trifles. "Think nothing of it," he said grandly. "It was Avshar we were after, not you." That, though, served to remind him of the pursuit and its grievous outcome. He subsided, feeling like a blockhead.

Vones cocked his head to the side and watched the Roman out of one eye, for all the world like some bright-eyed little sparrow. "How curious," he said. "You of all people are the last I'd expect to find hobnobbing with the Namdaleni."

"Why don't you shut up, Taso?" Soteric said, but from his resigned tone he felt it would do no good. Evidently he knew the Khatrisher and, like so many, was used to giving him leeway. "I think you talk for the sake of hearing yourself."

"What better reason?" Vones returned with a smile.

He would have said more, but Marcus, his curiosity fired by Vones' comment, interrupted him. "What's wrong with these folk?" he asked, waving to encompass the courtyard and everyone in it. "We get on well with them. Is something amiss in that?"

"Easy, easy." The ambassador laid a warning hand on his arm, and he realized how loudly he'd spoken. "Why don't we take an evening stroll? The night-blooming jasmine is particularly sweet this time of year, don't you think?" He turned to Soteric. "Don't worry, my island friend. I shan't pick his pocket—I can guess what you have planned for later."

Soteric shrugged; he had gotten involved in a conversation with the Namdalener on his left, who was making a point about hunting dogs. "I don't like the hook-nosed breed," the man was saying. "It makes their mouths too small to hold the hare. And if they have gray eyes, too, so much the worse—they can't see to grab the beast in the first place."

"About that I'm not so sure," Soteric said, swigging. The more he drank, the more his island drawl came to the fore; his last word had sounded like "shoo-ah." He went on, "Gray-eyed hounds have keen noses, they say."

With scant interest in hunting dogs, gray-eyed or otherwise, Marcus was willing to follow Taso Vones as he sauntered out toward the darkness beyond the courtyard. The emissary kept up a nonstop chatter about nightflowers and other matters of small consequence until they had cleared the press. When he was satisfied no one could overhear, his manner changed. Giving the Roman more of that one-eyed study, he said, "I have yet to decide if you are the cleverest man or the greatest fool I've met lately."

"Do you always speak in riddles?" Marcus asked.

"Most of the time, actually; it's good practice for a diplomat. But forget me for the moment and look at yourself. When you met Avshar with swords, I felt sure our acquaintance would be short. But you won, and it seemed you knew what you were all about after all. And now this!"

"Now what?" the tribune wondered, thoroughly bewildered.

"You and your men beat the Namdaleni in your exercise. Well and good. You must have made Nephon Khoumnos proud and likely brightened the Emperor's day as well. The men of the Duchy are very good troops; Mavrikios will be glad to know he has loyal men who can stand against them at need."

He shot an accusing finger at Scaurus. "Or are you loyal? Having beaten them, what do you do? Boast of it? Hardly. You crack a bottle with them as if you and they were the best of friends. Are you trying to make the Emperor nervous? Or do you think the Sevastos will like you better now? After those herrings, I doubt it—yes, I saw you pause, and your stomach seems sound enough to me."

"What has Sphrantzes to do with—" Scaurus began. His mouth snapped shut before the question was done, for he knew the answer. The Namdaleni were mercenaries, of course, but what that meant had not struck him until now. It was not the present Emperor or his backers who employed foreign troops. That had been the policy of the bureaucrats of the capital, who used their hired swords to keep Gavras and his ilk in check while they ran the Empire for their own benefit. . . . And at their head was Vardanes Sphrantzes.

He swore, first in Videssian for Taso Vones' benefit, then in Latin to relieve his own feelings. "I see you understand me now," Vones said.

"This is nothing more than settling up a bet," Scaurus protested. Taso Vones lifted an eloquent eyebrow. No other comment was needed. The Roman knew how easy it was to judge a man by the company he kept. Caesar himself, in his younger days, had fallen into danger through his association with Marius' defeated faction.

Besides, there was no denying he did like the Namdaleni. They had a workmanlike approach to life, one rather like the

Romans'. They did not show the Videssians' touchy pride and deviousness, nor yet the dour fatalism of the Halogai. The men of the Duchy did the best with what they had, an attitude that marched well with the tribune's Stoic background. There are other reasons, too, he whispered deep inside himself.

He remarked, "It's rather too late to worry about it now, wouldn't you say?" Then he asked, "Why bother warning me? We hardly know each other."

Vones laughed out loud; like the patriarch Balsamon's, his laugh had real merriment in it. He said, "I've held my post in the city eight years now and I'm scarcely the oldest hand here—Gawtruz has been an ambassador for twice that long and more. I know everyone, and everyone knows me. We know the games we play, the tricks we try, the bargains we drive—and most of us, I think, are bloody bored. I know I am, sometimes.

"You, though, you and your Ronams—" He watched Marcus flinch, "—are a new pair of dice in the box, and loaded dice at that. It's whether you throw ones or sixes that remains to be seen." He scratched his fuzzy-bearded chin. "Which reminds me, we probably should be wandering back. Soteric won't talk about hook-nosed hounds forever, I promise you that."

When the tribune pressed him to explain himself, he refused, saying, "You'll see soon enough, I suspect." He headed toward the courtyard, leaving Scaurus the choice of staying behind by himself or following. He followed.

Taso Vones grunted in satisfaction when they rounded the last corner. "A little early," he said, "but not bad. Too early is better than too late, else we'd not find room at the games we favor—not for stakes we can afford, at any rate." Gold and silver clinked as he dug in his pouch for coins.

As he stared at the scene before him, Marcus wondered about his earlier analysis of Namdalener character. Were they fond of gambling because they believed in Phos' Wager, or had their theologians concocted the Wager because they were gamblers born? At the moment, he would have bet on the latter—and likely found an islander to cover his stake.

Most of the tables and benches had disappeared. In their places were circles chalked on the ground for dice-throwing, wheels of fortune, boards for tossing darts, others for hurling knives, a wide cleared space with a metal basin set in its center for throwing the dregs from winecups—as he expected, Scaurus saw Gorgidas there; the Greek was a dab hand at kottabos—and other games of skill or chance the tribune did not immediately recognize.

He rummaged in his own pouch to see what money he had. It was about as he had thought—some bronze pieces of irregular size and weight, some rather better silver, and half a dozen goldpieces, each about the size of his thumbnail. The older, more worn coins were fine gold, but the newer ones were made pale by an admixture of silver or blushed red with copper. With its revenues falling, the government, as governments will, had resorted to cheapening the currency. All its gold coinage, of whatever age, was nominally of equal value, but in the markets and shops the old pieces took a man further.

Videssian rules at dice, he had learned during the long winter at Imbros, were different from those at Rome. They used two dice here, not three, and Venus—a triple six, the best throw in the game he knew—would only have brought a hoot of derision even with a third dice allowed. A pair of ones—"Phos' little suns," they called them—was the local goal. You kept the dice until you threw their opposite—"the demons," a double six—in which case you lost. There were side bets on which you would roll first, how many throws you would keep the dice, and anything else an ingenious gambler could find to bet on.

The first time the dice came his way, Scaurus threw the suns three times before the demons turned up to send the little bone cubes on to the Namdalener at his left. That gave him a bigger stake to play with, one he promptly lost in his next turn with the bones—on his very first cast, twin sixes stared balefully up at him.

Shouts and applause came from the circle round the kottabos basin. Marcus looked up from his own play for a moment, to find it was just as he'd thought; with that deadly wristflick of his, Gorgidas was making the basin ring like a bell, flicking in the lees from farther and farther away. If he didn't get too drunk to stand, he'd own half the Namdaleni before the night was through.

Scaurus' own luck was mixed; he would win a little before dropping it again, get behind and make it up. His area of

attention shrank to the chalked circle before him—the money
in it, the dice spinning through, the men's hands reaching in to
pick up the cubes, gather in their winnings, or lay new bets.

Then, suddenly, the hand that took the dice was not masculine at all, but a smooth, slim-wristed lady's hand with painted
nails and an emerald ring on the forefinger. Startled, Marcus
looked up to see Komitta Rhangavve, with Thorisin Gavras
beside her. The Sevastokrator wore ordinary trousers and tunic
and could have been in the game an hour ago, for all Scaurus
had noticed.

Komitta slightly misinterpreted his surprise. Smiling pret-
tily at him, she said, "I know it's against custom, but I so love
to play myself. Do you mind?" Her tone warned that he had
better not.

That he really did not care made it easier. "Certainly not,
my lady." On the other hand, even if he had minded, he could
scarcely say so, not to the Sevastokrator's woman.

She won twice in quick succession, letting her stake ride
each time. When her third series of rolls ended by wiping her
out, she angrily hurled the dice away and cursed with unlady-
like fluency. The gamblers snickered. Someone found a new
pair of dice and from that moment she was an accepted
member of the circle.

With his landed wealth, Thorisin could easily have run the
other dicers from the game by betting more than they could
afford to cover. Remembering his hundred goldpiece bet with
Vardanes Sphrantzes, Marcus knew the Sevastokrator was not
averse to playing for high stakes. But, matched against men of
limited means, he was content to risk now a goldpiece, now
two, or sometimes a handful of silver. He took his wins and
losses as seriously as if he were playing for provinces—whatever he did, he liked to do well. He was a canny gambler, too;
before long, a good-sized pile of gold and silver lay before
him.

"Did you get that at swordpoint, or are they losing on purpose to curry favor with you?" someone asked the Sevastokrator, and Marcus was amazed to see Mavrikios Gavras standing
over his brother. The Emperor was no more regally dressed
than the Sevastokrator and attended only by a pair of Haloga
bodyguards.

"You don't know skill when you see it," Thorisin retorted.

"Hah!" He raked in another stake as the Namdalener across from him rolled the demons.

"Move over and let your elder show you how it's done. I've been listening to accountants since this morning and I've had a gutful of, 'I'm most sorry, your Imperial Majesty, but I cannot advise that at the present time.' Bah! Sometimes I think court ceremonial is a slow poison the bureaucrats invented to bore usurpers to death so they can sneak back into power themselves." He grinned at Marcus. "My daughter insists it's otherwise, but I don't believe her anymore."

With a murmured, "Thank you, sweetheart," he took a cup from a passing girl. The lass whirled in surprise as she realized whom she'd served. Mavrikios might not trust the Namdaleni where his Empire was concerned, Scaurus thought, but he certainly had no fears for his own person among them.

The Gavrai, naturally, were on opposite sides of every bet. As he'd been doing most of the evening, Thorisin won several times in a row after his brother sat down. "Go back to your pen-pushers and leave dicing to people who understand it," he said. "You'll get a fart from a dead man before you collect a copper from me."

Mavrikios snorted. "Even a blind hog stumbles across an acorn now and then. There we go!" he exclaimed. Marcus had just thrown suns, and Thorisin had bet against him. The Emperor turned to his brother, palm out. With a shrug, Thorisin passed the stake to him.

Marcus soon decided these were two men who should not gamble against each other. Both were such intense competitors that they took losing personally, and the good humor in their banter quickly disappeared. They were tight-lipped with concentration on the dice; their bets against each other were far greater than any others round the circle. Thorisin's earlier winnings vanished. When Mavrikios rolled the suns yet another time, his brother had to reach into his pouch to pay.

Mavrikios stared at the coins he produced. "What's this?" he said, flinging half of them to the ground. "You'd pay me with money from Yezd?"

Thorisin shrugged once more. "They look like gold to me, and finer than what we mint these days, for that matter." He scooped them up and tossed them far into the crowd. Glad cries said they were not lost for long. Seeing his brother's expression, Thorisin said, "If it won't pay my scot, what good is money to me?" Mavrikios slowly turned a dull red.

Everyone who saw or heard the exchange between the two brothers did his best to pretend he had not. Nevertheless, the camaraderie the dicing circle had enjoyed was shattered, and Marcus was not sorry to see the game break up a few minutes later. It could only bode ill for Videssos when the Emperor's brother showed him up in public, and he knew the story would do nothing but grow in the telling.

Climbing a stairway in the great building that housed the Grand Courtroom—the opposite side of the building from Nephon Khoumnos' workplace—Marcus wondered how much the story had grown in the past few days. Ahead of him on the stair was the thin clerk who had brought the tribune the invitation to this meeting, and ahead of *him* was a destination to which Scaurus had never thought to be bidden—the offices of Vardanes Sphrantzes.

"This way, if you please," the clerk said, turning to his left as he reached the top of the stairs. He led the Roman past a series of large rooms, through whose open doors Scaurus could see whole maniples of men busy with stylus and waxed tablet, pen, ink, and parchment, and the trays of reckoning beads with which skilled Videssians could calculate magically fast. The tribune was far more at home with the power of the barracks hall, but, watching the bureaucrats at work in this nerve center of Empire, he could not deny that power dwelt here too.

A pair of stocky nomads from the plains of Pardraya stood sentry at the door the clerk was approaching. Their faces, blank with boredom before, turned alert when they spied him and stormy when they recognized the Roman behind him. Scaurus had neither wanted nor had much to do with the Khamorth since coming to Videssos, but it was plain they felt he had brought disgrace down on them by exposing one of their number as Avshar's tool.

From the black looks they were giving him, Marcus got the notion they would have much preferred it if their countryman had succeeded in driving his demon-haunted blade hilt-deep in the Roman.

"The boss wants to see this?" one of them asked the tribune's guide, jerking his thumb at Scaurus in a deliberately offensive way. "You're sure?"

"Of course I'm sure," the clerk snapped. "Now stand aside, will you? You'll win no thanks for interfering in his business."

Insolently slow, the Khamorth gave way. As Scaurus stepped past them, one made a ghastly gurgle, like the dying gasp of a man with a slit throat. It was so horribly authentic the tribune whipped his head around before he could stop himself. The plainsman grinned nastily.

Furious at losing face before the barbarian, Scaurus cranked his defenses to the highest pitch of readiness as he walked into the Sevastos' office. When the functionary who led him announced his name, he bowed with the same puncti-liousness he would have shown the Emperor—not by any act of omission would he give Sphrantzes a moral advantage over him.

"Come in, come in, you are most welcome," the Sevastos said. As always, his smooth, deep voice revealed nothing but what he wanted in it; at the moment, a cultured affability.

Before Marcus could fully focus his suspicions on the Se-vastos, the office's other occupant, a gangling, scraggly-bearded fellow in his early twenties, bounced up from his seat to shake the tribune's hand. "A brilliant martial display, truly brilliant!" he exclaimed, adding, "I saw you beat the Namda-leni. Had it been crimson-handed war and not mere sport, the ground would have been a thirsty sponge to drink their blood. Brilliant!" he said again.

"Er—yes, of course," Scaurus muttered, at a loss to recon-cile this unwarlike-seeming youth with his gore-filled talk.

Vardanes Sphrantzes coughed drily. "One of the reasons I asked you here, my outland friend, was to present you to my nephew, the spatharios Ortaias Sphrantzes. Since your victory over the easterners, he's done nothing but pester me to arrange the meeting."

While spatharios had the literal meaing of "sword-bearer," it was a catch-all title, often with little more real meaning than "aide." In young Ortaias' case, that seemed just as well; he looked as if the effort of toting a sword would be too much for him.

He was, though, nothing if not an enthusiast. "I was fasci-

nated to see you successfully oppose the Namdaleni on foot,"
he said. "In his *Art of Generalship* Mindes Kalokyres recom-
mends plying them with arrows from afar and strongly implies
they are invincible at close quarters. It's a great pity he is a
century in his grave; I should have like to hear his comments
on your refutation of his thesis."

"That would be interesting, I'm sure, your excellency,"
Scaurus agreed, wondering how much of Ortaias' speech he
was understanding. The young noble spoke very quickly; this,
coupled with his affected accent and his evident love for long
words, made following his meaning a trial for someone with
the tribune's imperfect grasp of Videssian.

"Kalokyres is our greatest commentator on things military," Ortaias' uncle explained courteously. "Do sit down,
both of you," he urged. "Scaurus—" In Videssian it sounded
more like Scavros. "—take some wine if you will. It's a fine
vintage, from the western province of Raban, and rather hard
to come by in these sorry times."

The pale wine poured silkily from its elegant alabaster ca-
rafe. Marcus sipped once for politeness' sake, then a second
time with real appreciation; this was more to his liking than
any wine he'd yet sampled in Videssos.

"I thought you would enjoy it," Vardanes said, drinking
with him. "It's a touch too piquant for me to favor ordinarily,
but it is a pleasant change of pace." Scaurus gave the Sevastos
his reluctant admiration. It could hardly have been easy for
him to learn the Roman's taste in wine and then to meet it.
The obvious effort Sphrantzes was making to put him at his
ease only made him wonder further what the real object of this
meeting might be.

Whatever it was, the Sevastos was in no hurry to get
around to it. He spoke with charm and wit of bits of gossip
that had crossed his path in the past few days and did not spare
his fellow bureaucrats. "There are those," he remarked, "who
think the mark for a thing in a ledger is the thing itself."
Raising his cup to his lips, he went on, "It takes but a taste of
the wine to see how foolish they are."

The tribune had to agree, but noted how possessively
Sphrantzes' hand curled over the polished surface of the cup.

The Sevastos' office was more richly furnished than
Mavrikios Gavras' private chambers, with wall hangings of

silk brocade shot through with gold and silver threads and upholstered couches and chairs whose ebony arms were inlaid with ivory and semiprecious stones. Yet the dominant impression was not one of sybaritic decadence, but rather of a man who truly loved his comforts without being ruled by them.

In Rome Marcus had known men who enjoyed having fish ponds set in their villas' gardens, but he had never seen a decoration like the one on Sphrantzes' desk—a globular tank of clear glass with several small, brightly colored fish darting through waterplants rooted in gravel. In a strange way, it was soothing to watch. The tribune's eyes kept coming back to it, and Sphrantzes gazed fondly at his little pets in their transparent enclosure.

He saw Scaurus looking at them. "One of my servants has the duty of catching enough gnats, flies, and suchlike creatures to keep them alive. He's certain I've lost my wits, but I pay him enough that he doesn't say so."

By this time the Roman had decided Sphrantzes' summons masked nothing more sinister than a social call. He was beginning to muster excuses for leaving when the Sevastos remarked, "I'm glad to see no hard feelings exist between yourselves and the Namdaleni after your recent tussle."

"Indeed yes! That is most fortunate!" Ortaias said enthusiastically. "The tenacity of the men of the Duchy is legendary, as is their fortitude. When linked to the specialized infantry skills you Ronams—"

"Romans," his uncle corrected him.

"Your pardon," Ortaias said, flushing. Thrown off his stride, he finished with the simplest sentence Scaurus had heard from him. "You'll fight really well for us!"

"I hope so, your excellence," Marcus replied. Interested by Vardanes' mention of the islanders, he decided to stay a bit longer. Maybe the Sevastos would be forthcoming after all.

"My nephew is right," the elder Sphrantzes said. "It would be unfortunate if there were a lasting grudge between yourselves and the Namdaleni. They have served us well in the past, and we expect the same of you. There is already too much strife within our army, too much talk of native troops as opposed to mercenaries. Every soldier is a mercenary, but with some, paymaster and king are one and the same."

The tribune steepled his fingers without replying. The Sevastos' last statement, as far as he was concerned, was nonsense, and dangerous nonsense at that. Nor did he think Sphrantzes believed it any more than he did—whatever else he was, Vardanes Sphrantzes was no fool.

He also wondered how Vardanes was using his "we" and "us." Did he speak as head of the bureaucratic faction, as prime minister of all the Empire, or with the royal first person plural? He wondered if Sphrantzes knew himself.

"It's regrettable but true," the Sevastos was saying, "that foreign-born troops do not have the fairest name in the Empire. One reason is that they've so often had to be used against rebels from the back of beyond, men who, even on the throne, find no more dignity than they did in the hayseed robbers' nests from which they sprang." For the first time, his disdain rang clear.

"They have no breeding!" Ortaias Sphrantzes was saying. "None! Why, Mavrikios Gavras' great-grandfather was a goatherd, while we Sphrantzai—" The cold stare Vandanes sent his way stopped him in confusion.

"Forgive my nephew once more, I beg you," the Sevastos said smoothly. "He speaks with youth's usual exaggeration. His Imperial Majesty's family has been of noble rank for nearly two centuries." But by the irony still in his voice, he did not find that long at all.

The conversation drifted back toward triviality, this time for good. A curiously indecisive meeting, Marcus thought on his way back to the barracks. He had expected the Sevastos to show more of his mind but, on reflection, there was no reason why he should do so to a man he felt to be of the opposite side. Then too, with one slip of the tongue his nephew probably had revealed a good deal more than the senior Sphrantzes wanted known.

Two other things occurred to the tribune. The first was that Taso Vones was a lucky acquaintance. The little Khatrisher had an uncanny knowledge of Videssian affairs and was willing to share it. The second was a conclusion he reached while wondering why he still distrusted Vardanes Sphrantzes so much. It was utterly in character, he decided, for the Sevastos to delight in keeping small, helpless creatures in a transparent cage.

VIII

As the weeks passed after Mavrikios Gavras' ringing declaration of war against Yezd, Videssos began filling with warriors mustered to wage the great campaign the Emperor had planned. The gardens, orchards, and other open spaces which made the imperial capital such a delight saw tent cities spring up on them like mushrooms after a rain. Every street, it seemed, had its contingent of soldiers swaggering along, elbowing civilians to one side, on the prowl for food, drink, and women . . . or simply standing and gaping at the wonders Videssos offered the newcomer's eye.

Troops flowed in day after day. The Emperor pulled men from garrisons in towns he reckoned safe, to add weight to his striking force. A hundred men came from here, four hundred more from there, another two hundred from somewhere else. Marcus heard that Imbros' troops had arrived and wondered if Skapti Modolf's son was among them. Even the saturnine Haloga would be hard pressed to call the city a less pleasant place than Imbros.

The Empire's own soldiers were not the only ones to swell Videssos to the bursting point. True to his promise, Mavrikios sent his neighbors a call for mercenaries against Yezd, and the response was good. Videssian ships sailing from Prista, the Empire's watchport on the northern coast of the Videssian Sea, brought companies of Khamorth from the plains, and their steppe-ponies with them. By special leave, other bands of nomads were permitted to cross the Astris River. They came south to the capital by land, paralleling the seacoast and, in the latter stage of their journey, following the route the Romans had used from Imbros. Parties of Videssian outriders made sure the plainsmen did not plunder the countryside.

Khatrish, whose border marched with Videssos' eastern frontier, sent the Empire a troop of light cavalry. In gear and appearance they were about halfway between imperials and plainsdwellers, whose bloods they shared. Most of them seemed to have the outspoken cheeriness of Taso Vones. Scaurus had a chance to get acquainted with a fair number of them at a heroic feast the Khatrisher ambassador put together. Viridovix made the night memorable by throwing a Khamorth clear through a very stout wineshop door without bothering to open it first. Vones paid the repair costs out of his own pocket, declaring, "Strength like that deserves to be honored."

"Foosh!" the Celt protested. "The man was a natural-born damn fool, the which is proven by the hardness of his head. For no other reason did he make so fine a battering ram."

The Namdaleni also heeded the Empire's rallying cry. The Duchy's lean square-riggers brought Videssos two regiments to fight the Yezda. Getting them into the capital, however, was a tricky busines. Namdalen and the Empire were foes too recent for much trust to exist on either side. Mavrikios, while glad of the manpower, was not anxious to see Namdalener warships anchored at Videssos' quays, suspecting the islanders' piratical instincts might get the better of their good intentions. Thus the Namdaleni transshipped at the Key and came to the city in imperial hulls. The matter-of-fact way they accepted the Emperor's solution convinced Marcus that all Gavras' forebodings were justified.

"How right you are," Gaius Philippus agreed. "They don't so much as bother pretending innocence. If they got a quarter of a chance they'd jump Mavrikios without even blinking. He knows it, and they know he knows it. And on those terms they can deal with each other."

For the Romans, spring and early summer were a time of adjustment, a time to find and to make their place in their new homeland. Their position in the army was never in doubt, not after the win over the men of the Duchy in their mock-combat. Marcus became the oracle of infantry. Almost daily, high-ranking Videssians or mercenary officers would appear at the Roman drills to watch and question. The tribune found it flattering and ironically amusing, as he knew he was but an amateur soldier.

When other business kept him from leading the exercises, the duty of coping with observers fell on Gaius Philippus. The senior centurion got on well with fellow professionals, but did not suffer fools gladly. After one such meeting, he asked Scaurus, "Who's the lanky half-shaved whiffet always hanging about? You know, the fellow with the book under one arm."

"Ortaias Sphrantzes?" Marcus asked with a sinking feeling.

"That's the one. He wanted to know how I heartened the men before a battle; and before I could get a word out of my mouth, he started a harangue he must have written himself, the stupid puppy. To win a battle after that speech, he'd need to be leading a crew of demigods."

"You didn't tell him so, I hope?"

"Me? I told him he should save it for the enemy—he'd bore them to death and win without a fight. He went away."

"Oh." For the next few days the tribune kept expecting poison in the radishes, or at least a summons from Ortaias' uncle. But nothing happened. Either the young Sphrantzes had not told the Sevastos of his embarrassment, or Vardanes was resigned to his nephew stubbing his toes every now and again. Marcus judged it was the former; resignation was not an expression he could easily see on Vardanes Sphrantzes' face.

Just as the Romans changed Videssian notions of military practice, the Empire's way of life had its effect on them. To the tribune's surprise, many of his men began to follow Phos. While he had nothing against Videssos' faith, it also had no appeal for him. He worried lest the legionaries' adoption of the Empire's god was the first step in forgetting Rome.

Gaius Philippus shared his concern. "It's not right, hearing the lads go, 'Phos fry you!' when someone trips over their feet. We should order them to stop that nonsense right now."

Looking for more disinterested advice, the tribune put the question to Gorgidas. "An order? Don't be absurd. You can tell a man what to do, but even your iron-fisted centurion can't tell him what to think. They'll only disobey if he tries. And if they don't follow the one command, who's to say they'll follow the next? It's easiest to ride a horse in the direction he's already going."

Scaurus felt the sense of the doctor's words; the Greek articulated the conclusion he was reaching himself. But the certainty in Gorgidas' next remark rocked him back on his heels. "Of course we'll forget Rome—and Greece, and Gaul."

"What? Never!" Marcus said with unthinking rejection.

"Come now, in your head you know I'm right, say your heart what it will. Oh, I don't mean every memory of the world we knew will disappear; that's truly impossible. But as the years pass, Videssos will lay its hand on us all, gently, yes, but the day will come when you discover you've forgotten the names of half your parents' neighbors . . . and it won't really bother you." Gorgidas' eyes were far away.

The tribune shivered. "You see a long way ahead, don't you?"

"Eh? No, a long way behind. I tore my life up by the roots once before, when I left Elis to ply my trade at Rome. It gives me a sense of proportion you may not have.

"Besides," the Greek went on, "eventually we'll have a good many Videssians in our own ranks. Apokavkos is doing well, and we'll not find more Romans to make up the losses we'll take."

Scaurus did not reply; Gorgidas had a gift for bringing up things he would rather not think about. He did resolve to fix his every memory so firmly it could never escape. Even as he made the resolution, he felt the cold wind of futility at his back. Well, then, the best you can, he told himself, and was satisfied. Failure was no disgrace; indifference was.

Videssian usages also began to change what Marcus had thought a fundamental part of Roman military thinking—its attitude toward women. The army of Rome was so often on campaign that marriage during legionary service was forbidden as being bad for discipline. Neither the Videssians nor their mercenary soldiers followed that rule. They spent much of their time in garrison duty, which gave them the chance to form long-lasting relationships that could not have existed in a more active army.

As with the worship of the Empire's god, the tribune knew he could not keep his men from uniting with Videssos' women. He would have faced mutiny had he tried, the more so as the local soldiers enjoyed the privilege the legionaries

were seeking. First one and then a second of the four barracks
halls the Romans used was transformed by hastily erected par-
titions of wood and cloth into quarters where privacy could be
had. Nor was it long before the first proud Romans could
boast that they would be the fathers of fine sons—or so they
hoped—to take their places.

Gaius Philippus grumbled more than ever. "I can see us in
a few years' time—brats squalling underfoot, troopers brawling because their queans had a spat. Mars above, what are we
coming to?" To forestall the evil day, he worked the legionaries harder than before.

Scaurus had reservations too, but he noted that while most
of the Namdaleni had women, it did not seem to blunt their
edge. In a way, he could even see it as an advantage—with
such an intimate stake in Videssos' survival, the legionaries
might fight harder for the Empire.

Yet he also realized that acquiring mates was another tap
on the wedge Videssos was driving into the souls of his men,
another step in their absorption into the Empire. Every time
the tribune saw a Roman walk by with his attention solely on
the woman whose waist his arm encircled, he felt again the
inevitability of Gorgidas' words. The Romans were a drop of
ink fallen into a vast lake; their color had to fade with time.

Of all the peoples they came to know in the capital, the
legionaries seemed to blend best with the Namdaleni. It embarrassed Scaurus, who reserved his loyalty for the Emperor
and knew the men of the Duchy would cheerfully gut Videssos if ever they saw their chance. But there was no getting
around it—Roman and Namdalener took to one another like
long-separated relatives.

Maybe the skirmish and feast they had shared made friendship easier; maybe it was simply that the Namdaleni were less
reserved than Videssians and more willing to meet the
Romans halfway. Whatever the reason, legionaries were
always welcome in taverns that catered to the easterners, and
constant traffic flowed between the islanders' barracks and
those housing the Romans.

When Marcus worried his soldiers' fondness for the men of
the Duchy would undermine the friendships he'd built up with
the Videssians, Gaius Philippus put an arm round his

shoulder. "You want friends everywhere," he said, speaking like a much older brother. "It's your age, I suppose; everyone in his thirties thinks he needs friends. Once you reach your forties, you find they won't save you any more than love did."

"To the crows with you!" Marcus exclaimed, appalled. "You're worse than Gorgidas."

One morning, Soteric Dosti's son came to invite several of the Roman officers to that day's Namdalener drill. "Aye, you bettered us afoot," he said, "but now you'll see us at our best."

Marcus had watched the Namedaleni work before and had a healthy respect for their hard-hitting cavalry. He also approved of their style of practice. Like the Romans, they made their training as much like battle as they could, so no one would be surprised on the true field of combat. But from the smug grin Soteric was trying to hide, this invitation was to something special.

A few Khamorth were practicing archery at the drillfield's edge. Their short, double-curved bows sent arrow after arrow *whock*ing into the straw-stuffed hides they had set up as targets. They and the party Marcus led were the only non-Namdaleni on the field that day.

At one end stood a long row of hay bales, at the other, almost equally still, a line of mounted islanders. The men of the Duchy were in full caparison. Streamers of bright ribbon fluttered from their helms, their lances, and their big horses' trappings. Each wore over his chain mail shirt a surcoat of a color to match his streamers. A hundred lances went up in salute as one when the easterners caught sight of the Romans.

"Och, what a brave show," Viridovix said admiringly. Scaurus thought the Gaul had found the perfect word; this was a show, something prepared specially for his benefit. He resolved to judge it on that basis if he could.

The commander of the Namdaleni barked an order. Their lances swung down, again in unison. A hundred glittering leaf-shaped points of steel, each tipping a lance twice the length of a man, leveled at the bales of hay a furlong from them. Their leader left them thus for a long dramatic moment, then shouted the command that sent them hurtling forward.

Like an avalanche thundering down an Alpine pass, they started slowly. The heavy horses they rode were not quick to build momentum, what with their own bulk and the heavily armored men atop them. But they gained a trifle at every bound and were at full stride before halfway to their goal. The earth rolled like a kettledrum under their thuttering hooves; their iron-shod feet sent great clods of dirt and grass flying skywards.

Marcus tried to imagine himself standing in a hay bale's place, watching the horses thunder down on him until he could see their nostrils flaring crimson, staring at the steel that would tear his life away. The skin on his belly crawled at the thought of it. He wondered how any men could nerve themselves to oppose such a charge.

When lances, horses, and riders smashed through them, the bales simply ceased to be. Hay was trampled underfoot, flung in all directions, and thrown high into the air. The Namdaleni brought their horses to a halt; they began picking hay wisps from their mounts' manes and coats and from their own surcoats and hair.

Soteric looked expectantly to Scaurus. "Most impressive," the tribune said, and meant it. "Both as spectacle and as a show of fighting power, I don't think I've seen the like."

"Sure and it's a cruel hard folk you Namdaleni are," Viridovix said, "to beat poor hay bales all to bits, and them having done you no harm."

Gaius Philippus added, "If that was your way of challenging us to a return engagement on horseback, you can bloody well think again. I'm content to rest on my laurels, thank you very kindly." The veteran's praise made Soteric glow with pride, and the day, the islanders agreed, was a great success.

But the centurion was in fact less overawed than he let the Namdaleni think. "They're rugged, don't misunderstand me," he told Scaurus as they returned to their own quarters after sharing a midday meal with the easterners. "Good steady foot, though, could give them all they want. The key is keeping their charge from flattening you at the start."

"Do you think so?" Marcus asked. He'd paid Gaius Philippus' words less heed than he should. It must have shown, for Viridovix looked at him with mischief in his eye.

"You're wasting your breath if you speak to the lad of war, I'm thinking," he said to the centurion. "There's nothing in his head at all but a couple of fine blue eyes, sure and there's not. She'a a rare beauty lass, Roman; I wish you luck with her."

"Helvis?" Marcus said, alarmed his feelings were so obvious. He covered himself as best he could. "What makes you think that? She wasn't even at table today."

"Aye, that's true—and weren't you the disappointed one now?" Viridovix did his best to assume the air of a man giving serious advice, something of a wasted effort on his naturally merry face. "You're about it the right way, I'll say that. Too hard and too soon would do nothing but drive her from you. But those honied plums you found for her boy, now—you're a sly one. If the imp cares for you, how could the mother not? And giving them to Soteric to pass along will make him think the better of you too, the which canna hurt your chances."

"Oh, hold your peace, can't you? With Helvis not there, who could I give the sweets to but her brother?" But quibble as he would over details, in broad outline he knew the Celt was right. He was powerfully drawn to Helvis, but that was complicated by his guilt over his role, accidental though it was, in Hemond's death. Still, in the few times he had seen her since that day, she bore out her claim that she had no ill will toward him. And Soteric, for his part, would have had to be blind not to have noticed the attention Scaurus paid his sister, yet he raised no objections—a promising sign.

But that his feelings should be common knowledge, maybe—no, certainly—the subject of gossip through Videssos' community of soldiers, could only dismay the tribune, who did not much care to reveal himself to any but his friends.

He was relieved when Gaius Philippus returned to the conversation's original subject. "Stiffen your line with pikemen and give them a good volley of *pila* as soon as they come into range, and your fine Namdalener horsemen will have themselves a very warm time indeed. Horses know better than to run up against anything sharp."

Viridovix gave the centurion an exasperated glance. "You are the damnedest man for holding onto a worthless idea I ever did see. Here we could be making himself squirm like a worm in a mug of ale, and you go maundering on about nags, Epona preserve them." He named the Gallic horse-goddess.

"One day, maybe, it'll be you in the alepot," Gaius Philippus said, looking him in the eye. "Then we'll see if you're glad to have me change the subject."

While Mavrikios readied his stroke to put an end to Yezd once for all, the Empire's western enemy did not stand idle. As always, there was a flow of wild nomads down off the steppe, over the Yegird River, and into the northwest of what had been the land of Makuran. Thus had the Yezda entered that land half a century before. Khagan Wulghash, Marcus thought, was no one's fool. Instead of letting the newcomers settle and disrupt his state, he shunted them eastward against Videssos, urging them on with promises of fighting, loot, and the backing of the Yezda army.

The nomads, more mobile than the foe they faced, slid through Vaspurakan's mountain valleys and roared into the fertile plains beyond them, spreading atrocity, mayhem, and rapine. The raiders were like so much water; if checked at one spot, they flowed someplace else, always probing for weak spots and all too often finding them.

And at their head was Avshar. Marcus cursed and Nephon Khoumnos swore the first reports of him were lies, but soon enough they had to admit the truth. Too many refugees, straggling into Videssos with no more than they could carry, told a tale that left no room for doubt. Yezd's wizard-chieftain did not try to hide his presence. On the contrary, he flaunted it, the better to terrify his foes.

With the white robes he always wore, he chose to ride a great black charger, half again the size of his followers' plains-ponies. His sword hewed down the few bold enough to stand against him, and his mighty bow sent shafts of death winging farther than any normal man, any human man, could shoot. It was said that any man those arrows pierced would die, be the wound ever so tiny. It was also said no spear or arrow would bite on him, and that the mere sight of him unstrung even a hero's courage. Remembering the spell his good Gallic blade had turned aside, Marcus could well believe the last.

High summer approached and still the Emperor gathered his forces. Local levies in the west fought the Yezda without support from the host building in the capital. None of the Romans could understand why Mavrikios, certainly a man of action, did not move. When Scaurus put the question to Neilos Tzimiskes, the borderer replied, "Too soon can be worse than too late, you know."

"Six weeks ago—even three weeks ago—I would have said aye to that. But if matters aren't taken in hand soon, there won't be much of an Empire left to save."

"Believe me, my friend, things aren't as simple as they seem." But when Marcus tried to get more from Tzimiskes than that, Neilos retreated into vague promises that matters would turn out for the best. It was not long before the Roman decided he knew more than he was willing to say.

The next day, Scaurus kicked himself for not seeking what he needed to know from Phostis Apokavkos. The truth was, the former peasant had blended so well into the Roman ranks that the tribune often forgot he had not been with the legionaries in the forests of Gaul. His new allegiance, Marcus reasoned, might make him more garrulous than Tzimiskes.

"Do I know why we're not out on campaign? You mean to tell me you don't?" Apokavkos stared at the tribune. He plucked the air where his beard had been, then laughed at himself. "Still can't get used to this shaving. Answer to your question's a simple thing: Mavrikios isn't about to leave the city until he's sure he'll still be Emperor when he gets home."

Marcus thumped his forehead with the heel of his hand. "A pox on faction politics! The whole Empire is the stake, not who sits the throne."

"You'd think a mite different if it was your backside on it."

Scaurus started to protest, then thought back on the last decades of Rome's history. It was only too true that the wars against King Mithridates of Pontus had dragged on long after that monarch should have been crushed, simply because the legions opposing him were sometimes of Sulla's faction, sometimes of the Marians'. Not only was cooperation between the two groups poor; both kept going back to Italy from Asia Minor to fight another round of civil war. The Videssians were men like any others. It was probably too much to ask of them not to be fools like any others.

"You're getting the idea, all right," Apokavkos said, seeing Marcus' grudging agreement. "Besides, if you doubt me, how do you explain Mavrikios staying in the city last year and not going out to fight the Yezda? Things were even tighter then than they are now; he plain didn't dare leave."

The adopted Roman's comment made clear something Scaurus had puzzled over for some time. No wonder Mavrikios looked so bleak when he admitted his earlier inability to move against Yezd! The past year had seen the Empire's power vastly increase and, in the face of the Yezda threat, its unity as well. The tribune better understood Mavrikios' pouched, red-veined eyes; it was strange he dared sleep at all.

Yet power and unity still did not walk hand in hand in Videssos, as Marcus discovered a few mornings later. The tribune had urged Apokavkos to keep the street connections he'd made in the city. Marcus saw how the Namdaleni were excluded from the news and rumors always seething, and did not want his Romans similarly deprived. The report Phostis brought made him thankful for his forethought.

"If it didn't have us in it, too, I likely wouldn't tell you this," Apokavkos said, "but I think it'd be smart for us to walk small the next few days. There's trouble brewing against the damned easterners, and too many in town put us and them in the same wagon."

"Against the Namdaleni?" Marcus asked. At Phostis' nod, he said, "But why? They've quarreled with the Empire, true, but every one of them in the city now is here to fight Yezd."

"There's too many of 'em here, and they're too proud of themselves, the swaggering rubes." Phostis' conversion to Roman tastes did not stretch to the men of the Duchy. "Not only that, they've taken over half a dozen shrines for their own services, the damned heretics. Next thing you know, they'll start trying to convert decent folk to their ways. That won't do."

Marcus suppressed a strong impulse to scream. Would no one in this god-ridden world forget religion long enough to do anything needful? If the followers of Phos as sure victor over evil fought those who believed in Phos' Wager, then the only winners would be Skotos-worshippers. But when the Roman suggested that to Apokavkos, his answer was, "I don't know but what I'd sooner see Wulghash ruling in Videssos than Duke Tomond of Namdalen."

Throwing his hands in the air, Scaurus went off to pass the

warning to Soteric. The islander was not in his usual billet on the ground floor of the barracks. "He's with his sister, I think. You can probably find him there," offered one of the men whose bed was nearby.

"Thanks," the tribune said, heading for the stairway. As usual, the prospect of seeing Helvis made him skittish and eager at the same time. He was aware that more than once he'd invented excuses to visit Soteric in the hope of encountering his sister. This time, though, he reminded himself, his business with the Namdalener was real and urgent.

"By the Wager!" Soteric exclaimed when he saw who was knocking on Helvis' door. "Talk about someone and just see if he doesn't show up." That was an opening to take Scaurus clean out of play, especially since the Namdalener declined to follow it up and left Marcus guessing.

"Would you care for some wine, or some bread and cheese?" Helvis asked when the Roman was comfortable. She was still far from the vibrant lady who had caught his fancy a few weeks before, but time, as it always does, was beginning its healing work. The pinched look of pain that sat so wrongly on her lively features was not so pronounced now; there were times again when her smile would reach her eyes.

Malric darted into the livingroom from the bedchamber beyond. He was carrying a tiny wooden sword. "Kill a Yezda!" he announced, swinging his toy blade with three-year-old ferocity.

Helvis caught up her son and swung him into the air. He squealed in glee, dropping his play weapon. "Again!" he said. "Again!" Instead, his mother squeezed him to her with fierce intensity, remembering Hemond in him.

"Run along, son," Soteric said when his nephew was on his feet again. Grabbing up his sword, the boy dashed away at the same breakneck speed he'd used to come in. Recalling his own younger sisters growing up, Scaurus knew all small children were either going at full tilt or asleep, with next to nothing in between.

Once Malric was gone, the tribune told Soteric the story he had heard from Phostis Apokavkos. The islander's first reaction was not the alarm Marcus had felt, but rather smoldering eagerness. "Let the rabble come!" he said, smacking fist into palm for emphasis. "We'll clean the bastards out, and it'll give us the excuse we need for war on the Empire. Namdalen will inherit Videssos' mantle soon enough—why not now?"

Scaurus gaped at him, flabbergasted. He knew the men of the Duchy coveted the city and the whole Empire, but Soteric's arrogance struck him as being past sanity. Helvis was staring at her brother, too. As softly as he could, Marcus tried to nudge him back toward sense. "You'll take and hold the capital with six thousand men?" he asked politely.

"Eight thousand! And some of the Khamorth will surely join us—their sport is plunder."

"Quite true, I'm sure. And once you've disposed of the rest of the plainsmen, the Emperor's Haloga guards, and the forty thousand or so Videssian warriors in the city, why then all you need do is keep down the whole town. They'd hate you doubly—for being heretics and conquerors both. I wish you good fortune, for you'll need it."

The Namdalener officer looked at him as Malric would if he'd snapped the boy's toy sword over his knee. "Then you didn't come to offer your men as allies in the fight?"

"Allies in the fight?" If it came to a fight such as Soteric envisioned, Scaurus hoped the Romans would be on the other side, but he guessed the islander would be more furious than chastened to hear that. The tribune was still marveling at Soteric's incredible . . . there was no word in Latin for it. He had to think in Greek to find the notion he wanted: *hubris*. What tragedian had written, "Whom the gods would destroy, they first make mad"?

Gorgidas would know, he thought.

Some of the ravening glitter in Soteric's eye faded as he saw Marcus' rejection. He looked to his sister for support, but Helvis would not meet his glance. She was as ardent a Namdalener as her brother, but too firmly rooted in reality to be swept away by a vision of conquest, no matter how glowing.

"I came to stop a riot, not start a war," Marcus said into the silence. He looked for some reason he could use to draw Soteric from his dangerous course without making him lose face. Luckily, one was close at hand. "With Yezd to be dealt with, neither you nor the Empire can afford secondary fights."

There was more than enough truth in that to make Soteric stop and think. The smile on his face had nothing to do with amusement; it was more like a stifled snarl. "What would you have us do?" he asked at last. "Hide our beliefs? Skulk like cowards to keep from firing the rabble? The Videssians have no shame over throwing their creed in our faces. I'd sooner fight than kowtow to the street mob, and damn the consequences, say I!" But mixed with the warrior's pride in his speech was the frustrated realization that the outcome of such a fight likely would not be what he wished.

Marcus tried to capitalize on the islander's slowly emerging good sense. "No one would expect you to knuckle under," he said. "But a little restraint now could stop endless trouble later."

"Let the bloody Cocksures show restraint," Soteric snapped, using the Duchy's nickname for the orthodox of Videssos.

Continued contact with the Namdalener's hot temper was beginning to fray Scaurus' own. "There's the very thing I'm talking about," he said. "Call someone a 'Cocksure' once too often and you can be sure you'll have a scramble on your hands."

Up to this time Helvis had listened to her brother and the Roman argue without taking much part. Now she said, "It seems to me the two of you are only touching one part of the problem. The city people may like us better if we're less open about some things they don't care for, but what we do can only go so far. If Videssos needs our service, the Emperor— or someone—should make the people know we're important to them and should not be abused."

"Should, should, should," Soteric said mockingly. "Who would put his neck on the block for a miserable band of mercenaries?"

It was plain he did not think his sister would have a good answer for him. Thinking of the government leaders he knew, Marcus did not find it likely either. Mavrikios or Thorisin Gavras would sacrifice the men of the Duchy without a qualm if they interfered with the great campaign against Yezd. Nephon Khoumnos might sacrifice them anyway, on general principles. True, the Namdaleni were part of the power Vardanes Sphrantzes wielded against the Gavrai, but the Sevastos, Scaurus was sure, was too unpopular in the city to make his words, even if given, worth much.

But Helvis did have a reply, and one so apt Marcus felt like a blockhead for not finding it himself. "What of Balsamon?" she asked. "He strikes me as a good man, and one the Vides- sians listen to."

"The Cocksures' patriarch?" Soteric said incredulously. "Any Videssian blue-robe would send us all to the eternal ice before he'd lift a finger for us."

"Of most of them I would say that's true, but Balsamon has a different feel to him. He's never harassed us, you know," Helvis said.

"Your sister's right, I think," Marcus said to Soteric. He told him of the startling tolerance the prelate of Videssos had shown in the Emperor's chambers.

"Hmm," Soteric said. "It's easy enough to be tolerant in private. Will he do it when it counts? There's the rub." He rose to his feet. "Well, what are the two of you waiting for? We'd best find out—myself, I'll believe it when I hear it."

The ruthless energy Soteric had wanted to turn on Videssos now was bent against his sister and the tribune. Helvis paused only to pick up her son—"Come on, Malric, we're going to see someone."—and Marcus not at all, but they were not quick enough to suit Soteric. Scoffing at Helvis' idea at the same time as he pushed it forward, her brother had her and Scaurus out of the Namdalener barracks, out of the palace complex, and into the hurly-burly of the city almost before the Roman could blink.

The patriarchal residence was in the northern central part of Videssos, on the grounds of Phos' High Temple. The Roman had not cared to visit that, but some of his men who had taken to Phos marveled at its splendor. The High Temple's spires, topped with their gilded domes, were visible throughout the city; the only problem in reaching them was picking the proper path through Videssos' maze of roads, lanes, and alleys. Soteric led the way with assurance.

More by what did not happen than by what did, Marcus got the feel of how unwelcome foreigners had become in the capi- tal. It was as if the city dwellers were trying to pretend they did not exist. No merchant came rushing out of his shop to importune them, no peddler approached to ply his wares, no small boy came up to offer to lead them to his father's hostel. The tribune wryly remembered how annoyed he had been at not achieving anonymity after his fight with Avshar. Now he had it, and found he did not want it.

Malric was entranced by the colors, sounds, and smells of the city, so different from and so much more exciting than the barracks he was used to. Half the time he walked along among Helvis, Soteric, and Marcus, doing his short-legged best to keep up; they carried him the rest of the way, passing him from one to the next. His three constant demands were, "Put me down," "Pick me up," and, most of all, "What's that?" Everything drew the last query: a piebald horse, a painter's scaffold, a prostitute of dubious gender.

"Good question," Soteric chuckled as the quean sauntered past. His nephew was not listening—a scrawny black puppy with floopy ears had stolen his interest.

The High Temple of Phos sat in lordly solitude at the center of a large enclosed courtyard. Like the arena by the palace complex, it was one of the city's main gathering points. At need, lesser priests would speak to the masses assembled outside the Temple while the prelate addressed the smaller, more select audience within.

The residence of the patriarchs of Videssos stood just outside the courtyard. It was a surprisingly unassuming structure; many moderately wealthy traders had larger, more palatial quarters. But the modest building had a feeling of perpetuity to it that the houses of the newly wealthy could not hope to imitate. The very pine trees set round it were gnarled and twisted with age, yet still green and growing.

Coming from young Rome, whose history was little more than legend even three centuries before his own time, Marcus had never quite gotten over the awe Videssos' long past raised in him. To him, the ancient but vigorous trees were a good metaphor for the Empire as a whole.

When he said that aloud, Soteric laughed mirthlessly, saying, "So they are, for they look as if the first good storm would tear them out by the roots."

"They've weathered a few to come this far," Marcus said. Soteric brushed the comment away with a wave of his hand.

The door opened before them; a high-ranking ecclesiastic was ushering out a Videssian noble in white linen trousers and a tunic of lime-green silk. "I trust his Sanctity was able to help you, my lord Dragatzes?" the priest asked courteously.

"Yes, I think so," Dragatzes replied, but his black-browed scowl was not encouraging. He strode past Marcus, Helvis, and Soteric without seeming to notice them.

Nor did the priest pay them any heed until his gaze, which was following Dragatzes' retreating back, happened to fall on them. "Is there something I can do to help you?" he said. His tone was doubtful; Helvis and her brother were easy to recognize as Namdaleni, while Marcus himself looked more like a man of the Duchy than a Videssian. There was no obvious reason for folk such as them to visit the head of a faith they did not share.

And even after Marcus asked to speak with Balsamon, the priest at the door made no move to step aside. "As you must know, his Sanctity's calendar is crowded. Tomorrow would be better, or perhaps the next day. . ." Go away and don't bother coming back, Marcus translated.

"Who is it, Gennadios?" the patriarch's voice came from inside the residence. A moment later he appeared beside the other priest, clad not in his gorgeous patriarchal regalia but in a none too clean monk's robe of simple blue wool. Catching sight of the four outside his door, he let loose his rich chuckle. "Well, well, what have we here? A heathen and some heretics, to see me? Most honored, I am sure. Come in, I beg of you." He swept past the spluttering Gennadios to wave them forward.

"But, your Sanctity, in a quarter hour's time you are to see—" Gennadios protested, but the patriarch cut him off.

"Whoever it is, he'll wait. This is a fascinating riddle, don't you think, Gennadios? Why should unbelievers care to see me? Perhaps they wish to convert to our usages. That would be a great gain for Phos' true faith, don't you think? Or perhaps they'll convert *me*—and wouldn't that be a scandal, now?"

Gennadios gave his superior a sour look, clearly finding his humor in questionable taste. Soteric was staring at the patriarch in disbelief, Helvis in delight. Marcus had to smile, too; remembering his last meeting with Balsamon, he knew how much the prelate relished being outrageous.

Malric was in his mother's arms. As she walked by Balsamon, her son reached out for two good handsful of the patriarchal beard. Helvis stopped instantly, as much in alarm at what

* * *

bowed his way through the thick-packed
g Phos' High Temple. In his hand was a
rchment entitling him to one of the coveted
Temple itself to hear the patriarch Balsamon's
st had delivered it to the Roman barracks the
was sealed with the sky-blue wax that was the
the patriarch alone.

nd gear, Marcus drew some hard looks from the
e pushed by. A disproportionate number of them
e city toughs of the sort Scaurus had seen on the
met Phostis Apokavkos. They did not take kindly
rs at the best of times, but the sight of the Roman's
l pass was evidence enough for them that he stood
e regard of their well-loved prelate, and he had no
le making headway.

sian soldiers at the bottom of the broad stairways
up the Temple kept the mob from crowding rightful
ders out of their pews. They were nonplussed to find a
ary captain with a token of admisison, but stood aside
him pass. At the top of the stairs a priest relieved him of
rchment and lined through his name on a roll of ex-
d attenders. "May the words of our patriarch enlighten
" the priest said.

He enlightens me every time I hear him," Marcus replied.
e priest looked at him sharply, suspecting derision from this
nifest unbeliever, but the Roman meant what he said. See-
g that, the priest gave a curt nod and waved him into the
High Temple.

From the outside, Marcus had found the Temple rather
ugly, impressive for no other reason than sheer size. He was
used to the clean, spare architecture the Romans had borrowed
from Greece and found the Temple's heavy projecting but-
tresses clumsy, cluttered, and ponderous. Inside, though, its
architects had worked a miracle, and the tribune stood spell-
bound, wondering if he had been suddenly whisked to the
heaven Phos' followers looked to in the life to come.

The structure's basic plan was like that of Phos' main temple in Imbros: at its heart was a circular worship-area, surmounted by a dome, with rows of benches projecting off in
each of the cardinal directions. But Imbros' shrine was the

Balsamon might do as to keep him from being tugged with
her.

Her fright must have shown, for the patriarch laughed out
loud. "You know, my dear, I don't eat children—at least not
lately." He gently detached Malric's hands from their hold.
"You thought I was an old billy goat, didn't you?" he said,
poking the boy in the ribs. "Didn't you?" Malric nodded,
laughing in delight.

"What's your name, son?" the patriarch asked.

"Malric Hemond's son," Malric answered clearly.

"Hemond's son?" The smile slipped from Balsamon's face.
"That was a bad business, a very bad business indeed. You
must be Helvis, then," he said to Malric's mother. As she
nodded, Marcus was impressed—not for the first time—with
the patriarch's knowledge and memory of detail. Balsamon
turned to Helvis' brother. "I don't think I know you, sir."

"No reason you should," Soteric agreed. "I'm Soteric
Dosti's son; Helvis is my sister."

"Very good," Balsamon nodded. "Come with me, all of
you. Gennadios, do tell my next visitor I'll be somewhat delayed, won't you?"

"But—" Realizing the uselessness of any protest he might
make, Gennadios gave a sharp, short nod.

"My watchdog," Balsamon sighed as he led his visitors to
his chambers. "Strobilos set him on me years ago, to keep an
eye on me. I suppose Mavrikios would take him away if I
asked, but somehow I've never bothered."

"It must amuse you to bait the ill-humored fool, besides,"
Soteric said. Marcus had thought the same thing, but not in
the cruel way the Namdalener said it.

Helvis laid her hand on her brother's arm, but Balsamon
did not seem disturbed. "He's right, you know," the patriarch
told her. He looked musingly at Soteric, murmuring, "Such a
pretty boy, to have such sharp teeth." Soteric flushed; Marcus
was reminded that the patriarch could care for himself in any
battle of wits.

Balsamon's audience room was even more crowded with
books than Apsimar's had been back at Imbros, and far less
orderly in the bargain. Volumes leaned drunkenly against the
shabby chairs that looked like castoffs from the Academy's

refectory. Others jammed shelves, swallowed tables, and did their best to make couches unusable for mere human beings.

Peeping out from the few spaces parchment did not cover was a swarm of ivories, some no bigger than a fingernail, others the size of a big man's arm. They were comical, ribald, stately, furious, what have you, and all carved with a rococo extravagance of line alien to the Videssian art Scaurus had come to know.

"You've spied my vice, I fear," Balsamon said, seeing the tribune's eye roam from one figurine to the next, "and another, I admit unjust, cause for my resentment against Yezd. These are all the work of the Kingdom of Makuran that was; under its new masters, the craft does not flourish. Not much does, save only hatred.

"But you didn't come to hear me speak of ivories," the patriarch said, clearing things enough for them to sit. "Or if you did, I may indeed become a Gambler, from sheer gratitude." As usual, what would have been a provoking name in another's mouth came without offense from his. His hands spread in a gesture of invitation. "What do you think I can do for you?"

Helvis, Soteric, and Marcus looked at each other, none of them anxious to begin. After a few seconds of silence, Soteric took the plunge, blunt as always. "We've had reports the people of Videssos are thinking of violence against us because of our faith."

"That would be unfortunate, particularly for you," Balsamon agreed. "What am I to do about it? And why ask me to do anything, for that matter? Why should I? After all, I am hardly of your faith." He pointed at the patriarchal robe draped untidily over a chair.

Soteric drew in a breath to damn the prelate for being the stiff-necked fool he'd thought him, but Helvis caught the gleam of amusement in Balsamon's eye her brother missed. She, too, waved at the crumpled regalia. "Surely your flock respects the office you hold, if nothing else," she said sweetly.

Balsamon threw back his head and laughed till the tears came, clutching his big belly with both hands until his wheezes subsided. "One forgets what a sharp blade irony has —until stuck with it, that is," he said, still chuckling. "Yes, of

course I'll pour w
ism enough to c
else, you deserve
those who could be

The patriarch tur
"What are you, the sile

"If you like." Unlike
no intention of being draw
knowing it could only have

Helvis thought he had
policy, and came to his defe
trouble brewing," she said.

"You have good sources, my
the Roman, "but then I already
that was your role here—it's too
islanders to have caught the smel
working on this sermon more than a

"What?" Marcus shouted, jolted
solved to maintain. Soteric and Helvis
had been almost asleep in his mother's
sudden noise, he began to cry. Helvis ca
cally, but most of her attention was still on

"Give me some credit for wits, my you
patriarch smiled. "It's a poor excuse for a pri
know what his people are thinking. More tha
called me a poor excuse for a priest, but that was

He rose, escorting his astounded guests to a d
from the one they'd used to enter. "It would be best
this way," he said. "Gennadios was right, as he all
is—I do have another visitor coming soon, one wh
blink at the company some of you keep."

Thick hedges screened the side door from the front o
patriarchal residence. Peering through the greenery, Mar
saw Gennadios bowing to Thorisin Gavras. Balsamon w
right—the Sevastokrator would not be pleased to see the trib
une with two Namdaleni.

"Right?" Soteric exclaimed when Scaurus remarked on it. The islander was still shaking his head in wonder. "Is he ever wrong?"

work of a not very gifted child when compared to this great jewel of a building.

First and most obvious, the craftsmen of the imperial capital had the advantage of far greater resources to lavish on their creation. The High Temple's benches were not of serviceable ash but sun-blond oak, waxed and polished to glowing perfection and inset with ebony, fragrant red sandalwood, thin layers of semi-precious stones, and whole sheets of shimmering mother of pearl. Gold leaf and silver foil ran riot through the Temple, reflecting soft sheets of light into its furthest recesses. Before the central altar stood the patriarch's throne. For Balsamon that throne alone should have made the High Temple a place of delight, for its tall back was made up of a score of relief-carved ivory panels. Scaurus was too far away to see their detail but sure only the best was tolerated in this place.

He tried to calculate what sum the erection of this incredible edifice must have consumed. His mind, however, dazzled by this Pelion on Ossa of wonders, could make no coherent guess, but only continue to marvel at the prodigies his eyes reported.

Dozens of columns, sheathed in glistening moss agate, lined the Temple's four outthrusting wings. Their acanthus capitals, while more florid than the ones Marcus was familiar with, were in keeping with the extravagance of the Temple as a whole. Its interior walls were of purest white marble, turquoise, and, at east and west, pale rose quartz and orange-red sard, reproducing the colors of Phos' sky.

Halfway up the eastern wall was a niche reserved for the imperial family. A screen of elaborate filigreework drawn around the enclosure allowed Emperors and their kin to see without being seen themselves.

For all the treasure lavished on the Temple, it was its splendid design that emerged triumphant. Columns, walls, arches, ancillary semidomes—all smoothly led the eye up to the great dome, and that was a miracle in itself.

It seemed to float in midair, separated from the real world echoingly far below by flashing beams of sunlight streaming in through the many windows which pierced its base. So bulky from the outside, it was light, soaring, graceful—almost disembodied—when seen from within. It took a distinct effort of will to think of the tremendous weight that freestanding dome represented, and of the massive vaults and piers on which it rested. Easier by far to believe it light as a soap-bubble, and so delicately attached to the rest of the Temple that the faintest breeze might send it drifting away and leave Phos' shrine open to the air.

The play of light off the dome's myriad tesserae of gold-backed glass further served to disembody it, and further emphasized the transcendence of Phos' image at its very zenith. The Videssians limned their god in many ways: kind creator, warrior against the darkness, bright youth, or, as here, severe almighty judge. This Phos watched over his congregation with a solemn yet noble face and eyes so all-seeing they seemed to follow Scaurus as he moved beneath them. Videssos' god held his right hand upraised in blessing, but in his left was the book wherein all good and evil were recorded. Justice he would surely mete out, but mercy? The tribune could not find it in those awesome eyes.

More than a trifle daunted, he took a seat. He could not help sneaking glances toward the stern omnipotence high above and noted hard-faced Videssian nobles, who must have seen that Phos hundreds of times, doing the same thing. It was, quite simply, too powerful to ignore.

The Temple filled steadily; latecomers grumbled as they slid into seats far from the central altar. Yet the floor sloped almost imperceptibly down toward the center, and no one was denied a view.

Soteric strode in, wearing his dignity as proudly as the wolfskin cape and tight breeches that marked him for a Nam-dalener. Catching Scaurus' eye, he sketched a salute. But even his sangfroid showed signs of cracking when he locked eyes with the god in the dome. Under the weight of that gaze his shoulders' proud set lowered a touch, and he sat with evident relief. Marcus did not think less of him for it; he would have been beyond humanity's pale to remain unmoved by first sight of that omniscient, commanding frown.

The low mutter of conversation in the Temple died away as a choir of blue-robed monks filed in to range themselves round the altar. Joined by their audience and the pure tones of handbells from behind the tribune, they sang a hymn in praise of Phos.

Marcus had to content himself with listening, as he did not

know the words. Nor did listening profit him much, for the canticle was in so archaic a dialect of Videssian that he could understand only a word here and there. A trifle bored, he wanted to crane his neck rudely to watch the bell players perform; he forbore only with reluctance. They were wonderfully skilled, their music clean and simple enough to appeal even to the tribune.

The High Temple's thick walls had muffled the noise of the crowd outside. As the hymn's last sweet notes faded, the throng's clamor swelled, growing like the roar of the surf when the tide walked up the beach. All questions as to the reason for the increasing uproar disappeared when Balsamon, preceded by a pair of censer-swinging acolytes, came into the Temple. His face was wreathed in smiles as he made his way toward the altar.

Everyone rose at first sight of the patriarch. Out of the corner of his eye Marcus caught a flicker of motion from behind the screen guarding the imperial family's box. Even the Emperor paid homage to Phos' representative, at least here in the Temple, the heart of Phos' domain on earth.

The tribune would have sworn Balsamon winked at him as he walked past. He doubted himself a second later; with every step the patriarch took toward his throne, he assumed a heavier mantling of distinction. He did not contradict the figure he cut in private, but there was more to him than his private self.

He sank into the patriarchal throne with a silent sigh. Marcus had to remind himself that Balsamon was not a young man. The patriarch's mind and spirit were so vital it was hard to remember his body might not always answer.

Balsamon pushed himself up out of the throne in less than a minute; the packed Temple had remained on its feet for him. He raised his hands to the mighty image of his god on high and, joined by his entire congregation, intoned the prayer Marcus had first heard from the lips of Neilos Tzimiskes northeast of Imbros, though of course he had not understood it then: "We bless thee, Phos, Lord with the right and good mind, by thy grace our protector, watchful beforehand that the great test of life may be decided in our favor."

Through the murmured *Amens* that followed, Scaurus heard Soteric firmly add, "On this we stake our very souls." Glares flashed at the Namdalener from throughout the Temple, but he stared back in defiance—that the men of the Empire chose to leave their creed incomplete was no reason for him to do likewise.

Balsamon lowered his arms; the worshippers took their seats once more, though necks still turned to catch sight of the bold heretic in their midst. Marcus expected the patriarch, no matter how forbearant his personal beliefs were, to take some public notice of Soteric's audacity.

And so, indeed, he did, but hardly in the way the Roman had looked for. Balsamon looked to the Namdalener almost in gratitude. "'On this we stake our very souls,'" he repeated quietly. His eyes darted this way and that, taking the measure of those who had stared hardest at Soteric. "He's right, you know. We do."

The patriarch tapped gently on the top of his throne's ivory back; his smile was ironic. "No, I am not speaking heresy. In its most literal sense, the Namdalener's addition to our creed is true. We have all staked our souls on the notion that, in the end, good shall triumph over evil. Were that not so, we would be as one with the Yezda, and this Temple would not be a place of quiet worship, but a charnel house where blood would flow as does our wine and, instead of incense, the stinking smoke of scorched flesh would rise to heaven."

He looked about him, defying anyone to deny his words. Some of his listeners shifted in their seats, but no one spoke. "I know what you are thinking but will not say," the patriarch continued: "'That's not what the cursed barbarian means by it!'" He brought his voice down to a gruff baritone, a parody of half the Videssian officers in the audience.

"And you're right." His tones were his own again. "But the question still remains: When we and the men of the Duchy quarrel at theology, when we damn each other and fling anathemas across the sea like stones, who gains? The Phos we all revere? Or does Skotos, down there in his frozen hell, laugh to see his enemies at strife with one another?

"The saddest part of the disagreement between us is that our beliefs are no further apart than two women in the streets. For is it not true that, while orthodoxy is indeed my doxy, heterodoxy is no more than my neighbor's doxy?" Balsamon's listeners gaped in horror or awestruck admiration, each according to his own temperament.

The patriarch became serious once more. "I do not hold to the Wager of Phos, as do the islanders—you all know that, even those who like me none too well. I find the notion childish and crude. But by our standards, the Namdaleni *are* childish and crude. Is it any wonder they have a doctrine to fit their character? Merely because I think them mistaken, must I find them guilty of unpardonable crimes?"

His voice was pleading as he looked from one face to the next. The noise of the crowd outside the Temple had died away; Marcus could hear a great-voiced priest reading the patriarch's words to the multitude.

Balsamon resumed, "If the men of the Duchy have their faith founded on true piety—and that, no reasonable man could doubt—and if they grant us our customs in our own land, what cause have we to worry? Would you argue with your brother while a thief was at the door, especially if he'd come to help hold that thief at bay? Skotos is welcome to the man who'd answer yes.

"Nor are we Videssians without blame in this senseless squabble over the nature of our god. Our centuries of culture have given us, I fear, conceit to match our brilliance. We are splendid logic-choppers and fault-finders when we think we need to criticize our neighbors, but oh! how we bawl like branded calves when they dare return the favor.

"My friends, my brothers, my children, if we stretch out our arms in charity, even so little charity as would hardly damage the soul of a tax-collector—" No matter how solemn the moment, Balsamon would have his joke, and the sudden, startled laughter from outside when the reader reached it showed it had struck its intended audience. "—surely we can overlook disagreements and build goodwill. The seeds are there—were it otherwise, why would the men of Namdalen sail from overseas to aid us against our foe? They deserve our grateful thanks, not tumult readied against them."

The patriarch looked about one last time, begging, willing his listeners to reach for something bigger than themselves. There was a moment of stony silence before the applause began. And when at last it came, it was not the torrent Balsamon—and Scaurus—would have wished for. Here a man clapped, there another, off to one side several more. Some looked sour even as they applauded, honoring the patriarch but at best tolerating the message for the sake of the man.

Mavrikios was not one of those. He had risen and pushed aside the ornamental grillwork, loudly acclaiming Balsamon. At his side, also clapping, was his daughter Alypia. Thorisin Gavras was nowhere to be seen.

Marcus found a moment to worry over the Sevastokrator's absence. He could not recall seeing the two Gavrai together since their unfortunate meeting at dice. One more thing to plague the Emperor, he thought. It was a dreadful time for Mavrikios to be at odds with his peppery brother.

And not even the Emperor's open approval could make the notables in the High Temple warm to Balsamon's sermon. The same confused, halfhearted applause came from the larger audience outside. Marcus remembered what Gorgidas had said; even the patriarch had trouble turning the city from the direction it had chosen.

He did win some measure of success. When Soteric emerged from the High Temple, no one snarled at him. Indeed, a couple of people seemed to have taken Balsamon's words to heart, for they shouted "Death to the Yezda!" at the mercenary. Soteric grinned savagely and waved his sword in the air, which won him a few real cheers.

Such lukewarm victory left him dissatisfied. He turned to Scaurus, grumbling, "I thought that when the patriarch spoke, everyone leaped to do as he said. And by what right does he call the men of the Duchy children? One fine day, we'll show him the sort of children we are."

Marcus soothed his ruffled feathers. Having expected no improvement in the situation, the tribune was pleased with whatever he got.

Back at the Roman barracks that night, Scaurus did some hard thinking about Soteric. Helvis' brother could be alarming. He was, if anything, more headstrong than Thorisin Gavras—and that was saying something. Worse, he lacked the Sevastokrator's easy charm. Soteric was always in deadly earnest. Yet there was no denying his courage, his energy, his military skill, or even his wit. The tribune sighed. People were as they were, not as he wished they'd be, and it was stupid—especially for someone who thought himself a Stoic —to expect them to be different.

Nevertheless, he recalled the adage he'd mentally applied to Soteric when the islander proposed seizing Videssos in despite of the whole imperial army. He sought Gorgidas. "Who was it," he asked the Greek, "who said, 'Whom the gods would destroy, they first make mad'? Sophokles?"

"Merciful Zeus, no!" Gorgidas exclaimed. "That could only be Euripides, though I forget the play. When Sophokles speaks of human nature, he's so noble you wish his words were true. Where Euripides finds truth, you wish he hadn't."

The tribune wondered whose play he'd watched that afternoon.

IX

THE FELLOW-FEELING BALSAMON LABORED SO VALIANTLY TO create crumbled, as things would have it, under the fury of an outraged section of his own clergy—the monks. All too few had Nepos' compassion or learning; most were arrogant in their bigotry. From their monasteries they swarmed forth like angry bees to denounce their patriarch's call for calm and to rouse Videssos once more to hatred.

Marcus was leading a couple of Roman maniples back from the practice field when he found his way blocked by a large crowd avidly taking in one such monk's harangue. The monastic, a tall thin man with a pocked face and fiery eyes, stood on an upended crate in front of a cheese merchant's shop and screamed out his hatred of heresy to everyone who would listen.

"Whoever tampers with the canons of the faith sells—no, gives!—his soul to the ice below! It is Phos' own holy words the foul foreigners pervert with their talk of wagers. They seek to seduce us from the way of truth into Skotos' frigid embrace, and our great patriarch—" In his rage, he fairly spat the word "—abets them and helps the demon spread his couch.

"For I tell you, my friends, there is, there can be, no compromise with evil. Corrupters of the faith lead others to the doom they have chosen for themselves, as surely as one rotten pear will spoil the cask. Balsamon prates of toleration—will he next tolerate a temple to Skotos?" The monk made "tolerate" into an obscenity.

His voice grew shriller yet. "If the eastern barbarians will

186

not confess the truth of our faith, drive them from the city, I say! They are as much to be feared as the Yezda—more, for they wear virtue's mask to hide their misbelief!"

The audience he had built up shouted its agreement. Fists waved in the air; there were cries of "Dirty barbarians!" and "The pox take Namdalen!"

"We may be having to break their heads to get through, if himself pushes the fire up any more," Viridovix said to Marcus.

"If we do, we'll set the whole city ablaze," the tribune answered. But he could see his men loosening swords in their scabbards and taking a firmer grip on the staves they were carrying in lieu of spears.

Just then the monk looked over the heads of the throng before him and caught sight of the Romans' unfamiliar gear. He probably would not have recognized a true Namdalener had he seen one, but in his passion any foreigner would serve. He stretched out a long bony finger at the legionaries, crying, "See! It is the men of the Duchy, come to cut me down before my truth can spread!"

"No, indeed!" Marcus shouted as the crowd whirled to face the Romans. Behind him he heard Gaius Philippus warning, "Whether the mob does or not, I'll have the head of the first man who moves without orders!"

"What then?" the monk asked Scaurus suspiciously. The crowd was spreading out and edging forward, readying itself for a rush.

"Can't you tell by looking? We're the surveying party for that temple to Skotos you were talking about—do you know where it's supposed to go?"

The monk's eyes bulged like a freshly boated bream's. The members of the would-be mob stopped where they stood, gawping at the Roman's insolence. Scaurus watched them closely—would they see the joke or try to tear the Romans to pieces for blasphemy?

First one, then another, then three more in the crowd burst into guffaws. In an instant the whole fickle gathering was shrieking with laughter and running forward, not to attack the legionaries, but to praise their leader's wit. Suddenly deserted by his audience, the monk, with a last malice-filled glance at

Scaurus, clambered down from his makeshift podium and disappeared—to spread his hatred elsewhere, Marcus was sure.

That, though, left his former throng discontented. The monastic had entertained them, and they expected the same from Scaurus. The silence stretched embarrassingly; with the tribune's one quip gone, his mind seemed blank.

Viridovix filled the breach in magnificent style, bursting into a borderer's song about fighting the cattle-thieves from Yezd. Only Marcus' thorough lack of interest in music had kept him from noticing what a fine voice Viridovix owned. Even his Gallic accent brought song to his speech. Someone in the crowd had a set of pipes; the Celt, the Videssians, and those Romans who knew the tune's words sang it through at the top of their lungs.

When it was done, one of the city men began another ditty, a ribald drinking song everyone in the crowd seemed to know. More legionaries could sing along with this one; Marcus himself had spent enough time in taverns to learn the chorus: "The wine gets drunk, but you get drunker!"

After two or three more songs it seemed as if the Romans and Videssians had been friends forever. They mingled easily, swapping names and stories. Marcus had no trouble continuing back to the barracks. A couple of dozen Videssians walked most of the way with the legionaries; every few blocks someone would think of a new song, and they would stop to sing it.

Once inside their hall at last, four of Scaurus' men discovered their belt pouches had been slit. But even Gaius Philippus, who under most conditions would have gone charging back into the city after the thieves, took the loss philosophically. "It's a small enough price to pay for dousing a riot," he said.

"Small enough for you, maybe," one of the robbed legionaries muttered, but so softly the centurion could not tell which. He snorted and gave them all an impartial glare.

"Sure and that was quick of you, to stop the shindy or ever it started," Viridovix said to Scaurus. "Was your honor not afraid it might set the spalpeens off altogether?"

"Yes," Marcus admitted, "but I didn't think we would be much worse off if it did. There wasn't time to reason with them, or much hope of it, for that matter—not with that madman of a monk egging them on. I thought I had to shock them, or make them laugh—by luck, I managed to do both at once. You helped a bit yourself, you know; you sing very well."

"Don't I, now?" the Celt agreed complacently. "Aye, there's nothing like a good tune to make a man forget the why of his ire. There's some fine songs in this Videssian tongue, too. That first one I sang reminds me of a ditty I knew at home—kine-stealing's almost a game with us, for pride and honor's sake, and we're fond of singing over it.

"Or we were," he added bleakly. For a rare moment, he let Marcus see the loneliness he usually hid so well.

Touched, the tribune reached out to clasp his shoulder. "You're among friends, you know," he said. It was true—there was not a Roman who had anything but liking for their former foe.

Viridovix knew that, too. "Aye," he said, tugging at his long mustaches, "and glad I am of it, but there's times when it's scarce enough." He said something in his own tongue, then shook his head. "Even in my ears the Celtic speech grows strange."

The riots against Namdalen began in earnest the next day, incited, as Marcus had feared, by the monks. The day was one sacred to Phos. Processions of worshippers marched through the streets carrying torches and gilded spheres and discs of wood as they hymned their god. As the tribune learned much later, one such parade was wending its way down Videssos' chief thoroughfare—the locals, with their liking for simple names, called it Middle Street—when it happened to pass a small temple where the Namdaleni were celebrating the holiday with their own rites.

Seeing a party of islanders enter the schismatic chapel infuriated the monks heading the procession. "Root out the heretics!" they cried. This time no jests or soft words distracted their followers. Phos' torches torched Phos' temple; believer slew believer, believing him benighted. And when the Namdaleni sallied forth from their smoke, as brave men would, Videssian blood, too, crimsoned the cobbles of Middle Street.

The mob, made brave only by numbers, was rabid when a few from among those numbers fell. "Revenge!" they screamed, ignoring their own guilt, and went ravening through the city for Namdaleni to destroy. As riots will, this one quickly grew past its prime purpose. Burning, looting, and rape were sports too delightful to be reserved for the islanders alone; before long, the swelling mob extended their benefits to natives of the city as well. Nevertheless, the men of the Duchy remained chief targets of the rioters' attention.

The mob's distant baying and the black pillars of smoke shooting into the sky brought news of the tumult to the Romans. Scaurus was always thankful the city did not erupt until noon, Phos' most auspicious hour. The early-rising legionaries had already finished their drill and returned to the palace complex before the storm broke. It could have gone hard for them, trapped in a labyrinth the Videssian rioters knew far better than they.

At first Scaurus thought the outbreak minor, on the order of the one that had followed his own encounter with Avshar's necromancy. A few battalions of native soldiers had sufficed to put down that disturbance. The tribune watched the Videssians tramping into action, armed for riot duty with clubs and blunt-headed spears. Within two hours they were streaming back in disarray, dragging dead and wounded behind them. Their smoke-blackened faces showed stunned disbelief. Beyond the palace complex, Videssos was in the hands of the mob.

Sending inadequate force against the rioters proved worse than sending none. The howling pack, buoyed up by the cheap victory, grew bolder yet. Marcus had gone up onto the roof of the Roman barracks to see what he could of the city and its strife; now he watched knots of ill-armed men pushing through the lush gardens of the palace quarter itself, on the prowl for robbery or murder.

Still far away but terribly clear, he could hear the mob's battle cry: "Dig up the bones of the Namdaleni!" The call was a bit of lower-class city slang; when Videssos' thieves and pimps were displeased with someone, they wished him an unquiet grave. If the Roman needed further telling, that rallying-cry showed him who the rioters were.

Scaurus put a maniple of battle-ready legionaries around his soldier's barracks. Whether the bared steel they carried deterred the mob or the Videssians simply had no quarrel with the Roman force, no rioters tested them.

Sunset was lurid; it seemed grimly appropriate for Phos' symbol to be reduced to a ball of blood disappearing through thick smoke.

Like dragons' tongues, flames licked into the night sky. In their island of calm the Romans passed the hours of darkness at full combat alert. Marcus did not think the Videssians would use his men against the rioters, judging from their past practice, but he was not nearly so sure the mob would keep giving immunity to the legionaries.

The tribune stayed on his feet most of the night. It was long after midnight before he decided the barracks probably would not be attacked. He sought his pallet for a few hours of uneasy sleep.

One of his troopers roused him well before dawn. "What is it?" he asked blearily, only half-awake. Then he jerked upright as full memory returned. "Are we under assault?"

"No, sir. It's almost too quiet, what with the ruction all around us, but there's no trouble here. Nephon Khoumnos says he needs to speak with you; my officer thinks it sounds important enough for me to get you up. If you like, though, I'll send him away."

"Who's out there? Glabrio?"

"Yes, sir."

Marcus trusted that quiet young centurion's judgment and discretion. "I'll see Khoumnos," he said, "but if you can, hold him up for a couple of minutes to let me get my wits together."

"I'll take care of it," the legionary promised and hurried away. Scaurus splashed water on his face from the ewer by his bed, ran a comb through his sleep-snarled hair, and tried to shake a few of the wrinkles from his cloak before putting it on.

He could have omitted his preparations, sketchy as they were. When the Roman guardsman led Nephon Khoumnos into the barracks hall, a glance was enough to show that the Videssian officer was a man in the last stages of exhaustion. His usual crisp stride had decayed into a rolling, almost drunken gait; he seemed to be holding his eyes open by main force. With a great sigh, he collapsed into the chair the Romans offered him.

"No, no wine, thank you. If I drink I'll fall asleep, and I can't yet." He yawned tremendously, knuckling his red-tracked eyes at the same time. "Phos, what a night!" he muttered.

When he sat without elaborating, Marcus prompted him, "How are things out there?"

"How do you think? They're bad, very bad. I'd sooner be naked in a wood full of wolves than an honest man on the streets tonight. Being robbed is the best you could hope for; it gets worse from there."

Gaius Philippus came up in time to hear him. Blunt as always, he said, "What have you been waiting for? It's only a mob running wild, not an army. You have the men to squash it flat in an hour's time."

Khoumnos twisted inside his shirt of mail, as if suddenly finding its weight intolerable. "I wish things were as simple as you make them."

"I'd better turn around," Gaius Philippus said, "because I think you're about to bugger me."

"Right now I couldn't raise a stand for the fanciest whore in the city, let alone an ugly old ape like you." Khoumnos drew a bark of laughter from the senior centurion, but was abruptly sober again. "No more could I turn the army loose in the city. For one thing, too many of the men won't try very hard to keep the mob from the Namdaleni—they have no use for the islanders themselves."

"It's a sour note when one part of your fornicating army won't help the next," Gaius Philippus said.

"That's as may be, but it doesn't make it any less true. It cuts both ways, though: the men of the Duchy don't trust Videssian soldiers much further than they do any other Videssians."

Scaurus felt like turning around himself; he had caught Nephon Khoumnos' drift, and did not like it. The imperial officer confirmed the tribune's fears with his next words. "In the whole capital there are only two bodies of troops who have the respect of city-folk and Namdaleni alike: the Halogai, and your men. I want to use you as a screen to separate the mob and the easterners, while Videssian troops bring the city as a whole under control. With you and the Halogai keeping the main infection cordoned off, the riot should lose force quickly."

The tribune was anything but eager to use his troops in the street-fighting that wracked Videssos. He had already learned the mercenary commander's first lesson: his men were his capital, and not to be spent lightly or thrown away piecemeal in tiny, meaningless brawls down the city's back alleys. Unfortunately, what Khoumnos was proposing made sense. Without the excitement of heretic-hunting, riot for the sake of riot would lose much of its appeal. "Are you ordering us into action, then?" he demanded.

Had Nephon Khoumnos given him an imperious yes, he probably would have refused him outright—in the city's confusion, Khoumnos could not have enforced the order. But the Videssian was a soldier of many years' standing and knew the ways of mercenaries better than Scaurus himself. He had also come to know the tribune accurately.

"Ordering you?" he said. "No. Had I intended to give you orders, I could have sent them through a spatharios. I came to ask a favor, for the Empire's sake. Balsamon put it better than I could—the fight against Yezd makes everything else trivial beside it. No matter what the idiot monks say, that's true. That fight can't go forward without peace here. Will you help bring it?"

"Damn you," Scaurus said tiredly, touched on the weak spot of his sense of duty. There were times, he thought, when a bit of simple selfishness would be much sweeter than the responsibility his training had drilled into him. He considered how much of his limited resources he could afford to risk.

"Four hundred men," he decided. "Twenty squads of twenty. No units smaller than that, unless my officers order it—I won't have a solitary trooper on every corner for the young bucks to try their luck with."

"Done," Khoumnos said at once, "and thank you."

"If I said you were welcome, I'd be a liar." Shifting into Latin, Scaurus turned to Gaius Philippus. "Help me find the men I'll need. Keep things tightly buttoned here while we're gone and in the name of the gods don't throw good men after bad if we come to grief. Even if we should, you'd still have better than a cohort left; that's a force to reckon with, in this world of useless infantry."

"Hold up, there. What's this talk about you not coming back, and what I'd have if you didn't?" the centurion said. "I'm going out there myself."

Marcus shook his head. "Not this time, my friend. I have to go—it's by my orders we're heading into this, and I will not send men into such a stew without sharing it with them. Too many officers will be out in the city as is; someone here has to be able to pick up the pieces if a few of us don't come back. That's you, I fear. Curse it, don't make this harder than it is; I don't dare risk both of us at once."

On Gaius Philippus' face discipline struggled with desire and finally threw it to the mat. "Aye, sir," he said, but his toneless voice accented instead of concealed his hurt. "Let's get the men picked out."

The colloquy between Khoumnos, the tribune, and Gaius Philippus had been low-voiced, but once men were chosen to go out into Videssos and they began to arm themselves, all hope for quiet vanished. As Scaurus had feared, Viridovix woke up wildly eager to go into the city and fight.

The tribune had to tell him no. "They want us to stop the riot, not heat it further. You know your temper, Viridovix. Tell me truly, is that the task you relish?"

Marcus had to give the big Gaul credit; he really did examine himself, chewing on his mustaches as he thought. "A plague on you for a cruel, hard man, Marcus Aemilius Scaurus, and another for being right. What a cold world it is, where a man knows himself too hot-blooded to be trusted with the breaking of heads."

"You can stay here and wrangle with me," Gaius Philippus said. "I'm not going either."

"What? You?" Viridovix stared at him. "Foosh, man, it'd be the perfect job for you—for a good soldier, you're the flattest man ever I've met."

"Son of a goat," the centurion growled, and their long-running feud was on again. Scaurus smiled inside himself to hear them; each, he knew, would take out some of his disappointment on the other.

When the selection was done, and while the legionaries

chosen were readying themselves for action, the tribune asked Khoumnos, "Where are you sending us?"

The Videssian officer considered. "There's a lot of newly come Namdaleni in the southern harbor district, especially round the small harbor; you know, the harbor of Kontoskalion. My reports say the fighting has been vicious there—city people murdering islanders, and islanders murdering right back when the odds are in their favor. It's a running sore that needs closing."

"That's what we'll be there for, isn't it?" Marcus said. He made no effort to pretend an enthusiasm he did not feel. "The harbor district, you say? Southeast of here, isn't it?"

"That's right," Khoumnos agreed. He started to say more, but the tribune cut him off.

"Enough talk. All I want is to get this worthless job over. Soonest begun, soonest done. Let's be at it." He strode out of the barracks into the predawn twilight.

As the legionaries came to attention, he walked to the head of their column. There were a couple of warnings he felt he had to give his men before he led them into action. "Remember, this is riot duty, not combat—I hope. We want the least force needed to bring order, not the most, lest the riot turn on us. Don't spear someone for throwing a rotten cabbage at you.

"That's one side of things. Here's the other: if your life is on the line, don't spend it; if the choice is between you and a rioter, you count ten thousand times as much, so don't take any stupid chances. We're all the Romans there are here and all the Romans who ever will be here. Do your job, do what you have to do, but use your your heads."

He knew as he gave it the advice was equivocal, but it accurately reflected his mixed feelings over the mission Khoumnos had given him. As the sun rose red through the city's smoke, he said, "Let's be off," and marched his men away from their barracks, out of the palace complex, and into the strife-torn heart of the city.

Most times he savored Videssos' early mornings, but not today. Smoke stung his eyes and stank in his nostrils. Instead of the calls of gulls and songbirds, the dominant sounds in the city were looters' cries, the crack of glass and splintering of boards as houses and shops were plundered, and the occasional sliding rumble of a fire-gutted building crashing down.

The legionaries stayed in a single body on their way to the harbor of Kontoskalion. Scaurus did not intend to risk his men before he had to and reckoned the sight of four hundred armored, shielded warriors tramping past would be enough to make any mob think twice.

So it proved; aside from curses and a few thrown stones, no one interfered with the Romans as they marched. But theirs was a tiny, moving bubble of order drifting through chaos. Videssos, it seemed, had abandoned law's constraints for an older, more primitive rule: to the strong, the quick, the clever go the spoils.

Where there were few Namdaleni to hunt, the riot lost part of its savagery and became something of a bizarre carnival. Three youths pulled velvet-covered pillows from a shop and tossed them into the arms of a waiting, cheering crowd. Marcus saw a middle-aged man and woman dragging a heavy couch down a sidestreet, presumably toward their home.

A younger pair, using their clothes for padding, made love atop a heap of rubble; they, too, were cheered on by a rapt audience. The Romans passing by stared and shouted with as much enthusiasm as any Videssians. They clattered their shields against their greaves to show their enjoyment. When the couple finished, they sprang to their feet and scampered away, leaving their clothes behind.

In madness' midst, the occasional island of normality was strange in itself. Marcus bought a pork sausage on a bun from a vender plying his trade as if all were peaceful as could be. "Haven't you had any trouble?" the tribune asked as he handed the man a copper.

"Trouble? Why should I? Everyone knows me, they do. Biggest problem I've had is making change for all the gold I've got today. A thing like this is good for the city now and again, says I—it stirs things up, a tonic, like." And he was off, loudly crying his wares.

Two streets further south, the Romans came upon a double handful of corpses sprawled on the cobbles. From what could be seen through the blackened, congealed blood that covered them, some were Namdeleni while others had been city men. They were covered in little more than their blood; all the bodies, alien and citizen alike, had been stripped during the night.

Soon the sound of active combat came to the Romans' ears. "At a trot!" Scaurus called. His men loped forward. They rounded a corner to find four Namdaleni, two of them armed only with knives, trying to hold off what must have been three times their number of attackers. Another easterner was on the ground beside them, as were two shabbily dressed Videssians.

Their losses made the rioters less than enthusiastic about the fight they had picked. While the ones to the rear yelled, "Forward!" those at the fore hung back, suddenly leery of facing professional soldiers with weapons to hand.

The Videssians cried out in terror when they saw and heard the Romans bearing down on them. They turned to flee, throwing away their weapons to run the faster.

The men of the Duchy joyfully greeted their unexpected rescuers. Their leader introduced himself as Utprand Dagober's son. He was not a man Marcus had seen before; the tribune guessed he must be one of the newly come Namdalener mercenaries. His island accent was so thick he sounded almost like a Haloga. But if the tribune had trouble with his shades of meaning, there was no mistaking what Utprand wanted.

"Are you not after the devilings?" he demanded. "T'ree of my stout lads they kill already—we had the misfortune to be near their High Temple when they set on us and we've crawled through stinking alleys since, trying to reach our mates. Do for them, I say!" The other islanders still on their feet snarled agreement.

After some of the things he had seen in Videssos, Marcus was tempted to turn his men loose like so many wolves. Though it would do no good—and in the long run endless harm—it would be so satisfying. In this outburst the city folk had forfeited a great part of the respect he had come to feel for their state. He could also see the legionaries trembling to be unleashed.

He shook his head with regret, but firmly. "We were sent here to make matters better, not worse, and to form a cordon between you and the Videssians to let the riot burn itself out. It has to be so, you know," he said, giving Utprand the same argument he had used against Soteric. "If the imperial army moves against you with the mob, you're doomed, do what you will. Would you have us incite them to it?"

Utprand measured him, eyes pale in a gaunt, smoke-blackened face. "I never thought I could want to hate a clear-thinking man. Curse you for being right—it gripes my belly like a green apple that you are."

He and two of his men took up their fallen comrade and the dagger he had used in vain to defend himself. Marcus wondered where the dead man's sword might be and who would take the dagger to his kin. The three started toward their camp by the harbor. The fourth islander, Grasulf Gisulf's son, stayed behind with the Romans to point out the best places to seal off the harbor of Kontoskalion from the rest of the city.

The tribune posted his double squads where Grasulf recommended; most of them were stationed along major streets leading north and south. Scaurus had no reason to complain of Grasulf's choices. The Namdalener had an eye for a defensible position.

As he'd known he might have to, Marcus gave his under-officers leave to split their commands in half to cover more ground. "But I want no fewer than ten men together," he warned them, "and if you do divide your forces, stay in ear-shot of each other so you can rejoin quickly at need."

The Romans worked their way steadily west. They passed from a district of small shops, taverns, and cramped, untidy houses into a quarter inhabited by merchants who had made their fortunes at Videssos' harbors and still dwelt nearby. Their splendid homes were set off from the winding streets by lawns and gardens and warded further with tall fences or hedges of thorn. These had not always saved them from the mob's fury. Several were burned, looted wrecks. Others, though still standing, had hardly a pane of glass left in their windows. Many had an unmistakable air of desertion about them. Their owners, knowing how easily rioters' anger could turn from the foreign to the merely wealthy, had taken no chances and left for safety in the suburbs or on the western shore of the Cattle-Crossing.

By the time he had penetrated most of the way into this section of the city, Marcus had only a couple of units of legionaries still with him. He placed one between a temple of

Phos built solidly enough to double as a fortress and a mansion's outreaching wall. Along with Grasulf and his last twenty men, he pressed on to find a good spot to complete the cordon. The sound of the sea, never absent in Videssos, was sharp in his ears; a final good position should seal Videssians and Namdaleni from each other.

A spot quickly offered itself. Sometime during the night, the rioters had battered a rich man's wall to rubble and swarmed in to plunder his villa. The prickly hedge on the other side of the street still stood, unchallenged. "We can throw up a barricade here," the tribune said, "and stand off troubles from either side."

His men fell to work with the usual Roman thoroughness; a breastwork of broken brick and stone soon stretched across the roadway. Marcus surveyed it with considerable pride. Fighting behind it, he thought, the legionaries could stop many times their numbers.

That thought loosed another. The position the Romans had just made was so strong it did not really need twenty men to hold it. He could leave ten behind and push closer yet to the sea. It would be safe enough, he thought. This part of the city, unlike the turbulent portion he'd gone through before, seemed to be a no man's land of sorts. Most of the property owners had already fled, and, after the storm of looting passed by, neither the men of the city nor those of the Duchy were making much use of these ways to reach each other.

Taking heart in that observation, Marcus divided his small force in two. "I know just the place for you," Grasulf told him. He led the Romans to a crossroads between four mansions, each of them with strong outwalls at the edge of the street. The sea was very close now; along with its constant boom against the seawall, the tribune could hear individual waves slap-slapping against ships and pilings in the harbor of Kontoskalion.

The city was still troubled. New smokes rose into the noonday sky, and from afar came the sound of fighting. Scaurus wondered if the mob was battling Namdaleni, the Videssian army, or itself. He also wondered how long and how much it would take before Nephon Khoumnos—or, by rights, the Emperor himself—decided to teach the city's explosive populace a lesson it would remember.

In this momentary backwater it was easy to forget such things. The Romans stood to arms for the first couple of hours at their post, but when nothing more frightening came by than a stray dog and a ragpicker with a great bag of scraps slung over his back, the tribune did not see anything amiss in letting them relax a bit. While three men took turns on alert, the others sat in the narrow shade of the southern wall. They shared food and wine with Grasulf. The Namdalener puckered his lips at their drink's bite, though to Scaurus it was still too sweet.

Shadows were beginning to lengthen when the distant commotion elsewhere in Videssos grew suddenly louder. It did not take Marcus long to decide the new outbreak was due east of his position—and, from its swelling volume, heading west at an uncomfortable clip.

His men climbed to their feet at his command, grumbling over leaving their shadows for the sunshine's heat. As any good soldiers would, they quickly checked their gear, making sure their short swords were free in their scabbards and their shield straps were not so frayed as to give in action.

Videssos' twisting, narrow streets distorted sound in odd ways. The mob's roar grew ever closer, but until it was all but on him Scaurus did not think he was standing in its path. He was ready to rush his men to another Roman party's aid when the first rioters turned the corner less than a hundred yards away and spotted his little detachment blocking their path.

They stopped in confusion. Unlike the monk a few days before, they knew the warriors in front of them were not Namdaleni and had to decide whether they were foes.

Taking advantage of their indecision, Marcus took a few steps forward. "Go back to your homes!" he shouted. "We will not harm you if you leave in peace!" He knew how colossal the bluff was, but with any luck the mob would not.

For a heady second he thought he had them. A couple of men at the head of the throng, plump middle-class types who looked badly out of place among the rioters, turned as if to retreat. But then a fellow behind them, a greasy little weasel of a man, recognized Grasulf for what he was. "An islander!" he yelled shrilly. "They're trying to keep him from us!" The rioters rushed forward in a ragged battle line, brandishing a motley collection of makeshift or stolen weapons.

"Oh, bugger," one of the legionaries beside Marcus muttered as he drew his sword. The tribune had a sinking feeling in the pit of his stomach. More and more Videssians kept rounding that cursed corner. The Romans were professional soldiers, true, but as a professional Scaurus knew enough to mislike odds of seven or eight to one against him.

"To me, to me!" he shouted, wondering how many Romans he could draw to his aid and whether they would come too late and be swallowed up band after band by the mob.

Grasulf touched his arm. "Bring my sword home, if you can," he said. And with a wild cry the Namdalener charged forward against the mob. His blade swung in two glittering arcs; a pair of heads bounced from rioters' shoulders to the ground. Had his success gone on, he might have singlehandedly cowed his foes. But the same little sneakthief who had first spied him now darted up to plunge his dagger through the Namdalener's mail shirt and into his back. Grasulf fell; howling in triumph as they trampled his corpse, the mob stormed into the Romans.

The legionaries were well trained and heavily armed. They wore chain mail and greaves and carried their metal-faced semicylindrical shields. But their foes had such weight of numbers pushing them on that the Roman line, which by the nature of things could only be three men deep here, cracked almost at once. Then the fighting turned into a series of savage combats, in each of which one or two Romans were pitted against far too many opponents.

In his place at the legionaries' fore, Marcus had three men slam into him at once. One was dead as he hit, the tribune's sword twisting in his guts to make sure of the kill. But his momentum and that of his two living comrades bowled Scaurus to the ground. He pulled his shield over him and saved himself from the worst of the trampling as the mob passed over him, but it was only luck that no one aimed anything more deadly at him than a glancing blow from a club.

Striking out desperately in all directions with his sword, he managed to scramble to his feet after less than a minute on the cobblestones, to find himself alone in the midst of the mob. He slashed his way toward a wall that would cover his back. To judge from the noise and the flow of the action, the other Romans yet on their feet were doing the same.

A Videssian armed with a short hunting spear lunged at the tribune. His thrust was wide; its impetus propelled him into the Roman's shield. Marcus shoved as hard as he could. Taken off balance, the rioter stumbled backwards to trip up another of his fellows. Scaurus' sword made them both pay for the one's clumsiness.

Not all the rioters, luckily, were staying to fight the Romans. Some kept pressing west, in the hopes of finding Namdaleni to slaughter. Before long, only the mob's tail was still assailing the tribune. As the pressure against him eased, he began to hope he would live.

Through the din of fighting he heard the shouts and clatter of more Romans charging to the aid of the beleaguered squad. The rioters, without the discipline of real warriors, could not stand against their rush. Marcus started to call out to his men, but at that moment a stone rang off the side of his helmet, filling his head with a shower of silver sparks. As he staggered, his sword slipped from his hand. A rioter bent, snatched it up, and fled; newly armed or not, he had seen enough combat for this day.

Panic's chill wind blew through Marcus' brain. Had it been an ordinary Roman shortsword, he would have been glad enough to let the thief keep his booty. But this was the blade whose magic had brought him to this very world, the blade that stood against Avshar and all his sorceries, the blade that lent him strength. He threw his shield aside, drew his long-unused dagger, and gave chase.

He thanked his gods the fighting had almost passed him by. His hurled *scutum* decked one Videssian, a slash on his arm sent another reeling back. Then Scaurus was free of the crush and pounding after the sword-thief.

His pulse thudded in his ears as he ran; he would gladly have foregone the weight of his armor and his heavy boots. But his long strides were still closing the gap. The man bouncing along ahead of him was a short, fat fellow who seemed too prosperous to need to riot. Hearing himself pursued, he looked back over his shoulder and almost ran full tilt into a wall. He saved himself at the last instant and scurried down an alleyway, Marcus ten yards behind.

Strain as he would, the tribune could get no closer. Nor could his quarry shake free, though his zigzagging dash through backstreets and by-roads lost Scaurus in Videssos' maze.

The thief's knowledge of the city's ways was no more perfect than Marcus'. He darted halfway down an alley without realizing it was blind. Before he could mend his error, the tribune came panting up to cork the entrance.

Wiping the sweat from his face, the rotund thief brought his stolen sword up to the guard position. The awkward set of his feet and his tentative passes with the blade said he was no swordsman. Scaurus approached with caution anyhow. His opponent, after all, had three times his length of blade, clumsy or not.

He took another pace forward, saying, "I don't want to have to fight you. Lay my sword down and you can go, for all of me."

Scaurus never learned whether the other thought he spoke from cowardice and was thus emboldened, or whether he simply was afraid to be weaponless before the Roman. He leaped at Marcus, swinging the tribune's sword with a stroke that confirmed his ineptness. But even as Marcus' mind realized he was facing a tyro, his body responded with the motions long hours on the practice field had drilled into it. He ducked under the amateurish slash and stepped forward to drive his knife into his foe's belly.

The plump thief's mouth shaped a voiceless "Oh." He dropped the Roman's blade to clutch his wound with both hands. His eyes went wide, then suddenly showed only white as he sagged to the ground.

Marcus stooped to recover his sword. He felt no pride in his victory, rather self-disgust at having killed an opponent so little a match for him. He looked reproachfully down at the crumpled corpse at his feet. Why hadn't the fat fool had enough sense to bar his door and stay behind it, instead of playing at what he knew nothing about?

The tribune thought he could let his ears lead him back to the brawl between his man and the rioters, but retracing his path was not so simple. The winding streets kept leading himaway from the direction in which he needed to go, and that direction itself seemed to shift as he moved. The homes he walked by offered few clues to guide him. Their outer walls and hedges were so much alike that only a longtime resident of the neighborhood could have steered by them.

He was passing another not much different from the rest when he heard a scuffle from the far side of the wall. Scuffles today were a copper a handful; worrying about finding his way back to the Romans, Scaurus was on the point of ignoring this one until it was suddenly punctuated by a woman's scream.

The sound of a blow cut across it. "Quiet, bitch!" a rough male voice roared.

"Let her bleat," another replied, coldly callous. "Who's to hear, anyway?"

The wall was too high to see over and too high for a man encumbered by armor to hope to climb. Marcus' eye flashed to its gate. He ran at it, crashing into it with an iron-clad shoulder. It flew open, sending the tribune stumbling inside onto a wide expanse of close-trimmed grass.

The two men holding a woman pinned to that grass looked up in amazement as their sport was interrupted. One had hold of her bare shoulders; a ripped tunic lay nearby. The other was between her thrashing white legs, hiking her heavy skirt up over her waist.

The second man died as he was scrambling to his feet, Marcus' blade through his throat. The tribune had a moment's regret at giving him so easy an end, but then he was facing the dead man's comrade, who was made of sterner stuff. Though he looked a street ruffian, he carried a shortsword instead of a dagger, and from his first cut Scaurus saw he knew how to use it.

After that first slash failed to fell the Roman, his enemy chose a purely defensive fight and seemed to be looking for a chance to break and run. But when he tried to flee, the woman he had been holding down snaked out a wrist to trip him. Marcus ran the falling man through. Where he had regretted killing the miserable little fellow who ran off with his sword, now he felt nothing but satisfaction at ridding the world of this piece of human offal.

He knelt to wipe his blade on the dead man's shirt, then turned, saying, "Thank you, lass, the whoreson might have got away if you—" His mouth stayed open, but no more words emerged. The woman sitting up was Helvis.

She was staring at him, too, seeing for the first time who her rescuer was. "Marcus?" she said, as if in doubt. Then, sobbing wildly in reaction to the terror of a moment before, she ran to him. Of themselves, his arms tightened around her. The flesh of her back was very smooth and still cool from the touch of the grass to which she had been forced. She trembled under his hands.

"Thank you, oh, thank you," she kept repeating, her head pressed against his corseleted shoulder. A moment later she added, "There's so much metal about you—must you imprison me in an armory?"

Scaurus realized how tightly he was holding her to his armored front. He eased his grip a bit; she did not pull away, but still clung to him as well. "In the name of your Phos, what are you doing here?" the tribune demanded roughly. The stress of the moment made his concern sound angry. "I thought you safely back at your people's barracks by the palaces."

It was precisely because of Phos, he learned, that she was not at the Namdalener barracks. She had chosen to celebrate her god's holiday—was it only yesterday? Marcus wondered; that seemed impossible—by praying not at the temple near the barracks, but at another one here in the southern part of Videssos. It was a shrine popular with the Namdaleni, for it was dedicated to a holy man who had lived and worked on the island of Namdalen, though he was three hundred years dead before the northerners wrested his native land from the Empire.

Helvis continued, "When the riots started and the crowds were screaming, 'Dig up the Gamblers' bones!' I had no hope of getting back to my home through the streets. I knew my countrymen had an encampment by the harbor and decided to make for that. Last night I spent in a deserted house. When I heard the mob screaming down toward the harbor, I thought I should hide again.

"The far gate over there was open," she said, pointing. She ruefully went on, "I found out why all too soon. Those—" No word sufficed; she shuddered instead "—were ransacking the place, and I was just another lucky bit of loot."

"It's all right now," Scaurus said, stroking her tangled hair with the same easy motion he would have used to gentle a frightened horse. She sighed and snuggled closer. For the first time, he was actually aware of her half-clothed state and that their embrace was changing from one sort of thing to another altogether.

He bent his head to kiss the top of hers. Her hands stroked the back of his neck as he tilted her face up to his. He kissed her lips, her ear; his mouth trailed down her neck toward her uncovered breasts. Her skirt rustled as it slid over her hips and fell to the ground. His own coverings were more complicated, but he was free of them soon enough. He had a brief second of worry for his embattled men, but this once not all his discipline could have stopped him from sinking to the grass beside the woman waiting for him there.

There is almost always a feeling among first-time lovers, no matter how much they please each other, that their love will grow better as they come to know each other more. So it was here; there was fumbling, some awkwardness, as between any two people unsure of one another's likes. Despite that, though, for the tribune it was far sweeter than he had known before, and he was so close to his own time of joy he nearly did not notice the name Helvis cried as her nails dug into his back was not his own.

Afterward he would have liked nothing better than to lie beside her forever, wholly at peace with the world. But now the tuggings of his conscience were too strong to ignore. Already he felt guilt's first stir over the time he had spent pleasuring himself while his troopers fought. He tried to drown it with Helvis' lips but, as is ever the way, only watered it instead.

His armor had never felt more confining than when he redonned it now. He handed Helvis her slain attacker's shortsword, saying, "Wait for me, love. You'll be safer here, I think, even alone, than on the streets. I won't be long, I promise."

Another woman might have protested being left behind, but Helvis had seen combat and knew what Marcus was going to. She rose, ran her finger down his cheek to the corner of his mouth. "Yes," she said. "Oh, yes. Come back for me."

Like a man recovering from a debilitating fever, Videssos slowly came back to its usual self. The riots, as Khoumnos had predicted, died away after the Romans and Halogai succeeded in cordoning off the Namdaleni who were their focus. By the time a week had gone by, the city was nearly normal once more, save for the uncleared piles of rubble that showed where the mob had struck. Small, stubborn columns of smoke still rose from some of these, but the danger of great conflagrations was past.

Where the city was almost itself again, Scaurus' life changed tremendously in the couple of weeks following the riots. He and a party of his men had taken Helvis first to the Namdaleni based by the harbor of Kontoskalion and then, as Videssos began to calm, she was able to return to the islanders' barracks in the palace complex.

She did not stay there long, however. Their first unexpected union did not slake, but whetted, her appetite and the tribune's. It was only days before she and Marcus—and Malric—took quarters in one of the two halls the Romans reserved for partnered men.

While he was more eager to share her company than he had ever been for anyone else's, a few concerns still gave him pause. First and foremost in his mind was the attitude Soteric would take. The tribune had seen more than once how prickly Helvis' brother could be when he thought his honor touched. How would he react to the Roman's first taking his sister and then taking her away?

When he raised the question to Helvis, she disposed of it with a woman's practicality. "Don't trouble yourself over it. If anything needs saying, I'll say it; I doubt it will. You hardly seduced a blushing virgin, you know, and had you not been there, the dogs who had me likely would have slit my throat when they were too worn to have any other use for me. Dearest, your saving me will count for more with Soteric than anything else—and so it should."

"But—" Helvis stopped his protest with a kiss, but could not quiet his fretting so easily. Still, events proved her right. Her brother's gratitude for her rescue carried over to the rescuer as well. He treated Marcus like a member of his family, and his example carried over to the rest of the Namdaleni. They knew what the Romans had done for them in Videssos' turmoil; when the legionaries' commander fell in love with one of their women, it was yet another reason to treat him as one of themselves.

That problem solved, Marcus waited for the reaction of his own men to the new situation. There was some good-natured chaffing, for the Romans knew his acquiescence to their taking companions had been grudging, and here he was with one himself.

"Pay them no mind," Gaius Philippus said. "No one will care if you're bedding a woman, a boy, or a purple sheep, so long as you think with your head and not with your crotch." And after that bit of pungent but cogent advice the centurion went off to hone his troops once more.

It was, Scaurus found, a suggestion easier to give than to follow. He found himself wallowing in sensuality in a way unlike any he had known. Before, he was always moderate in venery—in vanished Mediolanum, in Caesar's army, and since his arrival in Videssos. When he needed release he would buy it, and he did not often seek the same woman twice. Now, with Helvis, he found himself making up for long denial and growing greedier of her with every night that passed.

She, too, took ever-increasing delight from their love. Hers was a simple, fierce desire; though she had looked at no man since Hemond's death, her body nonetheless craved what it had become accustomed to and reacted blissfully to its return. Marcus found he was sleeping more soundly than he had since he was a boy. It was lucky, he thought once, that Avshar's Khamorth had not come seeking him after he found Helvis. He surely would never have wakened at the nomad's approach.

Scaurus had wondered how Malric would adjust to the change in his life, but Helvis' son was still young enough to take almost anything in his stride. Before long he was calling the tribune "Papa" as often as "Marcus," which gave the Roman an odd feeling, half pride, half sorrow it was not so. The lad instantly became the legionaries' pet. There were few children around the barracks, and the soldiers spoiled them all. Malric picked up Latin with the incredible ease small children have.

There were days when the tribune almost forgot he was in a city arming for war. He wished there could be more of them; he had never been happier in his life.

X

"IT'S BLOODY WELL TIME," GAIUS PHILIPPUS SAID WHEN THE summons to the imperial council of war came. "The campaign should have started two months ago and more."

"Politics," Marcus answered. He added, "The riots didn't help, either. But for them, I think we'd be under way by now." With faint irony, he heard himself justifying the delays he had complained about not long before. He was much less anxious to begin than he had been then and knew why only too acutely. At the moment, it was as well such matters were not under his control.

The tribune had not been in the Hall of the Nineteen Couches since the night of his duel with Avshar. As always, the reception hall was couchless. A series of tables was joined end-to-end to form a line down its center. Atop the tables were maps of the Videssian army's proposed line of march; along them sat the leaders from every troop contingent in that army: Videssians, Khatrishers, nomadic Khamorth chieftains, Namdalener officers, and now the Romans too.

Mavrikios Gavras, as was his prerogative, sat at the head of the tables. Marcus was glad to see Thorisin at his brother's right hand. He hoped it meant their rift was healing. But the other two people by the Emperor made Scaurus want to rub his eyes to make sure they were not tricking him.

At Mavrikios' left sat Ortaias Sphrantzes. For all the young aristocrat's book-learning about war, Marcus would not have thought he had either the knowledge or the mettle to be part of this council, even if he was a member of the Emperor's faction instead of the nephew of Gavras' greatest rival. Yet here he was, using the point of his ornately hilted dagger to trace a river's course. He nodded and waved when he spied the entering Romans. Marcus nodded back, while Gaius Philippus, muttering something unpleasant under his breath, pretended not to see him.

The Emperor's daughter was on Thorisin Gavras' right, between him and Nephon Khoumnos. Alypia was the only woman at the gathering and, as was usually her way, doing more listening than talking. She was jotting something on a scrap of parchment when the Romans came into the Hall of the Nineteen Couches and did not look up until a servant had taken them to their assigned place, which was gratifyingly close to the table's head. Her glance toward Scaurus was cool, measuring, and more distant than the tribune had expected; he suddenly wondered if she knew of his joining with Helvis. Her face was unreadable, a perfect mask to hide her thoughts.

Marcus took his seat with some relief. He bent his head to study the map before him. If he read the spidery Videssian writing aright, it represented the mountains of Vaspurakan, the border land whose passes offered tempting pathways between the Empire and Yezd.

As had Apsimar's, the map looked marvelously precise, far more so than any the Romans made. Peaks, rivers, lakes, towns—all were portrayed in meticulous detail. Nevertheless, Scaurus wondered how trustworthy a chart it was. He knew how even well-intentioned and usually accurate men could go wrong. In the third book of his history, Polybius, as careful an investigator as was ever born, had the Rhodanus River going from east to west before it flowed south through Narbonese Gaul and into the Mediterranean. Having tramped along almost its entire length, the Roman was wearily certain it ran north and south throughout.

Mavrikios did not formally begin the council until an hour after the Romans arrived. Only when the last latecomers— Khamorth, most of them—were seated did he break his quiet conversation with his brother and raise his voice for the entire room to hear.

"Thank you for joining us this morning," he said. The hum of talk running along the tables as the gathered soldiers discussed their trade died away. He waited until it was quite gone before continuing, "For those who have marched and fought in the westlands before, much of what you'll hear today will be stale news, but there are so many newcomers I thought this council would be worthwhile for their sakes alone."

"Fewer new men are here than should be, thanks to your cursed monks," someone called, and Marcus recognized Utprand son of Dagober. The Namdalener still wore the same look of cold fury he'd had when the tribune rescued him from the riots; here, Scaurus judged, was a man not to be easily deflected from his purposes. Growls of agreement came from other easterners. Marcus saw Soteric well down at the junior end of the tables, nodding vehemently.

Ortaias Sphrantzes and Thorisin Gavras looked equally offended at Utprand's forthrightness. Their reasons, though, were totally different. "Blame not our holy men for the fruit of your heresy," Ortaias exclaimed, while the Sevastokrator snapped, "Show his Imperial Majesty the respect he deserves, you!" Up and down the tables, Videssians assented to one or the other—or both—of those sentiments.

The Namdaleni stared back in defiance. "What respect did we get when your holy men were murdering us?" Utprand demanded, answering both critics in the same breath. The temperature in the Hall of the Nineteen Couches shot toward the boiling point. Like jackals prowling round the edge of a fight, the Khamorth shifted in their seats, ready to leap on the battler they thought weaker.

Marcus felt the same growing despair he had known many times before in Videssos. He was calm both by training and temperament, and found maddening the quarrels of all the touchy, excitable people the Empire and its neighbors bred.

Mavrikios, it seemed, was cast from a similar mold. He laid one hand on his brother's shoulder, the other on that of Ortaias Sphrantzes. Both subsided, though Thorisin moved restively. The Emperor looked down the tables to Utprand, his brown eyes locking with the Namdalener's wolf-gray ones. "Fewer of you *are* here than should be," he admitted, "nor is the fault yours." Now it was Sphrantzes' turn to squirm.

The Emperor ignored him, keeping all his attention on Utprand. "Do you remember why you are here at all?" he asked. His voice held the same urgency Balsamon's had carried in the

Great Temple when he requested of Videssos a unity it would not grant him.

As Marcus had already seen, Utprand recognized truth when he heard it. The Namdalener thought for a moment, then gave a reluctant nod. "You're right," he said. For him that was enough to settle the matter. He leaned forward, ready to take part in the council once more. When a few hotheaded young Namdaleners wanted to carry the argument further, the ice in his eyes quelled them faster than anything the Videssians might have done.

"There is one hard case," Gaius Philippus whispered admiringly.

"Isn't he, though? I thought the same when I met him during the riots," Scaurus said.

"He's the one you talked of, then? I can see what you meant by—" The centurion broke off in mid-sentence, for the Emperor was speaking.

Calm as if nothing untoward had happened, Mavrikios said to Ortaias Sphrantzes, "Hold up that map of the westlands, would you?" The spatharios obediently lifted the parchment so everyone could see it.

On the chart, Videssos' western dominions were a long, gnarled thumb of land stretching toward the imperial capital and separating the almost landlocked Videssian Sea in the north from the great Sailors' Sea to the south.

The Emperor waited while a couple of nearsighted officers traded seats with colleagues near the map, then began abruptly, "I want to leave within the week. Have your troops ready to go over the Cattle-Crossing within that length of time, or be left behind." He suddenly grinned a most unpleasant grin. "Anyone who claims he cannot be ready by then will find himself ordered to the hottest, most Phos-forsaken garrison I can think of—he'll wish he were fighting the Yezda, I promise you that."

Mavrikios waited to let the sudden excited buzz travel the length of the tables. Marcus had the same eager stirring the Emperor's other officers felt—a departure date at last, and a near one, too! The tribune did not think Gavras would have to make good on his threat.

"For those of you who don't know," the Emperor resumed, "our western frontier against the Yezda is about five hundred miles west of the city. With an army as large as the one we've mustered here, we should be through Vaspurakan and into Yezd in about forty days." At a pinch, Scaurus thought his Romans could halve that time, but the Emperor was probably right. No army could move faster than its slowest members, and with a force of this size, the problem of keeping it supplied would slow it further.

Gavras paused for a moment to pick up a wooden pointer, which he used to draw a line southwest from Videssos to the joining of two rivers. "We'll make the journey in four stages," he said. "The first one will be short and easy, from here to Garsavra, where the Eriza flows into the Arandos. We'll meet Baanes Onomagoulos there; he'll join us with his troops from the southern mountains. He would be bringing more, but the fornicating pen-pushers have taxed too many of them into serfdom."

The map Ortaias Sphrantzes was holding did not let Scaurus see his face. That was a pity; he would have given a good deal to learn how the young aristocrat was reacting to the ridicule heaped on his family's policy. That map was beginning to quiver, too—it could not be comfortable for Ortaias, the tribune realized, sitting there with his arms out at full length before him. Sure enough, the Emperor was finding ways to put him in his place.

"From Garsavra we'll head west along the Arandos to Amorion, up in the plateau country. That's a longer stage than the first one, but it should be no harder." Marcus saw one of Alypia's eyebrows quirk upward, but the princess made no move to contradict her father. She scribbled again on her piece of parchment.

"There will be supply caches all along the line of march," Gavras went on, "and I'll not have anyone plundering the peasants in the countryside—or robbing them for the sport of it, either." He stared down the twin lengths of officers before him, especially pausing to catch the eyes of the Khamorth chieftains newly come from the plains. Not all of them spoke Videssian; those who did murmured translations of the Emperor's words for their fellow nomads.

One of the men from the Pardrayan steppe looked a question back at Mavrikios, who acknowledged him with a nod. "What is it?"

"I am Firdosi Horse-breaker," the nomad leader said in labored Videssian. "I and mine took your gold to fight, not to play the robber. Slaying farmers is woman's work—are we not men, to be trusted to fight as men?" Other Khamorth up and down the tables bowed their heads to their chests in their native gesture of agreement.

"That is well said," the Emperor declared. Without troops at his back, Marcus would not have trusted Firdosi or any of the other steppe-dwellers and was sure Mavrikios felt the same. But, he thought, this was hardly the time to stir up trouble.

Then Thorisin Gavras added lazily, "Of course, what my brother said should not be taken to apply only to our allies from the north; all foreign troops should bear it in mind." And he looked, not at the Khamorth, but at the Namdaleni.

They returned his mocking glance with stony silence, which filled the hall for a long moment. Mavrikios' nostrils dilated in an anger he could not release before his watching officers. As they had at Soteric's gambling party, men looked here and there to try to cover their discomfiture. Only Alypia seemed indifferent to it all, watching her father and uncle with what looked to Scaurus like amused detachment.

Making a visible effort, Mavrikios brought his attention back to the map Ortaias was still holding. He took a deep breath before carrying on. "At Amorion another detachment will meet us, this one headed by Gagik Bagratouni. From there we will move northwest to Soli on the Rhamnos River, just east of the mountain country of Vaspurakan, the land of princes—or so they claim," he added sardonically.

"That may be a hungry march. The Yezda are loose there, and I need not tell anyone here what they do in farming country, Phos blight them for it. If the earth does not produce its fruits, everyone—peasant, artisan, and noble alike—must perish."

Marcus saw two of the nomads exchange disdain-filled glances. With their vast herds and flocks, they had no need for the products of agriculture and felt the same hostility toward farmers as did their Yezda cousins. Firdosi had said it plainly —to the plainsmen, peasants were beneath contempt, and even to be killed by a true man was too good for them.

"After Soli we'll push into Vaspurakan itself," the Emperor

said. "The Yezda will be easier to trap in the passes than on the plain, and the loot they'll be carrying will slow them further. The Vaspurakaners will help us, too; the princes may have little love for the Empire, but the Yezda have raped their land time and again.

"And a solid win or two against Avshar's irregulars will make Wulghash himself come out from Mashiz with his real army; either that, or have the wild men turn on him instead." Anticipation lit Mavrikios's face. "Smash that army, and Yezd lies open for cleansing. And smash it we shall. It's been centuries since Videssos sent out a force to match the one we have here today. How can any Skotos-loving bandit lord hope to stand against us?"

More with his soldiers than with the crowd in the amphitheater, Mavrikios succeeded in firing imaginations—made his officers truly see Yezd prostrate at their feet. The prospect pleased them all, for whatever reason, political gain, religious purification, or simply fighting any booty in plenty.

When Ortaias Sphrantzes understood the Emperor was through at last, he put the map down with relief.

Marcus shared the officers' enthusiasm. Mavrikios' plan was in keeping with what the Roman had come to expect of Videssian designs—ponderous, but probably effective. He seemed to be leaving little to chance. That was as it should be, with so much soldiering in his past. All that remained was to convert plan to action.

As with everything else within the Empire, ceremony surrounded the great army's preparations for departure. The people of Videssos, who not long before had done their best to tear that army apart, now sent heavenward countless prayers for its success. A solemn liturgy was scheduled in the High Temple on the night before the troops were to leave.

Scaurus, as commander of the Romans, received the stamped roll of heavy parchment entitling him to a pair of coveted seats at the ritual. "Whom do you suppose I can give these to?" he asked Helvis. "Do you have any friends who might want them?"

"If that's meant as a joke, I don't find it funny," she replied. "We'll go ourselves, of course. Even though I don't fully share the Videssian creed, it would be wrong to start so important an undertaking without asking Phos' blessing on it."

Marcus sighed. When he asked Helvis to share his life, he had not anticipated how she would try to shape it into a pattern she found comfortable. He did not oppose the worship of Phos but, when pushed in a direction he did not want to take, his natural reaction was to dig in his heels.

Nor was he used to considering anyone else's wishes when planning his own actions. Since reaching the age of manhood he had steered his own course and ignored advice he had not sought. But Helvis was used to having her opinions taken into account; Scaurus remembered how angry she had been when he was close-mouthed over what the council of war decided. He sighed again. Nothing, he told himself, was as simple as it looked to be at its beginnings.

He held firm in his plans to avoid the service at the High Temple until he saw Neilos Tzimiskes' horror when he offered the Videssian the chance to go in his place. "Thank you for the honor," the borderer stammered, "but it would look ill indeed if you did not attend. All the great captains will be there—even the Khamorth will come, though they have scant use for Phos."

"I suppose so," Scaurus grumbled. But put in those terms, he could see the need for appearing; no less than Balsamon's unsuccessful sermon had been, this was an occasion for a public display of unity. And, he thought, it would certainly help the unity of his new household. There, at least, he was not mistaken.

That was as well; preparations for the coming campaign were leaving him exhausted and short-tempered at the end of every day. Roman discipline and order were still intact, so having his men ready was no problem. They could have left the day after Mavrikios' council—or the day before. But Videssian armies marched in greater luxury than a Caesar would have tolerated. As was true in the oriental monarchies Rome had known, great flocks of noncombatants accompanied the soldiers, including their women. And trying to get them in any sort of traveling order was a task that made Marcus understand the doom ordained for Sisyphos.

By the night of the liturgy, the tribune was actually looking forward to it and wondering how Balsamon would manage to

astound his listeners this time. When he entered the High
Temple, Helvis clinging proudly to his arm, he found she and
Tzimiskes had been right—he could not have afforded to miss
the gathering. The Temple was packed with the high officers
and functionaries of every state allied against Yezd and with
their ladies. It was hard to say which sex made a more gorgeous display, the men in their burnished steel and bronze,
wolfskin and leather, or the women showing off their gowns
of linen and clinging silk and their own soft, powdered flesh.

Men and women alike rose as the patriarch of Videssos
made his way to his ivory throne. When he and his flock
offered Phos their fundamental prayer, tonight there were
many Namadaleni to finish the creed with their own addition:
"On this we stake our very lives." At Marcus' side Helvis did
so with firm devotion and looked about defiantly to see who
might object. Few Videssians seemed offended; on this night,
with all kinds of heretics and outright unbelievers in the Temple, they were willing to overlook outlanders' barbarous practices.

When the service was done, Balsamon offered his own
prayer for the success of the enterprise Videssos was undertaking and spoke at some length of the conflict's importance and
the need for singleness of purpose in the face of the western
foe. Everything he said was true and needed saying, but
Marcus was still disapointed at his sermon. There was little of
Balsamon's usual dry wit, nor did his delivery have its normal
zest. The patriarch seemed very tired and halfhearted about his
sermon. It puzzled Scaurus and concerned him, too.

But Balsamon grew more animated as his talk progressed
and ended strongly. 'A man's only guide is his conscience—it
is his shield when he does well and a blade to wound him if he
falters. Now take up the shield of right and turn back evil's
sword—bow not to wickedness' will, and that sword can
never harm you!"

As his listeners applauded his words and calls of "Well
said!" came from throughout the Temple, above them rose the
massed voices of the choir in a triumhant hymn to Phos, and
with them the bell players whose music had intrigued Scaurus
before. Now he was sitting at an angle that let him watch them
work, and his fascination with them was enough to wipe away
a good part of the letdown at Balsamon's pedestrian address.

The twoscore players stood behind a long, padded table. Each had before him some half dozen polished bells of various sizes and tones. Along with their robes, the players wore kidskin gloves to avoid smudging the bright bell metal. They followed the direction of their bellmaster with marvelous speed and dexterity, changing and chiming their bells in perfect unison. It was, Marcus found, as entrancing to watch as to hear.

The bellmaster was a show in himself. A dapper little man, he led his charges with slightly exaggerated, theatrical gestures, his body swaying to the hymn he was conducting. His face wore a look of exaltation, and his eyes never opened. It was several minutes before Scaurus realized he was blind; he hardly seemed to need to see, for his ears told him more than most men's eyes ever would.

If the music of the bells impressed the unmusical tribune, it delighted Helvis, who said, "I've heard the Temple's bell players praised many times, but never had the chance to listen to them before. They were another reason I wanted to be here tonight." She looked at Marcus quizzically. "If I'd known you liked them, I would have used them as an argument for coming."

He had to smile. "Probably just as well you didn't." He found it hard to imagine being persuaded to go anywhere by the promise of music. Still, there was no doubt the bell players added spice to what otherwise would have been an unsatisfying evening.

The Emperor ordered criers through the streets to warn the people of Videssos to spend the following day at home. The major thoroughfares were packed tight with soldiers in full kit, with nervous horses and braying donkeys, wagons carrying the warriors' families and personal goods, other wagons driven by sutlers, and still others loaded with every imaginable sort of military hardware. Tempers shortened more quickly than the long files of men, animals, and wains inching toward the quays where ships and boats waited to take them over the Cattle-Crossing to the Empire's westlands.

The Romans, as part of Mavrikios' Imperial Guard, had little waiting before they crossed. Everything went smoothly as could be, except for Viridovix. The luckless Celt spent the entire journey—fortunately for him, one of less than half an hour—leaning over the galley's rail, retching helplessly.

"Every time I'm on the water it happens to me," he moaned between spasms. The usual ruddiness had faded from his features, leaving him fishbelly pale.

"Eat hard-baked bread crumbled in wine," Gorgidas recommended, "or, if you like, I have a decoction of opium that will help, though it will leave you drowsy for a day."

"Eat—" The very word was enough to send the Gaul lurching toward the rail. When he was through he turned back to Gorgidas. Tears of misery stood in hs eyes. "I thank your honor for the advice and all, but it'd be too late to do me the good I need. Dry dirt, bless it, under my feet will serve me better than any nostrum ever you made." He cringed as another wavelet gently lifted the ship's bow.

With their small harbors, Videssos' suburbs on the western shore of the Cattle-Crossing could not hope to handle the avalanche of shipping descending on them. The capital was the Empire's chief port and, jealous of its status, made sure no other town nearby could siphon business from it.

Nevertheless, the armada of sharp-beaked slim galleys, merchantmen, fishing boats, barges, and various motley small craft did not have to stand offshore to disembark its host. Videssian ships, like the ones the Romans built, were even at their biggest small and light enough to stand beaching without damage. For several miles up and down the coast, oars drove ships ashore so men and beasts could splash through the surf to land. Sailors and soldiers cursed together as they labored to empty hulls of supplies. That also lightened the beached craft and made them easier to refloat.

Viridovix was so eager to reach land that he vaulted over the rail before the ship was quite aground and came down with a splash neck-deep in the sea. Cursing in Gaulish, he floundered onto the beach, where he lay at full length just beyond the reach of the waves. He hugged the golden sand as he would a lover. Less miserable and thus more patient, the Romans followed him.

The imperial galley came ashore not far from where they were disembarking. First out of it were Mavrikios' ever-present Haloga guardsmen. Like the Romans, they left their vessel by scrambling down rope ladders and nets cast over the side. Then, watchful as always, they hurried to take up positions to ward off any sudden treachery.

For an Emperor, however, even one who set as little store in ceremony as Mavrikios Gavras, clambering down a rope would not do. As soon as his guards were in place, a gangplank of gilded wood was laid from ship to beach. But when the Emperor was about to step onto the sand, his booted foot came down on the hem of his long purple robe. He tripped and went to all fours on the beach.

Romans, Halogai, and Videssian seamen alike stared in consternation. What omen could be worse for a campaign than to have its leader fall before it began? Someone made a sign to avert evil.

But Mavrikios was equal to the occasion. Rising to his knees, he held aloft two fistsful of sand and said loudly, "Videssos, I have tight hold of you!" He got to his feet and went about his business as if nothing out of the ordinary had happened.

And, after a moment or two, so did the men who had witnessed the mishap. The Emperor's quick wits had succeeded in turning a bad omen into a good one. Discussing it that evening, Gaius Philippus gave Mavrikios his ultimate accolade. "Caesar," he declared, "couldn't have done it better."

Like a multitude of little streams running together to form a great river, the Videssian army gathered itself on the western shore of the Cattle-Crossing. The transfer from the capital had been far easier than Marcus had expected. There were, it seemed, some advantages after all to the minute organization that was such a part of life in the Empire.

That organization showed its virtue again as the march to Garsavra began. Scaurus doubted if Rome could have kept so huge a host fed without its pillaging the countryside and gave his men stern orders against foraging. But plundering for supplies never came close to being necessary. No Yezda had yet come so far east, and the local officials had no trouble providing the army and its hangers-on with markets adequate for their needs. Grain came by oxcart and rivercraft, along with herds of cattle and sheep for meat.

Hunters added to the meat bag with deer and wild boar. In the case of the latter, there were times when Scaurus was not sure the pig was truly wild. Videssian hogs shared with their boarish cousins a lean, rangy build, a strip of bristly hair down their backs, and a savage disposition. Stealing one of them could give a hunting party as lively a time as going after a wild boar. The tribune enjoyed gnawing the fat-rich, savory meat from its bones too much to worry over its source for long.

The first leg of the march from the city was a time of shaking down, a time for troops too long in soft billets to begin to remember how they earned their pay. For all the drills and mock fights Gaius Philippus had put the Romans through, they were not quite the same hard-bitten, hungry band who had fought in Gaul. Their belts had gone out a notch or two and, most of all, they were not used to a full day's march, even one at the slow pace of the army they accompanied.

At the end of each of the first few days out of the capital, the legionaries were glad to collapse and try to rub some life back into their aching calves and thighs. Gorgidas and the other medics were busy treating blisters, laying on a thick ointment of lard mixed with resin and covering the sores with bandages of soft, fluffy wool well sprinkled with oil and wine. The troopers cursed the medicine's astringent bite, but it served them well until their feet began to harden once more.

Marcus had expected all that sort of thing and was not put out when it happened. He had not really anticipated, however, how resentful his Romans would be when called on to create a regular legionary camp every night. Throwing up daily earthworks did not appeal to them after their comfortable months in the permanent barracks of Videssos.

Gaius Philippus browbeat the troops into obedience the first three nights on march, but an ever more sullen, half-hearted obedience. By the third night he was hoarse, furious, and growing desperate. On the next day a deputation of legionaries came to see Scaurus with their grievances. Had they been shirkers or men of little quality, he would have dealt with the matter summarily, punishing them and not listening for an instant. But among the nine nervous soldiers—one from each maniple—were some of his finest men, including the stalwart Minucius. He decided to hear them out.

For one thing, they said, none of the other contingents of the imperial army made such a production of their nightly stopping places. They knew they were deep in Videssian territory and altogether safe, and their tents went up in a cheerful, casual disarray wherever their officers happened to feel like pitching them. Worse yet, in a proper Roman camp there was no place for women, and many of the legionaries wanted to spend their nights with the partners they had found in Videssos.

The tribune could find no sympathy with the first of these points. He said, "What the rest of the army does is its own concern. It's too simple to go slack when things are easy and then never bother to tighten up again—until it costs you, and then it's too late. The lot of you are veterans; you know what I'm saying is true."

They had to nod. Minucius, his booming voice and open manner subdued by the irregular situation in which he'd put himself, said timidly, "It's not the work we mind so much, sir. It's just that well . . . once camp is made, it's like a jail, with no escape. My woman's pregnant, and I worry about her." His comrades muttered agreement; looking from one of them to another, Marcus saw they were almost all coupled men.

He understood how they felt. He had slept restlessly the past couple of nights, knowing Helvis was only a few hundred yards away but not wanting to give his troopers a bad example by breaking discipline for his private gratification.

He thought for a few seconds; less than a third of the Romans had women with them. If a party of about a hundred got leave each night, each soldier could see his lover twice a week or so. The improvement in morale would probably be worth more than the slightly loosened control would cost.

He gave the legionaries his decision, adding, "Leave will only be granted after all required duties are complete, of course."

"Yes, sir! Thank you sir!" they said, grinning in relief that he had not ordered them clapped in irons.

He knew they must not be allowed to think they could violate the proper chain of command on every whim. He coughed dryly, and watched the grins fade. "The lot of you are fined two weeks' pay for bringing this up without your officers' permission," he said. "See that it doesn't happen again."

They took the fine without a murmur, still afraid he might

condemn them to far worse. Under the law of the legions he could confiscate their goods, have them flogged, or give them over to the *fustuarium*—order them clubbed, beaten, and stoned to death by their fellow soldiers. When he snapped, "Get out!" they fell over themselves scrambling from his tent. In some ways, Roman discipline still held.

The order duly went out, and the grumbling in the ranks vanished or was transmuted into the ordinary grousing that has existed in every army since time began. "I suppose you had to do it," Gaius Philippus said, "but I still don't like it. You may gain in the short run, but over the long haul anything that cuts into discipline is bad."

"I thought about that," Scaurus admitted, "but there's discipline and discipline. To keep the vital parts, you have to bend the ones that aren't. The men have to keep thinking of themselves as Romans and *want* to think that way, or they— and we—are lost. If they decide they'd rather slip off and be peasants in the countryside, what can we do? Where can we find the legions, the generals, the Senate to back up our Roman discipline? Do you think the Videssians give a damn about our ways? I can't order us to feel like Romans; it *has* to come from within."

Gaius Philippus looked at him like a Videssian suddenly confronted with heresy. The centurion had kept himself—and, to a large measure, the rest of the legionaries, too—going by ignoring, as far as he could, the fact that Rome was gone forever. It rocked his world for Scaurus to speak openly of what he tried not even to think about. Shaking his head, he left the tribune's tent. A few minutes later Marcus heard him blistering some luckless soldier over a speck of rust on his greave. Scaurus made a wry face. He wished he could work off his own concerns so easily.

Letting the Romans out of camp at night proved to have one advantage the tribune had not thought of when he decided to allow it. It put them back in the mainstream of army gossip, as much a constant as that of the capital. The women heard everything, true or not, and so did the legionaries while with them. Thus it was that Scaurus learned Ortaias Sphrantzes was still with the army. He found it almost impossible to believe, knowing the mutual loathing the Gavrai and Sphrantzai had for one another, but on his way to see Helvis a night later he proved its accuracy by almost bumping into the spatharios.

"Your pardon, I beg," the young Sphrantzes said, stepping out of his way. As he had when Gaius Philippus rated him while he watched the Romans drill, he had a fat volume under his arm. "Yes, it's Kalokyres on generalship again," he said. "I have so much to learn and so little time to learn it."

The idea of Ortaias Sphrantzes as a general was enough to silence the tribune. He must have raised an eyebrow, though, for Ortaias said, "My only regret, my Roman—" He pronounced the word carefully. "—friend, is that I'll not have your formidable infantry under my command."

"Ah? What command is that, my lord?" Marcus asked, thinking Mavrikios might have given the youth a few hundred Khamorth to play with. The answer he got shook him to his toes.

"I am to lead the left wing," Sphrantzes replied proudly, "while the Emperor commands the center and his brother the right. We shall make mincemeat of the foe! Mincemeat! Now you must forgive me; I am studying the proper way to maneuver heavy cavalry in the face of the enemy." And the newly minted field marshal vanished into the warm twilight, paging through his book to the place he needed.

That night, Helvis complained Scaurus' mind was somewhere else.

The next morning the tribune told Gaius Philippus the ghastly news. The senior centurion held his head in his hands. "Congratulations," he said. "You just ruined my breakfast."

"He seems to mean well," Marcus said, trying to find a bright side to things.

"So does a doctor treating somebody with the plague. The poor bastard'll die all the same."

"That's not a good comparison," Gorgidas protested. "True, the plague is past my power to treat, but at least I'm skilled in my profession. After reading one book of medicine, I wouldn't have trusted myself to treat a sour stomach."

"Neither would anyone else with sense," Gaius Philippus said. "I thought Mavrikios had too much sense to give the puppy a third of his army." He pushed his barley porridge aside, saying to the Greek doctor, "Can you fix *my* sour stomach? The gods know I've got one."

Gorgidas grew serious. "Barley after you're used to wheat will give you distress, or so says Hippokrates."

"It never did before," Gaius Philippus said. "I'm disgusted, that's all. That bungling twit!"

The "twit" himself appeared later that day, apparently reminded of the Romans' existence by his encounter with Marcus. Sphrantzes looked dashing as he rode up to the marching legionaries; his horse had the mincing gait of a Videssian thoroughbred. His breastplate and helm were gilded to show his rank, while a deep-blue cape streamed out behind him. The only flaw in his image of martial vigor was the book he still carried clamped under his left arm.

Sphrantzes reined his horse in to a walking pace at the head of the Roman column. He kept looking back, as if studying it. Gaius Philippus' hostile curiosity soon got the better of him. He asked, "What can we do for you today, sir?" His tone belied the title of respect he'd granted Sphrantzes.

"Eh?" Ortaias blinked. "Oh, yes—tell me, if you would, are those the standards under which you fight?" He pointed at the nine tall manipular *signa* the standard-bearers proudly carried. Each was crowned by an open hand ringed by a wreath, representing faithfulness to duty.

"So they are. What of it?" Gaius Philippus answered shortly.

Marcus understood why the subject was a sore one. He explained to Sphrantzes, "We were only a detachment of a larger unit, whose symbol is the eagle. We have no eagle here, and the men miss it dearly."

That was an understatement, but no Videssian could hope to understand the feeling each legion had for its eagle, the sacred symbol of its very being. During the winter at Imbros there had been some talk of making a new eagle, but the soldiers' hearts were not in it. Their *aquila* was in Gaul and lost to them forever, but they wanted no other. The lesser *signa* would have to do.

"Most interesting," Ortaias said. His concern with the Romans' standards, however, was for a different reason. "Is your custom always to group like numbers of soldiers under each ensign?"

"Of course," Scaurus replied, puzzled.

"And why not?" his centurion added.

"Excuse me a moment," Sphrantzes said. He pulled out of the Roman line of march so he could stop his horse and use both hands to go through his tactical volume. When he found what he wanted, he sent the beast trotting back up to the Romans.

"I quote from Kalokyres," he said: "The first book, chapter four, part six: 'It is necessary to take care not to make all companies exactly equal in number, lest the enemy, counting one's standards, form an exact idea of one's numbers. Take heed in this matter: as we said, the companies should not be more than four hundred men, nor less than two hundred.' Of course, your units are smaller than the ones Kalokyres uses, but the principle, I should say, remains the same. Good day to you, gentlemen." He rode away, leaving the Romans speechless behind him.

"Do you know," Gaius Philippus said, "that's not a bad notion?"

"So it isn't," Marcus said. "In fact, it's a very good one. How in the world did Ortaias Sphrantzes ever come up with it?"

"It's not as if he thought of it himself," the centurion said, looking for a way out of his discomfiture. "This Kalo-what's-his-name must have had his wits about him. Yes." He tried to console himself with that thought, but still looked rattled.

Viridovix had watched the entire exchange with high glee. "Sure and there he is, the man who sucked in soldiering with his mother's milk—a centurion she was herself, I have no doubt—all tossed in a heap by the biggest booby ever hatched. It all goes to prove the Celtic way of fighting is the best—get in there and do it, for the more you think, the more trouble you're in."

Gaius Philippus was too graveled even to argue. "Oh, shut up," he muttered. "Where'd Gorgidas get to? My stomach's hurting again."

The coastal plain between the suburbs across from Videssos and the city of Garsavra was some of the most fertile land the Romans had ever seen. The soil was a soft black loam that crumbled easily in the hand and smelled rich, almost meaty, in its promise of growth. Scores of rivers and lesser streams ran down from the central plateau so that the soil could fulfill its promise. The warm rain fetched by the constant breeze off the Sailors' Sea watered those few stretches flowing water did not touch.

Viridovix' dire predictions about the weather, made months before, came true with a vengeance. It was so hot and humid the ground steamed each morning when the sun came up. The pale Halogai, used to the cool, cloudy summers of their northern home, suffered worse than most; day after day, they fainted in their armor and had to be revived with helmetsful of water.

"Red as a boiled crayfish, he was," Viridovix said of one sunstruck northerner.

Gorgidas cocked an eye at him. "You don't look any too good yourself," he said. "Try wearing a soft hat instead of your helmet on march."

"Go on with you," the Celt said. "It takes more than a bit of sun to lay me low." But Scaurus noticed he followed the physician's advice.

With fine soil, abundant water, and hot sun, no wonder the breadbasket of the Empire lay here. The land was clothed with the various greens of growing plants. There were fields of wheat, millet, oats, and barley, and others growing flax and cotton, which Gorgidas insisted on calling "plant wool." Orchards grew figs, peaches, plums, and exotic citrus fruits. As none of these last had been common in the western Mediterranean, Marcus had trouble telling one from the next—until the first time he bit into a lemon, thinking it an orange. After that he learned.

Vineyards were rare here; the soil was too good, and water too plentiful. Nor did Scaurus see many olive trees until the land began to rise toward the plateau a day or so outside of Garsavra.

The folk who farmed the fertile plain were as much a revelation to the tribune as their land. They were quiet, steady, and as industrious as any people he had seen. He was used to the tempestuous populace of Videssos the city, with their noisy, headlong pace, their arrogant assumption of superiority over all the rest of mankind, and their fickle swings of mood. He'd wondered more than once how the Empire had managed to prosper for so many centuries with such truculent material on which to build.

Gorgidas laughed at him for saying that one night. The Greek physician was always a part of the unending talk round the Roman watchfires. He seldom left camp after dusk had fallen. Scaurus knew he had no sweetheart, but used the company of men to hold loneliness at bay.

Now he commented, "You might as well judge Italy by the hangers-on at the lawcourts in Rome. For as long as Videssos has had its empire, the Emperors have spoiled the people of the capital to win their favor. You can hardly blame them, you know—reckoning by the riots a few weeks ago, their necks would answer if they didn't keep them happy. Don't forget, the Empire has lasted a long time; the city people think luxury their rightful due."

The tribune remembered Cato's complaint of over a century before his own time, that a pretty boy could cost more than a plot of land, and a jar of imported liquamen more than a plowman. Rome had not become less fond of pleasure in the intervening years. What was the joke about Caesar?—every woman's husband and every man's wife. Scaurus shook his head, wondering what his native capital would be like after hundreds of years as an imperial capital.

Garsavra, which the army reached on the ninth day out of Videssos, was a long way from imperial status. The town was, in fact, smaller than Imbros. Thanks to its river-junction site, it was a trade center for a good part of the westlands. Nevertheless, when the expeditionary force camped round the city, it more than doubled Garsavra's population.

There was something wrong with the town's outline as the Romans came up to it, but Marcus could not put his finger on its oddness. Gaius Philippus had never a doubt. "I will be damned," he said. "The bloody place is without a wall!"

He was right; Garsavra's houses, shops, and public buildings were open to the surrounding world, unprotected from any attack. More than anything else he had seen in the Empire, that brought home to Marcus Videssos' accomplishment. Imbros, even the capital itself, had to ward off barbarians from the north, but the land they shielded had known peace so long it had forgotten even fortcraft.

With his predator's mind, Viridovix was quick to see the other side of the coin. "Wouldn't the Yezda have a lovely time now, swooping down on a town so naked and all? They'd fair break their poor horses' backs with the booty they'd haul off."

The thought of Avshar's wolves laying waste this peaceful, fertile land was nearly enough to make Scaurus physically sick. Like vicious children loose in a pottery, they could wreck in minutes what had taken years to create and take only delight in the wrecking.

"That's why they pay us," Gaius Philippus said, "to do the dying so they can stay happy and fat."

Marcus found that notion little more appetizing than Viridovix'. It was not strictly fair, either; Videssians made up much the greatest part of Mavrikios' army, and several thousand more native troops were already here awaiting the Emperor's arrival.

There was, however, a grain of truth behind the centurion's cynical words. The men Baanes Onomagoulos had called up from the soldier-peasants of the countryside were all too plainly less soldier than peasant. Their mounts were a collection of crowbait, their gear old and scanty, and their drill next to nonexistent.

Their commander was something else again, a general out of the same school from which Mavrikios Gavras had come. Scaurus got a good look at him during the review the Emperor called to welcome the new contingent into his forces. Onomagoulos rode past the Romans on his way to Mavrikios; now and again he touched his spurs to his horse's flank to make the beast rear. He was not a very big man, but the way he sat his horse and the set of his hawk-nosed face proclaimed him a seasoned warrior nevertheless. He was well past forty; the years had swept most of the hair from his crown, but neither its remnants nor his pointed beard were frosted with gray.

Protocol demanded that he rein in, dismount, and perform a proskynesis before addressing the Emperor. Instead, he rode straight up to Mavrikios, who was also mounted, and cried, "Gavras, you old bastard, how have you been?"

Marcus waited for the world to fall to ruins, or at least for the Halogai at the Emperor's side to tear the offender limb from limb. Some of the younger guardsmen reached for their swords, but Zeprin the Red was watching Mavrikios. Seeing the Emperor was not angry, the mercenary officer made a quick hand signal, and his men relaxed.

Gavras smiled thinly. "I manage to keep busy—too busy, usually. Maybe you should have had the job after all." He brought his horse forward and slapped Onomagoulos on the back. Onomagoulos threw a lazy phantom punch at the Emperor, who ducked, his smile wider now.

The tribune suddenly understood a great deal. For Baanes Onomagoulos, Mavrikios Gavras was no distant omnipotent sovereign, but a fortunate equal, like a man who was lucky in love—and Scaurus thought of Helvis with a brief, warm glow. He wondered how long these two leaders had known each other and what they had seen together, for their friendship to survive the challenge of Mavrikios' imperial rank.

Baanes looked to Thorisin, asking, "And how are you, pup?"

"Well enough," the Sevastokrator answered. His tone was not as warm as his brother's. Marcus noted he made no move to join Baanes and Mavrikios.

"'Pup,' is it?" Viridovix breathed into Scaurus' ear. "Sure and it's a rare bold man to be calling Thorisin Gavaras a name like that, with himself so feisty and all."

"Onomagoulos has likely known him since before he could walk," the Roman whispered back.

"All the more reason for the name to rankle now. You have no older kin, I'm thinking?"

"No," Scaurus admitted.

"There's no one worse than your elder brother's friends. The first they see of you is a wee pulling lad, and they never forget it, not when you're taller than the lot of them." There was an edge to the Celt's voice Marcus had seldom heard; when he looked round, Viridovix was thoroughly grim, as if chewing on a memory whose taste he did not like.

The Arandos river bounced down from the plateau into the flatlands over a series of cataracts, past which the army marched as it made its way westward. Churning down over the great boulders in the streambed, the Arandos hurled rainbow-catching spray hundreds of feet to either side of the riverbanks. The fine droplets drying on the faces of the soldiers slogging west were almost the only relief they got from the burning heat.

The central highlands were a very different place from the

lush coastal plain. The land was baked a dirty gray-brown by the sun and crisscrossed by gullies, dry nine parts of the year but rampaging torrents the tenth. Wheat grew here too, but only with reluctance when compared to the riot of fertility to the east.

Long stretches of land were too poor for agriculture of any sort, supporting only a thin cover of grass and spikey shrubs. Herdsmen drove vast flocks of sheep, cattle, and goats across the rugged terrain, their way of life more akin to that of the nomadic Khamorth than to that practiced elsewhere in the Empire.

For the first time, the supply problems Marcus had feared began showing up. Bread from the lowlands still followed the army up the Arandos, portaged past the rapids. It helped, for local deliveries of flour and grain were spotty and small. Some of the shortfall was made up from the herds, which gave the Romans something new to gripe about. On campaign they preferred a largely vegetarian diet, feeling that eating too much meat made them hot, heavy, and slow.

Most of the Videssians, used to a climate like Italy's, had similar frugal tastes. The Halogai and their Namdalener cousins, on the other hand, gorged themselves on roast mutton and beef—and, as always, suffered more from the heat than did the rest of the army.

The Khamorth ate everything edible and did not complain.

Marcus grew more thankful for the Arandos with every day that passed. Without it and its occasional tributaries, the plateau would have been a desert in which nothing could survive. Its water was blood-warm and sometimes muddy, but never failed or slackened. The tribune found nothing more exquisite on a scorching afternoon than dipping up a helmetful and pouring it over his head. So thirsty was the air for moisture, though, that half an hour later he would have to do it again.

By the middle of the third week of the march, the army was beginning to become a real unit, not the motley collection of forces that had set out from Videssos. Mavrikios sped the process with a series of drills, rushing the men from column formation into line of battle, now ordering them to defend against the front, now the right, and again the left.

The maneuvers were exhausting when carried out in that heat, but the men started to know each other and to know what they could expect in battle from their comrades: the iron courage of the Halogai, the Romans' steadiness, the overwhelming charges of the Namdaleni, the dash of the little company of light horse from Khatrish, the Khamorth bands' speed and ferocity, and the all-around competence of most of the Videssian majority—though not so specialized in their techniques as their allies, the Videssians were more versatile than any other troops.

The army's left wing seemed no slower to deploy than the right or the center and no clumsier in its evolutions. Marcus began to think he had done Ortaias Sphrantzes an injustice. Then one day he heard Nephon Khoumnos' bull voice roaring out on the left, overriding Sphrantzes' reedy tones but careful to preface each command with, "Come, on, you lugs, you heard the general. Now—" and he would shout out whatever was needed.

Gaius Philippus heard him too, and said, "There's a relief. At least now we know things won't fall apart on our flank."

"True enough," Scaurus agreed. His solid respect for Mavrikios' wits increased once more. The Emperor had managed to give the young scion of the rival faction a position that seemed powerful, but no authority to go with his rank. Sometimes Videssian subtlety was not to be despised.

As he and his men were slowly making their way to the Roman position in column after an exercise, the tribune caught sight of a familiar plump figure atop a donkey. "Nepos!" he called. "I didn't know you were with us."

The fat little priest steered his mount over to the Romans. A conical straw hat protected his shaven pate from the sun's wrath. "There are times I'd sooner be lecturing at the Academy," he admitted. "My fundament was not designed for days on end in the saddle—oh, a horrid pun there. I crave pardon —it was unintentional." He shifted ruefully, continuing, "Still, I was asked to come and so here I am."

"I would have thought the Emperor could find enough priests to take omens, hearten the men, and suchlike without pulling you away from your research," Gorgidas said.

"And so there are," Nepos said, puzzled at the physician's slowness. "I do such things, to be sure, but they are hardly my reason for being here."

"What then, your honor?" Viridovix asked with a sly grin. "Magic?"

"Why, of course," Nepos replied, still surprised anyone needed to put the question to him. Then his brow cleared as he remembered. "That's right—in your world, magic is more often talked of than seen, is it not? Well, my friends, answer me this—if not for magic, how and why would you be marching through some of the least lovely land in the Empire of Videssos? How would you be talking with me now?"

Viridovix, Gorgidas, and the Romans in earshot looked uncomfortable. Nepos nodded at them. "You begin to understand, I see."

While his mates were still wrestling with Nepos' words, Gaius Philippus drove to the heart of the problem. "If you use magic in your fighting, what can we poor mortals expect? Hordes of demons shrieking out of the sky? Man-sized fire-balls shot from miles away? Gods above, will the very earth crack under our feet?"

Nepos frowned at the centurion's oath, but saw from his listeners' faces how alarming the prospect of the unknown was. He did his best to reassure them. "Nothing so dramatic, I promise you. Battle magic is a very chancy thing—with men's minds and emotions at the pitch of combat, even the most ordinary spells often will not bite. For that matter, sorcerers are often too busy saving their own skins to have the leisure they need for magecraft.

"And you must bear in mind," the priest went on, "that both sides will have magicians with them. The usual result is that they cancel each other's work and leave the result to you armored ruffians. In short, you have little to fear. I think my colleagues of the Academy and I should be able to keep our sorcerous friend Avshar quite well checked and perhaps give him more than he bargained for."

Nepos sounded confident. Yet for all the priest's assurances of wizardry's small use in battle, Marcus could not help remembering the talking corpse in the armory of Videssos' sea-wall, could not stop himself from recalling the black rumors swirling round Avshar's name in the fighting thus far. His hand slid to the hilt of his good Gallic sword. There, at least, was something to be counted on to hold dire sorceries at bay.

XI

THE FIRST SIGNS VIDESSOS WAS A LAND UNDER ATTACK showed themselves several days' march east of Amorion. A string of plundered, burned-out villages said more clearly than words that Yezda raiders had passed this way. So did abandoned farms and a gutted monastery with its ravaged fields. Some of the destruction was very fresh; a pair of starving hounds still prowled round the monastery, waiting for masters who would not return.

The damage the nomads had done elsewhere was not much worse than any land could expect in wartime. For the Empire's god, though, the Yezda reserved a special fury. The small chapel by the monks' living quarters was viciously desecrated. The images on its walls were ripped to bits, and the altar chopped up and used for stovewood. As a final act of insult, the bandits had stabled their horses there.

If the Yezda thought to strike terror into their enemies by such tactics, they failed. The Videssians already had good cause to hate their western neighbors. Now the same hatred was inculcated in the mercenaries who followed Phos, for Mavrikios made sure all his soldiers looked inside the profaned chapel. The Emperor made no comment about what they saw. None was needed.

The devastation upset Marcus for another reason. He had long since decided Yezd was a foe worth fighting. Any land that placed one such as Avshar high in its councils was not one with which decent men could hope to live at peace.

What the tribune had not realized was how strong Yezd

was. The imperial army was not much more than halfway to Videssos' western frontier, yet already the land bore the marks of the strokes the nomads were hurling at the Empire. And what they were seeing today was but the weakest, furthest touch of the Yezda. What would the land be like five days further west, or ten? Would anything grow at all?

That night there were no complaints over setting up the usual Roman field fortifications, with ditch, earth breastwork, and palisade of stakes. Not a Yezda had been seen, but the entire imperial force made camp as if in hostile country.

Scaurus was glad it was the turn of his group of legionaries to visit their women. As he and his men strolled from their camp to that of the women, he looked askance at local notions of what a fortified camp should be. He always did.

True, the women's tents were surrounded by a palisade of sorts, but it was no better than other Videssian productions. There were too many large, haphazardly trimmed tree trunks —as soon as two or three foes could combine to pull one away from its fellows, the palisade was breached. The Romans, on the other hand, each carried several stakes, which they set up each night with their branches intertwining. They were hard to uproot, and even if one was torn free, it did not leave a gap big enough for a man to enter. He'd mentioned the matter to the Videssians several times; they always sounded interested, but did nothing.

Nervous sentries challenged the Romans half a dozen times in the five-minute walk. "Use your wits, fool!" Marcus snapped to the last of the challengers. "Don't you know the Yezda fight on horseback?"

"Of course, sir," the sentry answered in injured tones. Scaurus hesitated, then apologized. Any sort of ruse was possible, and the last thing he should do was mock a man's alertness. He was more on edge than he'd thought; tonight he badly needed the peace Helvis could bring him.

Yet it was not easy for him to find that peace, though Helvis sent Malric to sleep with some friends he had made on the march. Scaurus was so long out of the habit of unburdening himself to anyone—and perhaps especially to a woman— that he spoke not of his concerns, but merely of the day's march and other matters of little importance. Not surprisingly,

Helvis sensed something was wrong, but the tribune's shield was up so firmly she could not tell what it was.

Even their love that night could not give the Roman the relief he sought. He was too much within himself to be able to give much, and what passed for lovemaking had a hesitance and an incompleteness it had not known before. Feeling all the worse because he had hoped to feel better, the tribune slipped into uneasy sleep.

The next he knew, he was in a Gallic clearing he remembered only too well, in the midst of his little band of legionaries as the Celts began their massacre. He stared wildly about him. Where was Videssos, the Emperor, the baking plain he and the survivors of this very night had been crossing? Or were there any survivors? Was the Empire but a fantasy of a man driven from his wits by fear?

Here came Viridovix, swinging the long blade that was twin to Scaurus' own. The tribune raised his sword to parry, or so he thought, but the hand he brought up over his head was empty. The Celt's blade hurtled down—

"What is it, darling?" The touch on his cheek was not the bite of a blade, but Helvis' hand. "Your thrashing woke me, and then you cried out loud enough to rouse half the camp."

Marcus lay on his back for several seconds without answering. The night was nearly as hot as the day had been, but there was cold sweat on his chest and shoulders. He looked up to the ceiling of the tent, his mind still seeing torchlight glittering off a Celtic sword.

"It was a dream," he said, more to himself than to Helvis.

"Of course it was," she answered, caressing his face again. "Just a bad dream."

"By the gods, how real it felt! I was in a bad dream inside a nightmare, dreaming Videssos was but a dream, and me about to die in Gaul—as I should have, by any sane man's rules.

"How real it was!" he said again. "Was that the dream, or is this? What am I doing here, in this land I never imagined, speaking its tongue, fighting its wars? Is Videssos real? Will it—oh, the dear gods, will you—vanish, too, one day, like a soap-bubble when a needle pricks it? And am I doomed to soldier on, then, for whatever new king I find, and learn his ways as well?"

He shuddered; in the hours when one day was long dead

and the next far from born, the vision had a terrifying feel of probability to it.

Helvis pressed her warm naked length against him. "The nightmare is gone when you wake. This is real," she said positively. "You see it, you feel it, you taste it—what more could there be? I am no one's dream but my own—though it gives me joy you share it." In the darkness her eyes were enormous.

"How tight you are," she said, her fingers exploring his chest, the side of his neck. "Roll over!" she ordered, and Scaurus turned obediently on his belly. She straddled his middle; he grunted in pleasure as her strong hands began to knead the tension from his back. Her massage always made him want to purr like a kitten, never more so than now.

After a few minutes he rolled to his back once more, careful not to dislodge her from atop him. "What are you doing?" she asked, but she knew the answer. He raised himself on his elbows to kiss her more easily. A strand of her hair was between them; she brushed it aside with a laugh. Her breath sighed out as she lowered herself onto him.

"*This* is real, too," she whispered as she began to move. The tribune could not argue, nor did he want to.

Three days later the army saw its first live Yezda, a small band of raiders silhouetted against the sky to the west. The Emperor gave chase with a squadron of Videssian horse, but the nomads on their steppe ponies eluded the hunters.

Ortaias Sphrantzes was intemperate in his criticism of Mavrikios' choice. He told everyone who would listen, "Kalokyres plainly states that only nomads should be employed in the pursuit of other nomads since, being accustomed to the saddle from infancy, they are superior horsemen. Why have we Khamorth with us, if not for such a purpose as this?"

"If himself doesna cease his havering anent his precious book, the Gavras will be after making him eat it one fine day," Viridovix said. Marcus thought the same, but if the Emperor was displeased he gave no immediate sign.

The morning after the Yezda were spotted, Scaurus was returning to the Roman camp from the women's quarters when someone called his name. He turned to find Thorisin Gavras behind him. The Sevastokrator was swaying slightly; he looked to have had quite a night of it.

"Good morning, your Highness," Scaurus said.

Thorisin raised a mocking eyebrow. "'Good morning, your highness,'" he mimicked. "Well, it's good to see you can still be polite to the hand that feeds you, even if you do sleep with an island wench."

Marcus felt his face grow hot; the flush was all too noticeable with his fair skin. Catching sight of it, Thorisin said, "Nothing to be ashamed about. The lass is far from homely, I give you that. She's no fool, either, from what I've heard, whether or not her brother eats nails every morning."

"That sounds like Soteric." Marcus had to smile, struck by the aptness of Thorisin's description.

Gavras shrugged. "Never trust a Namdalener. Deal with them, yes, but trust? Never," he repeated. He walked slowly up to Scaurus and then around him, studying the bemused Roman as he might a horse he was thinking of buying. Marcus could smell the wine on the Sevastokrator's breath. Thorisin considered silently as he walked, then burst out, "So what's wrong with you?"

"Sir?" When faced with a superior in an unpredictable mood, least said was best. The tribune knew that lesson as well as the lowliest of his troopers.

"What's wrong with you?" It seemed Thorisin could only keep track of his thoughts by saying them over again. "You damned Romans keep company with the islanders by choice; Skotos' frozen beard, you take to them like flies to dead meat." Despite the unflattering simile, there was no rancor in the Sevastokrator's voice, only puzzlement. "By rights, then, you should be bubbling with seditions, rebellions, and plots to put one Scaurus on my brother's throne, with his skull for a drinking goblet."

Now genuinely alarmed, the Roman started to protest his loyalty. "Shut up," Thorisin said, with the flat authority power and drink can sometimes combine to put in a voice. "You come with me," he added, and started back to his own tent, not looking to see whether the tribune was following.

Marcus wondered if he should disappear and hope the Sevastokrator would forget their meeting once sober. He could not take the chance, he decided; Thorisin was too experienced a drinker to go blank that way. Feeling nothing but trepidation, he trailed along after Mavrikios' brother.

Gavras' tent was of blue silk, but not a great deal larger than the canvas and wool shelters of the Videssian army's common soldiers. The Sevastokrator was too much a warrior to care for extravagance in the field. Only the pair of Haloga bodyguards in front of the opening gave any real indication of his rank. They snapped to attention when they caught sight of their master. "Sir," said one, "the Lady Komitta has been asking for you for the past—"

Komitta Rhangavve herself chose that moment to poke her head out of the tent. Her lustrous black hair was pulled back from her face, accenting her aquiline features. She looked, in fact, like a barely tamed angry falcon, and the tirade she loosed at Thorisin did nothing to lessen the resemblance.

"Where have you been, you worthless rutting tinpot?" she shrilled. "Out swilling again, from the look of you, with the mountain men and the goatherds, and tumbling their women —or their goats! I am of noble kin—how dare you subject me to this humiliation, you—" and she swore with the same aptness Scaurus had heard from her when she gambled with the Namdaleni.

"Phos' little suns," Thorisin muttered, giving back a pace under the blast. "I don't need this, whether she's right or not. My head hurts already."

The two guards stood rigid, their blank faces caricatures of unhearingness. The Roman's efforts along the same line were not so successful, but then, he thought, the poor guards likely got more practice.

He had to admire the way the Sevastokrator pulled himself together and returned his irascible mistress' barrage. "Don't bite the thumb at me, slattern!" he roared, his baritone pounding through her soprano curses. "Give me peace, or I'll warm your noble backside!"

Komitta kept on at full bore for another few seconds, but when Thorisin Gavras stalked toward the tent with the evident intention of carrying out his threat, she turned and ducked back inside, only to emerge a moment later. Proud as a cat, she strode stiff-backed past Thorisin. "I shall be with my cousins," she informed him with icy hauteur.

"Good enough," he replied amicably; Marcus thought his

anger mostly assumed. Gavras suddenly seemed to remember the Roman standing by his side. "True love is a wonderful thing, is it not?" he remarked with a sour grin. A few seconds later he added, "If you pray to Phos, outlander, tack on a prayer that he deliver you from a taste for excitable women. They're great fun, but they wear . . . oh, they wear."

The Sevastokrator sounded very tired, but he was brisk again when he said to one of his bodyguards, "Ljot, fetch my brother for me, will you? We have a few things to discuss with this lad here." He stabbed a thumb at Marcus. Ljot, who proved to be the guard on the right, hurried away.

Thorisin pulled the tent flap back for the Roman to precede him. "Go on," he said, returning to the ironic tone with which he'd begun the encounter. "If not the Avtokrator's throne, will the Sevastokrator's mats please your excellency?"

Scaurus stooped to enter the tent; the air inside was still musky with Komitta's perfume. He sank to the silk-lined mat flooring, waiting for the Sevastokrator to follow. Thorisin's gamesome mood, his half-threats and sardonic compliments, only served to make the tribune jittery. As he had in the Emperor's chambers, he felt caught up in an elaborate contest whose rules he did not understand, but where the penalty for a misplay could be disastrous.

The Sevastokrator and the Roman had waited only a couple of minutes when the guardsman Ljot returned. "His Majesty asked me to tell you he will be delayed," the Haloga reported. "He is at breakfast with Baanes Onomagoulos and will join you when they are through."

If Thorisin Gavras had put on anger to match Komitta's, there was mistaking his real wrath now. "So I'm less important than that bald-headed son of a smith, am I?" he growled. "Ljot, you take your arse back to Mavrikios and tell him he and his breakfast can both climb right up it."

The Emperor's own head appeared inside the tent, a wide grin on his face. "Little brother, if you're going to commit lese majesty, never do it by messenger. I'd have to execute him too, and it's wasteful."

Thorisin stared, then started to laugh. "You are a bastard," he said. "Come on, set that stringy old carcass of yours down here." Mavrikios did so; the tent was a bit cramped for three but, thanks to its thin silk walls, not unbearably stuffy.

Opening a battered pine chest no finer than any private soldier might have owned, Thorisin produced an earthenware jug of wine, from which he swigged noisily. "Ahh, that's good. Phos willing, it will make my headache go away." He drank again. "Seriously, brother, you shouldn't use Baanes to twit me—I remember too well how jealous of him I was when I was small."

"I know, but the chance to listen to you fume was too good to pass up." Mavrikios sounded half-contrite, half-amused at his practical joke's success.

"Bastard," Thorisin said again, this time with no heat.

Marcus looked from one of the brothers Gavras to the other; though he'd had nothing to drink, he could feel the world starting to spin. Much of what he'd thought he under-stood of Videssian politics had just fallen to pieces before his eyes. Where was the feud that had the Gavrai so at odds with each other they rarely spoke?

"Oh dear," Mavrikios said, spying the bewilderment Scaurus was doing his best to hide. "I'm afraid we've man-aged to confuse your guest."

"Have we, now? Well, I'm damned if I'll apologize to any Namdalener-loving barbarian." Thorisin's words were fierce enough to make the tribune start up in fright, but he accompa-nied them with an unmistakable wink. Marcus sagged back to his haunches, altogether muddled.

"'Only right he should be confused," the Sevastokrator went on, warming to his theme. "He and his whole crew like the easterners so bloody well this whole camp should be buzz-ing with talk they're ganging together to kill us all. Phos knows we've paid enough good gold to sniff out the rumors."

"We didn't find any, either," Mavrikios said accusingly. "Which leads to one of two conclusions: either you're clever beyond compare, or else you may be loyal in spite of your perverse choice of friends."

"I don't think he looks all that bright, Mavrikios," Thorisin said.

"You don't look any too well yourself, little brother," the Emperor retorted, but again the tone of the badinage was what would be expected from two brothers who liked each other well.

With the persistence too much wine can bring, Thorisin

said, "If he's not so smart as to be able to fool us all, he's most likely loyal. Who would have thought it, from a friend of the Namdaleni?" He shook his head in amazement, then belched softly.

"The gods be thanked," Marcus murmured to himself. When both Gavrai eyed him questioningly, he realized he'd spoken Latin. "I'm sorry you had any reason to doubt me," he told them, returning to Videssian, "and very glad you don't any longer."

His relief was so great all of his defenses slid down at once, along with the guards on his tongue. "Then the two of you aren't quarreling with each other?" he blurted, then stopped in worse confusion than before.

The brothers Gavras suddenly looked like small boys whose secret has been discovered. Mavrikios plucked a hair from his beard, looked at it musingly, and tossed it aside. "Thorisin, he may be smarter than he seems."

"Eh?" Thorisin said blurrily. "I should hope so." He was sprawled out on his side and fighting a losing battle with sleep.

"Lazy good-for-nothing," Mavrikios smiled. He turned back to Scaurus. "You're quite right, outlander. We are having a little play, and to a fascinated audience, I might add."

"But I was there when you first quarreled, gambling against each other," the tribune protested. "That couldn't have been contrived."

The Emperor's smile slipped a notch. He looked at his brother, but Thorisin was beginning to snore. "No, it was real enough," he admitted. "Thorisin's tongue has always been more hasty than is good for him, and I own he made me spleenish that night. But next morning we made it up—we always do."

Mavrikios' smile broadened again. "This time, though, my contrary brother chose to make a donkey of himself in front of a hundred people. It was less than no time before the vultures started gathering over the corpse of our love." He cocked an eyebrow at the Roman. "Some of them flapped near you, I've heard."

"So they did," Scaurus agreed, remembering the odd meeting he'd had with Vardanes Sphrantzes.

"You know what I mean, then," Mavrikios nodded. "You

were far from the only one sounded, by the way. It occurred to Thorisin and me that if we lay very still and let the vultures land, thinking they were about to pick our bones, why then we might have the makings of a fine buzzard stew for ourselves."

"I can follow all that," Marcus allowed. "But why, having laid your trap, did you give Ortaias Sphrantzes the left wing of your army, even with Khoumnos to keep him in check?"

"He is an imbecile, isn't he?" the Emperor chuckled. "Nephon has his eye on him, though, so have no fear on that score."

"I've noticed that. But why is he here at all? Without his precious book he know less about soldiering than his horse does, and with it he's almost more dangerous, because he thinks he knows things he doesn't."

"He's here for the same reason he has his worthless command: Vardanes asked them of me."

Marcus was silent while he tried to digest that. At last he shook his head; the crosscurrents of intrigue that could make the Sevastos request such a thing and the Emperor grant it were too complex for him to penetrate.

Mavrikios Gavras watched him struggle and give up. "It's good to find there are still some things you don't understand," he said. "You have more skill at politics than most mercenary soldiers I know."

Thinking of the ruling Roman triumvirate of Caesar, Crassus, and Pompey—each of whom gladly would have torn the hearts from the other two could he have done so without plunging his country into civil war—Scaurus said, "I know something of faction politics, but yours, I think, are worse." He waited to see if Mavrikios would solve the riddle for him.

The Emperor did, with the air of a professor giving a demonstration for an inexperienced student who might have talent. "Think it through. With Ortaias here, Vardanes gets an eye in the army—not the best of eyes, perhaps, because I know it's there, but an eye just the same. And who knows? Even though Khoumnos has the real power on the left, Ortaias may eventually learn something of war and become more useful to his uncle in that way. Clear so far?"

"Clear enough, anyway."

"All right. If I'd said no to Vardanes, he wouldn't have stopped plotting against me—he could no more do that than stop breathing. I thought it safer to have Ortaias here where I could keep an eye on him than involved in Phos knows what mischief back in the city."

"I follow the logic well enough. From what little I've seen of Vardanes Sphrantzes, I'd say it was sound, but you know him far better than I."

"He's a serpent," Mavrikios said flatly. His voice grew grim. "There's one other reason to let Ortaias come along. If worse comes to worse, he's worth something as a hostage. Likely not much, when I recall how conveniently Evphrosyne died, but something." Still in the role of instructor, he spread his hands, palms out, as if he had just proven two lines in a complex figure parallel after all.

His, though, were not the pale soft hands of a sheltered don. Spear, sword, and bow had scarred and callused them, and sun and wind turned them brown and rough. They were the hands of a warrior, yes, but a warrior who also showed his skill in another arena, one where the weapons were the more deadly for being invisible.

The Emperor saw Scaurus' admiration, dipped his head in acknowledgment of it. "Time the both of us got back to work," he said. "Look angry when you come out. I've dressed you down, and Thorisin and I have been snapping at each other again. It would never do for people to think we like each other."

"Are you odd-looking people, uh, Romans?" The speaker was a smilingly handsome, swarthy young man on a stocky, fast-looking horse. A girl of about his own age, her silver-braceleted arms round his middle, rode behind him.

Both were in typical Videssian horseman's gear, a light, long-sleeved tunic over baggy woolen trousers tucked into boots. Each of them wore a sheathed saber; he had a bow and a felt quiver slung over his back.

They led a packhorse loaded with gear, prominent among it a wickerwork helmet, a bundle of javelins, and a fine pandoura, its soundbox decorated with elaborate scrollwork and inlays of mother of pearl.

The young fellow's Videssian had a slight guttural accent. He wore a leather cap with three rounded projections toward the front, a broad neckflap and several streamers of bright ribbon trailing off behind. Marcus had seen a good many Vaspurakaners with such headgear—quite a few of them had settled in these lands not far from their ancestral home. On most of them the cap seemed queer and lumpy, but the stranger somehow gave it a jaunty air.

His flashing smile and breezy way of speech were wasted on Gaius Philippus, who frowned up at him. "You don't look any too good yourself," he growled, unconsciously echoing Mavrikios speaking to Thorisin. "If we are Romans, what do you want with us?"

The centurion's sour greeting did not put off the horseman. He answered easily, "You may as well get used to me. I am to be your guide through the passes of my lovely homeland. I am Prince Senpat Sviodo of Vaspurakan." He drew himself up in the saddle.

Marcus was pleased he'd guessed the young man's people, but more alarmed than anything else at the prospect of having to deal with a new and unfamiliar royalty. "Your Highness—" he began, only to stop, nonplused, when Senpat Sviodo and his companion burst into gales of laughter.

"You *are* from a far land, mercenary," he said. "Have you never heard Vaspurakan called the princes' land?"

Thinking back, the tribune did recall some slighting reference of Mavrikios' during the briefing before the imperial army left Videssos. Of its significance, however, he had no idea, and said so.

"Every Vaspurakaner is a prince," Sviodo explained. "How could it be otherwise, since we are all descendants of Vaspur, the first and most noble of the creations of Phos?"

Scaurus was instantly sure the Videssians did not take kindly to that theology. He had little time to ponder it, though, for the girl was nudging Senpat, saying, "Half-truths, and men's half-truths at that. Without the princesses of Vaspurakan, there would be no princes."

"A distinct point," Senpat Sviodo said fondly. He turned back to the Romans. "Gentlemen," he said, looking at Gaius Philippus as if giving him the benefit of the doubt, "my wife Nevrat. She knows Vaspurakan and its pathways at least as well as I do."

"Well, to the crows with *you*, then," someone called from about the third rank of Romans. "I'd follow her anywhere!"

The legionaries who heard him whooped agreement. Marcus was relieved to see Senpat Sviodo laugh with them, and Nevrat too. She was a comely lass, with strong sculptured features, a dark complexion like her husband's, and flashing white teeth. Instead of Senpat's distinctive Vaspurakaner cap, she wore a flower-patterned silk scarf over her black, wavy hair.

Lest the next gibe have a less fortunate outcome, the tribune made haste to introduce some of his leading men to the Vaspurakaners. Then he asked, "How is it you are in Videssos' service?"

Senpat Sviodo told his story as they traveled west; it was not much different from what Scaurus had expected. The young man was of a noble house—his fine horse, his elegant pandoura, and the silver Nevrat wore had already made the tribune sure he was no common soldier.

"Being a noble in Vaspurakan these past few years was not an unmixed blessing," he said. "When the Yezda came sweeping through, our peasants could flee, having little to lose by taking shelter here inside the Empire. But my family's estates had rich fields, wealth besides from a small copper mine, and a keep as strong as any. We chose to fight to hold them."

"And well, too," Nevrat added. "More than once we drove the raiders off our lands licking their wounds." Her slim hand touched the hilt of her saber in a way that told Marcus she meant "we" in the most literal sense.

"So we did," Senpat agreed with a smile. But that smile faded as he thought of the grinding fight he had waged—and lost. "We never drove them far enough, though, or hard enough. Season by season, year by year, they wore us down. We couldn't farm, we couldn't mine, we couldn't go more than a bowshot from the keep without being attacked. Two years ago a Videssian regiment passed by our holding chasing Yezda, and Senpat Sviodo, prince of Vaspurakan, became Senpat Sviodo, imperial scout. There are worse fates." He shrugged.

He tugged at the rope by which he led his packhorse. When the beast came forward, he plucked the pandoura from its back and struck a fiery chord. "Worse fates indeed!" he shouted, half singing. "Wolves of the west, beware! I come to take back what is mine!" Nevrat hugged him tightly, her face shining with pride.

The Romans thought well of his display of spirit, but it had a special purport for Gorgidas. Familiar with the strife-torn politics of Greek cities, he said, "That one and his wife will do well. It's so very easy for an exile to leave hope behind along with his home. The ones who somehow bring it with them are a special breed."

As the army halted for the night, Senpat Sviodo and his wife, like so many before them in the Empire of Videssos, walked up to observe with unfeigned admiration as the Romans created their camp. "What a good notion!" he exclaimed. "With fieldworks like these, it would be easy to stand off attackers."

"That's the idea behind them," Scaurus agreed, watching his men toss the dry, reddish-brown plateau soil up from the ditch they were digging to form the camp's breastwork. "You'll have officer's status among us, so your tent will be one of those in front of mine, along the *via principalis*—" At Senpat's blank expression, he realized he'd used the Latin name and hastily translated: "The main road, I should say."

"Well enough, then," the Vaspurakaner said. Lifting the three-peaked cap from his head, he used a tunic sleeve to wipe caked sweat and dust from his forehead. "I could use a good night's sleep—my behind isn't sorry to be out of the saddle."

"Yours?" Nevrat said. "At least you had a saddle to be out of—I've been astride a horse's bumpy backbone all day, and my stern is petrified." She gave her husband a look full of meaning. "I hope you don't plan on being out of the saddle the whole night long."

"Dear, there are saddles, and then there are saddles," Senpat grinned. His arm slid round her waist; she nestled happily against him.

Seeing their longing for each other, Scaurus muttered a Latin curse—Videssian was too new in his mouth for comfortable swearing. Until that moment he had forgotten the rule he'd imposed against women in the camp. If it stood for his own men, he could hardly break it for these newcomers. As gently as he could, he explained his edict to the Vaspurakaners.

They listened in disbelief, too amazed to be really angry.

Finally Senpat said, "Watching your soldiers building this camp convinced me you were men of no common discipline. But to enforce that kind of order and have it obeyed—" He shook his head. "If your Romans are fools enough to put up with it, that's their affair and yours. But I'm damned if we will. Come on, love," he said to Nevrat. And their tent went up, not within the Roman stockade, but just outside it, for they preferred each other's company to the safety of trench, earthwork, and palisade. Alone inside his tent later that evening, Marcus decided he could not blame them.

His own sleep came slowly. It occurred to him that Phostis Apokavkos might well be able to tell him much more than he already knew about the strong-willed folk who came out of Vaspurakan. Apokavkos was from the far west and presumably had dealt with Vaspurakaners before.

The adopted Roman was not sleeping either, but throwing knucklebones with a double handful of men from his maniple. "You looking for me, sir?" he asked when he saw Marcus. "Won't be sorry if you are—I've got no luck tonight."

"If you're after an excuse to get out of the game, your luck just turned," the tribune said. He spoke in his own language, and Apokavkos had no trouble understanding him; when the onetime peasant-soldier tried to speak Latin, though, his lisping Videssian accent still made him hard to follow. But he stuck with it doggedly, and his progress was easy to see.

Scaurus took him back to his own tent and asked him, "Tell me what you know of Vaspurakan and its people." Recalling Apokavkos' dislike of the Namdaleni for their heterodox beliefs, he made himself ready to discount as prejudiced some of what the other would reply."

"The 'princes'?" Phostis said. "About their land I can't tell you that much—where I grew up, it was no more than mountains on the northern horizon. Beastly cold in winter, I've heard. They raise good horses there, but everybody knows that."

Even Scaurus had heard good things about Vaspurakaner horseflesh, and he had the traditional Roman attitude toward the equestrian art—that it was a fine skill, for other people. He was intellectually aware that the use of stirrups made horsemanship a very different thing from the one he knew, but still found it hard to take the idea seriously.

Apokavkos proceeded to surprise him, for he spoke of the Vaspurakaners themselves, not with suspicion, but with genuine and obvious respect. "It's said three 'princes' working together could sell ice to Skotos, and I believe it, for work together they would. I don't know where they learned it, unless being stuck between countries bigger'n they are taught it to them, but they take care of their own, always. They'll fight among themselves, aye, but let an outsider meddle in their affairs and they're tight as trap jaws against him."

To Marcus that seemed such plain good sense as hardly to be worth comment, but Phostis Apokavkos' voice was full of wistful admiration. "You—*we*, I mean—Romans are like that too, but there's plenty of Videssians who'd hire on Skotos himself, if it meant paying their enemies back one."

The tribune's thoughts went to the decayed heads he had seen at the foot of the Milestone in Videssos, generals who rebelled with Yezda backing, both of them. He also thought, uneasily, of Vardanes Sphrantzes. Apokavkos had a point.

Trying to shake the worrisome pictures from his mind, Scaurus decided to tease Phostis a bit, to see what he would do. "How can you speak so well of heretics?" he asked.

"Because they're good people, religion or no," Apokavkos said at once. "They aren't like your precious islanders—begging your pardon, sir—always chipping away at other people's ideas and changing their own whenever the wind shifts. The 'princes' believe what they believe and they don't care a horseturd whether you do or not. I don't know," he went on uncomfortably, "I suppose they're all damned—but if they are, old Skotos had better watch himself, because enough Vaspurakaners in his hell and they might end up taking it away from him."

The first raid on the imperial army came two days before it got to Amorion. It was a pinprick, nothing more—a handful of Yezda waylaying a Videssian scout. When he was missed, his comrades searches until they found his body. The Yezda, of course, had plundered it and stolen his horse.

There was a slightly larger encounter the next day, when a small band of Khamorth traded arrows with the Yezda until reinforcements drove the enemy away. Trivial stuff, really, Marcus thought, until he remembered the Emperor promising the journey from Garsavra to Amorion would be as easy as that from the capital to Garsavra. More invaders were loose in the Empire than Mavrikios had thought.

And Amorion, when the army reached it, proved to have suffered badly. Lying on the northern bank of the Ithome, a tributary of the Arandos River, Amorion, like most towns in Videssos' westlands, had long ago torn down its walls for their building stone. Yezda raiders took full advantage of the city's helplessness, ravaging its suburbs and penetrating almost to the river bank in several places. As the army approached, the plundered areas were barren and rubble-strewn, in stark contrast to the fertility the river brought neighboring districts.

The contingent Gagik Bagratouni had gathered to reinforce Mavrikios was not as large as the one under Baanes Onomagoulos, but it was, Marcus soon decided, made up of better men. Most were Vaspurakaners like their commander—dark, curly-haired men with bushy beards, usually heavier of build than the Videssians they lived among. They wore scale-armor; many had helmets of wicker like Senpat Sviodo's, often ornamented with plaited horns or wings. Almost all of them looked like veterans.

"So we should," Senpat Sviodo said when Marcus remarked on this. "At least as much as the Empire's *akritai*, we have stood in Yezd's way these past years and been Videssos' shield. Believe me, it was not what we wanted, but being set where Phos chose to place his princes in this world, we had no choice."

He shrugged, then went on, "My people tell a fable about a little lark who heard the sky was about to fall. She turned on her back with her legs in the air to catch it. 'Have you become a tree, then?' all the other animals asked. 'No,' she answered, 'but still I must do all I can.' So did she, and so do we."

Just as it had for Onomagoulos, the army arranged itself in review to honor Gagik Bagratouni. As the general rode up on a roan stallion, Scaurus found himself impressed by the man's sheer physical presence. If Caesar had been a bird of prey, a human expression of Rome's eagle, Gagik Bagratouni was a lion.

His tawny skin, his mane of coal-black hair, and the thick dark beard that covered his wide, high-cheekboned face almost to the eyes were enough in themselves to create that impression. The steady gaze from those eyes, a hunter's look, added to the image, as did the thrust of his nose—it was thicker and fleshier than the typical Videssian beak, but no less imperious. He even sat his horse strikingly, as if posing for an equestrian statue or, more likely, conscious that many eyes were on him.

Bagratouni held that impassive seat as he walked his horse past unit after unit. The only acknowledgment the troops got that he was so much as aware of their presence was a flick of his eyes across their ranks, the slightest dip of his head as he passed by each commander. Mavrikios himself was not nearly so imperial of demeanor, yet it was plain Gagik Bagratouni meant no slight to the Emperor, but was merely acting as he always did.

When he came to the Romans, drawn up next to the Emperor's Haloga guard, Bagratouni's thick brows rose—these were men whose like he had not seen. He looked them over appraisingly, studying their equipment, their stance, their faces. Whatever his judgment was, he did not show it. But when he saw Senpat and Nevrat Sviodo standing with the Romans' officers, his heavy features lit in the first smile Scaurus had seen from him.

He shouted something in his own tongue. His voice was in keeping with the rest of him, a bass roar. Senpat answered in the same speech; though altogether ignorant of it, Marcus heard the name "Sviodo" several times. Gagik Bagratouni cried out again, then jumped down from his horse and folded Senpat Sviodo in a bearhug, kissing him on each cheek. He did the same to Nevrat, with a different kind of gusto.

"Sahak Sviodo's son!" he said in thickly accented Videssian, switching languages out of courtesy to the Romans around him, "and with such a lovely bride, too! Lucky you are, both of you! Sahak was a great one for pulling Yezd's beard, yes, and the Emperor's too, when in our affairs he stuck it. You have the very look of home—I knew him well."

"I wish I could say the same," Senpat answered. "He died before my beard sprouted."

"So I heard, and a great pity it was," Bagratouni said. "Now you must tell me—who are these strange men you travel with?"

"Have you noticed, Scaurus darling," Viridovix said, "that every one of these Vaspurakaner omadhauns who sets eyes on you and yours is after calling you funny-looking? Right rude it is, I'm thinking."

"Likely they saw you first," Gaius Philippus put in, drawing a glare from Viridovix.

"Enough, you two," Marcus said. Perhaps luckily, the Gaul and the centurion preferred Latin as a language for bickering, and the Vaspurakaners could not understand them. Scaurus named his men for Bagratouni, introduced some of his officers and, as he had done so often by now, briefly explained how they had come to Videssos.

"That is most marvelous," Gagik Bagratouni said. "You— all of you—" His expansive gesture took in everyone the tribune had presented to him. "—must to my home come this evening for a meal, and more of your tale to tell me. I would have it now, but things are piling up behind me."

He spoke the truth there; the procession he headed, which was made up of his contingent's officers and some of the leading officials and citizens of Amorion, had halted in confusion when he dismounted. Its members were variously standing about or sitting on horseback while waiting for him to continue. One of them in particular, a tall harsh-faced priest who had a fierce hound on a lead of stout iron chain, was staring venomously at Bagratouni. The Vaspurakaner affected not to notice, but Scaurus stood near enough to hear him mutter, "Plague take you, Zemarkhos, you shave-pated buzzard."

Bagratouni remounted, and the army of functionaries moved on toward the Emperor. When the priest started forward once more, his dog balked, setting itself on its haunches. He jerked at its chain. "Come on, Vaspur!" he snapped, and the beast, choked by its collar, yelped and followed him.

Marcus was not sure he believed his ears. Clearly, not all Videssians shared the liking Phostis Apokavkos had for the folk of Vaspurakan—not when a priest would name his dog for the Vaspurakaners' eponymous ancestor. Senpat Sviodo stood tight-lipped beside Scaurus, plainly feeling the insult's sting. The Roman wondered how Gagik Bagratouni put up with such calculated insolence.

Unlike Baanes Onomagoulos at Garsavra, Bagratouni dismounted and performed a full proskynesis before the Em-

peror, followed by everyone accompanying him. Even in the
formal act of submission to his overlord he was still a commanding figure, going to his knees and then to his belly with
feline dignity and grace. Scaurus noted with amusement that,
by comparison, the churlish priest Zemarkhos looked a poorly
built stick man.

After Mavrikios' brief speech of thanks for the men Bagratouni had collected, the Vaspurakaner general and his party
performed the proskynesis once more, then retired from the
imperial presence. He held up their withdrawal for a moment
to give Senpat Sviodo and Scaurus directions to his dwelling.
Zemarkhos had never seen Romans before, but, from the look
he gave them, their willingness to be a Vaspurakaner's guests
was enough to brand them agents of Skotos.

When Senpat Sviodo and his wife met the Romans who
were going with them to Bagratouni's, they had exchanged
their traveling garb for more elegant attire. He wore a spotless
white tunic coming almost to his knees, baggy trousers of
reddish-brown wool, and sandals with golden clasps. On his
head was the familiar Vaspurakaner cap; his pandora was
slung across his back.

Nevrat was in a long gown of light blue linen, its cut subtly
different from Videssian designs. The dress set off her dark
skin magnificently, as did her massy silver bracelets, neck-
lace, and earrings.

Senpat stared at the Romans in amazement. "What matter
of men have I fallen in with?" he cried. "Do you satisfy each
other? Where are your women, in Phos' sacred name?"

"It's not our usual custom to bring them, unbidden, to a
feast," Marcus answered, but he shared an apprehensive look
with Quintus Glabrio. The junior centurion was partnered to a
fiery-tempered Videssian girl named Damaris. She and Helvis
would not be pleased to learn they had been excluded from a
function which they could have attended.

The rest of the Roman party was more sanguine about
being by themselves. "Sure and there'll be a lass or three fair
famished for the sight of a Celtic gentleman," Viridovix said.
"It's not as if I'm thinking to return alone."

Gaius Philippus was in most ways an admirable man but,
as Marcus knew, women were of no use to him out of bed.

He looked back at Senpat Sviodo with as much incomprehension as the Vaspurakaner directed toward him.

"Are you looking at me?" Gorgidas asked Senpat. "I hold with the idea of Diogenes, a wise man of my people. When he was asked the right time for marriage, he said, 'For a young man, not yet; for an old man, never.'"

"What of you, though?" Senpat asked. "You're neither one nor the other."

"I manage," Gorgidas said shortly. "Right now, I manage to be hungry. Come on, shall we?"

Gagik Bagratouni's home was half villa, half fortress. Its grounds were spacious and well kept, with little groves of citruses, figs, and date palms placed artfully among flowerbeds full of bright blooms. But the main house was a thick-walled stronghold seemingly transplanted from Vaspurakan's hills, set behind outworks that would have delighted the commander of any border keep.

As he greeted his guests by the massive, metal-clad gate, Bagratouni noticed the tribune taking the measure of the place and Gaius Philippus' frank stare of professional appraisal. "This is not what I would want," he said, waving at the forbidding gray stone walls. "But I fear too many in Amorion delight not in seeing prosper the princes. But prosper I do, and I am able for myself to care."

That, if anything, was an understatement, for Gagik Bagratouni did not rely on walls alone for protection. His personal guard manned them, a picked group of young Vaspurakaners as formidable as any band of warriors Scaurus had seen.

"Do not worry about such things," the general said. "Come into my courtyard; eat, drink, talk, laugh."

Bagratouni's house was laid out in a basic style Marcus knew well, for it was popular among the wealthy in Italy. Instead of facing out onto the world, the home's focus was directed inward to a central court. But the structure was more a bastion than any Roman home Marcus knew. Only a few windowslits were directed outward, and those as much for arrow-fire as for view. The gates that led from the outer grounds into the courtyard were almost as stoutly made as those protecting the estate as a whole.

Lanterns hung from trees inside the courtyard. Their glass

panes were of many colors; as twilight deepened, beams of gold and red, blue and green danced in the foliage. The main tables in the courtyard's center, though, were brightly lit, to call attention to the feast they bore.

Vaspurakaner cookery was nothing like Videssian cuisine, which emphasized seafood and sauces of fermented fish. The main course was a roasted kid, spiced with a glaze of tarragon, mint, and lemon, and garnished with shreds of sharp yellow cheese. There was also a stew of ground lamb and hard-boiled eggs, made flavorful with onion, coriander, and cinnamon, and extended with chickpeas. Both dishes made the eyes water along with the mouth, but both were delicious.

"Whoo!" Viridovix said, fanning his face with his hand. "There's a lot going on in there." To quell the flames, he downed his winecup and reached for the decanter before him. Of all Bagratouni's guests, the big Celt probably felt the food's tang the most. Beyond vinegar, honey, and a few pale-flavored herbs, northern Gaul had little to offer in the way of spices.

Scaurus sat at Gagik Bagratouni's right, between the general and his chief aide, a man of early middle years named Mesrop Anhoghin, who was even more thickly bearded than his commander. At Bagratouni's left, confirming Senpat Sviodo's words, was the general's wife Zabel, a plump, comfortable lady whose few words of Videssian were mostly an apology for not knowing more. Anhoghin's command of the imperial tongue was not much better. As a result, Gagik Bagratouni had the tribune's conversation almost entirely to himself, something Marcus soon began to suspect he had arranged deliberately.

The general—*nakharar*, he styled himself in his own language; it meant warrior-prince—had a hunger for knowledge of the world's far reaches that rivaled Gorgidas'. Perhaps, thought Scaurus, it sprang from his effort to grow beyond the limits of the isolated land in which he'd come to manhood. Whatever the reason, he bombarded the Roman with questions not only touching on matters military, but also about his native land, its people, what the city of Videssos was like, even what it was like to see the ocean. "Never have I seen it," he remarked sadly. "Rivers, yes, lakes, those yes, too, but never the sea."

"Did I see his honor ask you about the sea?" asked Virido-vix, who was a few seats away. At Marcus' nod, the Gaul said earnestly, "Tell him it's a fit province for lunatics, and precious little else. A boat's no more than a prison, with the risk of drowning besides."

"Why says he that?" Gagik asked. "On rivers and lakes I enjoy to fish in a boat."

"He suffers from seasickness," Scaurus answered, and then had to explain the concept to Bagratouni. The Vaspurakaner tugged his beard as he considered the Roman's words; Marcus wondered if he thought he was being made sport of.

Dessert consisted of fruit and some interesting pastry balls, a mixture of wheat flour, ground dates, and minced almonds, covered over with powdered sugar. This last was a discovery for the Romans, for the Videssians sweetened with honey, even as they did themselves. Reaching for about his fourth, Gorgidas remarked, "It's as well I don't see these more often, lest I bulge with lard."

"Bah!" Gaius Philippus said. "Why is it always the skinny ones who complain?" Only the hard life he led kept the centurion from losing the battle with his belly.

"Not only are they very good," said Quintus Glabrio, licking his fingers, "but they look as if they'd keep well, and they're so rich a few would feed a man for some time. They'd be good travelers' fare."

"So they would and so they are. You are one who sees the importance in things, then? That is good," Bagratouni rumbled approvingly. "We of Vaspurakan often on journeys carry them."

"The Videssians do, too," Senpat Sviodo told him with a grin. "They call them 'princes' balls.'" The Romans and most of the Vaspurakaners snorted; Gagik Bagratouni looked blank. Senpat translated the pun into his native language. The *nakharar* blinked, then he and his wife began to laugh at the same time. When Zabel laughed it was easy to see how the lines had come to crease her features; her face was made for laughter. Gagik smiled at her fondly. She was far from beautiful, but in her own way lovely.

"Do they indeed?" her husband chuckled. "Do they indeed?"

After the dessert was finished, someone called to Senpat,

"Give us a tune, there, since you've brought your pandoura along."

"Fair enough," he said. "Who's with me?" One of the Vaspurakaners had a flute; a quick search of the house turned up a small hand-drum for another volunteer. And with no more ado than that they struck up a song of their mountain homeland. All the Vaspurakaners seemed to know the words and clapped out the beat with their hands. Senpat's fingers danced over the strings of his instrument; his strong clear tenor helped lead the singers. Gagik Bagratouni sang with enthusiasm and great volume, but even Marcus could tell that the *nakharar* could not carry a tune in a bucket.

The tribune felt isolated, both by his indifference toward music in general and his ignorance of this music in particular. He wondered what Helvis would make of it and had another twinge of conscience over not bringing her with him. To his untrained ear, most of the songs had a defiant air to them, as befit the resilient folk who gave them birth.

As the musicians played on, the Vaspurakaners got up from the table one by one and began to dance, either with the ladies who accompanied them or with some of Gagik Bagratouni's servinggirls. The slates of the courtyard rang to boot heels stamping in intricate rhythms. Bodies swayed, sinuous and sinewy at the same time. The dancers were a physical expression of what they heard, Marcus thought with surprise, and began to understand the grip strong music could take, even if he failed to feel it himself.

Viridovix, now, was taken hard by it, watching and listening as if in a trance. When at length Senpat and his fellows struck up a particularly sprightly tune, the Celt could stand—or rather sit—no more. He rose to join the dancers.

He did not try to imitate their steps, dancing instead in his native Gallic style. Where their upper bodies shifted to the music, he was almost still above the waist, his arms motionless at his sides while his legs and feet twinkled in the complex figures of his dance. He leaped, spun, checked himself seemingly in midair, spun in the other direction, leaped again. His movements were utterly dissimilar to those of the dancers round him, yet strangely complementary as well.

A few at a time, the Vaspurakaners formed a circle around Viridovix, clapping him on. The musicians played faster and faster, but the Gaul was equal to the challenge, whirling and capering like a man possessed. As the music reached a fiery pitch, he capped his dance by springing almost his own height into the air. He let out a great shout at the top of his leap and came back to earth with a final splendid flourish.

The clapping turned from time-keeping to applause, in which all those still in their seats heartily joined. "Marvelous, marvelous!" Gagik exclaimed. "That step I should like to learn, were I less stiff in knee and thick of belly. Marvelous!" he repeated.

"I thank your honor," Viridovix panted; his exertions had deeply flushed his fair skin. He brushed sweat from his forehead. "Thirsty work it is, too. Would you be so kind as to fetch me a cup of wine, love?" he asked one of the serving-maids in the circle around him. Marcus noticed he chose a girl who had hardly been able to keep her eyes off him as he danced. The big Celt might be slipshod about some things, but where wenching was concerned he noted every detail.

"Thank you, lass," the Gaul purred as the girl brought his drink. He slipped an arm around her in what could have passed for no more than thanks, but when she moved closer to him instead of away he gathered her in with practiced efficiency.

"Your friend is as good as his word," Senpat Sviodo remarked to the tribune.

"I was thinking the same thing myself," Marcus laughed.

One of Bagratouni's retainers came trotting into the courtyard with some word for his master. He spoke in throaty Vaspurakaner, so Scaurus, sitting by the *nakharar*, could not understand what he said, but the Roman did catch the name Zemarkhos mentioned several times. Gagik Bagratouni's black brows lowered in anger. He asked a curt question of his guardsman, who nodded.

Bagratouni's scowl grew darker yet. He sat a moment in thought, his hands tangled in his thick beard. Then he snapped out a string of quick orders. The guard, startled, repeated the first one in a questioning voice, then broke into a toothy grin as Gagik explained. The man hurried away.

"Forgive me my rudeness, I pray you," the *nakharar* said, turning back to Scaurus. "When rises my temper, I forget the Empire's speech."

"So do I," the tribune admitted. "You've shown me much kindness tonight. I heard your man name the priest who hates you. Can I help you in your trouble? I think the Emperor would hear me if I asked him to make the man leave you at peace—Mavrikios is not one to sacrifice the Empire's unity for the sake of a priest's feelings."

"I need no man to fight my battles for me," was Gagik's instant response, and Scaurus was afraid he had offended the proud *nakharar*. But Bagratouni was hesitating, embarrassment on his leonine face—an expression that did not sit well there. "But by bad luck this foul priest wants not to speak with me, but with you and yours."

"With me? Why?" The prospect was alarming; Marcus had seen enough fanatical priests in Videssos to last him a lifetime.

"To read the mind of a cur, one must a cur be. It is better not to try. Do you wish to have words with him?"

The tribune's first impulse was to say no at once and have done. But to do so might leave his host in the lurch. "Whatever would serve you best," he replied at last.

"You are a good man, my friend. Let me think." The *nakharar* rubbed his forehead, as if trying to inspire wisdom.

"It might be better if you saw him," he decided. "Otherwise this Zemarkhos can claim I kept you from him. To me this matters not so much, for I shall Amorion be leaving with you and the Emperor. But for my people who stay behind, no end of trouble could he cause."

"All right, then." Marcus quickly rounded up Gaius Philippus, Quintus Glabrio, and Gorgidas, but Viridovix had contrived to disappear. Looking around, Scaurus also failed to see the serving wench the Celt had chosen as his quarry for the evening. He decided not to go chasing after Viridovix; he did not judge it likely that Zemarkhos knew the exact nature of the Roman party.

"I'd gladly trade places with the Gaul, sir," Glabrio grinned.

"I'm senior to you, puppy," Gaius Philippus said. "You wait your turn."

Ignoring their byplay, Gorgidas asked Scaurus, "What does the priest want with us?"

"To tell us we're all damned, I suppose. I'm glad you're here tonight; you're good at theological arguments."

"My favorite amusement," Gorgidas said, rolling his eyes in despair. "Oh, well, we'd best get this over with, I suppose —our host is growing impatient." That was true enough; like a caged hunting-beast, the *nakharar* was pacing up and down the courtyard, now and again smacking fist into palm.

When he saw the Romans finally ready, Bagratouni led them out through his fragrant gardens to the front gates of his estate. On their way to the gates, they were joined by the retainer who had brought Bagratouni word of Zemarkhos' arrival. Heavy leather gauntlets sheathed the man's arms, which were full of what looked like canvas sheeting. His face bore an expression of anticipation.

The gates were closed, as against any enemy. At the *nakharar's* impatient gesture, his men unbarred them and swung them wide. And, as if entering a conquered city in triumph, Zemarkhos strode onto the Vaspurakaner's land, his hound at his side.

He caught sight of Gagik Bagratouni before noticing the Romans behind him. "So," he said, "you dare not let these ignorant foreigners learn the truth, but seek only to enmesh them in your evil schemes?"

Bagratouni almost visibly swelled with wrath. Fists clenched, he stepped toward the priest. Zemarkhos' dog growled in warning; the hair stood up along its back. Zemarkhos took a tighter grip on the leash. "Stay, Vaspur!" he ordered, but that command was hardly one to make him better loved by the man he confronted.

Trying to avert the explosion, Marcus hastily brought his companions up past the *nakharar* so Zemarkhos could see them. "We are here, as you asked," he told the priest, "and at our kind host's urging as well. What do you have to say that would be of such importance for men you never met?"

"From your strange gear and now from your speech, I see you are a foreigner and know no better than to enter into this house of iniquity. My duty to your soul and those of your men has brought me to rescue you from the clutches of the infamous heretic who lured you here."

The tribune reluctantly admired Zemarkhos' misplaced courage. No faintheart would speak so boldly at his foe's very threshold. But, as with too many clerics Scaurus had met in Videssos, the priest's dogmas blinded him to the worth of any man who did not share them.

He answered as politely as he could. "As we did not discuss religious matters, the subject of heresy never came up."

"Oh, he is a sly one, cunning as the fox, hungry as the jackal. The ice will take him even so." Bagratouni's men muttered angrily as they listened to Zemarkhos revile their overlord, but the *nakharar* stood still and silent, as if carved from stone. His face was thunderous, but he did not answer the priest.

Gorgidas spoke up. His passionate interest in everything he came across had led him to examine Videssos' sacred writing as soon as he could read them, even if he could not accept their precepts. Now, with his facility for an apt quotation, he asked Zemarkhos, "Is it not written in the forty-eighth chapter: 'Let fury be suppressed! Put down violence, you who would assure yourselves, through righteousness.'?"

But quoting holy scriptures to the priest was letting him fight on ground of his own choosing. His reply was quick and sure. "Aye, and it is also written in the thirty-third chapter, 'Whoever works evil on the wicked pleases Phos and fulfills his will.' The Emperor may think he is doing a great thing in sallying forth against the heathen of Yezd. He could do better inside Videssos itself, by purifying it of the poisonous misbelievers within our borders!"

Bagratouni shoved past the Romans. "Priest, hatred you spew like a drunk his dinner. All this on my land you have done. Give I my men leave, and they treat you as you deserve."

Zemarkhos touched his dog's lead. In an instant the beast was leaping at Bagratouni, only to be brought up short by the leash. It snapped viciously, a growl rumbling in its throat. The priest laughed. "Send your dogs against mine—they'll have their tails between their legs soon enough."

"Why did you name that beast Vaspur? Tell me this," Bagratouni asked, tone deceptively mild.

"Why?" the priest jeered. "What better name for a dog?"

With that last insult, all Gagik Bagratouni's patience blew away. His voice was lion's roar indeed as he bellowed a command in his birth-tongue at the warrior who carried the roll of canvas. Deft as a net-wielding gladiator, the man jumped forward to pop his huge bag of heavy cloth over Zemarkhos' head. Screeching curses, the priest fell thrashing to the ground.

The hound Vaspur sprang snarling to protect its master. But Bagratouni's retainer was ready for the dog. Though tumbled about by its charge, he lodged one gauntleted arm between its gaping jaws while hugging the beast to his armored chest with the other. The snarl turned to a half-throttled whine.

The Vaspurakaner stooped to lift up the open end of the sack, which was now, of course, around Zemarkhos' flailing feet. Dodging a fusillade of kicks, he pushed the dog into the bag with its owner, then dropped the flap once more.

Zemarkhos' shrieks took on a sudden, desperate urgency as Vaspur, crazed with fear, began snapping wildly at everything near it—which, at the moment, consisted almost entirely of the priest. Great satisfaction on his face, Bagratouni came up to deliver a couple of sharp kicks to the bag. The dog yelped, the priest cried out even louder than before, and the gyrations within the flopping canvas were astonishing to behold.

Vaspurakeners came up to enjoy the spectacle of their enemy thus entrapped and to add a kick or two of their own. "What was it you said, priest?" Bagratouni shouted. "'Whoever works evil on the wicked pleases Phos'? Phos tonight is mightily pleased."

From the noises inside the sack, it sounded as if Zemarkhos was being torn to pieces. Scaurus had no love for the fanatic priest, but did not think he deserved so bitter a death. "Let him go," he urged Bagratouni. "Alive, he could not hate you and yours more than he already does, but slain he would be a martyr and a symbol for vengeance for years to come."

The *nakharar* looked uncomprehendingly at the Roman, almost like a man interrupted in the act of love. His eyes filled with reluctant understanding. "In that young head an old mind you have," he said slowly. "Very well. It shall be as you ask."

His men moved with the same unwillingness their overlord displayed, but move they did, cutting the bag apart so its occupants could free themselves. The moment the hole they made was wide enough to let out the dog Vaspur, it darted through. The Vapurakaners jumped back in alarm, but there was no fight left in the terrified beast. It streaked away into the night, its chain clattering behind it.

When Zemarkhos at last got loose from the swaddling canvas, he was a sight to glut even an appetite starved for revenge. There were deep bites on his arms and legs, and half of one ear was chewed away. Only luck had saved his face and belly from his animal's fangs.

Gorgidas leaped to his side at the sight of those wounds, saying, "Fetch me strips of cloth and a full winejug. We may be satisfied the dog was not mad, but the bites must be cleaned, lest they fester." When no Vaspurakaner stirred, the physician speared one with his eyes and snapped, "You! Move!" The man hurried back toward Bagratouni's house.

But Zemarkhos, lurching to his feet, would not let Gorgidas treat his injuries. "No heathen will lay hands on me," he said, and limped out through the gate of Bagratouni's estate. His priestly robe, torn by his dog's teeth, hung in flapping tatters around him. The *nakharar*'s men hooted in delight as the darkness swallowed up their chastised foe.

Viridovix came loping up to the gate with the Vaspurakaner Gorgidas had sent back for bandages. "What's all the rumpus in aid of? This omadhaun is after understanding my Videssian, but not a word of his can I make out."

When the Gaul learned of the stir he'd missed, he kicked at the ground in frustration. If he enjoyed anything more than his venery, it was combat. "Isn't that just the way of it? Another good shindy wasted because I was off friking in the bushes! It scarce seems fair."

"It's your own fault, you know. You could have been here with us if you hadn't gone skirt-chasing," Gaius Philippus said unkindly.

And Gorgidas demanded, "Is that all this would have been to you? Entertainment? Only a cruel man could take pleasure in watching the outcome of others' hatreds."

"Oh, get on with you," the Celt retorted. "You're only angry the now because that rascally priest ran off without letting you do the patching of him." There was just enough truth in that slander to reduce Gorgidas to sputtering fury.

Quintus Glabrio said quietly, "You needn't feel you lost out on a chance to take a risk, Viridovix. Or can you truly tell me you think loving any less dangerous than fighting?"

The Celt stared blankly, but Gordigas' eyes narrowed in thought, as if he were seeing the young centurion for the first time. And when Gagik Bagratouni had the exchange translated—for most of it had been in Latin—he put his arm round Glabrio's shoulder, saying, "Clever I knew you were. Many men are clever, but now I see as well you are wise. This is a rarer and more precious thing. Scaurus, of this one you must take good care."

"Up to now he's been pretty well able to take care of himself, which is as it should be," Marcus answered. Thinking back, he realized just how true that was. Glabrio was so silently competent that days would sometimes go by with the tribune hardly noticing him, but the maniple he led was always perfectly drilled and, now that Scaurus was putting his mind to it, it seemed his men had fewer disciplinary problems than the other Romans. A good man to have around, Marcus thought, a very good man indeed.

XII

In a way, the tribune was disappointed when neither Helvis nor Amorion flared up as he had expected. His lady was so caught up by his account of Gagik Bagratouni's revenge on Zemarkhos that she forgot to be angry at not having been there. That the priest was of the orthodox Videssian faith only made his fall sweeter to her.

"More of them should be treated thus," she declared. "It would take their conceit down a peg."

"Is it not as wrong for you to rejoice in their downfall as it is for them to oppress your fellow believers?" Marcus asked, but her only reply was a look as blank as the one Viridovix had given Quintus Glabrio. He gave up—she was too convinced of her beliefs' truth to make argument worthwhile.

Amorion would have risen against its Vaspurakaners with the slightest word of encouragement from the Emperor, but that was not forthcoming. When Zemarkhos appeared at Mavrikios Gavras' tent to lay charges against Bagratouni, Gavras already had the accounts of the *nakharar* and the Romans. He sent the cleric away unhappy, saying, "Priest or no, you were unwelcome on the man's land and incited him by gross insult. He is not blameworthy for taking action against you, nor should he and his be liable to any private venture of vengeance."

More direct, his brother Thorisin added, "As far as I can see, you got what you deserved for meddling where you didn't belong." That was the feeling of most of the army, which appreciated the rough wit of Gagik's device. A chorus of barks and howls accompanied Zemarkhos as he limped out of the camp. His every glance was filled with hate, but the Emperor's threat restrained him while the army resupplied at Amorion.

Scaurus had the distinct feeling Mavrikios begrudged every minute he spent in the plateau town. The conflict between Zemarkhos and Gagik Bagratouni, serious under most circumstances, was now but an unwelcome distraction to him. He had been like a horse with the bit between its teeth since the first skirmish with the Yezda and seemed on fire to join the great battle he had planned.

Yet it was as well that his host paused to refit before pushing northwest toward Soli. The journey, shorter than either of the first two stages, was worse than both of them rolled together. Whatever caches of food the local Videssian authorities managed to store up for the army had fallen instead to the invaders. The Yezda did their best to turn the land to desert, torching fields and destroying the canals that shared out what little water there was.

The nomads Yezd was funneling into the Empire were perfectly at home in such a desert. Trained to the harsh school of the steppe, they lived with ease where the Videssian army would have starved without the supplies it carried. More and more of them shadowed the imperial forces. When they thought the odds were in their favor they would nip in to raid, then vanish once more like smoke in a breeze.

Their forays grew bolder as time passed. About midway between Amorion and Soli, one band of about fifty broke through the army's screen of Khamorth outriders and dashed across the front of the marching column, spraying arrows into it as they rode.

Marcus saw the cloud of dust come rolling out of the west, but did not think much of it. Maybe, he thought, the scouts had spotted a good-sized Yezda party and were sending messengers back for aid.

Gaius Philippus disagreed. "There's too many there for that." His face went suddenly grim. "I don't think those are our men at all."

"What? Don't be absurd. They'd have to have—" Whatever argument the tribune was about to make died unspoken when one of the legionaries cried in pain and alarm as an arrow pierced his arm. The range was ungodly long, but quickly closed as the nomads, riding their light horses for all they were worth, zipped past the column's head, emptying their quivers as fast as they could. At their heels was a troop of Khamorth in imperial service.

"All maniples halt!" Gaius Philippus' battlefield roar rang out. "Shields up!" The Romans unslung their *scuta* and raised them to cover their faces.

There was nothing else they could do; the Yezda were racing by, far out of *pilum*-range. Adiatun and his slingers let fly with a few hasty bullets, but they fell short. What the Khamorth had thought all along, then, was true—the nomads' bows easily outranged any weapons the Romans had. Scaurus filed the fact for future worry.

The raiders broke up into groups of four and five and scattered in all directions. They had done nothing that could be called damage, but had managed to throw an army a thousand times their number into confusion.

Videssos' mercenary cavalry were still after the Yezda. More and more raced up to join the chase. Marcus was hard-pressed to tell friend from foe. In the swirling dust ahead, the nomads who fought under Yezd's banner looked little different from the Empire's hirelings. Perhaps the Khamorth themselves had the same problem, for not a handful of Yezda were brought down before the rest made good their escape.

The officers' meeting the Emperor called that night was not happy. The raiders' bravado stung Mavrikios, who was further infuriated by its going all but unpunished. "Phos' suns!" the Emperor burst out. "Half a day's march wasted on account of a few scraggly, unwashed barbarians! You, sirrah!" he barked at Ortaias Shprantzes.

"Your Majesty?"

"What was that twaddle you were spouting? Something about the only people to catch nomads are other nomads?" The Emperor waited ominously, but Sphrantzes, with better sense than Scaurus had thought he owned—or was it simply terror?—kept silent.

Prudent though it was, his silence did not save him. "Those were your bloody nomads the Yezda rode through, boy. If they do it again, you can forget your precious left wing—you'll be back at the rear, in charge of horsedung pickup." When angry,

Mavrikios was plainly Thorisin's brother. The Sevastokrator himself was saying no more than Ortaias Sphrantzes, but from his grin he was enjoying every bit of Mavrikios' tirade.

When the Emperor was through, Ortaias rose, bowed jerkily, and, muttering, "I'll certainly try to do better," made an undignified exit from the imperial tent.

His departure only partly pacified Mavrikios. He rounded on Sphrantzes' nominal subordinate Nephon Khoumnos: "You'll be right there with him, you know. I put the two of you together so your way of doing things would rub of on him, not the other way around."

"Anything can go wrong once," Khoumnos said stolidly. As was his style, he shouldered the blame without complaint. "They burst out of a wash and caught us napping. If it happens again, I deserve to be shoveling horseballs, by Phos."

"We'll leave it at that, then," the Emperor nodded, somewhat mollified.

Khoumnos was as good as his word, too; his cavalry pickets foiled ambush after ambush the rest of the way to Soli. The march slowed nonetheless. Skirmishes with the invaders were constant now, skirmishes that in a lesser campaign would have been reckoned full-scale battles. Time after time the army had to push the Yezda aside before it could press on.

The country through which it passed grew ever more barren, devastated. Save for the Videssian host and its foes, the land was nearly uninhabited, its farmers and hersdmen either dead or fled. The only substantial remaining population was in walled towns. There were not many of these after the long years of peace, nor were all of them unscathed. Where field and farm could not be worked, towns withered on the vine.

The army passed more than one empty shell of what had been a city but now housed only carrion birds—or, worse, Yezda who based themselves in abandoned buildings and fought like cornered rats when attacked.

Here as elsewhere, the invaders reserved their worst savagery for Phos' temples. Their other barbarities paled next to the fiendish ingenuity they devoted to such desecrations. Not all altars were so lucky as to be hacked to kindling; the bloody rites and sacrifices celebrated on others made mere desecration seem nothing more than a childish prank. As seasoned a veteran as Nephon Khoumnos puked up his supper after emerging from one ravaged shrine. Where before the Emperor had encouraged his troops to view their enemies' handiwork, now he began ordering the polluted fanes sealed so as not to dishearten them further.

"Such foulness points to Avshar, sure as a lodestone draws nails," Gorgidas said. "We must be getting near him."

"Good!" Gaius Philippus said emphatically. He had commanded the Roman party ordered to guard a sealed temple and used the privilege of his rank to break the seals and go inside. He came bursting out through the door an instant later, face pale beneath his deep tan and sweat beading on his forehead. "The sooner such filth is cleaned from the world, the better for all in it—aye, including the poor damned whoresons who follow him."

Marcus did not think he had heard his senior centurion ever speak thus of a foe. War was Gaius Philippus' trade, as carpentry might be another man's, and he accorded his opponents the respect their skills merited. Curious, the tribune wondered aloud, "What was it you saw in that temple?"

Gaius Philippus' face froze, as if suddenly turned to stone. Through clenched teeth he said, "If it please you, sir, never ask me that again. The gods willing, I may forget before I die."

The imperial army reached Soli a joyless force. What they found there did nothing to raise their spirits. The new town, wall-less in the fashion of so many Videssian cities, had snuggled against the Rhamnos River's turbid yellow waters, the better to lure trade. Old Soli on the hills above, a garrison against Makuran for hundreds of years, was all but deserted . . . until the Yezda came.

Then the new city fell in fire and death—sacked repeatedly, in fact, over the years, until nothing was left to loot. And Old Soli, far down the road to extinction, had a modest rebirth as survivors from the riverbank town patched its dilapidated walls and began to repair the tumbledown buildings from which their six-times-great-grandsires had sprung.

Heedless of the omens his men might draw, Mavrikios made camp amidst the ruins of the dead city by the Rhamnos. An army the size of his needed more water than Old Soli's wells and cisterns could provide, and the river was the logical place to get it. It made perfect military sense, but also made the soldiers edgy.

"Sure and there's bound to be angry ghosts about," Viridovix said, "all crying out for revenge on them that slew 'em. There!" he exclaimed. "Do you hear the keening of them?" Sure enough, a series of mournful cries came from the darkness outside the Roman camp.

"That's an owl, you great booby," Gaius Philippus said.

"Och, aye, it *sounds* like an owl." But the Gaul was anything but convinced.

Marcus shifted uneasily in his seat by the fire. He told himself he did not believe in ghosts and was able to convince the front part of his mind that he spoke the truth. Deeper down, he was not so sure. And if there were ghosts, they would surely live in such a place as this.

Most of the buildings of murdered Soli had perished either at the hands of the Yezda or through time's decay, but here and there a tower or a jagged section of some well-made building still stood, deeper blacknesses against the night sky. It was from these the owls' plaintive notes and the whirring call of the nightjar emanated—if that was what the noises were. No one seemed anxious to investigate, nor was the tribune inclined to ask for volunteers.

As if the place was not eerie enough, a thin mist crept up from the Rhamnos as the night wore on, half shrouding the imperial camp. Now it was Gaius Philippus' turn to fret. "I don't like this a bit," he declared as the fog swallowed one watchfire after another. "Belike it's some sending of Avshar's, to veil his attack till it's on us." He peered out into the rolling mist, trying to penetrate it by will alone. Inevitably he failed, which only increased his unease.

But Marcus had grown up in Mediolanum, hard by the Padus River's tributary the Olonna. He had to shake his head. "Mist often rises from a river at night—it's nothing to worry over."

"Quite so," Gorgidas agreed. "Nature has provided that particles go up into the air from oceans and streams. This fog is but the forerunner of a cloud. When the vapor rises to meet opposite emanations coming down from the ether which holds the stars, it will condense into a true cloud."

The Epicurean account of cloud formation did nothing to

reassure the centurion. Viridovix tried to tease him back to
good humor. "You didna trouble yoursel' when you saw the
very land steam or ever we came to Garsavra. Of course," he
added cunningly, "a good deal further from the Yezda we were
then."

Not even the imputation of cowardice could get much response from Gaius Philippus. He shook his head, muttering,
"It's this bloody place, that's all; even without fogs it's like
camping in a tomb. We couldn't leave too soon to suit me."

But for all the senior centurion's wholehearted desire to be
gone, the imperial army did not set forth at once. Scouts spying out the ways through Vaspurakan reported that the land
west of Soli was a desolation stripped bare of almost every
living thing.

Senpat Sviodo and his wife were among the riders who
went into Vaspurakan. "There will be a reckoning for this, if it
takes a thousand years," he said. What he had seen in his
birthland had burned some of his youth away forever. The
cold fury in his voice and on his face seemed better suited to a
man of twice his years.

"Our poor people survive only in the mountain forests and
in a few fastnesses," Nevrat said. She sounded weary beyond
belief; her eyes were full of sorrow too bitter for tears. "The
meadows, the farmlands—nothing moves there but Yezda and
other beasts."

"I had hoped to bring a band of princes back with me, to
fight under the Emperor's banner against the invaders," Senpat continued, "but no one was left to bring." His hands shook
in impotent fury.

Marcus studied the harsh lines newly etched on either side
of Senpat's mouth. The jolly youngster he'd met a few short
days before would be a long time reappearing, and the tribune
was not sure he cared for this grim almost-stranger who had
taken his place. Nevrat clasped her husband's hands in her
own, trying to draw the pain from him, but he sat staring
straight ahead, only the vision of his ravaged homeland before
him.

In such territory the army could not hope to live off the
land; it would have to carry its own provisions through the
wasteland. Mavrikios gave orders for grain to be brought up

the Rhamnos from the coastal plain to the north, and then had to wait with his men until the boats arrived.

The onerous delay in such dismal surroundings strained the Emperor's disposition to the breaking point. He had been short-tempered since the handful of Yezda raiders disrupted the army's march. Now, stymied again, frustration ate at him when each day failed to see the coming of the needed supplies. Men walked warily around him, fearful lest his pent-up rage lash out against them.

The abcess burst on the fifth day at Soli. Scaurus happened to be close by. He wanted to borrow a map of Vaspurakan from the collection Mavrikios kept in his tent, the better to follow Senpat Sviodo's description of the land through which they would be passing if the supply ships ever came.

Two Halogai of the Imperial Guard pushed through the tentflaps, dragging a scrawny Videssian soldier between them. Three more Videssians nervously followed the northerners.

"What's this?" the Emperor demanded.

One of the guardemen answered, "This worthless piece of offal has been filching coppers from his mates." He shook his prisoner hard enough to make the teeth snap in his head.

"Has he now?" The Emperor looked up at the Videssian soldiers behind the Halogai. "You three are witnesses, I suppose?"

"Your Majesty, sir?" said one of them. All three had been gaping at the luxurious interior of the tent, its soft bed and cleverly designed light furnishings—Mavrikios was of less spartan taste than Thorisin.

"Witnesses, are you?" the Emperor repeated. By his tone, his patience was very short.

Between them, they got the story out. The prisoner, whose name was Doukitzes, had been caught emptying a coin pouch when his three fellows unexpectedly returned to the tent the four of them shared. "We thought a few stripes would make him keep his fingers off what don't belong to him," one of the soldiers said, "and these fellows," he pointed to the Halogai, "happened to be coming by, so—"

"Stripes?" Gavras interrupted. He gestured contemptuously. "A thief forgets stripes before they're done healing. We'll give him something he'll remember the rest of his days." He turned back to the Halogai and snapped, "Take his hand off at the wrist."

"No! Phos have mercy, no!" Doukitzes shrieked, twisting free of his captors to fall at Mavrikios' feet. He seized the Emperor's knees and kissed the hem of his robe, babbling, "I'll never do it again! By Phos I swear it! Never, never! Mercy, my lord, I beg, mercy!"

The luckless thief's tentmates looked at the Emperor in horror—they'd wanted their light-fingered comrade chastised, yes, but not mutilated.

Marcus was equally appalled at Gavras' Draconian judgment. In theory, thievery in the Roman army could be punished by death, but hardly over the trifling sum at issue here. He stood up from the mapcase through which he'd been searching. "Your Majesty, is this justice?" he asked through Doukitzes' wails.

Save only the prisoner, everyone in the imperial tent—Mavrikios, the Haloga guards, the Videssian soldiers, and the Emperor's ubiquitous servants—turned to stare at the Roman, amazed anyone would dare call the sovereign to account.

The Emperor was chilly as the eternal snow topping the peaks of Vaspurakan. "Captain of mercenaries, you forgot yourself. You have our leave to go." Never before had Mavrikios used the imperial "we" to the tribune; it was a manifest note of warning.

But Scaurus' ways were those of a land that knew no king, nor was he trained from birth to accept any one man as the embodiment of authority and law. Still, he was glad to hear the steadiness in his voice as he replied, "No, sir. I recall myself better than you. In your worry over great affairs, you are letting rancor get the better of you in small ones. To take a man's hand for a few coppers is not justice."

The tent grew very still. The imperial servitors flinched away from Scaurus, as if not wanting to be contaminated by his blasphemous practice of speaking the truth as he saw it. The Halogai might have been carved from wood; the Videssian common soldiers, even Doukitzes, faded from the tribune's perception as he waited to see if Mavrikios would doom him too.

The Emperor slowly said, "Do you know what I could do to you for your insolence?"

"No worse than Avshar could, I'm sure."

A chamberlain gasped, somewhere to Scaurus' left. He did not turn his head, keeping his attention only on the Emperor. Gavras was studying him as intently. Without removing his eyes from the tribune, Mavrikios said to the Halogai, "Take this grizzling fool—" He stirred Doukitzes with his foot. "—outside and give him five lashes, well laid on, then let his mates take him back."

Doukitzes scuttled across the floor to Marcus. "Thank you, great lord, oh thank you!" He offered no resistance as the Halogai led him away.

"Does that satisfy you, then?" Mavrikios asked.

"Yes, your Majesty, completely."

"First man I've ever seen go happy to a whipping," the Emperor remarked, raising an ironic eyebrow. He was still watching Scaurus closely. "It wasn't just pride, then, was it, that made you refuse me the proskynesis back in Videssos all those months ago?"

"Pride?" That had never occurred to the Roman. "No, sir."

"I didn't think so, even then," Mavrikios said with something like respect. "If I had, you'd've regretted it soon enough." He laughed mirthlessly.

"Now get out of here," he went on, "before I decide I should have you killed after all." Scaurus left quickly, only half-sure he was joking.

"You were very brave, and even more foolish," Helvis said that night. Lazy after love, they lay side by side in her tent, his hand still curled over her breast. Her heartbeat filled his palm.

"Was I? I didn't really think about being either at the time. It didn't seem right, though, to have all Mavrikios' wrath come down on that poor wretch. His worst fault wasn't stealing a few pennies, it was being in the Emperor's way at the wrong time."

"His anger could have condemned you as easily as that worthless Videssian." Helvis sounded thoroughly afraid. She might come from a folk freer than the Empire's, Marcus thought, but she took the Avtokrator's absolute power as much for granted as any of Videssos' citizens.

Her fear, though, did not spring from any such abstract

reason, but a far more basic concern. Her hand took his, guided it down the smooth softness of her belly. "You were a featherbrain," she said. "Would you want your child to grow up fatherless?"

"My . . . ?" The tribune sat up on the soft sleeping-mat, looked down at Helvis, who still held his hand against her. She smiled up at him. "You're sure?" he asked foolishly.

Her warm rich laughter filled the small tent. "Of course I am, simpleton. There is a way of knowing such things, you know." She sat up, too, and kissed him.

He returned the embrace eagerly, not from the lust but sheer gladness. Then something struck him funny. "How could I know this morning that I might be making my child an orphan, when I didn't know there was a child?"

Helvis poked him in the ribs. "Don't you go chopping logic with me, like some priest. *I* knew, and that's enough."

And so perhaps it was. Good omens had been scarce lately, but what could be better before a battle than the creation of new life?

The next morning, the patrols Mavrikios sent riding north finally met the supply barges toiling their way upstream. The squat, ugly vessels reached Soli late that afternoon. Their journey had not been easy; marauding Yezda along both banks of the Rhamnos had made it impossible to use horses to tow the boats, and their arrows made life hellish for the barges' rowers.

One had lost so many men it could no longer make headway against the stream and drifted aground in the shallows by the riverbank. The rest of the fleet picked up its surviving crew, but the Yezda gleefully burnt the stricken craft to the waterline.

That night there was no time for worry over haunted surroundings. Men labored till dawn, hurling sacks of grain into hundreds of wagons. When the sun rose, the army rumbled over the great stone bridge spanning the Rhamnos and pushed its way into Vaspurakan.

Marcus soon saw what had moved Senpat Sviodo to such bitter hatred. The Yezda had done their worst in Videssos, but the destruction they wrought there was but the work of a few seasons. Vaspurakan had felt the invaders' hand far longer and far more heavily; in some frequently ravaged passes, fair-sized second growth was already springing up to shroud the ruins of what, in happier times, were farm and villages.

The raiders had come so often to the princes' land, they were beginning to think of it as their proper home. Just as he had outside Imbros, the tribune watched herdsmen drive their flocks up into the mountains at the first sight of the army. But these were not Videssians afoot with their herd dogs; they were nomad archers mounted on shaggy steppe ponies, looking uncomfortably like the Khamorth with the imperial forces.

In Vaspurakan even walled cities were under Yezda control, either stormed or, more often, simply starved into submission. Mavrikios' host came to the first of these two days out of Soli—a town called Khliat, whose shadow in the afternoon sun ran long down the valley through which the army was traveling.

The Yezda commander refused surrender with a brusque message eerily close to Scaurus' retort to the Emperor: "If you conquer, you could do me no worse harm than my lords would, should I yield."

Gavras did not waste time in further negotiations. Using what light remained, he surrounded Khliat, quickly driving the Yezda skirmishers back inside the city's walls. Once the encirclement was complete, he rode round the town just out of bowshot, deciding where it was most vulnerable to siege engines.

Again the night was furiously busy, this time with soldiers unloading the precut timbers and other specialized gear of the siege train. At the officers' council that night, the Emperor declared, "Our assault party tomorrow will be made up of Romans and Namdaleni. As the most heavily armed troops we have, they are best suited to forcing their way through breached walls."

Marcus gulped. Mavrikios' reasoning was probably sound, but the attacking force's casualties could well be hideous. The Namdaleni would fill their ranks with new recruits from the Duchy, but where was he to find new Romans?

"May your Majesty it please," Gagik Bagratouni spoke up, "but I the privilege of leading this assault would beg for my men. It is their homes they are freeing. Their armors may be lighter, but their hearts shall be so too."

Mavrikios rubbed his chin. "Be it so, then," he decided. "Spirit has raised more than one victory where it had no right to grow."

"Well, well, the gods do look out for us after all," Gaius Philippus whispered behind his hand to Scaurus.

"You've been in this wizards' land so long you've taken up mindreading," Marcus whispered back. The centurion bared his teeth in a silent chuckle.

After the meeting broke up, Soteric fell into step beside the tribune. "How interesting," he said sardonically, "and how lucky for you, to be chosen to share the butcher's bill with us. The Emperor is glad of our help, aye, and glad to bleed us white, too."

"Weren't you listening? The Vaspurakaners are going in our stead."

Soteric gestured in disgust. "Only because Bagratouni has more honor than sense. True, we're spared, but not forgotten, I promise you. Everyone knows what Mavrikios thinks of the men of the Duchy, and you did yourself no good when you stood up to him yesterday. You'll pay—wait and see."

"You've been talking to your sister again," Marcus said.

"Helvis? No, I haven't seen her today." Soteric eyed the tribune curiously. "By the Wager, man, don't you know? Every blasted Videssian is buzzing over how you saved twelve men from having their heads chopped off."

Scaurus exchanged a consternation-filled glance with Gaius Philippus. No matter how much he tried to evade the role, it seemed he was being cast as the Emperor's opponent. That notwithstanding, though, he thought Soteric was wrong. Mavrikios Gavras might be devious in his dealings with his foes, but there was never any doubt who those foes were.

When he said as much to the Namdalener, Soteric laughed at his naiveté. "Wait and see," he repeated and, still shaking his head over what he saw as the Roman's gullibility, went off about his business.

Gaius Philippus gave thoughtful study to the islander's re-treating back. He waited until Soteric was too far away to hear him before delivering his verdict. "That one will always see the worst in things, whether or not it's there." Coming from the centurion, a pessimist born, the statement was startling.

Gaius Philippus glanced warily at Scaurus; after all, the

man he was dispraising was the brother of the tribune's
woman. Even so, Marcus had to nod. The characterization
was too apt to gainsay.

Matching their commander's defiance, the Yezda inside
Khliat roared their war cries at the Videssian army from the
city's walls. The rising sun glinted bloodily off their sabers. It
was a brave show, but not one to frighten the professionals in
the audience. "This will be easy," Gaius Philippus said.
"There aren't enough of them by half to give us trouble."

Events quickly proved him right. The imperial army's bolt-
throwing engines and the strong bows of the Khamorth sent
such floods of darts against Khliat's defenders that the latter
could not stop Videssian rams from reaching the wall in three
separate places. The ground shook as each stroke did its pul-
verizing work.

One ram was put out of action for a time when the Yezda
managed to tear some skins from its covering shed and
dropped red-hot sand on the men who worked it, but new
troops rushed forward to take the place of those who fell. The
sheds' green hides were proof against the burning oil and fire-
brands the nomads flung down on them, and many defenders
bold enough to expose themselves in such efforts paid for their
courage with their lives.

The wall crumbled before one ram, then, only minutes
later, before a second. Yezda on the battlements shrieked in
terror and anguish as they slid through crashing stones to the
ground below. Others, cleverly stationed behind the masonry
the rams were battering, sent withering volleys into the siege
engines' crews.

Then the Vaspurakaners were rushing toward the riven
wall, Gagik Bagratouni at their head. Their battlecries held a
savage joy, a fierce satisfaction in striking back at the invaders
who had worked such ruin on their homeland.

A Yezda wizard, an angular figure in flapping blood-
colored robes, clambered onto shattered masonry in one of the
breaches to hurl a thunderbolt at the onstorming foe. But
Marcus learned what Nepos had meant when he spoke of battle magic's unreliability. Though lightning glowed from the
mage's fingertips, it flickered and died less than an arm's

length from his body. At his failure, one of his own soldiers sabered him down in disgust.

The fight at the breaches was sharp but short. The Yezda were not natural foot soldiers, nor was there any place for their usual darting cavalry tactics in the defense of a fortified town. More heavily armored than their opponents, the Vaspurakaners hammered their way through the nomads' resistance and into Khliat.

When he saw the enemy forces heavily committed against the "princes," Mavrikios gave the order for a general assault. Like a sudden bare-branched forest, ladders leaped upward at Khliat's walls. Here and there still-resolute defenders sent them toppling over with a crash, but soon the imperial forces gained a lodgement on the wall and began dropping down into the city itself.

The Romans were involved in little that deserved the name of fighting. The very heaviness of their panoplies, an advantage in close combat, made them slow and awkward on scaling ladders. The Emperor wisely did not use them thus until most danger was past. Khliat was largely in imperial hands by the time they entered it, a fact which brought advantages and disadvantages both. Their only casualty was a broken foot suffered when a legionary tripped and fell down a flight of stairs, but they found little loot, and some grumbled.

"Men are fools to complain over such things," Gorgidas remarked, bandaging the injured soldier's foot. "Think how much more booty there would be if the Yezda had killed everyone who got into the city before us, and how sorry we should be to have it."

Gaius Philippus said, "For a man who's followed the army a while, you're trusting as a child. Most of these lads'd cheerfully sell their mothers if they thought the old gals would fetch more than two coppers apiece."

"You may be right," Gorgidas sighed, "though I still like to think otherwise." Turning back to the Roman with the fracture, he said, "If you can, stay off that foot for three weeks. If you put your weight on it before it's healed, it may pain you for years. I'll change the dressings day after tomorrow."

"I thank you kindly," the legionary said. "I feel like a twit, falling over my own feet like that."

Gorgidas checked to make sure the bandage was not tight enough to risk necrosis in the Roman's foot. "Enjoy your rest while you can get it—you'll be back at your trade too soon to suit you, I promise you that."

The bravado of the Yezda cracked when it became plain they could not hold Khliat. They began surrendering, first one by one and then in groups, and were herded together like cattle in the city's marketplace. Some of the Videssians crowding round wanted to massacre the lot of them, but Mavrikios would hear none of it. In the glow of victory he was prepared to be merciful.

He threw a cordon of Halogai and Romans around the prisoners, then ordered the defeated enemy's common soldiers disarmed and sent back to Soli under guard. There they could await disposition until he had finished beating their countrymen. Most of them fought for Yezd instead of Videssos only because their wanderings first brought them to that land.

The chieftains were another matter. They knew full well the master they served and did so with open eyes. Yet their choice of overlord did not make the Yezda officers any less dauntless. Mavrikios came up to their commander, who was sitting dejectedly on the ground not far from where Marcus stood.

That captain and a handful of men had holed up in a house and would not yield until the Videssians threatened to burn it over their heads. Looking at him now, Scaurus did not think him wholly of the steppe blood, as were most of the warriors he led. He was more slimly built and finer of feature than they, with large liquid eyes; perhaps there were native Makuraners in his ancestry.

Thorisin Gavras was at his brother's side. "Rise for the Emperor, you!" he barked.

The Yezda did not move. "Were our positions reversed, I do not think he would rise for me," he said. His Videssian was fluent and almost without accent.

"Why, you impudent—" The Sevastokrator was furious, but Mavrikios checked him with a gesture. Not for the first time, Marcus saw the respect the Emperor gave forthrightness.

Mavrikios looked down at his captive. "Were our places reversed, what would you do with me?"

The Yezda stared back unflinchingly. He thought for a moment, then said, "I believe I would have you whipped to death."

"Keep a civil tongue in your head, filth!" said Zeprin the Red, hefting his axe. The Haloga officer tolerated the Romans treating Mavrikios with less than due ceremony; they were, after all, allies. This insolence from a prisoner he would not stomach.

The Emperor was unperturbed. He told the Yezda commander, "I will not be as harsh as you. You are a brave man —will you not renounce the evil you followed and join us in rooting it out?"

Something flickered in the Yezda's expressive eyes. Perhaps it was temptation. Whatever it was, it was gone before Marcus was sure he'd seen it. "I can no more foreswear myself than you could, were you sitting in this dust," the officer said, and won grudging nods of approval from both Thorisin Gavras and Zeprin the Red.

"As you wish," Mavrikios said. The quality of the man he faced made the Emperor eager to win him to his side. "I will not cast you in prison, though I will ship you to an island for safekeeping until I've beaten your khagan and his sorcerous minister. Then, maybe, your mind will change."

Scaurus thought the Yezda was, if anything, being treated too leniently, but the man only shrugged. "What you do to me does not matter. Avshar will dispose of me as he pleases."

The Emperor grew irritated for the first time. "You are under my control now, not your wizard-prince's." The Yezda shrugged again. Mavrikios spun angrily on his heel and strode away.

The next morning he sent men to take charge of the officer and ship him east. They found him dead, his lips burned from the poison he had swallowed. His stiff fist still clutched a tiny glass vial.

The news raised an unpleasant question in Marcus' mind. Had the Yezda killed himself for fear of the vengeance he thought Avshar would take on him, or was his suicide itself that vengeance? The implications were distasteful in either case.

* * *

Despite the questionable omen, the next two weeks went well for the imperial forces. Using Khliat as a base of operations, Mavrikios captured several other Yezda-held towns: Ganolzak and Shamkanor to the north, Baberd in the southeast, and Phanaskert due south of Khliat.

None of them put up a prolonged or difficult resistance. The Yezda were far more formidable on horseback than confined inside city walls, and the Videssian siege train proved its worth time and again. Moreover, the Vaspurakaners inside the towns hated their nomadic oppressors and betrayed them to the imperial forces at every opportunity. Large numbers of prisoners went trudging unhappily into the east; Videssian garrisons took their place.

Marcus noticed that Mavrikios Gavros was using troops of doubtful worth or loyalty to hold the newly captured cities, and appointing as garrison commanders officers whose allegiance he suspected. Gaius Philippus saw the same thing. He said, "He's stripping us down for the real action, right enough. Better to put the fainthearts where they might be useful than have them turn tail and run when he really needs them."

"I suppose so," Marcus agreed. Still, he could not help recalling the grief he'd come to by dividing his Romans on riot duty in Videssos.

Phanaskert was a good-sized city, though badly depopulated by the raids of the Yezda and their occupation. When Mavrikios took the rest of his forces back to Khliat, he left more than half his Namdaleni behind to hold the town's long circuit of walls against possible counterattack from the west.

Soteric was one of the islanders ordered to garrison duty. He invited his sister and Scaurus to share an evening meal with him before the bulk of the Videssian army returned to its base. Over captured Vaspurakaner wine—even thicker and sweeter than Videssian vintages—the Namdalener said to Marcus, "You see now what I meant outside the Emperor's tent. By one trick or another, Mavrikios finds ways to be rid of us."

Pretending not to take his meaning, the tribune answered, "Are you unhappy with your assignment? Holding a town from the inside strikes me as softer duty than fighting your way into one."

Soteric exhaled in exasperation at the Roman's dullness, but Helvis was coming to know him well enough to realize when he was dissembling. She said, "Must you always speak the Emperor fair? You have to see that the only reason he has for using the men of the Duchy so is his fear for our faithfulness."

Marcus usually dismissed Soteric's complaints over the Emperor's policies as the products of a slightly obsessed mind, but the more he thought about this one, the more likely it seemed. He knew Mavrikios thought along the lines Soteric was sketching; the Emperor had said as much himself, when talking of Ortaias Sphrantzes.

The tribune suddenly laughed out loud. Even people who always thought themselves persecuted could be right sometimes.

The joke fell flat when he made the mistake of trying to explain it.

Scaurus was drilling his men outside the walls of Khliat when he spied a horseman approaching the town from out of the west. "A nomad he is, from the look of him," Viridovix said, shading his eyes against the afternoon sun. "Now, will he be one of ours, or a puir lone Yezda struck from his wits by the heat and out to kill the lot of us at once?"

The rider was not hostile. He had ridden long and hard; his horse was lathered and blowing, and caked sweat and dust begrimed his clothes. Even so, he was so urgent to deliver his news that he reined in as he came up to the exercising Romans. He gave Marcus a tired wave that was evidently meant as a salute.

"Artapan son of Pradtak I am, a scout of Baan Onomag's army," he said, clipping the general's name in plainsman fashion. "I am not ot the west—our watchword is 'Phos' light.'"

Onomagoulos had pushed west ten days before with a quarter of Mavrikios' remaining troops to seize the city of Maragha, which sat athwart the army's way into Yezd. "What word do you bring?" the tribune asked.

"Water first, I beg. This past half-day I rode with dry canteen," Artapan said, showing Marcus the empty waterskin at his belt. He swallowed the warm stale water from Scaurus' canteen as if it were chilled wine of ancient vintage, then wiped his mouth. "May the spirits be kind to you for that. Now you must take me into the city—Onomag is attacked, is pinned down less than a day's march from Maragha. We cannot go forward; no more can we go back. Without more men, we perish."

"Awfully bloody eager, isn't he?" Gaius Philippus said suspiciously. "If I were setting a trap, he's sprouting the very story I'd use to send an army running pell-mell into it."

Marcus considered. The Yezda might well have had the chance to pick off an outrider and torture the password from him. Still— "There must be men inside Khliat who know this fellow, if he is in imperial service. He'd be a fool to think he wouldn't have his story checked. And if it's true—if it's true," the tribune said slowly, "then Mavrikios has done just what he hoped he would, and made the Yezda stand and fight."

In some excitement, he turned back to Artapan, but the nomad was no longer there. Impatient with the colloquy in a language he did not understand—for both the centurion and Scaurus had spoken Latin—he had booted his horse into a worn-out trot for the city.

"Out of our hands now," Gaius Philippus said, not altogether displeased at being relieved of the responsibility of choice. "Still, it's as you say—Mavrikios is too canny by half to sit down without looking first to see whether he's plunking his tail onto an anthill."

That the Emperor took Artapan's message seriously soon became clear. Marcus had been back from drills less than an hour when an orderly summoned him to an urgent officer's council.

"The Khamorth *is* genuine, then, sir," Quintus Glabrio guessed. The same enthusiasm that had gripped the tribune before was now beginning to run through his men.

Doing his best to present the calm front befitting a senior officer, Scaurus shrugged, saying merely, "We'll know soon enough, either way."

For all his efforts at impassiveness, he could not help feeling a tingle of excitement when he saw Artapan Pradtak's son seated close by the Emperor in what had been the main hall of

Khliat's *hypasteos* or city governor. Another nomad, this one with a bandaged shoulder, was next to Artapan.

Scaurus and Gaius Philippus slid into chairs. Their curiosity, fired by the earlier meeting with the Khamorth scout, made them among the firstcomers. Their seats were the light folding type of canvas and wood, obviously from the imperial camp, not part of the hall's original furnishing.

The table at which they sat was something else again, being massively built from some heavy dark wood and looking as if it had held its place for centuries. It had the stamp of a Vaspurakaner product, calling to mind Gagik Bagratouni's fortress of a dwelling back in Amorion. The "princes" had become so used to life at bay that their very arts reflected their constant search for protection and strength.

The Yezda must have used the *hypasteos'* office as their headquarters before the Videssians drove them from Khliat, for the table was scarred with swordcuts and crude carvings. One symbol recurred constantly: twin three-pronged lightning bolts. Marcus thought nothing of them until Nephon Khoumnos sat down beside him and cursed when he saw them. "Filthy swine," he said, "putting Skotos' brand everywhere they go." The tribune remembered the dark icon in Avshar's suite at the capital and nodded in understanding.

Mavrikios brusquely called the meeting to order by slamming his palm down on the table. The low-voiced buzz of conversation disappeared. Without further preamble, the Emperor declared, "Baanes Onomagoulos has run into a nestful of Yezda a bit this side of Maragha. Without help, he says, he doesn't think he'll be able to hold out for long."

Heads jerked up in surprise—the Emperor had not announced the purpose of the meeting he was calling. Marcus felt smug at not being caught unawares.

"How did you learn that?" someone asked.

Gavras pointed to the nomad scouts. "You can thank these two—they slipped through the invaders to bring word. Spatakar—" That was the bandaged Khamorth. "—came in just now with a written report of situation from Onomagoulos. The seals it bears have been checked—they're genuine. Not only that, both Spatakar and his fellow Artapan here are well known to their clansmen here in Khliat. This has also been checked. In short, gentlemen, this is what we've waited for."

Gaius Philippus touched Marcus' arm and whispered, "You were right." He need not have been so discreet. The whole room was in an uproar, with everyone talking at once, some exclaiming to their neighbors, others shouting questions at the Emperor.

The voice of Thorisin Gavras cut through the uproar. "Or, at any rate, it may be what we've waited for. As for me, I'm inclined to wait a trifle longer."

"Oh, Phos, here we go again," Nephon Khoumnos groaned.

Scaurus scratched his head at the sudden reversal of roles the two Gavrai were displaying. Thorisin was ever the impetuous one, with Mavrikios more inclined to wait on events. Yet now the Emperor was all for pushing ahead, while the Sevastokrator spoke out for caution. The tribune could make no sense of it.

Thorisin, having gained the council's attention, went on, "I would think three times before I set our whole army thundering to Baanes Onomagoulos' rescue because of his first reports of trouble. He may be a very able officer, but he is regrettably inclined to caution."

Baanes is a coward, Marcus translated. The Roman did not know Onomagoulos well, but did not think the Sevastokrator's thinly veiled charge was true. He grew surer he was right when he remembered Thorisin's longstanding jealousy of his older brother's comrade. Yes, things were clearer now. Nephon Khoumnos, who knew the Gavrai, must have seen all this from the moment Thorisin opened his mouth.

So, of course, did Mavrikios. He snapped, "Were it Khoumnos or Bagratouni out there, Thorisin, instead of Baanes, would you be counseling prudence?"

"No," his brother said at once. "And were it our good friend Ortaias here—" He did not bother hiding his contempt for young Sphrantzes. "—would you go pounding after him?"

Mavrikios ground his teeth in frustration. "That is a low blow, Thorisin, and well you know it."

"Do I? We'll see." The Sevastokrator shot questions at Onomagoulos' Khamorth, and, indeed, their answers seemed to show his forces were not in such grim straits as it first appeared. His interrogation, though, reminded Marcus of nothing so much as a skilled lawyer at work, eliciting from

witnesses only the facts he was after. But whether that was so
or not, Thorisin succeeded in raising enough doubts in the
council that it retired without taking any action at all.

"Grudges," Gaius Philippus said as he and Scaurus made
their way to the Roman encampment. He put such a wealth of
feeling in the word that it came out fouler than any swearing.

"You talk as if Rome were immune to them," the tribune
answered. "Remember when Sulla and Gaius Flavius Fimbria
each fought Mithridates without taking the other into account?
When they joined forces, so many of Fimbria's men went over
to Sulla that Fimbria killed himself from the sheer disgrace of
it."

"And good riddance to him, too," Gaius Philippus said
promptly. "He incited a mutiny against his commander to take
charge of that army in the first place, the swine. He—" The
centurion broke off abruptly, made a gesture full of disgust.
"All right, I see your point. I still don't like it."

"I never said I did."

The next morning passed in anticipation, with the imperial
forces in Khliat wondering whether Baanes Onomagoulos had
managed to wriggle free of the Yezda trap . . . and if the trap
was there at all. Around noon Scaurus got the summons to
another council of war.

This time Onomagoulos' messenger was no Khamorth, but
a Videssian officer of middle rank. His face was pinched with
exhaustion and, but for the area his helm's nasal had covered,
badly sun-blistered. Mavrikios introduced him to the assembled commanders as Sisinnios Mousele, then let him speak for
himself.

"I thought all our riders must have been caught before they
reached you," he said between swallows of wine; as was true
of Artapan Pradtak's son, his journey had left him dry as the
baking land round Khliat. "But when I made my way here, I
learned two Khamorth were a day ahead of me.

"Why are you not on the move," he demanded, "when my
news preceded me? Aye, we're holding our little valley
against the Yezda, but for how long? The stream that carved it
is only a muddy trickle in summer—we have almost no water
and not much food. And the barbarians are thick as locusts in
a wheatfield—I'd not thought there were so many Yezda in all

the world. We could break out, perhaps, but they'd tear us to pieces before we got far. In Phos' holy name, brothers, without aid all of us will die, and die for nothing."

While Mousele was speaking, Mavrikios looked stonily at his brother. He made no public recrimination, though, over the day the army had lost to Thorisin's envious suspicion of Onomagoulos. In a way, Marcus thought, that was encouraging—in the face of real crisis, the pretended feud between the Gavrai fell away.

Thorisin bore that out, asking the counsil, "Is there anyone now who feels we should not march? I own I was wrong yesterday; with your help and your men's, perhaps we can make good my mistake."

After Sisinnios Mousele's plea, there was almost no debate among the officers. The only question was how soon the army could start moving. "Don't worry, Sisinnios, we'll get your boys out!" a Videssian captain called.

Only when Mousele made no reply did all eyes turn toward him. He was asleep where he sat; his message delivered, nothing would have kept him awake another minute.

XIII

K̲HLIAT THAT AFTERNOON WAS LIKE A BEEHIVE POKED WITH A
stick. To speed the army's departure, Mavrikios promised a
goldpiece to each soldier of the contingent first ready to leave.
Men frantically dashed here and there, dragging their
comrades from taverns and whorehouses.

There were also hurried farewells by the score, for the Emperor had no intention of delaying his advance with sutlers,
women, children, and other noncombatants. Not a man complained; if they lost, better to have their loved ones safe behind Khliat's walls than in a battlefield camp at the mercy of
an onstorming foe.

Helvis was a warrior's brother and a warrior's widow. She
had sent men into battle before and knew better than to burden
Scaurus with her fears. All she said was, "Phos keep you safe
till I see you again."

"Bring me back a Yezda's head, Papa?" Malric asked.

"Bloodthirsty, aren't you?" Marcus said, hugging Helvis'
son. "What would you do with it if you had it?"

"I'd burn it all up," the boy declared. "They're worse than
Videssian heretics, Mama says. Burn it all up!"

The tribune looked quizzically at Helvis. "I won't say she's
wrong. If I bring my own head back, though, that will be
about enough for me."

The Romans won the Emperor's prize, as Marcus had been
sure they would—fighting the Yezda was a less fearful prospect than facing Gaius Philippus after losing. But the rest of
the army was close behind them, galvanized by the thought of

rescuing their fellows from the Yezda. To the tribune's amazement, Khliat's gates swung wide an hour before sunset, and the last soldier was out of it before twilight left the sky.

In his urgency, Mavrikios kept the army moving through the early hours of the night. The endless drumbeat of marching feet, the clatter of iron-shod hooves, and the squeaks and rattles of hundreds of wagons filled with supplies and munitions were so pervasive the ear soon refused to hear them. Only the curses and thumps that followed missteps in the darkness really registered, in the same way that a skipped heartbeat demands attention while a steady pulse can be ignored.

Marcus was impressed by the amount of ground the imperial forces were able to make in that first, partial, day's march, despite the unfamiliar ground and the darkness. "You've forgotten what it's like, being with an army that's ready to fight," Gaius Philippus said. "I only hope Mavrikios doesn't wear us down by going too fast too soon."

"Och, the gods forfend!" said Viridovix. "I'm near as worn the now as ever I was when first we set out from Videssos all that while ago."

"You'd be in better shape if you hadn't said good-bye so thoroughly," the centurion pointed out. "You could hardly walk when you saw fit to come back to us."

"And can you think of a better way to pass a summer's afternoon?"

"No, damn you," Gaius Philippus said, and the patent envy in his voice drew laughter from around the Roman campfire.

The hot fire of enthusiasm kept the army surging westward the next day, and the next. Resistance was light. Onomagoulos' force had largely cleared the Yezda from the imperial line of march, and the small bands re-entering the territory between Khliat and Maragha were no match for Mavrikios' grand expedition. Most chose flight over combat.

In those first two heady days of travel, the host covered more than half the distance to Onomagoulos' embattled troops. But then, as Gaius Philippus had feared, the drive began to slow. The soldiers, pushed past their limits by non-stop marching, had to slow down. Their officers urged them to greater efforts, but they were as exhausted as their men.

Marcus lived in a hot gray world, his thoughts reaching no

further than his next footsore stride, his cuirass chafing his shoulders, his sword bumping the outside of his thigh with every step he took. He found brief moments to be thankful the Romans marched at the imperial column's head; they kicked up dust for others to breathe instead of breathing it themselves.

When the army paused at night, he fell instantly into a slumber as deep as Sisinnios Mousele's. He woke dull and slow, as if he had been drugged.

In midmorning of the fourth day out from Khliat, Khamorth scouts rode in from the west to report a dustcloud, as of many marching men, approaching the Videssian force. Mavrikios took no chances, ordering his men to deploy from marching column into line of battle. Marcus felt a weary exultation when the command reached the Romans. One way or another, he thought, his ordeal would be over before long. He was so tired he hardly cared what the outcome would be.

Soon the Videssian army's main body could see the tan smudges of dust on the western horizon. Men looked to their weapons. Here and there a soldier spoke earnestly to his linemate, giving last instructions should he not survive the fight.

The dustclouds hid whoever stirred them up. The Emperor dispatched a couple of hundred Kharmorth to learn what was ahead. Scaurus watched them shrink to black dots and vanish into the dust. The few minutes that passed before they came racing back seemed far longer.

As they galloped toward the imperial army, it was easy to see their excitement. They were wheeling and rearing their horses, and waving their fur caps—never abandoned, no matter what the weather—above their heads. They were shouting something, too, over and over. At last they were close enough for Marcus to understand it: "Onomag! Onomag!"

The tribune was worn out, but still felt a thrill course through him. Xenophon, he thought, must have known that same thrill when, from the rear of his battered Greek army, he heard men ahead crying, *"Thalassa! Thalassa!* The sea! The sea!"

Not only Onomagoulos' warriors were out ahead; Yezda were there too, harrying their retreat. Mavrikios flung cavalry against them—Videssians, Khamorth, Khatrishers, and finally Namdaleni. The islanders' powerful charge sent the lighter-armed enemy scattering in dismay and let the survivors of Baanes' division rejoin their comrades.

The army's joy at the meeting was short-lived; the first glimpse of the men staggering back through their lines dispelled it. The groans and cries of the wounded, and the sight of their distress, brought home all too vividly the dangers Mavrikios' force had yet to taste.

Onomagoulos himself was brought to safety in a litter, a great gash in his thigh bound up in the rags of his cloak.

"You will excuse me," Gorgidas said to Scaurus. "These poor devils need help." Without waiting for the tribune's leave, he hurried off to give the injured what aid he could.

Marcus' eyes, though, were on the warriors whose bodies had taken no blows. He liked none of what he saw. If ever any were, these were beaten troops. It showed in their eyes, in the haggard, numb bewilderment on their faces, in their slumped shoulders and dragging weapons. They had the look of men who tried in vain to stand against an avalanche.

Two words were on their lips. One was "Water!" Whenever a canteen was offered, it was tilted, drained, and, with gasped thanks, given back empty.

The other word was spoken softly. The defeated did not make it a warning to spread alarm through their rescuers. Marcus thought they would sooner have left it unsaid. But as often as little bands of them stumbled past his legionaries, he heard their voices drop and grow fearful. Because it was whispered, it took him a few minutes to catch the name of Avshar. After that, he understood.

Marcus saw his men's marching order thrown into disarray by Onomagoulos' fugitives. The sun was nearing the western horizon; rather than push forward under such unpromising circumstances, the Emperor ordered camp made so he could safely advance come morning.

His main body of troops fell to with a will. Marcus had to admit they did better work under the threat of imminent attack. Palisades and rough earthen barricades were built with a speed even the Romans could not fault, while the cavalry who had earlier driven the Yezda from Onomagoulos' men now screened them from the campsite.

They did not have an easy time of it. The iron charge of the Namdaleni had knocked the Yezda back on their heels, but not out of the fight. Constantly joined by more horsemen from the west, they made a battle of it, with all the confusion usual in big cavalry engagements. Squads of horsemen dashed back and forth, arrows flew in clouds, and sabers gleamed as they rose and fell.

"It's a good thing our works are going up fast," Gaius Philippus said, peering through the dusty haze to the west. "I don't think our horse is doing any too well out there. Those bloody bastards can ride—and how many of them are there, anyway?"

To that Scaurus could offer no reply. The dust and distance made numbers impossible to judge. Moreover, both the Yezda and their Khamorth cousins who fought under the Emperor's banner had strings of horses for each man, assuring them of a fresh mount each day and also making them seem far more numerous than they really were.

Numbers aside, the centurion was grimly correct. The Namdaleni might be the masters of the Yezda at close quarters, and the Khamorth their equals in speed. But the Videssians who formed the bulk of the imperial cavalry could neither crush them in close nor stay with them in a running fight. Slowly at first, Mavrikios' cavalry began drawing back toward and then into the field fortifications their comrades were still completing.

Marcus could hear horse shouts of triumph as the Yezda gave chase. Too many for all to enter at once, the Videssians and their mercenaries jammed together at the six gates of the imperial camp. Their foes, whooping with glee, sent flight after flight of arrows into those tempting targets. Men toppled in slow motion from their saddles; horses screamed as they were hit. The wounded beasts bolted in all directions, adding to the chaos round the gates.

Worse yet, in the turmoil and the fading light there was no way for the army to tell Khamorth friends from Yezda foes. More than a few invaders got into the camp in the guise of allies, then went on killing rampages until shot from their horses. Scaurus watched in horrified admiration as a Yezda sabered down three Videssian footsoldiers in quick succession, then leaped his horse over the breast-high palisade and into dusk's safety.

Khamorth were killed too, mistaken for enemies by panicky Videssians. Once or twice their clan-brothers, seeing comrades die before their eyes, took summary revenge. War within the Emperor's army was suddenly as real a threat as the enemy outside.

Much later, Marcus would hear Phostis Apokavkos retell the story of that dreadful night and say, "I'd sooner be dead than live through another time like that." From the proud, confident host that had set out from Videssos, the army was reduced in the early hours of that evening to little more than a terror-stricken mob, huddling behind the flimsy barricades that were all that kept it from the clutches of its foes.

If the Yezda had mounted an assault then and there, Marcus thought the Videssian force would have broken before them like so many dry sticks. But the nomads were leery of attacking a fortified camp, and perhaps the constant motion inside—in reality as meaningless as the scurrying of ants when their hill is disturbed—looked from outside like the preparations of battle-ready troops. The onslaught did not come, and little by little the Emperor began to get his men in hand once more.

He seemed everywhere at once, not in robes of state now but gilded armor above the crimson imperial boots. He dragged skulkers to the palisade from the false security of their tents. His army's position was hardly enviable, but he was far too much a soldier to quit without a fight.

When he came to the Roman section of the camp, weary approval lit his face. "Very neat," he complimented Scaurus. "Ditch, rampart, stakes—aye, and water too, I see—just like a drill. Are your men's spirits holding up?"

"Well enough, your Majesty," the tribune replied.

"There's no need to fret over that," Viridovix put in. "The lot of these Romans are too thick-skinned to be afraid."

Gaius Philippus bristled instinctively, but the Emperor waved him to silence. "Easy, there. On a night like this, you'd be better off if that were so. Phos knows, I wish I could say it." Not even the ruddy campfires could bring much color to his face; in their flickering light he looked wan and old. Shoulders bent as if under a heavy load, he turned and went his way.

His brother the Sevastokrator was rallying the staggered army too, in his own more direct fashion. "Phos' left hairy nut!" Marcus heard him shouting not far away. "Give me that bow, you worthless crock of dung!" A bowstring thrummed; Thorisin cursed heartily at a miss. He shot again. Somewhere in the gloom a horse gave a contralto shriek of agony. "There!" the Sevastokrator said. "That's how it's done!"

Strangely enough, Ortaias Sphrantzes also helped pull the Videssian army back together. He went wandering through the camp declaiming such pedantries as, "Wisdom-loving men— for I name you philosophers rather than soldiers—should show the barbarians that their eagerness is deathless," and, "The souls of the Yezda are not double, nor are their bodies made of adamant. They, too, are initiated into the mysteries of death."

The performance should have been ludicrous, and indeed it was. Men smiled to hear the young noble mouthing his platitudes, but in that place smiles were hard to come by. Moreover, however long-winded Sphrantzes was, he also spoke the truth, and those who took the time to listen were not worse for it.

Priests circulated, praying with the soldiers and re-swearing them to loyalty to the Empire. No one seemed to care this night if a Namdalener added a clause to the creed Videssos followed, or if a man of Vaspurakan styled himself a son of Phos' firstborn. In the face of peril, everyone was for once united.

When asked, the pagan Khamorth, too, took fresh oaths of allegiance. No priests would hear them, but before some of Mavrikios' scribes they swore by their swords to hold faith with the Emperor. Their very reluctance after the mishaps at the gates convinced Scaurus their word was good. Had they intended betrayal, he thought, they would have made their vows more readily, the better to deceive.

"Hello, hello." That was Nepos, who had been standing at the tribune's elbow for a couple of minutes without managing to be noticed. The little priest looked as somber as his plump, merry features would allow. He said diffidently, "Might I ask you and yours to join the rest of this army in pledging your loyalty to Videssos? I hold no suspicions and mean no offense, but this seems a time for renewing faith."

"Of course," Scaurus nodded. Had the Romans been singled out for such treatment he would have taken it ill, but, as the priest said, every man in the camp was reaffirming his loyalty. "What oath would satisfy you, though? Most of us do not follow your ways."

"Hmm." Nepos scratched his shaven head. "A poser—have you any suggestions?"

Marcus thought for a moment, then said, "It is our custom, when taking service in a legion, for one man to take the oath, and everyone swear to follow his example. If I swear that oath again, this time by my gods and your own, would it suffice?"

"I fail to see how I could ask for anything more."

"All right." At the tribune's command, the buccinators sounded their horns to gain the legionaries' attention. The clear trumpet notes cut through the tumult; Romans snapped their heads around to see what the matter was.

When Marcus saw they were all watching him, he asked if there was any man unwilling to give the promise Nepos asked. No one spoke. "Very well, then," he told them. "By the gods we brought from Rome and by the god we met here, I pledge myself to obey the Emperor and do his bidding as best I can. Do you now swear to do the same as I?"

"*Iuramus!*" they cried in the same Latin they had used when first joining their legions. "We swear it!" Nepos might not understand the word, but its meaning was unmistakable. He bowed his thanks to Marcus and hurried away to confirm some other unit's allegiance.

The din outside the camp was unbelievable. Not quite bold enough to storm its ramparts, the Yezda did everything they could to bring terror to the men within. Some rode up close to scream threats in broken Videssian, while others contented themselves with wordless shrieks of hate.

Worse still, Marcus thought, were the great drums that boomed around every Yezda campfire like the irregular heart-beats of a dying, demented god. The vibration came through the ground as much as through the air and seemed to echo and re-echo inside a man's bones.

To sleep in such circumstances was a forlorn hope, even for the phlegmatic Scaurus. He welcomed the messenger announcing Mavrikios' nightly council with enough eagerness to send the man off shaking his head in confusion. There was no need for directions to the Emperor's tent. Not only was it bigger than any other, it also stood on the highest ground in the campsite, to let Mavrikios have as good a view as he could of the surrounding terrain.

Reaching it, though, was like fighting through the crowds that always filled the forum of Palamas in the imperial capital. Men were on the move all through the camp, some with purposeful strides, others wandering aimlessly, using the simple fact of their motion as an anodyne against thought. Despite having a definite goal, the tribune also paid less attention to his surroundings than he might have. Gaius Philippus' warning was too slow to keep him from bumping into a Haloga from behind.

The blond giant swung round in annoyance; he wore a leather patch over his right eye. "Watch your feet, you oafish—" He stopped short.

"Skapti!" Marcus exclaimed. "I did not think you were with the Emperor's army. You should have visited us long ago."

"When I saw you last, I said we'd meet again." The commander of the Imbros garrison shrugged. To himself more than the Romans, he went on, "A man's weird is a strange thing— if he will not come to it, it comes to him instead."

He took Scaurus' hand in both his own in the Haloga fashion, then shook his head, rueful amusement on his face. Giving the Romans no time to puzzle out his riddle, he turned and went on his way, tall, lonely, and proud.

Staring at his back, Gaius Philippus said, "I've seen men with that look to them before. Fey, Viridovix would call him."

"Aye, and he seems to think somehow I'm part of his fate —may the gods prove him wrong." Something else struck Scaurus. "When did you, of all people, take to borrowing words from the Celt?"

The centurion wore the same expression Skapti Modolf's son had shown a moment before. "It does fit, though, doesn't it?"

"That I can't argue. Come on—let's see if Mavrikios' wizards have come up with a way to give us all wings and get us out of this pickle."

No wizards were at the battle conference, with or without word of wings. Mavrikios had brought them with his force, to be sure, but more to foil enemy sorcery than to use his own as a weapon of offense—he was a man of arms by birth and training. The fight he faced now might not be on the terms he wanted, but he did not intend to dodge it.

Indeed, he was surprisingly cheerful, saying to Ortaias Sphrantzes, "I don't think this is the way Kalokyres would have recommended luring the enemy into battle, but it shouldn't work out too badly. Unless I miss my guess, the nomads will be so pumped up from today's fighting that they'll stand against us for once. And when they do, we'll break them. In hand-to-hand they don't have a prayer against us."

Marcus thought the Emperor had every chance of being right. From what he had seen of the Yezda, victory would make them reckless. They would probably be so eager to finish off the Videssians as to be easy to snare.

The Emperor's thoughts were running along the same lines. He gave his orders to his brother and Sphrantzes accordingly, "You two on the wings will be crucial in making this work, since you have most of the light cavalry. Spread wide—funnel the Yezda down to the center. The heavy troopers there will stop them; once they're well engaged, close the wings like this." He brought his outstretched arms together in front of his body. "We'll surround them on three sides or, Phos willing, all four, and that should do it."

Thorisin quietly listened to Mavrikios' outline, now and then nodding as the Emperor made a point. "He's cool enough, isn't he?" Gaius Philippus murmured to Scaurus.

"Why not? This scheme can't be news to him. He and Mavrikios likely have been working it through since sundown."

Ortaias Sphrantzes was hearing it all for the first time, and his eyes glowed with excitement. "A classic ploy, your Majesty," he breathed, "and surely a trap to catch the undisciplined barbarian rabble." Scaurus was inclined to agree with the first part of what he said, but rather resented the rest. Mavrikios' plan reminded him of Hannibal's at Cannae, and that trap had closed around Romans.

The Emperor was pleased by the praise. "Thank you, Ortaias," he said graciously. "I look to you to hearten your men tomorrow with a fine rousing speech." Mavrikios was in a confident mood indeed, thought Marcus, if he was willing to be so courteous to his rival's nephew.

"I shall! I've prepared one against the day of need, nicely calculated to raise martial ferocity."

"Excellent."

Next to Scaurus, Gaius Philippus rolled his eyes and groaned, but so low in his throat only the tribune could hear. The senior centurion had listened to part of that speech, Marcus recalled, and was anything but impressed. It did not really matter. Scaurus had watched Nephon Khoumnos, well down in the formal order of precedence, listening to Mavrikios' scheme, and could fairly see the old warhorse plan its execution. Everyone—save possibly Ortaias Sphrantzes—knew the left wing was really his.

Out in the darkness beyond the encircled camp, the drums paused in their discordant pounding, were silent for a moment, then began anew, this time all together: *thump-thump, thump-thump, thump-thump*. The two-beat phrase, repeated endlessly, maddeningly, made teeth rattle in their sockets, brought dull pain to the head. The harsh voices of the Yezda joined the drums: "Avshar! Avshar! Avshar! Avshar!"

Marcus felt his hands curl into fists when he understood the invaders' chant. He glanced over to see Mavrikios' reaction. The Emperor met his eye, quirked an eyebrow upward. "All the pieces are on the board," he said. "Now we can play."

The day dawned clear and hot, the brassy sun fairly leaping into a sky of flawless blue. The tribune's eyes were gritty as he spooned up his breakfast porridge. The drums had not stopped throbbing all night, and what sleep he'd had was shallow and shot through with evil dreams. All through the Videssian camp, men yawned while they ate.

Quintus Glabrio scoured his empty bowl with sand, put it back in his pack. He was yawning too, but not worried about it. "Unless all the men out of Yezd are deaf, they had as much trouble sleeping as I did," he said. Marcus nodded, appreciating his sense of proportion.

Yezda tents lay scattered over the plain like multicolored toadstools. There were more of them to the west of the Videssian camp; many were grouped around a great pavilion of jet-black felt. Without need for conscious thought, Scaurus was sure it was Avshar's. Yezda streamed toward it. The tribune watched their battle line begin taking shape.

As he had feared, the nomads tried to keep the imperial army besieged in its camp, but Mavrikios was equal to that. Archers from behind the palisade made them keep their distance, and, when three or four dart-throwing catapults added their fire, the Yezda drew back toward their own lines. The Emperor then used his light horse as he had before, to form a curtain behind which his main force could deploy.

Sweat already beginning to make his shoulders raw under his cuirass, Scaurus led his Romans to their place in the Videssian line. They anchored the left flank of Mavrikios' strong center; to their own left was the cavalry contingent from Khatrish, which linked the center to Ortaias Sphrantzes' left wing.

The Khatrisher commander, a slim, pockmarked man named Laon Pakhymer, waved when he saw the tribune. Marcus waved back. Ever since his first encounter with Taso Vones, he had liked the Khatrishers. He also preferred them on his flank to their Khamorth cousins. Some of the men from the plains of Pardraya were in a sullen mood, and Scaurus could scarcely blame them after their allies had shot at them by mistake.

Viridovix looked out over the barren plain toward the gathering enemy. He scratched his nose. His fair skin suffered under the fierce Videssian sun, burning and peeling without ever really tanning. "Not much like the last shindy the two of us were in, is it now?" he said to Marcus.

"It isn't, is it? Morning instead of night, hot instead of mild, this naked rockpile instead of your Gallic forest . . . why, we're even on the same side now."

"So we are." Viridovix chuckled. "I hadna thought of that. It should be a fine brawl all the same." Scaurus snorted.

Pipes whistled and drums thumped, ordering the imperial forces forward. The Romans did without such fripperies, except for their rallying horncalls, but the tribune was rather glad of the martial music surrounding his men. It made him feel less alone, less as if all the Yezda ahead were marking him as their target.

The invaders were advancing too, not in the neat articulated units of the Videssian army, but now here, now there, like a wave up an uneven beach. It was easy to recognize Avshar, even at the distance between the two forces. He chose to lead his host from the right rather than from the center like

Mavrikios. His white robes flashed brightly against the sooty coat of the huge stallion he rode. Yezd's banner flapped lazily above his head.

"That is an evil color for a standard," Quintus Glabrio said. "It reminds me of a bandage soaked with clotted blood." The image was fitting, but surprising when it came from the Roman officer. It sounded more like something Gorgidas would say.

Gaius Philippus said, "It suits them, for they've caused enough to be soaked."

The two forces were about half a mile apart when Mavrikios rode his own roan charger out ahead of his men to address them. Turning his head left and right, Marcus saw Ortaias Sphrantzes and Thorisin doing the same in their divisions of the army. The Yezda, too, came to a halt while Avashar and their other chieftains harangued them.

The Emperor's speech was short and to the point. He reminded his men of the harm Yezd had inflicted on Videssos, told them their god was fighting on their side—the tribune was willing to bet Avshar was making the same claim to his warriors—and briefly outlined the tactics he had planned.

The tribune did not pay much attention to Mavrikios' words—their draft was plain after five or six sentences. More interesting were the snatches of Ortaias Sphrantzes' address that a fitful southerly breeze brought him.

In his thin tenor, the noble was doing his best to encourage his men with the same kind of sententious rhetoric he had used inside the Videssian camp the night before. "Fight with every limb; let no limb have no share of danger! The campaign of Yezd has justice opposed to it, for peace is a loathsome thing to them, and their love of battle is such that it honors a god of blood. Injustice is often strong, but it is also changed to ruin. I will direct the battle, and in my eagerness for combat engage the aid of all—I am ashamed to suffer not suffering . . ."

On and on he went. Marcus lost the thread of Sphrantzes' speech when Mavrikios finished his own and the men of the center cheered, but when their shouts subsided Ortaias was still holding forth. The soldiers on the left listened glumly, shifting from foot to foot and muttering among themselves. What they expected and needed was a heartening fierce speech, not this grandiloquent monologue.

The Sevastos' nephew built to his rousing conclusion. "Let no one who loves luxury's pleasures share in the rites of war and let no one join in the battle for the sake of loot. It is the lover of danger who should seek the space between the two armies. Come now, let us at last add deeds to words and let us shift our theory into the line of battle!"

He paused expectantly, waiting for the applause the two Gavrai had already received. There were a few spatters of clapping and one or two shouts, but nothing more. "He does have the brain of a pea," Gaius Philippus grumbled. "Imagine telling a mercenary army not to loot! I'm surprised he didn't tell them not to drink and fornicate, while he was at it."

Dejectedly, Sphrantzes rode back into line. Nephon Khoumnos was there to slap his armored back and try to console him—and also, Marcus knew, to protect the army from his flights of fancy.

It would not be long now. All speeches done at last, both armies were advancing again, and the forwardmost riders were already exchanging arrows. Scaurus felt a familiar tightening in his guts, suppressed it automatically. These moments just before fighting began were the worst. Once in the middle of it, there was no time to be afraid.

The Yezda came on at a trot. Marcus saw the sun flash off helmets, drawn swords, and lanceheads, saw their banners and horse-tail standards lifted high. Then he blinked and rubbed his eyes; around him, Romans cried out in amazement and alarm. The oncoming line was flickering like a candle flame in a breeze, now plain, now half-seen as if through fog, now vanished altogether. The tribune clutched his sword until knuckles whitened, but the grip brought no security. How was he to strike foes he could not see?

Though it seemed an eternity, the Yezda could not have remained out of sight more than a few heartbeats. Through the outcry of his own men, Scaurus heard counterspells shouted by the sorcerers who accompanied the imperial army. The enemy reappeared, sharp and solid as if they had never blurred away.

"Battle magic," the tribune said shakily.

"So it was," Gaius Philippus agreed. "It didn't work, though, the gods be thanked." He spoke absently, without turning to look as Scaurus. His attention was all on the Yezda, who, their ploy failed, were riding harder now, bearing down on the Videssians. "Shields up!" the centurion shouted, as arrows arced their way toward the Romans.

Marcus had never stood up under arrow fire like this. An arrow buzzed angrily past his ear; another struck his *scutum* hard enough to drive him back a pace. The noise the shafts made as they hissed in and struck shields and corselets was like rain beating on a metal roof. Rain, though, never left men shrieking and writhing when it touched their soft, vulnerable flesh.

The Yezda thundered forward, close enough for the tribune to see their intent faces as they guided their horses toward the gaps their arrows had made. "*Pila!*" he shouted, and, a moment later, "Loose!"

Men pitched from saddles, to spin briefly through the air or be dragged to red death behind their mounts. So stirrups had drawbacks after all, Scaurus thought. Horses fell too, or ran wild when bereft of riders. They fouled those next to them and sent them crashing to the ground. Warriors behind the first wave, unable to stop their animals in time, tripped over the fallen or desperately pulled back on their reins to leap the sudden barrier ahead—and presented themselves as targets for their foes.

The Roman volley shook the terrifying momentum of the Yezda charge, but did not, could not, stop it altogether. Yelling like men possessed, the nomads collided with the soldiers who would bar their way. A bushy-bearded warrior slashed down at the tribune from horseback. He took the blow on his shield while he cut at the nomad's leg, laying open his thigh and wounding his horse as well.

Rider and beast cried out in pain together. The luckless animal reared, blood dripping down its barrel. An arrow thudded into its belly. It slewed sideways and fell, pinning its rider beneath it. The saber bounced from his loosening grip as he struck.

A few hundred yards to his right, Marcus heard deep-voiced cries as the Namdaleni hurled themselves forward at the Yezda before them. They worked a fearful slaughter for a short time, striking with swords and lances and bowling the enemy over with the sheer weight of their charge. Like snapping wolves against a bear, the nomads gave way before them, but even in retreat their deadly archery took its toll.

Again the Yezda tried to rush the Romans, and again the legionaries' well-disciplined volley of throwing spears broke the charge before it could smash them. "I wish we had more heavy spearmen," Gaius Philippus panted. "There'd be nothing like a line of *hastati* to keep these buggers off of us." The *hasta*, though, was becoming obsolete in Rome's armies, and few were the legionaries trained in its use.

"Wish for the moon, while you're at it," Marcus said, putting to flight a nomad who, fallen from horse, chose to fight on foot. The Yezda scuttled away before the tribune could finish him.

Viridovix, as always an army in himself, leaped out from the Roman line and, sidestepping an invader's hacking swordstroke, cut off the head of the nomad's horse with a single slash of his great blade. The Romans cried out in triumph, the Yezda in dismay, at the mighty blow.

The rider threw himself clear as his beast foundered, but the tall Celt was on him like a cat after a lizard. Against Viridovix's reach and strength he could do nothing, and his own head spun from his shoulders an instant later. Snatching up the gory trophy, the Gaul returned to the Roman ranks.

"I know it's not your custom to be taking heads," he told Scaurus, "but a fine reminder he'll be of the fight."

"You can have him for breakfast, for all I care," the tribune shouted back. His usual equanimity frayed badly in the stress of battle.

The legionaries' unyielding defense and the exploit of the Celt, as savage as any of their own, dissuaded the Yezda from further direct assaults. Instead, they drew back out of spearrange and plied the Romans with arrows. Marcus would have like nothing better than to let his men charge the nomads, but he had already seen what happened when a Vaspurakaner company, similarly assailed, ran pell-mell at the Yezda. They were cut off and cut to pieces in the twinkling of an eye.

Still, there was no reason for the Romans to endure such punishment without striking back. Scaurus sent a runner over to Laon Pakhymer. The Khatrisher acknowledged his request with a flourish of his helmet over his head. He sent a couple of squadrons of his countryman forward, just enough to drive the Yezda out of bowshot. As the nomads retreated, Marcus moved his own line up to help cover the allies who had protected him.

He wondered how the fight was going. His own little piece of it was doing fairly well, but this was too big a battle to see all at once. The numbers on both sides, the length of the battle line, and the ever-present smothering dust made that hopeless.

But by the way the front was bending, Mavrikios' plan seemed to be working. The Yezda, squeezed on both flanks, were being forced to hurl themselves at the Videssian line's center. Deprived of the mobility that gave them their advantage, they were easy meat for the heavy troops the Emperor had concentrated there. The great axes of his Haloga guardsmen rose and fell, rose and fell, shearing through the nomad's light small shields and boiled-leather cuirasses. The northerners sang as they fought, their slow, deep battle chant sounding steadily through the clamor around them.

Avshar growled, deep in his throat, a sound of thwarted fury. The Videssian center was even stronger than he had expected, though he had known it held his foes' best troops. And among them, he suddenly recalled, was the outlander who had bested him at swords. He seldom lost at anything; revenge would be sweet.

Three times he fired his deadly bow at Scaurus. Twice he missed; despite terrified rumor, the weapon was not infallible. His third shot was true, but a luckless nomad rode into the arrow's path. He fell, never knowing his own chieftain had slain him.

The wizard cursed to see that perfect shot ruined. "A different way, then," he rumbled to himself. He had intended to use the spell against another, but it would serve here as well.

He handed his bow to an officer by his side, calmed his horse with his knees till it stood still—the spell required passes with both hands at once. As he began to chant, even the Yezda holding the bow flinched from him, so frigid and terrible were his words.

Marcus' sword flared dazzlingly bright for an instant. It chilled him, but many magics were loose on the field today.

He waved to the buccinators to call a lagging maniple into position.

Avshar cursed again, feeling his sorcery deflected. His fists clenched, but even he had to bow to necessity—back to the first plan, then. Yezda scouts had watched the imperial host drill a score of times and brought him word of what they had seen. Of all the men in that host, one was the key—and Avshar's spell would not go awry twice.

"There you go! There you go! Drive the whoresons back!" Nephon Khoumnos shouted. He was hoarse and tired, but increasingly happy over the battle's course. Ortaias, Phos be praised, was not getting in his way too badly, and the troops were performing better than he'd dared hope. He wondered if Thorisin was having as much success on the right. If he was, soon the Yezda would be surrounded by a ring of steel.

The general sneezed, blinked in annoyance, sneezed again. Despite the sweltering heat, he was suddenly cold; the sweat turned clammy on his body. He shivered inside his armor— there were knives of ice stabbing at his bones. Agony shot through his joints at every move. His eyes bulged. He opened his mouth to cry out, but no words emerged. His last conscious thought was that freezing was not the numb, painless death it was supposed to be.

"They appear to be stepping up the pressure," Ortaias Sphrantzes said. "What do you think, Khoumnos? Should we commit another brigade to throw them back?" Getting no reply, he turned to glance at the older man. Khoumnos was staring fixedly ahead and did not seem to be giving any heed to his surroundings.

"Are you all right?" Sphrantzes asked. He laid a hand on the general's bare arm, then jerked it back in horror, leaving skin behind. Touching Khoumnos was like brushing against an ice-glazed wall in dead of winter, but worse, for this was a cold that burned like fire.

Startled at the sudden motion, the general's horse shied. Its rider swayed, then toppled stiffly; it was as if a frozen statue bestrode the beast. A hundred throats echoed Sphrantzes' cry of terror, for Khoumnos' body, like a statue carved from brittle ice, shattered into a thousand frozen shards when it struck the ground.

"A pox!" Gaius Philippus exclaimed. "Something's gone wrong on the left!" Sensitive to battle's changing tides as a deer to the shifting breeze, the centurion felt the Yezda swing to the offensive almost before they delivered their attack.

Pakhymer caught the scent of trouble, too, and sent one of his riders galloping south behind the line to find out what it was. He listened as his man reported back, then shouted to the Romans, "Khoumnos is down!"

"Oh, bloody hell," Marcus muttered. Gaius Philippus clapped his hand to his forehead and swore. Here was a chance the Emperor had left unreckoned—responsibility for a third of the Videssian army had just landed squarely on Ortaias Sphrantzes' skinny shoulders.

The Khatrisher who brought the news was still talking. Laon Pakhymer heard him out, then spoke so sharply the Romans could hear part of what he said: "—mouth shut, do you under—" The horseman nodded, gave him an untidy salute, and rode back into line.

"Sure and I wonder what all that was about," Viridovix said.

Gaius Philippus said, "Nothing good, I'll warrant."

"You're a rare gloomy soul, Roman dear, but I'm afraid you have the right of it this time."

When his left wing faltered, Mavrikios guessed why. He sent Zeprin the Red south as fast as he could to rescue the situation, but the Haloga marshal found himself caught up in confused and bitter fighting that broke out when a band of Yezda cracked the imperial line and rampaged through the Videssian rear. The northerner's two-handed axe sent more than one of them to his death, but meanwhile Ortaias Sphrantzes kept command.

Like a ship slowly going down on an even keel, the left's plight grew worse. The various contingents' officers led them as best they could, but with Nephon Khoumnos gone their overall guiding force disappeared. Ortaias, in his inexperience, frantically rushed men here and there to counter feints, while failing to answer real assaults.

The left was also a liability in another way. Despite Pakhymer's silencing his messenger, rumors of how Khoumnos died soon ran through the whole Videssian army. They were confused and sometimes wildly wrong, but Avshar's name was writ large in all of them. Men in every section of the line looked south in apprehension, awaiting they knew not what.

The Emperor, seeing the failure of his scheme and the way the Yezda were everywhere pressing his disheartened soldiers back, ordered a withdrawal back to the camp he had left so full of hope. Using their superior mobility and the confusion on the left, the Yezda were beginning to slip small parties round the imperial army's flank. If enough got round to cut the Videssians off from their base, what was now nearly a draw could quickly become disaster.

Mavrikios did not intend to give up the fight. The Videssians could regroup behind their field fortifications and return to the struggle the next morning.

For a moment Marcus did not recognize the new call the drummers and pipers were playing. "Retreat," for obvious reasons, was not an often-practiced exercise. When he did realize what the command was, he read Mavrikios' intentions accurately. "We'll have another go at them tomorrow," he predicted to Gaius Philippus.

"No doubt, no doubt," the centurion agreed. "Hurry up, you fools!" he shouted to the legionaries. "Defensive front— get out there, you spearmen! Hold the losels off us." His fury came more from habit than need; the Romans were smoothly moving into their covering formation.

"Is it running away we are?" Viridovix demanded. "There's no sense of it. Aye, we've not beaten the spalpeens, but there's no one would say they've beaten us either. Let's stay at it and have this thing out." He brandished his sword at the Yezda.

Gaius Philippus sighed, wiped sweat from his face, rubbed absently at a cut on his left cheek. He was as combative as the Celt, but had a firmer grip on the sometimes painful realities of the field. "We're not beaten, no," he said. "But there's wavering all up and down the line, and the gods know what's going on over there." He waved his left arm. "Better we move back under our own control than fall apart trying to hold."

"It's a cold-blooded style of fighting, sure and it is. Still and all, there's a bright side to everything—now I'll have a chance to salt this lovely down properly." He gave a fond pat to the Yezda head tied to his belt. That was too much even for the hard-bitten centurion, who spat in disgust.

A deliberate fighting retreat is probably the most difficult maneuver to bring off on a battlefield. Soldiers equate withdrawal with defeat, and only the strongest discipline holds panic at bay. The Videssians and their mercenary allies performed better than Marcus would have expected from such a heterogeneous force. Warded by a bristling fence of spears, they began to disengage, dropping back a step here, two more there, gathering up the wounded as they went, always keeping a solid fighting front toward their foes.

"Steady, there!" Marcus grabbed the bridle of Senpat Sviodo's horse. The young Vaspurakaner was about to charge a Yezda insolently sitting his horse not thirty yards away.

"Turn me loose, damn you!"

"We'll get this one tomorrow—you've done your share for today." That was nothing less than the truth; Sviodo's fine wickerwork helm was broken and hanging loosely over one ear, while his right calf bore a rude bandage that showed the fighting had not all gone his way.

He was still eager for more, touching spurs to his mount to make it rear free of the tribune's grip.

Scaurus held firm. "If he hasn't the stomach to close with us, let him go now. All we have to do is keep them off us, and we'll be fine."

He glared up at the mutinous Vaspurakaner. To his legionaries he could simply give orders, but Senpat Sviodo was a long way from their obedience—and, to give him his due, he had better reason to hate that grinning Yezda than did the Romans. "I know how happy it would make you to spill his guts out on the dirt, but what if you get in trouble? To say nothing of your grieving your wife, we'd have to rescue you and risk getting cut off while the rest of the army pulled back."

"Leave Nevrat out of this!" Senpat said hotly. "Were she here, we'd fight that swine together. And as for the rest of it, I don't need your help and I don't want it. I don't care about the lot of you!"

"But want it or not, you'd have it, because we care about you, lad." Marcus released his hold on the bridle. "Do what you bloody well please—but even Viridovix is with us, you'll notice."

There was a pause. "Is he, now?" Senpat Sviodo's chuckle was not the blithe one he'd had before the army entered ruined Vaspurakan, but Marcus knew he'd won his point. Sviodo wheeled his horse and trotted it back to the Roman line, which had moved on another score of paces while he and Scaurus argued.

The tribune followed more slowly, studying as best he could how well the army was holding together. It really was going better than he'd dared hope; even the left seemed pretty firm. "You know," he said, catching up to the Vaspurakaner, "I do believe this is going to work."

Avshar watched Ortaias Sphrantzes canter down the Videssian left wing toward the center. Behind the robes that masked him, he might have smiled.

"Dress your lines! Keep good order!" Sphrantzes called, waving energetically to his men. This business of war was as exciting as he'd thought it would be, if more difficult. Decisions had to come at once, and situations did not easily fit into the neat categories Mindes Kalokyres outlined. When they did, they changed so quickly that orders were often worthless as soon as they were given.

The noble knew he had been outmaneuvered several times and lost troops as a result. It pained him; these were not symbols drawn on parchment or pieces to be taken cleanly from a board, but men who fought and bled and died so he could learn his trade.

Still, on the whole he did not think he had done badly. There had been breakthroughs, yes, but never a serious one— he did not know he still held command because of one of those breakthroughs. His mere presence, he thought, went a long way toward heartening his men. He knew what a fine warlike picture he made with his gilded helmet and armor, his burnished rapier with its jeweled hilt, and his military cape floating behind him in the breeze.

True, there had been that terrible moment when Avshar's sorcery reached out to slay Nephon Khoumnos. But even the white-shrouded villain was according him the respect he deserved, always shadowing him as he rode up and down the line.

He had done everything, in short, that a general could reasonably be expected to do . . . except fight.

Horns blared in the enemy ranks. Sphrantzes' lip curled at the discords they raised. Then the disdain vanished from his face, to be replaced by dread. A thousand Yezda were spurring straight at him, and at their head was Avshar.

"Ortaias!" the wizard-prince cried, voice spectrally clear through the thunder of hoofbeats. "I have a gift for thee, Ortaias!" He lifted a mailed fist. The blade therein was no bejeweled toy, but a great murdering broadsword, red-black with the dried blood of victims beyond number.

First among all the Videssians, Ortaias Sphrantzes in his mind's eye penetrated Avshar's swaddling veils to see his face, and the name of that face was fear. His bowels turned to water, his heart to ice.

"Phos have mercy on us! We are undone!" he squealed. He wheeled his horse, jabbed his heels into its flanks. Hunched low to ride the faster, he spurred his way back through his startled soldiers—just as Avshar, taking his measure, had foreseen. "All's lost! All's lost!" he wailed. Then he was past the last of his men, galloping east as fast as his high-bred mount would run.

A moment later the Videssian line behind him, stunned by its general's defection, smashed into ruin under the wizard's hammer-stroke.

Take a pitcher of water outside on a cold winter's day. If the water is very pure and you do not disturb it; it may stay liquid long after you would expect it to freeze. But let a snowflake settle on the surface of this supercooled water, and it will be ice clear through in less time than it takes to tell.

So it was with the Videssian army, for Ortaias Sphrantzes' flight was the snowflake that congealed retreat into panic. And with a gaping hole torn in its ranks, and Yezda gushing through to take the army in flank and rear, terror was far from unwarranted.

"Well, that's done it!" Gaius Philippus said, angry beyond profanity. "Form square!" he shouted, then explained to Marcus, "The better order we show, the less likely the sods

are to come down on us. The gods know they'll have easier
pickings elsewhere."

The tribune nodded in bitter agreement. The amputated left
wing of the army was already breaking up in flight. Here and
there knots of brave or stubborn men still struggled against the
nomads who were enveloping them on all sides, but more and
more rode east as fast as they could go, throwing away
shields, helms, even swords to flee more quickly. Whooping
gleefully, the Yezda pursued them like boys after rabbits.

But Avshar kept enough control over the unruly host he led
to swing most of it back for the killing stroke against the
Videssian center. Assailed simultaneously from front and rear,
many units simply ceased to be. They lacked the Romans'
long-drilled flexibility and tore their ranks to pieces trying to
redeploy. Even proud squadrons of Halogai splintered beyond
repair. The Yezda surged into the gaps confusion created and
spread slaughter with bow and saber. Survivors scattered all
over the field.

Under the ferocious onslaught, the motley nature of the
Videssian army became the curse Marcus had feared. Each
contingent strove to save itself, with little thought for the army
as a whole. "Rally to me!" Mavrikios' pipers signaled desperately, but it was too late for that. In the chaos, many regiments
never understood the order, and those that did could not obey
because of the ever-present, ever-pressing hordes of Yezda.

Some units held firm. The Namdaleni beat back charge
after charge, until the Yezda gave them up as a bad job.
Fighting with a fury born of despair, Gagik Bagratouni's
Vaspurkaners also stopped the invaders cold. But neither
group could counterattack.

As Gaius Philippus had predicted, the good order the
Romans still kept let them push on relatively unscathed. Indeed, they attracted stragglers—sometimes by squads and
platoons—to themselves, men seeking a safe island in a sea
of disaster. Marcus welcomed them if they still showed fight.
Every sword, every spear was an asset.

The additions came none too soon. One of the Yezda captains was wise enough to see that any organized force remained a potential danger. He shouted a word of command,
wheeled his men toward the Romans.

Drumming hooves, felt through the soles as much as heard

... "They come, aye, they come!" Viridovix yelled. Ruin all around him, he still reveled in fighting. He leaped out against the onrushing Yezda, ignoring arrows, evading swordstrokes that flashed by like striking snakes. The nomad captain cut at him. He jerked his head away, replied with a two-handed stroke of his own that sheared through boiled-leather cuirass and ribs alike, hurling his foe from his saddle to the dust below.

The Romans cheered his prowess, those not busy fighting for their own lives. *Pila* were few now, and the Yezda charge struck home almost unblunted. For all their discipline, the legionaries staggered under the blow. The front edge of the square sagged, began to crumple.

Marcus, at the fore, killed two Yezda in quick succession, only to have two more ride past on either side of him and hurl themselves against the battered line.

A mounted nomad struck him on the side of the head with a spearshaft swung club-fashion. It was a glancing blow, but his vision misted, and he slipped to one knee. Another Yezda, this one on foot, darted forward, saber upraised. The tribune lifted his shield to parry, sickly aware he would be too slow.

From the corner of his eye he saw a tall shape loom up beside him. an axe bit with a meaty *chunnk*; the Yezda was dead before his dying cry passed his lips. Skapti Modolf's son put a booted foot on the corpse, braced, and pulled the weapon free.

"Where are your men?" Scaurus shouted.

The Haloga shrugged. "Dead or scattered. They gave the ravens more bones to pick than their own." Skapti seemed more a wolf than ever, an old wolf, last survivor of his pack.

He opened his mouth to speak again, then suddenly stiffened. Marcus saw the nomad arrow sprout from his chest. His one good eye held the Roman. "This place is less pleasant than Imbros," he said distinctly. His fierce blue stared dimmed as he slumped to the ground.

Scaurus recalled the fate the Haloga had half foretold when the Romans left his town. He had little time to marvel. Legionaries were falling faster than replacements could fill the holes in their ranks. Soon they would be an effective fighting force no more, but a broken mob of fugitives for the invaders' sport.

The tribune saw Gaius Philippus' head whipping from side to side, searching vainly for new men to throw into the fight. The centurion looked more harassed than beaten, annoyed over failing at something he should do with ease.

Then the Yezda shouted in surprise and alarm as they in turn were hit from behind. The killing pressure eased. The nomads streamed away in all directions, like a glob of quicksilver mashed by a falling fist.

Laon Pakhymer rode up to Marcus, a tired grin peeking through his tangled beard. "Horse and foot together do better than either by itself, don't you think?" he said.

Scaurus reached up to clasp his hand. "Pakhymer, you could tell me I was a little blue lizard and I'd say you aye right now. Never was any face so welcome as yours."

"There's flattery indeed," the Khatrisher said dryly, scratching a pockmarked cheek. He was quickly serious again. "Shall we stay together now? My riders can screen your troops, and you give us a base to fall back on at need."

"Agreed," Scaurus said at once. Even in the world he'd known, cavalry was the Romans' weakest arm, always eked out with allies or mercenaries. Here the stirrup and the incredible horsemanship it allowed made such auxiliaries all the more important.

While the Romans struggled for survival on the left center, a larger drama was building on the Videssian right wing. Of all the army, the right had suffered least. Now Thorisin Gavras, shouting encouragement to his men and fighting in the first rank, tried to lead it back to rescue his brother and the beaten center. "We're coming! We're coming!" the Sevastokrator's men cried. Those contingents still intact in the center yelled back with desperate intensity and tried to fight their way north.

It was not to be. The charge Thorisin led was doomed before it truly began. With Yezda on either side of them, the Sevastokrator's warriors had to run the cruelest kind of gauntlet to return to their stricken comrades. Arrows tore at them like blinding sleet. Their foes struck again and again, ruthless blows from the flank that had to be parried at any cost—and the cost was the thrust of the attack.

Thorisin and Thorisin alone kept his men moving forward

against all odds. Then his mount staggered and fell, shot from under him by one of the black shafts Avshar's bow could send so far. The Sevastokrator was a fine horseman; he rolled free from the foundering beast and sprang to his feet, shouting for a new horse.

But once slowed, even for the moment he needed to re-mount, his men could advance no further. Against his will, one of his lieutenants literally dragging his mount's bridle, the younger Gavras was compelled to fall back.

A great groan of despair rose from the Videssians as they realized the relieving attack had failed. All around them, the Yezda shouted in hoarse triumph. Mavrikios, seeing before him the ruin of all his hopes, saw also that the last service he could give his state would be to take the author of his defeat down with him.

He shouted orders to the surviving Halogai of the Imperial Guard. Over all the din of battle Marcus clearly heard their answering, "Aye!" Their axes gleamed crimson in the sunset as they lifted them high in a final salute. Spearheaded by the Emperor, they hurled themselves against the Yezda.

"Avshar!" Mavrikios cried. "Face to face now, proud filthy knave!" The wizard-prince spurred toward him, followed by a swarm of nomads. They closed round the Halogai and swallowed them up. All over the field men paused, panting, to watch the last duel.

The Imperial Guard, steady in the face of the doom they saw ahead, fought with the recklessness of men who knew they had nothing left to lose. One by one they fell; the Yezda were no cowards and they, too, fought under their overlord's eyes. At last only a small knot of Halogai still stood, to the end protecting the Emperor with their bodies. The wizard-prince and his followers rode over them, swords chopping like cleavers, and there were only Yezda in that part of the field.

Whatever faint hopes the Videssian army had for survival died with Mavrikios. Men thought no further than saving themselves at any price and abandoned their fellows if it meant making good their own escape. Fragments of the right were still intact under Thorisin Gavras, but so mauled they could do nothing but withdraw to the north in some semblance of order. Over most of the battleground, terror—and the Yezda—ruled supreme.

More than anyone else, Gaius Philippus saved the Romans during that grinding retreat. The veteran had seen victory and defeat both in his long career and held the battered band together. "Come on!" he said. "Show your pride, damn you! Keep your ranks steady and your swords out! Look like you want some more of these bastards!"

"All I want is to get away from here alive!" a panicky soldier yelled. "I don't care how fast I have to run!" Other voices took up the cry; the Roman ranks wavered, though the Yezda were not pressing them.

"Fools!" The centurion waved his arm to encompass the whole field, the sprawled corpses, the Yezda ranging far and wide to cut down fugitives. "Look around you—those poor devils thought they could run away too, and see what it got *them*. We've lost, aye, but we're still men. Let the Yezda know we're ready to fight and they'll have to earn it to take us, and odds are they won't. But if we throw away our shields and flap around like headless chickens, every man for himself, not a one of us will ever see home again."

"You couldn't be more right," Gorgidas said. The Greek physician's face was haggard with exhaustion and hurt. Too often he had watched men die from wounds beyond his skill to cure. He was in physical pain as well. His left arm was bandaged, and the bloodstains on his torn mantle showed where a Yezda saber had slid along a rib. Yet he still tried to give credit where it was due, to keep the heart in others when almost without it himself.

"Thanks," Gaius Philippus muttered. He was studying his troops closely, wondering if he had steadied them or if stronger measures would be needed.

Gorgidas persisted, "This is the way men come off safe in a retreat, by showing the enemy how ready they are to defend themselves. Whether you know it or not, you're following Socrates' example at the battle of Delium, when he made his way back to Athens and brought his comrades out with him."

Gaius Philippus threw his hands in the air. "Just what I need now, being told I'm like some smockfaced philosopher. Tend to your wounded, doctor, and let me mind the lads on their feet." Ignoring Gorgidas' injured look, he surveyed the Romans once more, shook his head in dissatisfaction.

"Pakhymer!" he shouted. The Khatrisher waved to show he'd heard. "Have your riders shoot the first man who bolts." The officer's eyes widened in surprise. Gaius Philippus said, "Better by far to lose a few at our hands than see a stampede that risks us all."

Pakhymer considered, nodded, and threw the centurion the sharpest salute Marcus had seen from the easygoing Khatrishers. He gave his men the order. Talk of flight abruptly ceased.

"Pay Gaius Philippus no mind," Quintus Glabrio told Gorgidas. "He means less than he says."

"I wasn't going to lose any sleep over it, my friend," the physician answered shortly, but there was gratitude in his voice.

"The soft-spoken lad has the right of it," Viridovix said. "When he talks, that one—" He stabbed a thumb toward Gaius Philippus. "—is like a fellow who can't keep his woman happy—things spurt out before he's ready."

The senior centurion snorted, saying, "I will be damned. This is the first time you've been on the same side of an argument as the Greek, I'll wager."

Viridovix tugged at his mustache as he thought. "Belike it is, at that," he admitted.

"And so he should be," Marcus said to Gaius Philippus. "You had no reason to turn on Gorgidas, especially since he was giving you the highest praise he could."

"Enough, the lot of you!" Gaius Philippus exclaimed in exasperation. "Gorgidas, if you want my apology, you have it. The gods know you're one of the few doctors I've seen worth the food you gobble. You jogged my elbow when I was in harness, and I kicked out at you without thinking."

"It's all right. You just paid me a finer compliment than the one I gave you," Gorgidas said. Not far away, a legionary cursed as an arrow pierced his hand. The physician sighed and hurried off to clean and bandage the wound.

He had fewer injuries to treat now. With their battle won, the Yezda slipped beyond even Avshar's control. Some still hunted Videssian stragglers, but more were looting the bodies of the dead or beginning to make camp among them; sunset was already past and darkness coming on. Sated, glutted with combat, the nomads were no longer eager to assail those few companies of their foes who still put up a bold front.

Somewhere in the twilight, a man screamed as the Yezda caught up with him at last. Scaurus shivered, thinking how close the Romans had come to suffering the same fate. He said to Gaius Philippus, "Gorgidas had the right of it. Without you we'd be running for cover one by one, like so many spooked cattle. You held us together when we needed it most."

The veteran shrugged, more nervous over praise than he had been when the fighting was hottest. "I know how to run a retreat, that's all. I bloody well ought to—I've been in enough of them over the years. You signed on with Caesar for the Gallic campaign, didn't you?"

Marcus nodded, remembering how he'd planned a short stay in the army to further his political hopes. Those days seemed as dim as if they had happened to someone else.

"Thought as much," Gaius Philippus said. "You've done pretty well yourself, you know, in Gaul and here as well. Most of the time I forget you didn't intent to make a life of this—you handle yourself like a soldier."

"I thank you," Scaurus replied sincerely, knowing that was as fulsome a compliment from the centurion as talk of Socrates was from Gorgidas. "You've helped me more than I can say; if I am any kind of soldier, it's because of what you've shown me."

"Hmp. All I ever did was do my job," Gaius Philippus said, more uncomfortable than ever. "Enough of this useless chitchat." He peered out into the dusk. "I think we've put enough distance between us and the worst of it to camp for the night."

"Good enough. The Khatrishers can hold off whatever raiders we draw while we're digging in." Scaurus spoke to the buccinators, who trumpeted out the order to halt.

"Of course," Pakhymer said when the tribune asked him for a covering force. "You'll need protection to throw up your fieldworks, and they will shelter all of us tonight." He cocked his head at the Roman in a gesture that reminded Scaurus of Taso Vones, though the two Khatrishers looked nothing like each other. "One of the reasons I joined my men to yours was to take advantage of your camp, if we saw today end with breath still in us. We have no skill at fortcraft."

"Maybe not, but you ride like devils loosed. Put me on a horse and I'd break my backside, or more likely my neck." The feeble jest aside, Marcus looked approvingly at the Khatrisher. It had taken a cool head to see ahead till nightfall in the chaos of the afternoon.

It was as well the Yezda did not press an attack while the camp was building. The Romans, dazed with fatigue, moved like sleepwalkers. They dug and lifted with slow, dogged persistence, knowing sleep would claim them if they halted for an instant. The stragglers who had joined them helped as best they could, hampered not only by exhaustion but also by inexperience at this sort of work.

Most of the non-Romans were merely faces to Scaurus as he walked through the camp, but some he knew. He was surprised to see Doukitzes busily fixing stakes atop the earthen breastwork the legionaries had thrown up. He would not have thought the skinny little Videssian whose hand he'd saved likely to last twenty minutes on the battlefield. Yet here he was, hale and whole, with countless tall strapping men no more than stiffening corpses . . . Tzimiskes, Adiatun, Mouzalon, how many more? Spying Marcus, Doukitzes waved shyly before returning to his task.

Zeprin the Red was here too. The burly Haloga was not working; he sat in the dust with his head in his hands, a picture of misery. Scaurus stooped beside him. Zeprin caught the motion out of the corner of his eye and looked up to see who had come to disturb his wretchedness. "Ah, it's you, Roman," he said, his voice a dull parody of his usual bull roar. A great bruise purpled his left temple and cheekbone.

"Are you in much pain?" the tribune asked. "I'll send our physician to see to you."

The northerner shook his head. "I need no leech, unless he know the trick of cutting out a wounded recall. Mavrikios lies dead, and me not there to ward him." He covered his face once more.

"Surely you cannot blame yourself for that, when it had to be the Emperor himself who sent you from him?"

"Sent me from him, aye," Zeprin echoed bitterly. "Sent me to stiffen the left after Khoumnos fell, the gods save a spot by their hearthfire for him. But the fighting was good along the way, and I was ever fonder of handstrokes than the bloodless business of orders. Mavrikios used to twit me for it. And so I was slower than I should have been, and Ortaias the bold—" He made the name a curse. "—kept charge."

Anger roughened his voice, an anger cold and black as the stormclouds of his wintry home. "I knew he was a dolt, but took him not for coward. When the horseturd fled, I wasn't yet nearby to stem the rout before it passed all checking. Had I paid more heed to my duty and less to the feel of my axe in my hands, it might be the Yezda who were skulking fugitives this night."

Marcus could only nod and listen; there was enough truth in Zeprin's self-blame to make consolation hard. With bleak quickness, the Haloga finished his tale: "I was fighting my way back to the Emperor when I got this." He touched his swollen face. "Next I knew, I was staggering along with one arm draped over your little doctor's shoulder." The tribune did not recall noticing Gorgidas supporting the massive northerner, but then the Greek would not have been easy to see under Zeprin's bulk.

"Not even a warrior's death could I give Mavrikios," the Haloga mourned.

At that, Scaurus' patience ran out. "Too many died today," he snapped. "The gods—yours, mine, the Empire's, I don't much care which—be thanked some of us are left alive to save what we can."

"Aye, there will be a reckoning," Zeprin said grimly, "and I know where it must start." The chill promise in his eyes would have set Ortaias Sphrantzes running again, were he there to see it.

The Roman camp was not so far from the battlefield as to leave behind the moans of the wounded. So many lay hurt that the sound of their suffering traveled far. No single voice stood out, nor single nation; at any moment, the listeners could not tell if the anguish they heard came from the throat of a Videssian grandee slowly bleeding to death or a Yezda writhing around an arrow in his belly.

"There's a lesson for us all, not that we have the wit to

heed it," Gorgidas remarked as he snatched a moment's rest before moving on to the next wounded man.

"And what might that be?" Viridovix asked with a mock-patient sigh.

"In pain, all men are brothers. Would there were an easier way to make them so." He glared at the Celt, daring him to argue. Viridovix was the first to look away; he stretched, scratched his leg, and changed the subject.

Scaurus found sleep at last, a restless sleep full of nasty dreams. No sooner had he closed his eyes, it seemed, than a legionary was shaking him awake. "Begging your pardon, sir," the soldier said, "but you're needed at the palisade."

"What? Why?" the tribune mumbled, rubbing at sticky eyes and wishing the Roman would go away and let him rest.

The answer he got banished sleep as rudely as a bucket of cold water. "Avshar would have speech with you, sir."

"What?" Without his willing it, Marcus' hand was tight round his swordhilt. "All right. I'll come." He threw on full armor as quickly as he could—no telling what trickery Yezd's wizard-prince might intend. Then, blade naked in his hand, he followed the legionary through the fitfully slumbering camp.

Two Khatrisher sentries peered out into the darkness beyond the watchfires' reach. Each carried a nocked arrow in his bow. "He rode in like a guest invited to a garden party, your honor, he did, and asked for you by name," one of them told Scaurus. With the usual bantam courage of his folk, he was more indignant over Avshar's unwelcome arrival than awed by the sorcerer's power.

Not so his comrade, who said, "We fired, sir, the both of us, several times. He was so close we could not have missed, but none of our shafts would bite." His eyes were wide with fear.

"We drove the whoreson back out of range, though," the first Khatrisher said stoutly.

The druids' marks graven into Marcus' Gallic blade glowed yellow, not fiercely as they had when Avshar tried spells against him, but still warning of sorcery. Fearless as a tiger toying with mice, the wizard-prince emerged from the darkness that was his own, sitting statue-still atop his great sable horse. "Worms! You could not drive a maggot across a turd!"

The bolder-tongued Khatrisher barked an oath and drew back his bow to shoot. Scaurus checked him, saying, "You'd waste your dart again, I think—he has a protecting glamour wrapped round himself."

"Astutely reasoned, prince of insects," Avshar said, granting the tribune a scornful dip of his head. "But this is a poor welcome you grant me, when I have but come to give back something of yours I found on the field today."

Even if Marcus had not already known the quality of the enemy he faced, the sly, evil humor lurking in that cruel voice would have told him the wizard's gift was one to delight the giver, not him who received it. Yet he had no choice but to play Avshar's game out to the end. "What price do you put on it?" he asked.

"Price. None at all. As I said, it is yours. Take it, and welcome." The wizard-prince reached down to something hanging by his right boot, tossed it underhanded toward the tribune. It was still in the air when he wheeled his stallion and rode away.

Marcus and his companions skipped aside, afraid of some last treachery. But the wizard's gift landed harmlessly inside the palisade, rolling until it came to rest at the tribune's feet. Then Avshar's jest was clear in all its horror, for staring sightlessly up at Scaurus, its features stiffened into a grimace of agony, was Mavrikios Gavras' head.

The sentries did shoot after the wizard-prince then, blindly, hopelessly. His fell laugh floated back to tell them how little their arrows were worth.

With his gift for scenting trouble, Gaius Philippus hurried up to the rampart. He wore only military kilt and helmet, and carried his *gladius* naked in his hand. He almost stumbled over Avshar's gift; his face hardened as he recognized it for what it was. "How did it come here?" was all he said.

Marcus told him, or tried to. The thread of the story kept breaking whenever he looked down into the dead Emperor's eyes.

The senior centurion heard him out, then growled, "Let the damned wizard have his boast. It'll cost him in the end, you wait and see. This—" He gave Mavrikios a last Roman salute. "—doesn't show us anything we didn't already know. Instead of wasting time with it, Avshar could have been finishing

Thorisin. But he let him get away—and with a decent part of
army, too, once they start pulling themselves together."

Scaurus nodded, heartened. Gaius Philippus had the right
of it. As long as Thorisin Gavras survived, Videssos had a
leader—and after this disaster, the Empire would need all the
troops it could find.

The tribune's mind went to the morning, to getting free of
the field of Maragha. The legionaries' discipline would surely
pay again, as it had this afternoon; overwhelming triumph left
the Yezda almost as disordered as defeat did their foes. Now
he had the Khatrisher horse, too, so he could hope to meet the
nomads on their own terms. One way or another, he told himself, he would manage.

He stared a challenge in the direction Avshar had gone,
said quietly, "No, the game's not over yet. Far from it."

ABOUT THE AUTHOR

Harry Turtledove is that rarity, a lifelong southern Californian. He is married and has two young daughters. After flunking out of Caltech, he earned a degree in Byzantine history and has taught at UCLA and Cal State Fullerton. Academic jobs being few and precarious, however, his primary work since leaving school has been as a technical writer. He has had fantasy and science fiction published in *Isaac Asimov's, Amazing, Analog, Fantasy Book,* and *Playboy.* His hobbies include baseball, chess, and beer.